# SLOW TRAIN TO ARCTURUS
## BY
# ERIC FLINT AND DAVE FREER

SLOW TRAIN TO ARCTURUS

Copyright © 2008 by Eric Flint & Dave Freer


A Baen Books Original

Baen Publishing Enterprises
P.O. Box 1403
Riverdale, NY 10471
www.baen.com

ISBN: 0-978-1-4391-3348-4

Cover art by David Mattingly

First Baen paperback printing, April 2010

Distributed by Simon & Schuster
1230 Avenue of the Americas
New York, NY 10020


Library of Congress Cataloging-in-Publication Data:
2008020727


Printed in the United States of America

10 9 8 7 6 5 4 3 2 1

# ACKNOWLEDGMENTS

*Slow Train to Arcturus* was born out of a discussion between Eric and me about the classic "slowship" novels, and of how, besides being slow, these ships would face the problem that when they got to their target and found the worlds orbiting that sun uninhabitable, they'd have to start all over again . . . And the idea of colonizing space, not worlds, and of a ship that never went fast—but never slowed down either—came into being.

From there the discussion moved on to societies and what might go wrong in centuries of travel and isolation. The Slowtrain took shape with, of all things, fisheries biology furnishing the beads with an internal structure. But the Slowtrain is an engineering construct. Now, Eric is a historian by training, and I was a biologist. If this was going to be a novel worth reading, we would have to draw on those fields of expertise, as well as expertise in a number of fields in which biologists and historians are generally a little weak: engineering, astrophysics, astronomy . . . To get the engineering and space science side of the idea plausible, I turned to fellow writer and engineer Darwin Garrison, Dr. William D. Sears and Richard Knott. The errors are ours and the moments of genius due to their help, for which we are deeply grateful. Many people had a hand in the book, but to mention and thank a few special contributors for their input: Martin Bentley, Jonathan Rollins (at last, an astronomer who spoke English), Dr. Ginger Tansey, Mike Kabongo, and last and most of all, Barbara Freer.

One of the biggest faults with the concept of a one-shot slower-than-light colony mission was the proportion of the time spent accelerating and slowing down. Take Barnard's star, for example. At 5.9 light-years away, with a ship capable of 0.3 lights, a plausible speed for a ramscoop . . . you'd be there in 19.7 years, right?

Wrong. It all depends on acceleration. High-speed acceleration is expensive and creates engineering stresses, to say nothing of the stresses on the biological matter. A slow steady push is best. You accelerate slowly for at least a third of your trip. And then you have to slow down again. If you're going to visit a number of systems, this adds *hugely* to travel time. What's more, the momentum you've lost has to be built again.

Momentum is expensive. It is energy. Energy, whether taken from solar-pumped lasers or A-bombs is a consumable. Even if it is "free" solar power, it still costs to get it into a usable form, and once it has been used, it is gone. A metal space habitat has a finite lifespan—but it is an enormous one. The depreciating cost, amortized over its space-life, divided by its carrying capacity, makes it the cheapest vehicle humanity ever built.

However: Building the momentum needed to travel between the stars is too expensive to waste on one stop journeys, or even on leapfrogging between stars. Once the colony ship accelerates, it must never slow down again. Never. It will drop space habitat modules at each sun. But it must itself just keep cruising along, a slow train to the stars.

From: *Slowtrain: The Stars Within Our Grasp*, Conquist, A., Mordaunt Scientific Press, NY. 2090.

# 1

. . . More than any other space-used technique, the blowing of nickel-iron bubbles changed engineering. From ship hulls to habitats, it was the death of the 'plate-and-rivet' technology that had dominated since the nineteenth century. Bubbles blown from space-melted m-type asteroids altered nearly all the dynamics, both economically and in engineering terms.

From: *An Introduction to Space Engineering,* Vol. 1. 2202, Braun, W.J. and Casern, D. (ed.) SoCalTech Press (pub.)

In the Miran spacecraft now rapidly approaching the enormous alien starship, Kretz swam up from the drug induced trance-hibernation. He opened his eyes and looked at the cramped room, and up at Selna, the ship-physician, leaning over him.

"We're on the final intercept approach," said Selna, beaming down at him. From the transit-massage couch, Kretz smiled back, a little wary, a little confused.

That was to be expected. It would take his livers time to clear the drugs out of his system. Selna was much closer to sexual changeover than he was, and was therefore bigger and had more body, and more liver, available to deal with the trance-drugs. It was a reason to be wary with him. Moods were even less stable than sexuality, at this stage. Selna would only get worse until he became fully female, and settled down.

Well, thought Kretz, eventually he'd get there himself. It was odd to think of being sedentary and child-rearing. Selna had better watch his hormone supplements, though. There was no space on the intercept ship for a nesting territory, let alone a creche. Anyway, it would all smell wrong.

Kretz sat up. He was still giddy, but the excitement was beginning to push aside the drugs that had allowed them to make the six-year journey.

Selna lent him a hand, helping him to his feet. The physician-communications specialist's eyes were alive with excitement. "And have I got news for you, my xeno-biologist-engineering friend! It looks like both of your specialties may just be needed."

Incredulously, Kretz turned on him. "There is something alive on the alien craft? It is not just a probe?"

Selna laughed. "To hear Leader Zawn, you'd think it will be full of aliens."

Kretz had to laugh too. "Probably fluffy and pink with tentacles."

"Well, he has detected beamed laser signals coming from one of the spheres. The sixth. I've started computer analysis of the signal."

"It's just an automated signal system. Look, when they started checking the back-record from Astronomy, they found signs of the alien ship as far back as two hundred years ago. It'll be a treasure trove, all right, but Zawn's archaeology will have more of a role to play than my xenobiology."

By this time they'd walked forward down the narrow passage to the science deck. Kretz was glad to flop into a chair. Leader Zawn was peering intently at some instruments, so absorbed that he didn't even look up. He just waved a hand in greeting. His mouth was stretched into a beam of pure delight.

Kretz stared at the forward viewscreens as Selna handed him a high-energy drink, designed to stimulate the mind, flush the body of trance-drug metabolites and, naturally, taste vile. The alien ship filled the entire viewscreen, although they must be at least seven light-seconds away from it. It looked even more like a string of white beads—beads moving at nearly a third of the speed of light, but beads none-the-less. Of course there was not much light out here to reflect, but the infrared view confirmed that the thing was, by comparison to space, quite warm. The machinery inside must still function, somehow. No matter how well you insulated anything it would—eventually—leak heat.

"Behind the ramscoop is a fusion plant," said Zawn, looking up from his instruments and not bothering with niceties like asking how his xenobiologist felt after trance-sleep. The answer was always the same anyway: *awful*.

"And behind that the spectroscope confirms the next object is water-ice. Probably a whole comet. Now what do you think they'd want that for, Kretz?"

Kretz hid his smile. "Fuel?" he said just for the sheer joy of watching Zawn's face. The poor fellow almost showed his teeth before realizing that he was being teased.

"Someone will kill you in a mating fight, Kretz. Don't be more obstructive than you have to be. Replenishment, that's what. Replenishment of lost materials. There will be some leakage, but this gives the lie to Melka's ideas. Of course there could still be life, even if his calculation of the effectiveness of seals is correct. They just brought replenishments along. A lot of replenishments. The third object is nitrogen ice and carbon dioxide."

"Well, they're transporting water, nitrogen and $CO_2$ along does suggest that they're not the sort of alien life-forms Melka and Ferni proposed," said Kretz. Zawn had a habit of leaping to conclusions. Archeologists had to, he supposed. Often there wasn't that much to go on. But the combination was indeed promising for life as they knew it on Miran. Perhaps the theories of what the basic conditions for the formation of life were, were about to be proved. The theories of evolutionary convergence were another matter entirely. Yes, they worked within a planetary sphere, but out here . . .

Why should two legs and two eyes be a norm? He already knew the answer: because function shapes form. But even if there was a remnant of life on the alien ship, it was going to be *very* different. Excitingly different, beyond his wildest dreams.

Zawn leaned in, beamed, and came up with his clincher. "And it is very plain that they're using energy. Quite a lot of energy for a ship full of machinery or even sleepers. Each of those beads is rotating. There are small ion-jets on the equatorial ridge of each bead to keep them spinning."

Spin. Centrifugal force would provide the effect of gravity. And why should gravity matter to machinery, or, as had been postulated by the excitable fringe media on Miran, to a spacecraft full of frozen aliens?

There might be a huge cargo of trance-state aliens on that ship . . . but if so, where were they heading for? The ship showed no signs of slowing. The initial theory had been that the vessel's purpose was to deploy probes, and that that had caused the flash that had originally caught astronomers' attention. Objects moving at considerably higher fractions of C had been detected relatively soon after that.

But this was a different prospect altogether. A vastly different prospect. There could even be live "minders" on the alien string of pearl-like beads. The idea frightened and excited Kretz, as the rest of the Miran expedition crew were brought out of trance and the distance to the alien ship closed, hour after hour. Laser streams of data hurtled back toward Miran. Kretz could imagine the newscasts getting it all wrong, and a whole generation of young males wishing that they were on this grand adventure themselves, and the nest-mothers being terribly glad that their young males weren't out here.

The amount of information going back now was nothing to what they'd send when they actually made physical contact. That would take the greater proportion of their reaction mass . . . and was giving both the steersman and navigator sleepless rest-periods, and relentless computing.

"It'll have to be the distal pole of the last bead," said Steersman Kastr firmly. "I'm sorry, Leader Zawn. The spin means we have to land on a pole—and the link between the beads means only the last pole is an option.

Besides, deep-radar suggests that the surface at the pole is exposed metal, whereas we think most of the rest is covered by some form of film—possibly a coating on an inner regolith layer. The sixth from last bead may be transmitting laser signals, but we can't land the intercept there."

"The lifecraft?" said Zawn desperately.

"Possibly. Once we've matched velocity . . . well, all things are relative," said Kastr, in his *this is another one of your stupid ideas, archeologist* voice.

Kretz knew Zawn well enough to suspect that, stupid idea or not, the lifecraft, intended to provide their final stage home, would be attempting the journey to the sixth bead. It had been a possibility in the design phase, Kretz knew. There was a crawler in the hold too. It had seemed like a waste of space to Kretz, but then it had been difficult to guess what they'd need to explore an alien artifact moving at 0.3 lights. The only obvious answer seemed to be: You need whatever you haven't thought of. Kretz was cynically sure that that was as certain to be true as Selna suggesting a little recreational sex next rest period. It was one of those thing about approaching change. Selna's hormones were in a riot, just like his moods and his temper. And the ship had three of its crew heading that way . . . full of hormone supplements to avoid sex-change.

"It's an airlock," Kretz said, looking at the shape of the alien structure that Zawn had projected up onto the screen. "That much is obvious, Leader Zawn. Engineering convergence is as inevitable as biological convergence. A bridge looks like and works like a bridge —within certain limits—no matter where on our world it was built, by whatever linguistic group or culture."

Zawn looked thoughtful. "And tetrahedronous religious building and tomb-structure are more of a sign of structural and material dictates than historical contact. True. But the question remains. Do we attempt to open this airlock?"

"It's what we came for," said Selna, caressing Kretz's back.

"Not strictly speaking," said Kretz. "We came to investigate an alien artifact, assumed long dead, or to be a probe. Yes, I'd love to see an alien life-form. But it is also true that whatever is in there may not care to be disturbed. And we are the interlopers."

Selna snorted, stopping his distracting activity. "Look," he said, "what are we going to do? Come nearly 1.8 light-years and then go home wringing our hands and grimacing, just in case the occupant might be showing their teeth, and not welcoming visitors to their nest? We are males. Some of you are even quite attractive." His hand trailed down Kretz's back again.

The physician didn't see things quite the way a behavioral biologist did. "They might not have two sexes," said Kretz. "Maybe three. Or only one."

Selna laughed. "No. Convergent evolution dictates that they'll have at least two. Females to tell the males what to do. Males to ignore them."

"And get killed," said Kretz.

Selna laughed again. "Well, we'd have overpopulation problems if males were as nest-minded as females."

"I think they're going to be very small and very different, or else in cyronic preservation," Kretz said firmly. "Look at the size of the each of those beads. They're not really big enough to be bio-viable."

"I thought that the consensus was that they'd have to be at least of roughly equal cranial capacity to us to allow for the evolution of sentience," said Selna, betraying that he'd read far more than he admitted to. After the existence of the alien artifact had been confirmed, theories had proliferated like bacteria. The cranial capacity one had quite caught the public eye. Of course it assumed that aliens would have a cranium . . .

"Only assuming that their biology is close to ours. If the brain is not convoluted, for example, they'd need about three times the cranial capacity—assuming their nervous system works even remotely like ours," said Zawn, showing that he'd read the same speculation.

"I personally hope that they're going to be dead sexy," said Selna, getting up and walking off in search of new prey, with one of his sudden mood-swings. "You're all too boring."

Selna's absence did make rational conversation easier. "So," said Kretz to Leader Zawn. "I suppose what you are really trying to ask me is how many people we should send in, and what dangers they can expect to face? I know you well enough to know you are going to go yourself."

Zawn smiled. "Yes," he said. "So long as you accept that the number will include me."

"Both of us," said Kretz. "We're relatively expendable."

Zawn was amused. "What a shocking thing to say to your leader."

"True enough, though. And as for the dangers . . . well, it is relatively unlikely that we're going to find any life in there, or that any contamination will survive contact with hard vacuum."

Zawn's lips stretched and narrowed in a smile. "And that pink furry tentacled aliens will come out and run off with Selna."

"He's being exhausting right now," admitted Kretz. The attention was flattering, but still . . .

"We'll all get there," said Zawn tolerantly.

"If we live that long. I'm quite looking forward to him changing and settling down in a nest-territory and never moving again," said Kretz.

"At the moment his promiscuity is a little tiring," said Zawn. "But spare me a territorial female to deal with as well. So: You and me, and maybe Abret. There is not much call for a deep-space radiation scientist. We have a spare pilot, besides him. And Selna can do his life-support work in a pinch."

There was more to Leader Zawn, thought Kretz, than mere boundless enthusiasm and a capacity to think the best of everyone. More than an encyclopedic knowledge of the historical artifacts of seventeen cultures, too. It must have been difficult for the expedition committee to chose a male to lead, but he was as good a candidate as you were likely to find this side of changeover. "My choice, exactly," he admitted. "So when do we go?"

"Now," said Zawn calmly. "Abret is just off getting some adjustments done to his suit. His growth has been slower than predicted while he was under the trance-drugs."

"In other words, you'd already made up your mind before you asked me," Kretz said.

"Well, not quite," admitted Zawn. "I wanted your opinion, and I wanted you along, of course. But I wasn't sure how expendable to engineering you considered yourself." Zawn showed the tact that had led to him being chosen to lead the alien artifact interception mission, over the heads of the obvious candidates in Navigation or Steering. He took Kretz by the arm and the two of them walked toward the passage to the outer airlock. "The decisions on risk profiles were actually taken back on Miran, before we left, you see. But a willing participant is always best." He looked mischievously at Kretz. "And if we go now, well, what Selna doesn't know he can't fuss over. He is not to be considered for any high-risk operations."

"A very good point," admitted Kretz.

The team had set up the laser-video links, before retreating on the Miran spacecraft. Kretz had had the frisson of knowing they would forever be the first Miran males who had finally penetrated an alien spacecraft. That laser relays would have those pictures on datafiles back home.

He'd also had the fear of walking into an alien airlock, and the knowledge that Selna was furious with him.

Abret painstakingly checked the atmosphere being pumped into the airlock. "We'd breathe this and live, you know," he said, looking at the readouts again. "More nitrogen and less carbon dioxide than we're used to. Traces of methane. And sulphur compounds . . . But the oxygen level is tolerable."

"Sorpon's prediction on the environmental requirement for intelligent life comes true," Kretz said regretfully, pausing in the setup of the radio repeater. "I'd have preferred you to prove him wrong, as I always thought his premises for the evolution of intelligence were simply too narrow. What's the temperature like?"

"Chilly," said the scientist. "Enough to make you sprout cilia, but not to kill you."

The inner airlock door beckoned. Aside from bridges and religious tetrahedrons . . . function demanded that a door look like a door. It was lower and wider than Miran would have made it, but it was still a door.

"Well?" asked Kretz. "Do we open it? Or do we examine this area carefully first?"

"Caution and good archeology suggests the latter," said Leader Zawn. "But I am still a young enough male to be foolish and reckless," he said, smiling. "Besides, our time is limited. If we follow good archeological principles we'll still be looking at the edge of the launchpad when the artifact heads on for the next star, and we'll have to go along for a one-way ride. I suggest we have laser pistols at the ready, but don't hold them obtrusively."

He began pulling on the wheel-device on the door. It responded. External sound pick-ups on the suit recorded a faint creak. But Kretz had not even had time to draw the laser pistol, when the door slid open. Inside . . .

Inside the alien ship was not, as some had suggested, a huge hollow space. They were in a large open area, true, but it was not high-roofed. An elderly female Miran would have had to duck her head. Before them, open entryways gaped. One passage was wide enough to take a lander, and had, Kretz noticed, a roof-rail. But most of them were narrow. Some were lit, as this area was, with a light that seemed a little too yellow and too bright. And they could see spindly green things there.

The truth dawned on Kretz then. "It's not a probe. Or a spaceship. It's a habitat. A space habitat. They've got away from the space-constraint issue with layering."

His engineering side was doing some hasty recalculation as to the surface area in the habitat. This would increase area by several thousand percent. True, it would be more than a little claustrophobic in the passages —walking closer they could see the walls were covered in growing things.

"I think it is both a habitat and a spaceship. Those inside have a small world to live in," said Zawn, slowly. "They must be a species far more adapted to life in space than us. Better able to tolerate enclosed spaces, for starters."

"But why?" asked Abret, peering around. "I mean, why build a ship that appears to do nothing but transport their habitat across maybe a hundred light-years? The ship isn't slowing. It hasn't slowed—according to examination of back data—for at least a hundred years. And yet . . . a species content to dwell in space habitats could make their home around any star. And there is more room around any one star than they could ever use."

It was quite a question, thought Kretz. "Maybe they like to travel or to explore, and this is just to provide them with a home while they do?"

"Could be, I suppose," said Zawn, staring around. "We make the arctic observatories as homelike as possible. Or maybe this is a failed colony ship. Do you think anything is still alive in here? Besides the plant-life that you're peering at, Kretz?"

"Could be too," said Kretz, peering at the divided leaves. The convergence was amazing! He clipped a tiny piece off with a monomolecular-edged sampling blade and dropped it into a sample holder on his belt. Of course it would have to be examined under the strictest quarantine conditions, even if the risks of biocontamination were minuscule. But he could hardly wait to get a microscope to it, and to begin investigating its chemical makeup.

"Then why aren't they here?" asked Abret, moving back nervously from the leafy passage-mouth.

"Maybe they're not expecting visitors in deep space," said Zawn, flippantly. "I don't think you should be damaging the flora, Kretz. It's their property. They might take offense—"

And then something moved, darting forward towards them.

Abret must have been nearer to the thin edge of panic than he'd let on, because he fired.

A piece of alien greenery was cut and fell, and something exploded and burst into flames briefly.

A stripe-faced creature, clad in green and brown mottling that had made it difficult to see, dropped something and raised its hands. So did two others that had been so perfectly hidden that none of the Miranese explorers had seen them.

Three Miran had faced three aliens for a long moment before Zawn said "Raise your hands too. It must be a greeting. See, empty palms, a gesture of friendship and peace."

The aliens stood like statues as Zawn and Kretz echoed the two-handed greeting, while Abret, obviously almost paralyzed with fear, stood with his laser pistol at the ready.

"Abret. Greet them," said Zawn, firmly. The frightened deep-space physicist responded slowly, raising just the one hand above his head, keeping his laser pointed at the aliens. They all stood like that for a very long time, looking at each other. They were disturbingly Miranshaped, and yet alien. Wrong. Yes, they were bipeds, and had the normal arrangement of arms and a head. Two eyes, a mouth and a nose. But the hands were wrong. Five digits instead of the normal three and opposable. It looked as if one of their digits—the inner one—might

be opposable. And the head and face were even more
wrong. The heads had filaments on them, as if the aliens
were suffering from extreme cold. And the face pigment-
stripes were all different. The position of the eyes, the
shape of the nares, the angle of the mouth were all
slightly different, and the external part of what was probably an ear was too low. At least they were not showing
their teeth. Eventually, Kretz said in whisper—
ridiculous, because the aliens couldn't hear their radio
transmissions and certainly couldn't understand them:
"Can we stop greeting now? My arms are getting very
tired."

Zawn slowly lowered his arms. The aliens looked at
each other and slowly did the same. And the external
mikes picked up the sound of alien speech.

Transcomp cut in. "Unknown but sequential pattern,"
the computer supplied. "Analyzing."

"So what do we do now?" asked Abret.

"Hope like hell that they're not too mad at the damage
you did shooting at them. Apologize," said Zawn.

"How do we do that?" asked Kretz.

"We repeat their words back them from Transcomp.
And then we do some miming," said Zawn. "It appears
as if we have similar meanings in our hand-gestures,
anyway."

What the expedition leader lacked in animal-behavior
knowledge he made up for in decisiveness. Personally,
Kretz thought that the miming could have meant nearly
anything from "sorry" to "if you move we'll shoot at you."
But the repeat-back of the Transcomp recorded words
had produced a flurry of more alienese. When this was
repeated back to them, one of the aliens had grasped
the situation and began pointing to objects and naming

them. They plainly were quick on the uptake. But that was what you'd expect from the builders of such a magnificent artifact.

What followed was the most exhausting and thrilling time period of Kretz's life. Transcomp got the names of objects quickly enough. Once they got the idea the aliens had even contrived to show actions and provide words. Kretz wasn't sure how much of the translation was getting through the other way. The aliens called all of them "Zawn." And they appeared willing to help, even if Abret had kept his distance, nervously, most of the time. Another thing had been noting the appearance of small 'bots of alien design which had eventually appeared and begun repairing the damage from Abret's shot. Obviously the alien ship's internal machinery still functioned well, if slowly.

It had been a triumphant and excited group that had returned to the ship.

The aliens were . . . alien.

And yet, less so than some of the scientists and the general public had expected. If they'd been blobs of slime they might have been more wary. If Transcomp, designed to provide interface between nests from any island or culture on Miran had proved less adaptable and successful, things might have been different too, admitted Kretz.

Everyone had wanted to be part of the next group, but Leader Zawn had taken that cautiously too. "We'll take four people next time. They seem friendly. I'm afraid, Kretz and Abret, I won't be able to take you two, this time."

Abret, in the nervous-moody stage before change, certainly didn't mind. Kretz too hadn't regretted it in the slightest. The systematic examination of the plant sample he'd taken took up most of that time. The others would merely have been part of the second contact. He'd been part of the first, and his monograph on the alien plants would ensure that his fame continued long after he'd mothered his sons and become a vast matriarch, too big to move without help. The structure of the plant had been like looking at a young student's first badly understood research of Miran vegetation. It was . . . similar in function, but obviously had arrived there from a different direction. The chemists would have fun with some of the long-chain organic molecules too, but they were carbon compounds. Evolution had a myriad possible paths to follow in theory, but perhaps in practice there were certain constraints. Kretz found himself intensely curious as to how these alien plants would taste. He resisted the crazy urge. Miran digestion was robust, but who knew what alien toxins would do to one's livers?

The second expedition came back bubbling with excitement at the friendliness of the aliens. "They want to meet all of us. It . . . seems they are rather vague on 'outside,' " said Zawn. "We're making huge strides with the language. I've decided: Except for Abret and Derfel, who will be taking the lander to the source of the laser pulses, and Leter and Guun, who will remain onboard the ship, we're all going in after next rest period. It's a veritable treasure house of alien life-forms and equipment, Kretz. And . . . you know what? We think it was supposed to be a colony ship. A whole series of them, rather. They say their bead was supposed to take them to a new sun. Obviously their astronomy must be far ahead of ours, to predict what suns would have habitable planets."

Kretz had been just as excited about the idea of more material to add to his biological firsts and keen on engineering discovery. He'd quietly taken along the better part of an engineering repairman toolkit.

He was expecting great things.

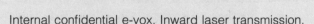

**2**

Internal confidential e-vox. Inward laser transmission.
From: Field Agent P. Firston, deep-space sector 3.
To: Agent Supervisor FJ Lu-Hellens
re: Weapons seizure.
Habitat unit 36 (Free Federation of Aryan Survivalists).

Illegal weapons detected with remote sensors in the personal effects of the attached list of embarkees. Will require at least four full enforcement units, and heavy ordnance and armor for confiscation before departure. Permission to schedule raid for 3.30 CMT, 11/1/2153

Internal confidential e-vox. Outward laser transmission.
From: Agent Supervisor FJ Lu-Hellens
To: Field Agent P. Firston, deep-space sector 3.
re: Weapons seizure.
**Permission denied.**

Attached vox: private
From: Fenella Lu-Hellens
To: Paul Firston.

Word from on high, Paul. Ignore it. Ignore anything smaller than tactical nukes. We've been tracking most of the stuff for months. Most of it is twentieth century, obsolete, but better out of the solar system than in it. The boss says: So long as they're taking it outsystem on a one-way trip, who cares? Maybe the stupid bastards will find something to shoot at out there. If not, they can always shoot each other.

Fen

---

The platter-table was stacked with . . . things. The scientist part of Kretz wanted to categorize them more precisely but . . . he really wasn't sure what they were. They steamed. The blackened bits looked . . . almost animal-like. As if someone had dismembered and charred some creature. A large creature, about the size of a small alien. They oozed red liquid. The aliens waved them forward.

"Zawn. What is going on here?" asked Borch.

The archeologist smiled. "I think that we are being invited to a feast. A gesture of hospitality."

"It looks like a burned alien hatchling," said Selna.

"Hush," said Zawn sternly. "They're bound to be offended by that, if their Transcomp picks it up."

"So what do we do?" asked someone. Most of the ship's crew was here now, and several of them were still very wary of the aliens.

Kretz didn't care what Zawn did. He wasn't getting too close to the things first. He noticed that Selna too had thought this out and was at the very back of the

Miran crew. The aliens had stepped back to give them a wide berth, a clear passage to the feast.

Zawn turned and smiled. "We go through the motions. Pretend. We can't really eat of course. But it is a primitive gesture of welcome common to most soc—"

Whatever Zawn had been about to say was cut off by the roar of flame, leaping from the nozzle of a device held by two of the aliens. The fiery blast engulfed the Miran party.

The fire died back and Kretz, still stunned with shock, saw how the bare handful of stripe-faced aliens that had welcomed them forward to the feast had somehow multiplied. Now they were a mob, swarming forwards, screaming, teeth exposed, knives and other strange objects brandished. Kretz had little time to think about it, though. The aliens were onto them, attacking, attempting to pull them down.

The suits had withstood the fire easily enough. They were made to survive vacuum and the temperature variations of deep space. The fabric was tough, self-healing. It would take more than some primitive knife to cut it, with one slash. But the aliens were gleeful about giving the Miran a death of a thousand cuts. And there were just so many of them. Even setting fire to their own environment with the flamethrower had not stopped them.

As he struggled with the aliens in this mad place of fire and smoke, Kretz heard Zawn desperately yelling over the radio for help from those still on the ship.

Knocked off his feet, pinned down with an alien stabbing repeatedly at his chest, Kretz hoped they'd come fast.

And then from somewhere closer at hand came other intervention. Selna had not obeyed Zawn's instructions about the laser pistols being left behind. And somehow he'd managed to get it out and pull the trigger.

Selna hadn't been aiming. His laser-bolt burned through several of their attackers—and navigator Borch.

The aliens should have fled. But instead the mob turned on Selna like a pack of blood-crazed feral animals.

Kretz staggered to his feet as the aliens charged at Selna. Selna was still firing as they struck him. The laser pistol discharged most of its charge into the now exposed stanchions as Selna and an alien fought for it, while others pulled him to the ground. Kretz, struggling with the shock, reacted like any Miran male in danger. He tried to run. The best he managed was to retreat into a fallen fold of vegetation-clad wall. He saw that Zawn too was miraculously still on his feet, trying to flee with Pelta clinging to him.

And then came the sound of Guul—one of the drive technicians who had been left on the ship—yelling down the radio.

"Some kind of projectile weapon . . . " And then the sound of a mighty explosion echoed down the earphones.

Nutrient splashed out of tubes severed by Selna's laser-pistol and hissed on the fires, as the alien mob pulled Selna down.

For a few seconds Kretz watched in horror.

The air was hazy with smoke. The little 'bots were trying to quench the flames. The crazy aliens didn't seem to care that they were destroying their own home. Warily, Kretz moved from behind the cover of the vegetation, heading across the gap. If he was to get back to his ship he'd have to get past them. They were dancing around Selna's body, kicking him and spitting on him. Making strange wild caterwauling noises. The sight was enough to make him want to rush in, to try to protect his companion.

But he knew that it was too late for that now. Instead he had to try to survive.

With relief he reached the next segment of luxuriant greenery. Nutrient fluid still dribbled from the pipes high up the flexible plastic wall, where Selna's last desperate laser-bolt had cut into it. The plants farther across were burned by the aliens' crude flamethrower, but in this area they still provided him with cover.

The piece of passage tore free of its stanchion under his weight. As he fell with it Kretz realized that cover did not equate with safety. That last bolt from Selna's weapon had not just cut nutrient tubes. And, worse still, the fall had drawn the aliens' attention.

Even through the helmet, Kretz could hear the yammering and baying of the stripe-faced aliens. Transcomp was beginning to cope with some of the words, adding to the vocabulary that they'd already established, and applying inductive logic to try to deduce meanings and words. It coped with this particular input. It appeared that they were all screaming "Kill it!"

The entire pack of aliens surged after him as he staggered and clambered into the next passageway full of greenery. All he could do was run. So he did. His legs were longer than theirs, but they knew their way around in these labyrinthine passages and he had barely an idea of which direction he was going in. There was no thought now about making his way back towards the ship. The only direction open to him was farther in, towards the core of the space habitat. He ran on down the endless coiled passages.

The baying hunters seemed almost frantic now.

Then an explosion knocked him flying.

Only his headlong sprint had saved his life, as there was now a smoking hole where the passage floor had been. This area was relatively unravaged otherwise. The walls of the passage were dense with hanging plant growth. Kretz crashed in among the fragile branches. Red fruits cascaded down onto him. An oddly lucid part of his stunned mind registered that these were the first fruiting bodies he'd seen. But this was hardly the time for exercising one of the specialties that had got him onto the intercept ship, xenobotany. He cowered back into the bush.

They were firing some kind of projectile weapon at him. The suit absorbed some of the impact, but some of the objects had cut it. He was bleeding. And his body took longer to mend than the self-repairing fabric of the suit.

A yell came from the direction where Kretz had hoped to find safety. Transcomp struggled. "Insufficient for present extrapolation," it said calmly. A computer could be calm. Kretz could not. He'd seen four of his companions killed before he and Selna had managed to flee. Zawn and Pelta had also fled in the opposite direction. Like Selna, they could also be dead by now. Or perhaps they'd gotten back to the ship. Desperately, Kretz wished he could be there too.

"He's ours," Transcomp supplied the Miranese words in a cool level computer voice. Transcomp would eventually learn to translate nuances, but it was struggling with a too small established vocabulary and an alien species.

There was a barricade across the passage, in the direction he'd planned to go. It seemed a sin to destroy alien technology and habitat, but, by the looks of it, they were

busy destroying it themselves. Kretz used the monomolecular-edged sampling-knife to cut through the tough
passage wall he was cowering into, making a narrow slit.
He squeezed through, as quietly as possible.

"He's getting away!" Transcomp supplied, dashing the
hope that he could escape unnoticed.

The passageway he'd forced his way into was severely
damaged. Unlike the spiral passage he'd come from, this
one was just dead. Lightless and lifeless. Using his headlight, he could see that the skeletal remains of the aliens'
plants still hung from the walls. Either a systems failure
or warfare had destroyed this part of the space habitat.
Kretz picked a direction to run at random. The direction
he wanted to go—back towards the end pole where the
Miran intercept ship stood—was not an option. He didn't
wait to find out if he was still being chased. Instead he
raced down the dark passage as fast as his feet would
carry him. He nearly fell to an unpleasant death as a
result. Once again the passage showed signs that it had
been damaged by some form of explosion. The incredibly
tough wall fabric hung in tatters and even the girders
that supported the spiral passages were twisted. Two
hung broken.

Cautiously, Kretz began climbing along them, and
then swung down to the remains of a small metal structure. It had been burned and pieces of blackened wire
dangled inside, showing that, at some stage, electronic
equipment had been ripped from it. Distantly, Kretz
could hear voices again. He crawled into the hanging
little chamber, and curled up against the back wall, willing himself to be small, if not invisible. Neither was
something he could really achieve, but there was nothing
else he could do. He was just too tired to run any farther,
right now.

Flickering light from the torches of his pursuit began to cut the darkness. They were using brands of burning vegetation, as if they had no other form of light. Kretz lay very still, hardly daring to breathe. He could hear the shouting clearly. Transcomp began translating, but Kretz hastily flicked the audio off, before the sounds could betray him. All he could do was lie there and listen to the beating of both his hearts and the clatter of the pursuing aliens clambering along the beams.

At length the sounds faded. They'd moved on. Obviously they expected him to keep running. Well, he would have done so, had he not been just too tired. He tongued a suit food-fluid nipple into place and drank. As energy slowly seeped back into his body from the glucose, Kretz began—for the first time since the alien owners of this space habitat had attacked them without reason or provocation—to actually think, not just to flee their brutality. Had the Miran said or done something wrong? Why had the aliens suddenly attacked them? It made no sense!

Hiding in the wreckage of an equipment console Kretz had to admit: they'd expected almost anything but the flamethrower ambush. And then the remaining crew from the ship had fallen into some kind of explosive trap when they'd tried to come to their rescue.

Kretz waited until the sound and light had gone. Then he hauled himself out of his refuge, and tried to decide where to go. The Miranese expedition had, as yet, established very little about the internal geography of the space habitats. Externally, of course, the string of habitats had been studied in some detail while they closed with them. He knew as much about that as any fascinated scientist could. Well, Zawn had been wrong. They should have explored the outer equatorial ridge first and studied the still-active motors giving the structure spin. But the alien airlocks had been too tempting, too simple and too logical to operate. And, after all, this had been why they'd come.

Now lost, hunted and frightened, Kretz knew a little more about the inner structure. It appeared to consist of an endless "gut" of passages, not just in layers, but spiraling around the ovoid habitat, winding inside each other again, making tier on tier of surface area for the plant-life of the habitat. It was almost like a ball of hollow string.

It was good biology. It was hell for a fugitive. It was impossible for Kretz to judge accurately, but it seemed to him that the pursuit had forced him away from the entry lock and into the labyrinth of passages. He'd broken the antenna on his suit some time back, so there was no way he could communicate to see if anyone else had escaped.

It could have been worse, he knew. Abret was right. The air of the alien's habitat was cooler and lower in oxygen than his own. But he could breathe it. The suit-punctures hadn't led to explosive decompression. However, that would at least have been mercifully quick. This wasn't. He might have contemplated suicide, had one thing not been painfully obvious: It was his duty to the people of Miran to warn them.

The aliens had lied about being friendly. There could be only one reason for the attack. The astronomers *had* detected some high-speed objects being launched as the alien artifact came close to each sun. Now it was clear. They weren't exploring probes, or ships of peaceful colonists looking for new worlds. This was a habitat full of conquerors. He had to survive to get back to the ship, to tell the people of Miran that a murderous plague was coming, infalling into their system. There hadn't been a war on Miran for millennia. They would need to prepare. Or it would be flamethrower time for all of them. He had to get back to that pole. To the airlock, and somehow, to the ship. He had some oxygen in his tank, and, given enough time, the fabric of his suit would knit. But he could not afford to ditch the heavy tank and rebreather system if he was ever to leave the airlock of this hell-hole, and he needed time. The alien hunters were determined not give him any.

**3**

Extract from the Transcript of the Sysgov. Space Development Agency Administration meeting 325:2120.

> Director Palin: "One of the problems with handing over man's greatest enterprise to a bunch of fanatics and lunatics is that most of them *are* fanatics and lunatics, not really the sort of people we should use for such a grand enterprise."

> Chief Director Morpet. "That's all very well, but the only people willing and ready to go are nutters by definition. Maybe we just have to shift that definition, or acknowledge that man's future among the stars lies in the hands of oddballs."

Extract from televid conference of Nest-Mothers.

"Most of the crew are severely mentally aberrant, but that simply can't be helped. Mass is an issue and quarters

will have to be cramped. Still, we need to be aware that
madness in one area spills into others."

—Senior Nest-mother Daleen

━━━━━━━

Abret almost wished that he'd offered to go into the alien
habitat again, rather than cope with being in the lifecraft
with Derfel. The aliens had scared him, but so did Derfel. The male loved crowds and small spaces. He kept
standing too close to Abret. Derfel was the spacecraft's
problem-child. The others had formed friendships and
cliques. Everyone felt sorry for Derfel, but not sorry
enough to sleep with him. Well, it wasn't going to happen
in this lifecraft either.

"It's not fair. They get to discover the exciting stuff
and they send us off on the boring missions," grumbled
Derfel. "I want to go inside."

"Well, you can't," said Abret, wishing that they'd sent
someone else with him. Guul. Or Kastr. Or Kretz. Of
course getting a crew at all for this expedition had been
fraught with difficulty. All of them had to be able to
cope with claustrophobia to a greater extent than 99%
of Miran. And they'd needed multiple skills, because
there hadn't—even with crowding—been enough space.
Abret had come simply because of the journey-phase.
Most of the others had been drugged comatose, their
metabolisms slowed to a crawl for the entire time. He'd
been awake and working for repeated periods along the
way. His field of expertise was deep space, and of course
he'd trained as a pilot so that he could work on his spe-
cialty. He'd taken a course in life-support maintenance
too, learning how to maintain the growth-vats protein,
and carbohydrate reformatters, just to earn a place on

the trip. The ship—silent except for the sound of life-support mechanisms—had not been too crowded. Now, with everyone awake, it had been uncomfortably full. Well, at least he would not be going into the alien habitat. Merely examining the laser-transmitter. It couldn't possibly send data back to where this ship had originated from. Ten light-years was about the ceiling for practical laser messaging.

They touched down on the polar plate of the alien habitat. It was an excellent landing, if he had to say so himself. They suited up and set out across the surface to the laser pod. It wasn't operative right then. As far as they'd been able to assess, it only fired once every rotation, aiming back at a specific place. They'd be close by when it next pulsed. Then with the equipment photographed and, hopefully, the purpose understood, they could go back.

Abret was no engineer in the way that Kretz was. He had little interest in taking alien machinery apart. He took the readings and left the incomprehensible sealed device alone. "It has pretty low power. Unless there is something less than two light-years back it isn't going to get there," he said to Derfel. "It must be a relic. Well, that was waste of a trip."

Derfel's eyes were wild. "It's not going to be," he said.

Abret realized that Derfel was holding a laser pistol.

"I'm going to be famous too," said Derfel. "All the females will want to mate with me. I am going to discover things. I get left out of everything. I'm not going to be left out this time."

Abret looked at the laser. It was true that Derfel had been left out of the second expedition to the aliens, and now this one. He was . . . not someone who you wanted on a first contact.

"Put it away, Derfel," he said, trying to keep calm. "Everyone who went on this expedition will be famous." *And most of them don't care*, he thought, but did not say.

"No!" said Derfel furiously. "We are going in. Going to see a different habitat. I will be the first!"

"You're crazy, Derfel."

"Don't say that," snarled the claustrophile. "Everyone else is getting famous. I'll be more famous. The aliens are friendly. These ones are trying to signal to us. Now move."

So, reluctantly, Abret did, secure at least in the knowledge that Derfel's craziness was being transmitted back to the spacecraft. Perhaps Zawn or someone could talk some sense into him.

They walked to the airlock, and Abret made yet another attempt to talk Derfel around to some common sense. "There is no record of your great arrival, Derfel."

"I have a recorder running."

Well, that wasn't surprising, communications was one of Derfel's specialties. He'd gotten onto this expedition, despite his mental instability, because he had so many of them.

The second airlock opened. The place was similar in structure to the alien habitat he had visited before. There were some major differences though. The last lot of alien vegetation had looked scraggly. This area looked manicured. The aliens they had met there had been hiding in the vegetation. These were working methodically. So methodically that they didn't notice the two Miran for a moment or two.

And when they did, they knelt and bowed.

All Abret could do was hope that this meant the same thing to them as it did to Miran. "Can we go back now,

Derfel?" he said, trying to keep calm. "You've met them and seen them. You're famous now."

For a moment he thought that he had won.

But then the aliens crowded closer. Not threatening. Fawning.

Looking at the expression on Derfel's face, Abret knew that he was in even deeper trouble.

And then the radio-call came. "This is Guul for Abret and Derfel. Return to the ship immediately! We need you to join us in a rescue attempt for Leader Zawn and his party. They've come under attack."

The aliens surrounding them suddenly looked very threatening.

**4**

Extract from the Transcript of the Slowtrain funding debate of Lower House, Sysgov.

" . . . What the representative from Ceres is missing is that the costs of this expedition are being offset in several ways. While it is hard to quantify, precisely, what sort of saving in Safety, Security and Monitoring we're talking about, I have been told that we're going to save approximately eighty-four percent of our humint bill alone. Besides we get rid of a lot of misfits. Frankly, there is no place for them in the system."

—Speaker of the ruling party,
System Secretary Pablo Paris

Creeping along the greenery-hung passages in what he hoped was the right direction, Kretz had every sense alert. He knew that he was badly equipped for this. Besides the fact that he'd never stalked up on anything in his life, there was his suit. The clothing of the aliens and their striped facial pigmentation made them hard to see in the junglelike corridors. Kretz's suit was designed to be seen. Seen clearly, so that there were no chances of an accident. One wanted bright—garishly bright—colors and contrasts, so that the user could be spotted from a safe distance. Right now the lights were dim, barely a glow, obviously some part of the plant-life environmental requirements. That would have helped Kretz, except that part of the suit was luminous. He'd draped branches over himself and tried to tie them in place, but they kept falling off. Other than the equipment belt, the suit had been designed to be as snag-proof as possible. That made sense. You didn't want hook up on something when you were operating in a dangerous environment. It also meant that camouflage, even dirt, would not stick to the suit.

That made hiding out very difficult, and trying to creep back toward the airlock even more so. The internal structure made the habitat just so much bigger than it appeared from the outside, and the airlock was certain to be guarded.

Tired and frightened, Kretz could see no other option but to try to get there anyway. He'd been trying to think of an alternative, but right now could see none. So he crept onward.

Into ambush.

He hadn't even spotted anything wrong. The rope noose had been cunningly hidden, and had snatched him off his feet, upside down, a full body-length into the air, so fast that he barely had time to scream.

The aliens came running out of hiding, showing teeth, weapons at the ready.

Reacting with the strength born of pure terror Kretz took the monomolecular sampling knife and slashed at the cord. The slash was in too much haste, and Kretz's sampling knife went flying, and, to Kretz's shock, buried itself in the shoulder of one of the advancing aliens. The alien screamed, just as the cord around Kretz's ankles snapped.

Kretz fell, and would have landed on his head if he had not hit an alien on the way. They went down together. Kretz squirmed and struggled to get away from the strange grasping hands. He struggled to his feet, kicked free of the grip on his foot and tried to run, again. He tripped over the remains of the noose around his ankles.

It saved his life. The projectile weapon that one of the alien crew fired was not just one of the little tubes they'd used before. It was a massive tube and spat fire and smoke with a roaring boom that almost deafened Kretz. It shredded a wall of greenery before the projectile exploded farther down the passage. Kretz didn't know how he'd gotten up and started running again. He just found that he had.

There was one alien with a raised hand-weapon ahead of him. The alien was yelling something, his striped face savage, his red mouth open and his odd square teeth exposed. Kretz was beyond thought. He just kept running.

The hammer-blow on his shoulder nearly stopped him. It did spin him. He staggered against the wall. Somehow he kept on running through the pain. Another shot hit him from behind. He nearly fell again, but his nervous system was on full overload by now, hormones released to cushion him from the shock, letting him run on, blood warm and wet on his shoulder and buttocks.

He ran until he fell.

Then he got up onto hands and knees and crawled.

Eventually he stopped, because there was nowhere to crawl to. There was just a hole. The volume of explosives used here must have been enormous . . . because the hole was huge. It appeared to go all the way to the skin of the habitat. It was wide enough to park the ship's lifecraft in.

He was lying there, panting, desperate, and with the pain beginning to overwhelm him at last, when something hard pressed into his back.

The alien said something in the guttural language they used. Kretz—logic no longer functioning but struggling against despair—turned Transcomp on.

Transcomp coped quite well. "Turn over, [untranslated]. Turn over or I'll blow your spine in half."

Slowly Kretz turned. "Not that way!" snapped his alien captor. "You'll fall over the edge. Ah [untranslated] just stay still." The alien stared down at him teeth exposed in aggression. "The [untranslated] wants you alive to beat some answers out of you. Kill the rest of you, [untranslated]."

Kretz was not a particularly brave male. But he knew that he had very little choice.

He rolled.

The alien tried to catch him as he went over the edge. And, perforce, fell with him.

Screaming together.

It was a long way down.

There was a moment of glancing impact. Pain.

And then . . . nothing.

When he woke up, Kretz had no idea how long he'd been lying there. The alien he'd fallen with would have no idea either. By the stillness and the odd angle of his head, Kretz guessed that he was dead. The alien had been less lucky about where he had landed. He was lying on a metal girder, and not half-buried in a mass of stinking, rotting, soft vegetation. Kretz tried to move.

The agony that came from his arm told him that he'd been a fraction less lucky than he had thought. Cautiously, using the other hand, he sat up. His toes still moved. So did his legs. Now if he could only get to his feet and back to the spacecraft and see Selna . . .

Then it hit him. Selna was dead. Kretz had seen him fall, had seen the alien mob kicking him and spitting on him. The physician wouldn't ever treat anyone again. The Miran spacecraft, the refuge, might just as well be on another planet. All he could do now was try to survive. Or maybe he should just die and prevent the aliens from making him tell them how to get into the Miran spacecraft.

Kretz struggled to his feet. He staggered through the debris, across the gap created by the explosion and into the darkness beyond.

Whatever had happened here had cut water and power to this section of the alien corridor labyrinth. After a short distance it was absolutely black. He had to turn his headlight on. It was plain from the bones and the skeletal remains of plants that this piece of the alien habitat had been dead for many years. The dust too was undisturbed. No one, neither alien nor their little robots, had been here for many years. Swaying, half delirious with pain and the loss of blood, Kretz made his way forward. There was a stair ahead, possibly the reason that this hole had been blown in first place. Kretz began climbing the stair, with painful slowness.

How many times he fell and how many steps he climbed Kretz could never be sure. Eventually he arrived at a point where there was no more up. Just a curving landing, a thick horizontal pole, layered in microtubules, and very little gravity from the spin.

Or it could be his head spinning. He'd lost a lot of blood.

Eventually, he realized that it wasn't a pole. It was the line, the cable, that linked the habitats. He was right at the center of the habitat, possibly near a pole. Off to one side of him—that was an elevator! An alien elevator, yes, but still function defined form. The explosion-hole he'd fallen down . . . someone must have blown out an elevator shaft. Possibly they had filled an elevator with explosives in the shaft, and then exploded it. The stair he'd followed had been a mere standby.

His mind had been drifting between extreme lucidity and delirium for some time. It was in one of its lucid phases just then. There had to be a reason for the stairs and the lift shaft being right there—and looking at the cable he could see it.

A door. A door set into the central cable, with the millions of microtubules that surrounded the core in brackets around the door to allow access to it. Well . . . it would have been a door—if there had been any sign of a handle. And off to the side was a wide passage with a rail set into it. With an odd start Kretz realized that he'd seen one like it before—at the airlock they'd come in by.

The engineering side of Kretz's mind clicked in. This was for heavy equipment transport. And it had to run between the central cable and airlock. The question was . . . which airlock? Had he ended up at the wrong end of the habitat? And mostly, what should he do now? He knew that he'd been shot by the aliens. The suit had of course protected him to some extent. But he was badly bruised and still losing blood, and he had a broken arm. He stood, swaying, indecisive. Eventually he set off down the wide corridor. It was not one of the greenhouse ones, and was lit only by small lights on one wall. It curved quite steeply downwards and he found himself desperately hoping that he'd found an unguarded way to the airlock. He had to stop and lean against the wall quite often. But at least he found no more of the murderous aliens. And it brought him out into an antechamber with an airlock.

A glance at the surrounding water-reservoir was enough to tell him it was the wrong airlock. There was no way that, in his present state, he could make it out and over the equatorial ridge. He doubted if he had the air for such a trip anyway. And—thinking slightly more coherently—he realized that it wouldn't have helped if this had been the airlock by which they'd come in, anyway, right now. His suit-fabric would knit and repair itself, but not in time. He needed a place to hide. Perhaps inside the airlock would do.

He was about to step forward when he heard alien voices. He turned and fled up the ramp again. In the darkness he felt slightly more secure, just wishing it wasn't all uphill. There were no exits off this tunnel either, which made escape awkward.

At last he came to the cable. Here were other passage-entrances. He could hide here in one of the dead areas, surely? And then in one of those odd moments of lucidity he had an idea. If he could open that handleless door, he could hide inside the cable. Surely the only reason for it being handleless was to keep the passengers out? It was big enough to hide in. And, if there was a similar door on the far end of the habitat core, well, that should take him to the other down-ramp to the airlock that he wanted to reach.

All he had to do was to open a handleless alien door, which seemed impossible. But he still had his tools. It was worth trying surely? The thought of a hiding-place where these alien murderers couldn't find him was attractive. The thought that it might just open into a vacuum also occurred. Well. That would kill him. And them.

He began an electromagnetic probing of the door with a basic electronic workman's remote. It detected the active circuits within easily enough. The question was—could he open it?

He gambled and used a pulsed signal to interrupt the circuit. It was just the first thing to try . . .

And it worked.

There was no rush of air into a vacuum as the door swung open. Just a puff of old, stale, cold air, at slightly higher pressure. There was perfectly ordinary handle on the inside.

He stood there, leaning against the thick door, and staring into the blackness inside. A transport tunnel. That's what it had to be. A way of replenishing lost water or air from the stockpiles that were just behind the rams-coop. One stockpile for the entire string of habitats, fed through this tube. Simple. Elegant. Alien. Did he dare crawl into it?

A wave of giddiness nearly overwhelmed him. And then an alien voice said "I told you those were his tracks. Shoot him before he gets away!" There was an explosion. Water from broken microtubules splashed onto him. As quickly as he could with one good arm, Kretz scrambled up into the tube, and pulled the door closed behind him. It shut with an audible click. And the sound of the alien voices was gone as if cut off with a knife.

They probably wouldn't have an electronic workman's remote with them, thought Kretz. It was then, to his horror, that he realized that he didn't have his, either. He must have dropped it. That set his hearts racing even faster. If they knew how to use it . . .

And then he panicked. The tube was too small for him to stand up in. And crawling with a broken arm *hurt.* He shuffled and somehow made his way away from that door. He wasn't too worried about where he was going. The crucial direction was . . . away. Away from aliens with guns.

It was much later, in the dark, with no sounds of pursuit behind him, that he finally thought of putting his headlight on. When he got to another door . . . he lay down. It was not sleep really. More like half coma, half delirium. But no one and nothing disturbed him until his thirst did. There was nothing left in his suit tank. He cursed. Lay there and shivered with the tube going around and around. He tugged feebly at the door handle. It opened. It was obviously not intended to be secure from the inside.

Kretz was reluctant to leave the sanctuary of his refuge. But he knew that he had to drink. Had to. And besides, all Miran were somewhat claustrophobic. Females far more so than males, but no Miran liked confined places that much. It seemed better to let them kill him in the open. He was sure that he was too near death for them to beat anything out of him now.

Getting out and onto the ground was a difficult process. He hurt himself so badly that he passed out for a while. When he finally managed to stand up, he saw to his horror that the door he'd come through had somehow closed.

But at least there were no aliens around. To his blurred senses this end of the pipe seemed more verdant. There were certainly no burned-out passages, and the air smelled different. Perhaps they had local air-current circulators. The Miran explorers had barely begun to fathom the engineering of the habitat before the attack. Kretz still found it nearly incomprehensible that the aliens were so cavalier about destroying their own habitat. It was almost as if they did not know, or care, about how fragile an enclosed environment was. Of course a huge, complex one like this had far more self-correcting biofeedback loops than a smaller environment, but still, there had to be a point at which those could not compensate, and then collapse would be swift. The aliens must be pushing that limit, he thought, deriving some savage satisfaction from the idea, as his feet seemed to become more wayward and distant.

Suddenly, there was a squeal in front of him. A squat, four-footed pink alien peered malevolently at him from the shelter of the bush it had been rooting behind. This side of the habitat was very different. There was soil underfoot, along with plant-cover, even in this, the wide passage with the overhead rail. And there were transverse passages here too.

The alien was unclothed and rather muddy. It looked at Kretz . . . and turned and ran. The last he saw of it was its curly tail disappearing around a corner, into a transverse passage. Kretz watched it from a sitting down position and through a haze of pain, because his legs had gone wobbly on him and deposited him on his butt—which, by the feel of it, had started the bleeding again, and had jarred his arm.

Still: it stirred a kind of hope. There was more than one species of alien. Perhaps they were not all evil. Or perhaps it had just gone to call its friends. Doing his best to hurry, Kretz pressed on downward. But by now his eyes were having trouble focusing. And he kept hearing things—whether they were real or imaginary—he was not too sure. But he had to hide every time, in case.

It couldn't be much farther . . . surely? In his present state every step felt an enormous distance. And everything seemed so confused. Looking around him at the plants laden with heavy pink and green fruit, Kretz realized that he'd somehow lost the passage with the roof-rail and wandered into some side passage.

He was lost even from the vague hope of a path he'd been keeping to.

It was a small blow but the final one. He fell into the staked plants, breaking the fragile stems to half-lie, half-sit against the growth matrix-wall full of plants.

When consciousness came back he was aware of the sound of footsteps. Instinctively he tried to cower back the broken plants. But there was nowhere to hide this time. And he could not get up to run, although he tried. He closed his eyes, as if not by looking at it, it would not see him.

When he finally opened his eyes, the alien loomed over him. It looked like the alien monsters that had killed his friends and companions and hunted him down, except that it was much bigger.

There was one other difference, too. Its face was not striped.

# 5

Internal e-memo.
Re Habitat 37.
Date: 2120-11-3 Time: 13:53 NMT
To: Chief Construction (Spacefitting) Officer M. Kabongo
From: Systems Engineer (Maintenance) W. Ankar
Mike,

If they don't want maintenance robots, we can't force them to take them. The micro-bots are in place already and the externals will be here within 24 hours. There are standby 'bots in storage. What they don't see, they won't complain about, and it's not like work and safety people are going to come after us. You know that environmental planning is only giving the 350 year plus habitats a less than 50 percent chance of survival anyway. Their lookout. Their religious convictions.

Wanda

As he stumped irritably through his corridors, inspecting the tomatoes that now flourished in the section of drip-irrigators that he'd repaired, Howard Dansson wished that if God indeed had a plan for him, that he'd show him what it was. Howard knew that the thought itself was blasphemy, but he was so angry and frustrated that he took a kind of perverse pleasure in thinking it.

*The brethren do not meddle with mechanical things. God gave us our hands to work with.*

"Oh yes, Brother Galsson, perhaps we should all just starve," muttered Howard savagely, looking at the bountiful crop he was going to produce. If God had made the drip-irrigators then they would have been perfect, not prone to clogging up. And if they were made by God and not intended to be touched by human hands then why did he make them so simple that anyone with half a brain could open them and clean them?

Deep inside himself knew what someone like Galsson would say to that:

*Idle hands! The devil makes work for those idle hands, puts those thoughts into your head.*

Howard felt guilty in spite of his anger. Some of those thoughts he'd agree with Brother Galsson about. But being twenty-eight and still unmarried did have something to do with it. It wasn't that he was ugly, precisely. Just . . . different. And, in New Eden, girls' fathers did not find that an attractive feature in a prospective son-in-law.

Always in trouble with the teachers, for asking too many irreligious questions—and once even for questioning holy writ. With the regional council, for making a barrow. Everyone used them now, but when Howard thought that he'd been so clever to devise the thing, it'd been called a device of Satan. Fortunately, someone had found pictures of the brethren using them on lost Earth before the unbelievers had driven the brethren off to found New Eden, so they could see the fulfillment of God's promise and have a world of their own. So, if they founded it, how could God have made the drip-irrigators?

And lately he'd found himself in trouble with the Council of Elders. The bucket yoke. It was just so *obvious*.

He sighed and bent to remove a growing tip, before continuing with his ruminations. It wasn't that he *meant* to breach holy writ, or to set people on end. It was just that he thought about things, and then did them without considering what others might think. It was a severe character flaw. But, like finding a man who would bestow his daughter's hand on someone with a reputation for trouble, and who had been given one of the worst holdings in all of New Eden, it was something he hadn't succeeded in changing.

It wasn't as if he hadn't prayed about both issues. With all his heart and soul, he'd prayed. Repented too. It might have resulted in his growing the best tomatoes in New Eden, but it hadn't changed anything else, he had to admit. And then the next question would come up, and his mind would race off and try to answer it, leading his body into all sorts of trouble, like his flying experiments near the core. He'd only wanted to work out what the wingspan of an angel had to be! Of course it had subsequently occurred to him—though he'd never dared to mention it to anyone—that angel bodies were almost certainly lighter than mortal ones. That realization had come to him while looking at a broken chicken bone.

He'd really love to do a comparison between bone thicknesses of flying creatures and walking ones . . .

As his mind started to steal off down far more interesting corridors than the latest fuss about his water-management—either with the buckets or with clearing the drip-irrigators—something stopped him dead in his tracks. In pure dismay, at first.

Broken tomato vines will do that to even the most heathenly inventive tomato-farmer. Near-ripe fruit lay scattered around and the dying plant lay on the walkway. Howard bit back a word that would have had Elder Galsson read him out from the altar at Sunday's meeting. It must be pigs. Feral pigs from up in low G! That was one of the reasons no one liked the holdings this close to the polar core. The beasts were dangerous, besides all the damage they could do to a man's crops. But it was unusual that they hadn't eaten the fruit.

And then he realized that it wasn't pigs—although pigs eating half his crop might just have been better than the thing that was lying against the corridor wall. Howard couldn't have missed it in those shades of purple and orange. That was the color of its clothing, anyway. The creature's humanlike face was a pale golden color.

And the blood of it was red.

There was quite a lot of blood, too, on the walkway and on the walls. Howard was about to run, when the thing it opened its eyes. It cowered back against the wall, its lips moving.

Howard would still have run if it hadn't said "help" quite so weakly. And then it said something else that finally persuaded him that he could not just leave it here in the ruins of his prize Romas: "Peace."

"Peace be with you too, stranger," Howard managed to croak back.

After that, he could hardly leave the thing there. Whatever it was, demon or angelic messenger, it was hurt. And it had asked him for help. Howard picked it up in his arms. It was light. The thought occurred to him: *As light as an Angel might have to be to fly.* But there were no wings.

At least there was no spiked tail or horns, either.

He carried the creature home, the strange face warm against his shoulder. Just short of his door he saw two of the younger boys making their way back from the reservoirs. They'd sneaked off to swim, no doubt. He'd done it himself when he was their age. It had seemed worth the chastisement, as he recalled.

He called them. For a moment, it looked as if the guilty parties might bolt. But the brethren did raise children to be obedient to their elders, even if their hair was still dripping and the elder was someone like Howard. They came, fearful at first and then wide-eyed when they saw his limp burden. He pointed with his head to the smaller of the two boys. "I need you to run to Elder Rooson's home. Tell him I have some . . . thing which is hurt. I need his counsel. And you—"

He fixed the freckle-faced larger boy with his stare. "You will go to the healer. To Sister Thirsdaughter. As fast as your legs can carry you."

## 6

The fault with early slowship concepts was simple: When you get there, the place may not be habitable. It may not even be terraformable. Maybe there won't even be a planet: And then one has to start the journey over. Even probes can let you down—arrive on the one habitable spot, or at the only habitable season. With space habitats, the equation changes. Man stops colonizing planets. He colonizes space around suns. There is a life zone and everything he will need from m-asteroids to ice around *every* star.

From: *Slowtrain: The Stars Within Our Grasp*,
Conquist, A., Mordaunt Scientific Press, NY. 2090.

Howard looked at the creature on his bed, and then covered it gently with an angora-wool blanket. The . . .

person was still breathing, anyway. It didn't seem right to call it a creature. It wore clothes and had the trappings of an intelligent being. Howard looked at it again, a troubled man. He looked at the large Bible open on the stand. He'd searched, and yet found no pleasantly direct, clear advice about what one should do with a clothed creature you found unconscious among your tomato plants.

There was a knock at his door. He walked across and opened it. He was not really surprised to find not just Elder Rooson, but Brother Galsson, and Sister Thirsdaughter too. It was inevitable that the Elder would bring at least one of his senior councilors with him. It was just as inevitable, now, that the news should spread through all of New Eden like wildfire. Brother Galsson could not have left his home without telling his wife, and Goodwife Galsson was the worst gossip in the entire universe. She could hardly be expected to keep something like this quiet.

And she could get any story chaotically wrong, too. Look at the affair with Goodwife Sanderson's twins! Somehow she'd turned that event—the greatest excitement in New Eden since the two-headed calf—into "an unnatural child, a visitation of Satan." The midwife had told her the birth was "something special," but refused to say more and of course Goody Galsson had embroidered the snippet of information in the wrong direction entirely.

"Peace be with you, brothers and sister." Howard greeted the Elder and the councilors with a heavy heart. He was in enough trouble without this. He was still under probation after the last incident. But what could he have done? Left it? The . . . being had plainly been in distress.

And those had been recognizable English words. "Help," and most importantly, "Peace." To have ignored them would have been contrary to his faith and his nature.

"And with you, Brother Dansson," said the old man, with a wry smile, his palm dry against Howard's sweaty hand.

Elder Rooson wasn't the worst. Howard shuddered to think what life in New Eden might be like under an Elder like Galsson. Everything would be forbidden, on principle.

"What strange thing have you brought upon us this time?" The Elder said, with gentle irony, indicating that he certainly hadn't forgotten the last time.

"A . . . stranger, Elder. As I said in my message. I found it—him—in my tomatoes."

Sister Thirsdaughter was amused. "Have you been experimenting on those too, young Howard? Is it a strange fruit—or a real man?"

She was all right. She'd never married. Maybe that was why. Or maybe her practice of medicine and midwifery needed a more pragmatic approach. "No, sister. Not a man. I undressed the being—"

Galsson interrupted. "You undressed a woman!" he said in righteous horror.

Inwardly, Howard restrained himself. "It's not a woman, brother." He kept his doubts on this to himself. He'd never actually seen a naked woman, but he didn't think that it was a woman. But it wasn't a man either, not in the sense that Galsson would have interpreted it, in the sense of being human. "I had to remove its garments to staunch its blood. It asked for help. What else could I do?"

"Let us see this . . . being," said the Elder, calmly, a raised hand silencing Galsson's incipient tirade.

So Howard led them through his front room, hoping they'd be too distracted to notice much there—his drawings were still on the table—and into his small bedroom.

They stood in silence looking at the occupant of Howard's bed. Even the face, all they could see above the bedclothes, did not look human.

Galsson was the first to react. "A demon!" he choked, backing off, his soft hands held up in a warding gesture.

The strange being's eyes opened. The eyes had no white in them at all. They were almost violet in color and the pupil was a double crescent, like a cat's eyes. The strange pupils flared and contracted as if trying to focus.

"Hush. It is trying to say something," said Sister Thirsdaughter.

In the sudden silence they all heard it, clearly. "Peace." The voice was oddly metallic and artificial sounding. But there was no doubt he'd said it. Howard saw his lips move.

"Peace be with you too, stranger," said Elder Rooson, his voice quavering slightly.

The only reply was an indistinct muttering. The vivid purple-blue eyes closed again.

"It's a demon, trying to entrap us," whispered Galsson, still backing fearfully towards the door.

"What is the extent of its injuries?" asked Sister Thirsdaughter, ignoring him. She came forward to peer at the golden face with its crestlike peak of golden hair.

"Various cuts. A bad one on the shoulder," said Howard, grateful for the calm matter-of-fact tone of the healer. "A hole that seems to be festering. There might be something in it. I also think that one arm is broken. I've splinted it as best I can. If you could have a look, sister?"

She nodded and stepped forward.

Galsson grabbed her arm. "On the peril of your soul, sister. Demons are masters of deception!"

She shook off his hand impatiently. "At this stage, it could be a demon or even an injured angel. And surely the hand of God is over anyone who treats an injured being, be they devil or angel."

He tried to get in front of her. "Sister, I implore you, do not touch it! It may be diseased. Or the contact may cause evil communications!"

She pushed him aside firmly, stepping up to the bed. "Then that has happened to Brother Dansson already, and we have touched him in greeting. It appears to be wearing his nightshirt, and he can hardly have put that on it without touching it." She seemed quite calm and imperturbable. "Howard, I will require boiled but cooled water, and some boiled cotton cloths."

Howard nodded. "I have the water cooling. And the bandage-cloths have been boiled. I sent a message to you, sister. So I prepared."

She smiled. "I was treating the Elder's hands when the boy brought your message to him." She looked him up and down, quizzically. "Are my wants that predictable, or is it just that you were the child who always had to be bandaged, splinted or sewed up?"

Howard flushed. He had indeed spent a disproportionate amount of his life being patched up. "The latter, sister," he admitted, feeling sheepish. "I'll go and get the cloths and bowls for you."

"Do that." She was already unrolling a neat little cloth package of instruments. "And some boiling water too. I'd better re-sterilize these."

Howard noticed that Elder Rooson had said nothing. But the old man's normally tranquil face wore a troubled expression. He looked a lot more like Brother Galsson than his usual tranquil self.

By the time Howard got back with the bandages and both the hot and cooled boiled water, Sister Thirsdaughter had laid out her instruments on his bedside table on a clean cloth, and folded back the blanket. The hands and feet that protruded from Howard's spare nightshirt had the wrong number of fingers and toes. But they lacked demonish talons. They lacked any form of nail at all. The toes were nearly as long as the fingers. Yet . . . they were clearly fingers—albeit three on each hand, with a broader almost central thumb, and too many joints.

The sight seemed to fill Brother Galsson with horror. Almost as much horror as Sister Thirsdaughter lifting Howard's nightshirt. "Sister! You shame yourself!"

She flicked an irritated glance at him. "I'm a midwife, Russ. I delivered you, among others. If this poor creature is male—then for once I may see something different. Give me a hand here, Howard. He's very heavy for an old woman to move."

"We need to roll him, sister," said Howard. "The principal injuries are to his back and . . . uh . . . buttocks. We must just have a care for his right arm."

She looked at the awkwardly bandaged arm. Shook her head. "You did your best, I suppose. Well, let's look at the rest first." She looked at Howard's sheet. "His blood is red enough, whatever he is."

Howard nodded. "If it had been say, black, I don't think I would have dared to touch him," he admitted. "But he seemed so helpless, and so hurt. I couldn't just leave him there."

"It might have been better to treat him first and move him afterwards, Howard," said Sister Thirsdaughter grimly. She was old enough to call nearly every person in New Eden by their first name. Howard wouldn't have dared to do the same to her.

He nodded again, shamefaced. "I know. I just didn't think. He was cold, and bleeding and he asked for help."

She smiled at him again. "What else could one of the Brethren do? But next time think with your head and not just your heart."

"His heart's in the right place," said Elder Rooson heavily. "It's his head that I am not too sure about. Do you need us for this, sister? I think I must convene a full council, to pray and discuss this matter."

"You do that, Elder," she said. "Tell them to pray for this poor fellow's survival." She looked at the exposed wound. "He may need all our prayers and all our skill. There is something lodged in there. I'm going to have to get it out. Ask Sister Melson to come please. I will need her skill with herbals. Not that we know what herbs may do to this . . . "

"Demon," supplied Galsson. "I shall stay here and protect you, sister."

"Well, then you may occupy yourself in boiling some more water," was all the reply he got.

The being moaned as she gently probed the wound with her forceps. They were old. The fine metalwork made Howard desperately envious. He had done some work in the forge making spades and axes, and he knew just what craftsmanship he was looking at.

"They're a relic of the first Eden," she told him.

Howard could only look at them in wonder. True, the brethren had been surrounded and repressed in that place, and evil had attacked them from all sides, threatening the faith and their way of life. But such craftsmanship . . .

She drew something out of the wound. A little red blood trickled out of the hole as she held it up, critically.

"What is it?" asked Howard, ever curious. He knew—enough people had told him—that it was his besetting sin.

"A piece of metal," said Sister Thirsdaughter. Her voice was curiously flat. She looked at it carefully. "It is something I have only seen in my medical text, that date from before the creation of New Eden. I think it is a bullet."

"What is that?" asked Howard.

Sister Thirsdaughter answered in the same expressionless voice. "A projectile driven at great speed by exploding gasses in a tube, I believe. The writers of the text seemed to assume that we would know about them. They were obviously common then, and intended to hurt or kill. Somewhere, someone tried to kill this . . . " She gestured with the forceps at the golden-skinned subject of her surgery. "Person."

Her watchers were nearly rigid with shock. Nothing could be more alien to the Society of Brethren.

"That's not possible," said Galsson, as usual, finding his wind first. "No one in New Eden would do such a thing."

Howard had to agree with him, for the first time ever.

Sister Thirsdaughter looked at both of them, silently. Then she said, "If that is the case, then he must have come from elsewhere. Outside."

If she'd said that all of Howard's neighbors were murderers and that Goody Galsson danced naked and sacrificed cats to the devil she could scarcely have had quite as stunning an effect.

Outside. Beyond New Eden. The first Eden had had evil, idolaters and unbelievers surrounding it. By the writings evil came right into the midst of the brethren, there. But nothing came to New Eden. Nothing ever had before anyway. Not in living memory.

"We have a tradition of keeping ourselves to ourselves," said Galsson stiffly. "It must go back to its kind."

Howard looked at the pale golden-skinned creature on his bed. To his eye it seemed to be developing goose bumps. So he covered it. "We also have a tradition of sanctuary," he said, quietly but with a firmness that surprised even himself. "If the outside is a place of evil, and they tried to kill him, perhaps he has repented, and tried to flee the world of sin."

"Perhaps he was too evil even for them," muttered Galsson.

"We also have a tradition of leaving God to judge," said Sister Thirsdaughter, "and of charity, and of healing the sick, and helping the weak. I," she said pointedly, "will not just pass by on the other side of the road."

"I think we must put it out of the airlock, and return it to its own kind," said Galsson. "I will speak to the council and say so. We have had no contact with the evils outside of New Eden, and we should not start now."

"First, however, let us heal it and allow it to speak for itself," said Sister Thirsdaughter firmly. "Is it not true, Brother Galsson, that there are things that evil cannot endure? Such as the name of the Lord?"

He blinked. That had, obviously, given him serious pause. "I shall go and confer with my fellow councilors on this. Perhaps we can banish evil by spiritual means."

Howard was very relieved to see the back of the man.

"Pass me the lint, Howard," was all Sister Thirsdaughter said. But her tone indicated that she too was pleased.

They worked on in relative silence, with barely a whimper of pain from their strange patient, as the healer adjusted and rebandaged the splint on the broken arm. Eventually they were finished. The elderly woman turned to her large helper and said, "Now, if I do not get a cup of your tea, I will fall over."

Howard tucked the blankets in around the patient's neck. "There are very strict injunctions against fallen women," he said solemnly, "so I'd better make you some."

The healer laughed. "You've a good sense of humor anyway, young man. It's an asset for someone who seems to spend his life in trouble. Come. We can leave him for a few minutes. He seems to be quiet. Whether it is sleep or unconsciousness, one cannot know."

They went through into the small kitchen. "Plenty of food for a bachelor," she said, looking at the strings of dried tomatoes and peppers. "And a clean and well-set up kitchen. I'd think you'd be a catch for any young woman looking for a husband, Brother Dansson."

"I thought it would work better like this," he said, hasty to explain the odd layout, rather than discuss his marital status. "I always needed water when I was cooking and I got tired of fetching it. And I grow fine crops. There is always excess."

"On a holding that was thought to be largely unusable," said Sister Thirsdaughter quietly. "You were expected to end up laboring for your keep."

"It was just a water problem, which I fixed," said Howard awkwardly, as he finished filling the kettle. "If I'd had to carry buckets, one at a time . . . then, yes, it would not be viable."

She twinkled at him "You've got the council in an uproar even without finding this strange being on your land. Did you know that despite the censure, a number of them want you to fix the water sprayers on their land?"

Howard looked gloomily at the next room. "The naysayers will claim this stranger is a punishment from God."

He bit his lip. "I still don't know what he is myself. Is he a demon or an angel?"

"He may be neither," said Sister Thirsdaughter. "In fact, Howard, I am not entirely sure he is a he."

Howard nearly dropped the mug he was holding. "But . . . but he . . . uh, it has . . . um . . . " he said, turning puce.

She nodded. "And also has a second orifice, and no external testicles. For all that it looks generally like a male, it may not be. Whatever it is, it isn't human. Unless the Lord made demons of baser flesh, and easily subject to wounding, I would say that the correct answer was neither angel nor devil, but quite frail, withal. I think it may die, Howard. We must say prayers for its soul."

"If it has a soul," said Howard. Such theology was beyond him. But was it not written that God had made man in his image?

"That is up to God to decide," she said tranquilly. "We must just do our best. Now, make us that tea."

**7**

External e-vox
from: Congress-Representative Frank Nalinno (sub-committee on system emigration support)
To: Dr. Anthony J. Jamieson, University of Nebraska

While you say that we do not appreciate what a legacy of traditions, culture, and of a living example of religious society for students to study we're throwing away here, what you may not appreciate, Dr. Jamieson, is what the general System-dwelling public think of these people, and their archaic belief systems. The truth is most of the public don't care, but SysGov has a sizable voting bloc—about fourteen percent from various interest groups—who do care. We've been under considerable pressure from a number of animal rights groups to have their traditional form of agriculture—which includes slaughter of meat animals instead of growing vat-protein—declared illegal. There are a number of women's rights groups who have campaigned to have them declared an illegal association, because their beliefs are patriarchal. Before you argue with me, my hands are tied. I know—for a small group—they retain under humane conditions a surprisingly large proportion of domesticated animal diversity, which, as pointed out by various studies, has declined catastrophically since protein vat-culture's inception. I've already had letters from your learned colleagues in zoological research. I know it's an open society with members choosing to live under a patriarchal system. It is simply not politically expedient to oppose the groups wishing to be rid of them. As a student of political history myself, this is a pattern which has frequently been repeated. I recall a similar problem with the anti-fox hunting legislation at the end of the twentieth century. Research and logic don't come into it. Voter sentiment does. Most people don't know, or have much contact with domestic animals, these days. Patriarchy is politically incorrect, and their holier-than-thou attitude gets up the voters' noses. They want our funds to get out of here? They're going to get them.

---

Kretz woke up, finding himself blessedly warm. He felt as if he hadn't been warm for a long, long time. Loss of blood, probably. Perhaps he was now in the final stages before death. Certainly things were strange enough to be hallucinations. He was in a room of some sort, and not in the endless plant-corridors. It was a starkly plain room, and was lit by a single flame burning on the end of some sort of yellowish stick. He was lying on something soft, under a cover. He felt curiously naked. And on the chair beside the bed sat one of the dreaded aliens.

Instinctively he attempted to get up and run away. His arm hurt as he moved. The alien pressed him back down. "It's all right. Calm down," Transcomp supplied.

Kretz lay still, rigid with fear, trying to gauge what to do now. His head swam with the pain, and the sudden exertion.

"Your arm is broken. It is splinted, but you mustn't use it," said the alien. "Do you want to sit up? I can help you."

Kretz closed his eyes. He remembered, now, through a haze of confusing pain, the escape from the aliens who had tried to kill him. He remembered this one, or one very like it, also without the face-stripes, saying "Peace."

"Can I give you something to drink?" asked the alien, via Transcomp.

Opening his eyes again, he saw that its clothes were also different from the mottled brown and green of the aliens he'd encountered previously. These were an unpatterned gray. It also seemed larger. Perhaps it was a female? Logic slowly came to his mind and to his rescue. If it had wanted to kill him, it could have done that while he was insensible. Whatever its intentions were, it was not going to kill him, at least not immediately. And the mention of drink did bring home to him just how incredibly thirsty he was.

"Drink," he said, and the Transcomp unit around his neck provided an alien sound. He reached his mouth for the water-nipple of his suit and realized he was not wearing it. Anyway, the water tank had been dry for some time.

"I will help you to sit up. You cannot drink lying down." The big alien hauled him up to lean back against something soft and gently yielding.

It lifted a container to his lips, while supporting his head, gently. "Here. Don't drink too much."

The water tasted a little odd. But it was wet. And if alien bacteria survived in his body . . . well, it was too late now. He'd been exposed to enough airborne bacteria, and without fluids he was not going to live for very long, even if the aliens didn't kill him.

He leaned back against the softness they had piled behind him. "What do you wish to do with me?"

The big alien looked at him. "You asked for help," it said.

Was that all that it took? But surely they had used the word before? Thinking back he was sure that Selna had called out for help before they'd shot him.

"Are you going to kill me?" he asked.

It was the alien's turn to back away, shaking its head. "We don't kill. That is why the Brethren left the Solar system. We are a people of peace."

Kretz, his mind flooding with the terrible images of destruction and the death of his fellows, struggled to reconcile this with the facts. "You killed my companions," he said.

The big alien shook its head. "The last person to commit the sin of Cain was Brother Lewisson in the year 79. He coveted his neighbor's wife. That was more than two hundred years ago."

Some of the words did not translate. "Years" was obviously some measure of time, and the reference to "his" made clear this was a bi-sexual species. But "Sin of Cain"? Transcomp made sense only of the middle word. If only Kretz didn't feel so weak and tired. Consciousness left him, blurring away into the horrors he'd been through.

When he next awoke there was another alien sitting beside him. A much smaller one, although the color of its clothing was similar. Was this one of the males? The aggressive sex? He eyed the alien warily. But it had nothing that was even reminiscent of the projectile flingers that the earlier aliens had all carried.

"Ah. I see that you are awake again, stranger," Transcomp supplied. "Peace be with you. I am Sister Thirsdaughter. Brother Dansson is out tending his crops."

Once again Transcomp struggled with some of the terms. "Sister" was confusing, given that the comparative size of the alien meant it was presumably male. But, whatever else, the word "peace" was a comforting one.

"What is your name?" The small alien inquired.

"Kretz."

"Do you want some more to drink, Brother Kretz? Perhaps some broth?"

"Yes. Drink."

So. "Brother" as well as "Sister." Clearly bi-sexual —but which sex was which?

The small alien got up and walked out, leaving the door open. Kretz knew he ought to seize this opportunity to get away. He was not constrained, in any way that he could see, constrained. Perhaps . . .

He tried to sit up, and found that there was one constraint—his arm was strapped and bandaged, and did not enjoy his attempt to move. He remembered, now, the fall. Weakly, he remained half-sitting, as the small alien returned. It—he? she?—carried a bowl that steamed. The alien saw what he had done and set the bowl down and put a careful hand under his armpit and helped him to sit up against the soft things. He remembered that he'd been sitting against them, when he'd drunk a little, earlier. He must have either slid down or been helped to lie down then. The little alien lacked the strength of the big one. It struggled with the task, and Kretz was too weak to help much.

Then the large alien came in to the room, and helped with no apparent effort. The little one said: "Well, I am glad you chose to get back just then, Howard. When you get to be as old as I am, you'll find strength isn't what it should be."

Kretz struggled with the rationale in this one. Surely the larger one was older? That was the only thing that made any biological sense. Even with his body in distress, and his person in all sorts of trouble, Kretz remained a biologist first. It was the reason he'd been considered insane enough to come on this mission.

The small, wrinkled-faced one must still be growing. Just like any young Miran, its skin was too large, still. The alien's statements about age were either a mistranslation or—a pleasant thought, this—a joke.

The small alien picked up the bowl while the larger one supported Kretz. The small one took a spoon—it was amazing how convergent some things were—and lifted a tiny quantity of the steaming stuff to his mouth. Alien scents assaulted his nares.

"I don't know if you can eat our food," said the little alien. "But you must eat something or you will die." Feeling his weakness Kretz realized that it was a true statement. He took a tiny sip.

It was hot! And salty. He spat weakly. Coughed. "Hot." he said, as soon as he could speak.

"Well, there goes Galsson's theory that you'd need boiling brimstone to survive," said the little one. "I'm going to add some cold water to this, Howard. And I think some honey."

"To soup?" the larger alien seemed taken aback.

The little wrinkled one nodded. "It will make something similar to the rehydration fluid I use on my patients with gastro."

Most of this made little sense to Kretz. But Transcomp was gathering vocabulary. Eventually, it would make complete linkages. The small alien went away again with the bowl, and the larger one allowed Kretz to settle back against the softness, only to sit him up again when the little one returned. Steam no longer rose from the bowl, but the scent rising from it was just as alien. Once again, the alien raised a small quantity to his lips. It was both sweet and salty and just vaguely reminiscent of the energy nutrient drink that he'd had from the suit-nipple. It stayed down. The little one patiently fed him more, and then, just when he was almost getting used to it, stopped.

"I have a feeling we'd better not overdo this," it said. "When did you last have food?"

Kretz struggled to think. Of course Transcomp would not have units of time for the alien language yet. "A long time," he said. It had been, he was vaguely aware, a very long time.

"Then we'll let you digest this for a bit," said the little one. "Is there anything else we can do for you?"

The little alien really seemed to have no ill intent. So he said: "My suit."

They looked at him, tilting their heads at an oddly Miranese-seeming angle. Perhaps this was another example of both convergent evolution and the effect of binocular vision, tilting the head like that when querying something. It was plain that they did not understand him. He used his good hand to take the sleeve of the large one. "My," he said.

The alien nodded—another commonality—and stretched its lips out as if in discomfort, showing her oddly shaped teeth.

Well, perhaps that expression differed in meaning. Kretz certainly hoped so!

"I washed it," said the alien. "I have it in my cupboard." Whatever that meant . . . "Do you want me to bring it to you?"

Kretz nodded, scarcely able to believe this. Were these the same kind as the aliens who had hunted him so mercilessly? Who had burned the others, and who he'd seen bring down Selna like a pack of predators? It seemed almost impossible. The only difference he could see was the absence of stripes on their faces, and the way that they dressed.

"You can bring it for him, Howard," said the little wrinkled one. "But he's not to put it on. It won't fit over the cast. Your arm"—it pointed one of its upper limbs—"is broken. I've set it as best I can. Your bones are not quite the same as ours. I had to guess what I was doing."

The biologist wondered just how different they were. The Miranese crewman side of him remembered reading of a similar concept in primitive Miran, where the bones would be positioned, immobilized and allowed to knit of their own accord. It should still work, he supposed, doubtfully. But it seemed amazingly primitive for a species that could traverse the depths of interstellar space.

The sugars and possibly some of the other nutrients were working on his mind, at least. Now, with a definitely clearer head, he knew that eating alien food had been taking an enormous chance. A ridiculous one. Simple sugars—and as pure as possible—would be safest, he supposed. But Kretz could not live on sugars alone, and it seemed unlikely that he could get chemically pure sucrose—or the glucose his body broke it into, from such primitive-seeming people.

Perhaps, it occurred to him with sudden insight, they really *were* primitive. Perhaps the aliens had once been a technologically advanced species, but weren't any more. He wished that he had a sociologist like Ferbren to discuss it with. Perhaps this was what happened if you isolated people totally.

Still, they must have been technological masters of immense skill, once. The Miran time record for a self-contained habitat was only ten years. This string of habitats had been traversing space for far, far longer. Perhaps longer than the Miran had realized. Some of the ideas he'd seen—the gutlike increase in surface area, the use of low-G capillary action—were so simple and elegant that he wondered how they'd not become part of the sealed habitat projects of Miranese mainstream science.

But the truth was, he had to admit, that Miran had devoted less energy to space each year. There wasn't the drive to build such a craft, or a craft of any sort for that matter. The expense of creating environments large enough to keep the average Miran from chronic claustrophobia was prohibitive. That was why it was necessary to find freaks like himself for this voyage. Space interest had definitely been dying.

At least, until an alien ship had been spotted by the astronomers.

The larger of the two aliens came back carrying his suit. It was shaking its head so violently the brownish tuft of hair looked in danger of flying off. "I was going to mend it. But look, sister. The holes are gone!"

"And there I merely thought that the fineness of the weave was miraculous," said the smaller wrinkled alien.

As bizarre as it seemed, Kretz was coming to the conclusion that the large alien was male and the small one female. That was the only explanation, at least, that matched their consistent use of the terms "brother" and "sister." But, at the moment, he was far more interested in the suit itself. The sight of the suit in its comforting high-visibility colors lifted Kretz's spirits. These aliens seemed disposed to be kind. Indeed, if anything they appeared to be scared of him. But . . .

The Miran had thought the aliens in the first habitat had been friendly, too, at first. He couldn't trust them too much.

A third alien appeared. This one was also small but had a facial mane, like the large male. Perhaps the males had multiple mates. That was an odd idea, but not beyond the limits of biological possibility. "You could have knocked," said the large one.

"I go where the work of the Lord takes me," said the newcomer. "I must watch over this spawn of Satan, this thing from cities of the plain."

"It's a pity your piety doesn't take you to your crops more often. They look as if the devil has been at them," said the big one. It was hard to judge aliens, but the two seemed to dislike each other.

"How dare you?" demanded the newcomer.

The small wrinkled alien held up her hands. "Peace. If you two wish to make a loud noise go out and do it in your corridors. The patient needs rest."

They looked at her and were still. A powerful and influential female this! Well, it could also be that they could see that when the loose skin filled out she was going to be larger than either of them.

*The patient needs rest*, thought Howard, might well be true, but the patient had slept virtually uninterrupted for three days now. Howard was very underslept himself, from trying to do his chores and share in the nursing of the patient. He understood that the council had placed them in quarantine. He understood why, too. But it was a busy time on the farm-corridors right now and there was the section where the sub-irrigation had failed. He had to carry a powerful number of buckets for that, and, after all the trouble he was in about it, he didn't dare to use his four bucket yoke, although then he could have got the job done much, much faster. He had to work at night, to avoid others on his walk through to the water.

Having Sister Thirsdaughter virtually living in his home didn't make things any easier, either. There was nowhere he could really even hide the drawings without her possibly finding them. At the moment they were rolled up under his underwear. It was very frustrating. Still, she'd saved him from getting into an open fight with Galsson—something that would have had them both up before the discipline committee. That was something he didn't need, as they were still mired in debating his bucket-yoke.

"The council has deputized me to keep an eye on this . . . " said Galsson quietly, after standing fulminating for a while. He pointed at the stranger with a shaking forefinger. "And him. It is my opinion that it is his un-Godly meddling with the drip irrigators that has brought this visitation upon us!"

"It is possible," said Sister Thirsdaughter. "But we do not know whether this visitation is a demon, an angel or merely a test of our faith. And you might say that Brother Dansson has had his just reward for what he has done to the drip-irrigators in his crops."

"But they're good crops!" protested Howard.

"Exactly," said the healer.

"We will test its faith," said Galsson, grimly. "And God moves in mysterious and not always direct ways, sister."

"And chooses his instruments as he wills, according to his purposes," said the sister tranquilly. "You may test his faith, Russ Galsson. But not now. He's been insensate for three days. Howard. Sit with him. Brother Galsson will escort me to meet with my fellow councilors, and we can discuss how best to proceed."

So Howard found himself left to sit with the stranger-creature. It didn't seem to be in any danger of slipping back into a coma-sleep just yet. Its eyes were wide open, and it had a wary look about it. Mind you, that could just be its way of looking happy for all he knew.

He tried smiling at it. It shrank back against the pillows; plainly, no matter what kind of creature it was, afraid. "I'm not going to hurt you," he said hastily. "It is all right. I promise."

The wariness was still there in posture. "Promise? Means?"

"I give my word."

The strange creature shook its head in a curious round bobbing motion. "Means?"

"I swear." He stepped over to the Bible on its stand. Put his hand on it. "On the Bible."

The occupant of his bed looked no less puzzled. "Means? Bible?"

"The holy book! It means what I say is true."

"True. You do not wish to hurt?" It was still plainly doubtful.

Howard decided to try logic. "I have given you help. I have given you my nightshirt, my bed, and I bandaged you up. Why would I do that if I wanted to hurt you?"

"Bandaged? Means?"

Howard pointed to the injured arm. "Like that."

The occupant of Howard's bed looked at his splinted arm. Nodded slowly. "It is the teeth," it said.

Without thinking, Howard pulled back his lips and felt them with his tongue. He was surprised to see the stranger-creature shrink back again. "I'm sorry," he said hastily. "I didn't mean to frighten you. I'm not going to eat you."

The creature sat silent for a time, as if absorbing this. "Peace," said Howard, trying all he could think of. "Peace."

It seemed to find that comforting. "Peace," it said. "Teeth to Miran mean to fight."

It was clear enough when you put it like that. "You Miran?"

The creature nodded again. "You name?"

"Howard. Howard Dansson," supplied Howard, careful not to show his teeth when he smiled.

The creature looked uncomprehendingly at the hand Howard had extended. "Drink?"

So Howard fetched it water, and helped it to sit enough to drink, cautiously.

"Who hurt you?" asked Howard, when it had finished and rested against the pillows again.

Miran looked at him for a long time. "Howard," he said finally. "Howard with stripy face. Howard tried to kill me. Kills my *distod*. Miran come in peace. Howard kill."

*Distod?* "Howard with a stripy face"? Howard blinked at the creature as he puzzled over these terms.

Miran looked suddenly afraid again. "Howard with a stripy face close?"

Howard shook his head, more in puzzlement than anything else.

Miran closed his eyes, making little mewling noises, almost as if it were crying, but there were no tears. Gradually the sound stopped and the breathing slowed. It appeared to have slipped back into either sleep or a coma. Howard wished he could leave, as he had a myriad chores to do and tasks to attend to, today. But he'd been told to stay and watch the being.

So he did. It was a long, solitary vigil, until Sister Thirsdaughter came back.

"How is the patient?" she asked, smiling at him, but with a little frown of worry between her eyes.

"If you smile at him, don't show your teeth," said Howard. "He's scared of teeth. And I think he believes that all men are called 'Howard.' He says Howard with a stripy face hurt him and killed his 'disdod,' whatever they are."

Sister Thirsdaughter shook her head ruefully. "All we need is him saying that to the council. As if your act of charity hadn't landed you in enough trouble. They're sending five members here. I hope Kretz wakes soon."

"Kretz?"

"That's his name."

"Oh." said Howard, disconcerted. "He told me it was Miran."

Sister Thirsdaughter cocked her head at him. "In the same conversation that you told him all humans are called Howard?"

"Uh, yes," he admitted, getting the drift. "You mean they're called Miran?"

"And his name is Kretz. Yes."

Obviously the sound of his name, or Howard's stifled laughter, was enough to wake the sleeper. His violet-blue eyes snapped open. "Greeting, Howard," he said respectfully to Sister Thirsdaughter on seeing her. She covered her eyes with her hand, and, after the briefest pause, he did likewise. "I think the council may almost deserve this," she said, her voice shaking a little. "Our greeting is 'Peace be with you,' Brother Kretz. This is Howard. Or rather Brother Howard. I am Sister Thirs-daughter. We are human. You are one Miran, right?"

## 8

"It's an opportunity to get rid of a major problem. If we can get the 'Great Leader' satisfied that we meet his conditions, and he'll meet ours, a space habitat is a small price to pay. It'll get rid of a festering sore and allow development in the Far Eastern sector of Earth to finally fulfill its promise. Yes, it will be tough on those he takes with him, but better a few should suffer than we all do. I do think we need to get him to leave his nukes behind though, Mister Chairman."

—Dillon Wan Chu, Senior Policy Advisor
to SysGov Chairman Thomas Barattachi:
Transcript of Secret Service recordings.

Abret admitted that he was scared out of his wits and that he had no idea what to do about it. The radio-silence from the main ship just made it worse. They'd been carried head high through the corridors by the thronging crowds, cheering, clapping and making various other less comprehensible noises. They'd certainly covered a great distance. Even if they could persuade the aliens—who admittedly had done them no harm—to put them down, Abret wasn't too sure they could find their way back . . . if he could persuade Derfel to even try. He appeared to be reveling in this. At least he, Abret, was no longer under the mentally disturbed male's gaze and gun. He'd liberated his own laser from the holster—not that it would do him any kind of good in a crowd this size.

They had been carried to a huge building. Every other structure that Abret had seen was tiny. This was vast. Columns and carved stonework fronted it. As they advanced, the shallow ponds and great banks of colored plant-matter were covered by the sea of aliens. They were carried to the front of the mob, which had stopped moving. Abret saw a small group of aliens, in odd brown, bright-buttoned clothes, standing or kneeling in the archway. They were pointing at the crowd with shiny metal objects that said "weapon" even if one didn't know what they were.

The crowd carried the two of them straight towards the brown uniforms. Everything had gone very ominously quiet.

There was an explosion. Something hit Abret. The suit wasn't punctured, but they'd shot a projectile at him. Hit him, too.

He reacted instinctively with the weapon in his hand.

The brown clothes with their bright buttons were not proof against laser.

Before Abret had time to fully grasp the horror of what he'd done, the crowd roared—a deafening sound—and surged forward over the remains of those he'd shot.

At the main door there was an alien that the crowd held back from. Standing dead still on a plinth, he was a sort greenish-brown all over. He stood there with a fist raised and held back the mob.

This solitary alien barred the way.

Derfel shot him. Severed his neck with his laser.

The head fell with a metallic clang.

The alien figurine still stood. But it no longer held back the crowd. They just skirted the fallen head with its angry staring eyes.

Then came the worst part.

They found a small, round-bodied alien, dressed in the same odd brown clothes.

He tried to run, but the alien crowd picked him up and tore him apart. Literally, limb from limb. Then they kicked and danced and stamped on the remains until there was nothing left. The bright buttons and brown uniform were shredded and scattered.

Abret did not know what to do.

There was no reply from the ship.

Derfel had gotten down and kicked the dead torso too.

They were carried again, and Derfel was seated in a great chair on a dais in an enormous hall. Another one was fetched for Abret—not quite as ornate, but close. Frightened and wary, Abret had sat almost comatose with terror.

Derfel got them to start teaching his Transcomp words.

Abret turned his off and looked, desperately, for a way to escape.

He could see none. Every possible space was taken up by aliens. Aliens come to stare. Aliens in brown uniforms like the ones he'd shot came through also. They were pushed and jostled by the crowd, but not treated as they had the rotund alien. The brown-uniformed ones knelt before Derfel and Abret and groveled on their faces.

Derfel said something in the language of the aliens, and the crowd cheered.

He had them. But all Abret had was abject terror, and a desperate desire to escape from the maddening crowd.

## 9

"To the primitive who spent six months hollowing out a log, the clinker-built longship was an advance so great as to be beyond comprehension. It carried so much more, and was so much more seaworthy—and measured per person involved and transported by it, cost less. Then the caulked planks of a medieval carrack carried a vast load, unthinkable to earlier sailors. Its untreated timbers meant a short few years use out of 150 year-old oak timbers. It took skilled craftsmen in the best shipyard in Europe eight months to build . . . and by 1570 AD there were ships of 400 ton capacity. To those sailors, a supertanker would have been an unimaginable vessel—carrying 250,000 tons. Yet, per ton carried over time, the supertanker was far cheaper than the carrack. The space habitat of the future will be far bigger still . . . and far cheaper per ton carried, with an infinitely longer depreciation. Stretch your minds, and start leaving everything you have learned about engineering behind. This isn't the just mechanical engineering of heavy machinery . . . it's that, metallurgy, architecture and trajectory computation, all in one big, new package."

> —Prof. Marcus T. Chede. Inaugural lecture on assuming the Chair of Space Science, University of Wisconsin.

Kretz blinked. "You have seen other Miran?" he asked, hopefully. Perhaps others of his group had somehow found their way to this apparently friendly group.

They both shook their heads. "Never."

Someone knocked and the tall male, Howard, went to let them in. He led in a group of these Howards . . . humans into the room. Some had facial hair and others did not, and most of their hair had obviously not begun to turn lustrous and colored yet. Some hadn't yet grown any hair at all, or just had a few wispy strands.

Kretz was—to his fellow Miran—unusually tolerant of closed-in spaces and crowded places. That didn't mean—like poor Derfel, who was completely mad as most Miranese would see it—that he enjoyed being crowded. All of these aliens around the bed made him feel very confined. Two of them were showing teeth, too. That, he had to remind himself, was one of the pieces of social display that didn't translate.

It wasn't a threat among the aliens, although, thinking back, it could be. Well. Politeness first, even if they were making him most uncomfortable. "Peace be with you," he said.

That seemed to startle them. Several of them raised a hand—not two hands, Kretz noted—as the stripe-faced aliens had. A single hand at about face level, and not above their heads. "Peace be with you too, stranger," said one in a slightly shaky voice.

"Sister Thirsdaughter. Why is his face that color?" asked another.

"I think he just is that color," said the small wrinkled female who had tended his hurts. "Why don't you ask Brother Kretz yourself, Brother Lee? Kretz, Brother Lee would like to know why you are that color? He does speak some English, Brother Lee, although I must warn you that he's obviously still learning it."

Kretz did his honest best to answer the question. He was sure that Transcomp would get some words wrong, but they had asked. "It is because of chromophores in the dermis . . . the skin," Kretz elaborated, seeing the alien shake his head. "Why do you not have striped faces like the other aliens that look quite like you?"

"I've never heard of anyone with a striped face," said the one called Brother Lee. "Where did you meet these?"

"It was when we came into the habitat from our spacecraft," explained Kretz earnestly. "We were met and later attacked by them. They pretended to be friendly. Peaceful. They are going to attack and kill my people at our home."

"And they hurt you like this?" asked Sister Thirsdaughter. "Bothers, sisters, as I told you, I think he was shot. Shot with a projectile that looks very like a bullet in medical texts from pre-New Eden."

Much of what the wrinkled little female said didn't translate. But Kretz had a good idea what she was trying to say. "The striped-faced ones used some kind of tube-weapon, that drove a projectile very fast. They tried to kill me." He could see that not all of it had translated either, but the part about trying to kill him that had got to them, by the reaction. "I think they killed my companions—the rest of my friends. I ran. I was very hurt. I lost a lot of blood. I did not know where I ran. Thank you for helping me."

The humans were silent for a bit, then another asked: "Where have you come from?"

That, at least, was easy. "From Miran. Our world." Looking at the shaking heads he realized it was not going to be quite so easy after all. Had they forgotten that there was anything outside?

"Are many of you going to come to New Eden?" asked another.

Kretz shook his head, hoping that he was reading the questioner aright. The posture—if they were behaviorally at all like Miran, and seemed to be—was defensive. "It is very far away. It took us much time to get here. You are going past us, very fast. We cannot do it again."

"This Miran place. Is it hot?" That came from one with a misshapen face.

"You mean full of brimstone, Brother Lewis?" asked the wrinkled physician.

"Let him answer the question, sister," said the one who'd asked. "I see he's huddled under blankets. Tell us about this Miran-place . . . stranger."

Kretz thought carefully. How did you explain a planet? "It is a place like this—with plants and things much like yours. It is a little warmer, but not very much."

"So, if it is such a good place, why have you come here?"

How could he explain? "We came to see what was here. Your . . . place shines like a star in the sky."

That plainly impressed them. "And your light shall be a beacon to the multitudes," said one. Transcomp filed away several more unknown words.

It didn't appear to satisfy the one who had worried about Miran being warmer than this place. "Are there many of you?" he asked, sticking his head forward like a predatory tunnel-worm. He had bristly cilia above his eyes.

Kretz gave him as fair an answer as possible. "I do not know. Do you mean on Miran or here? On Miran, many. Here, I do not know. I may be the last of my kind. The striped-faced ones killed my companions. Two of the others were due to go to bead six."

"And how do we know all of this is true?" asked the inquisitor, pursing his lips and looking at Kretz with narrowed eyes.

Kretz guessed that the pursed lips were not an invitation to sexual congress here. Truth? Well, he could use Howard's earlier words. The big male had seemed very intense about it when trying to reassure him. It was probably a way of indicating a deeply held belief in that truth.

"I swear on the Bible." he said, pointing to the object Howard had put his hand on. He hoped that he read the alien's expression right, and that the alien wasn't going to be piqued at the lack of response he got.

Nothing he'd managed to say thus far had the same effect. Male Miran are very observational about postural cues. It was how they survived the moodiness of those undergoing changeover. Several of the aliens visibly relaxed.

"Are you of our Faith?" asked the one who had wanted to know why he was that color.

Transcomp rendered the last word as it heard it, as it had no Miran equivalent or near equivalent yet. By the way the posture changed, and by the way they looked at him, this was an important question. "I do not understand the word 'faith.' Please explain," he said, playing for time and more clues. He was at their mercy, and he was still not sure if the Miran had done something wrong with the other aliens, to make them murder his companions. This group seemed friendly. But so had the stripy-faced ones, at first.

"Do you believe in Almighty God?" asked one. It didn't seem to be an explanation. But they were all leaning in on him.

"I do not understand 'Almighty God'? Please explain."

"Aha!" The one who was possibly piqued because of a lack of attention pointed a finger at him. "An emissary of Satan, just as Brother Galsson said! His words are all lies!"

"If they're all lies, then why didn't he lie about that?" asked Howard. "Brother, why not get him to swear on the Bible? If he's a demon it should burn him."

"Who asked you to speak?" snapped Kretz's chief inquisitor.

"It's a good idea, all the same, Brother Lewis," said one of the others. "I think we should do it." The small still-bald male picked the Bible-thing up and put it on the bed. Kretz felt that he would never get the hang of this alien hierarchy, let alone the questions they were putting to him.

"Put your uninjured hand on it and say the following words after me. 'I swear,' " instructed the small male.

Kretz did he was instructed. "I swear." The Bible-thing was a fascinating artifact. It looked reminiscent of a text-screen. Kretz wished, rather sadly, that Zawn could be there to examine it.

The man continued. "By Almighty God, to tell the truth and nothing but the truth, so help me God."

The words were confusing, but there seemed no harm in them, and no way to avoid saying them without causing offense. So Kretz repeated them.

"Well, he didn't burst into flames," said someone.

Kretz's leading inquisitor was either very promiscuous —or the facial expression which he gave the alien who said that meant something else entirely. The inquisitor turned his attention to Kretz: "I ask you directly. Are you a demon sent here by the evil one to lead the faithful in the ways of unrighteousness to perdition?"

Kretz was growing tired of all of this. He was sore, tired, confused, and suddenly sick at heart again, thinking of Zawn. If they wished to kill him, perhaps they should just do it. "I do not want to lead anyone. I am male. I want to go back to my kind and back to my spacecraft and back to my home." They could find their own way to this place they wanted to go to. It was proba-bly somewhere in the striped-faced ones' territory.

To his surprise he saw that his answer hadn't offended them at all. "I think it is our duty to send you there," said the one with the bald head.

"Immediately," said the inquisitor. It was hard to tell, but he seemed relieved.

"Not quite," said the wrinkled little human who had bandaged him with Howard. "He needs to recover at least slightly first. He's weak from a lack of blood, and his blood is as red as yours, brothers and sisters. He's also half starved. And we must try not to send him to his enemies. They shot him, remember. We give succor to the weak and helpless."

"As soon as possible!" said Kretz. "Can you get me back to my spacecraft? Please?"

They looked perplexed. "I'm not too sure what this 'spacecraft' is," said the bald one. "But you can certainly leave as soon as you wish."

"Yes," said the inquisitor. "The land of milk and honey is not for evil unbelievers. You should go."

That was comforting, at least. They seemed sincere enough, although it was hard to judge. It seemed that what they really wanted was for him to get out of their lives. They probably didn't want trouble with the striped-faces.

If they had some way to get him past them?

He looked at the 'Bible' on his legs. The black marking on the thin white sheets undoubtedly had some meaning . . . unless it was some collection of computer circuits. It could be. It could be anything. They plainly valued it, though. Was it what kept the striped-face ones away? It might be something he could learn about, that he could take back to his people as a defense. "Can you explain this thing to me?" he said. "I would learn about it and tell my people."

"If he's a demon, he's a clever one," said one of the aliens.

"It shows that the path to grace may yet be open," said the bald one.

They did speak in riddles. Perhaps the path they referred to led past the stripy-faced ones by a secret route. That would be very welcome. The thought of facing them again made him feel sick. Or it could just be the alien soup, he supposed. He wanted to rest now. He tried a traditional farewell. Surely that would be hint enough?

"May you all father many sons, and may your clan mothers always be large, gentle and wise."

Several of the facially-maned ones looked taken aback at this. The ones with no facial manes snorted oddly. They seemed to be having trouble breathing.

"Some of us," said the wrinkled young female who had treated his hurts, "cannot *father* children, Kretz."

Kretz cringed. You didn't talk about this kind of thing. Well, Miran didn't. But perhaps the human's sexual etiquette and taboos were different. Sterility didn't appear to worry them, even if to the average Miran male it was a nightmare. Perhaps they only grew that mane if they were sterile? They were the ones who seemed distressed.

"It happens sometimes in space," he said sympathetically. "Radiation. No matter how careful you are. It's one of the things that goes with being male, I suppose, before we settle down and have sons. It might be safer if females would do it, but they won't."

That seemed to confuse them even more. "What do you mean?" asked the inquisitor-human.

Kretz was really feeling his exhaustion now. He was too tired to wrestle with alien social behavior. "Young males like me and yourselves go out-venturing. When they become female they remain at home in their breeding territory."

His reply caused that odd snorting noise among some and a reddening in faces of others. "It looks like it is not just theology he needs help with understanding," said the still-bald one.

"I also think he needs to rest. Councilors, we can take this further another time," said the wrinkled female.

Kretz could only be grateful when they left.

He was drifting back into sleep already when Howard came back, still making odd snorting noises. He must find out what that meant sometime. Was it a respiratory ailment? It made him very red faced.

# 10

The Great Leader's grasp of science is not good. The laser sequence has been analyzed and decoded. We've started a retransmission of the signals from Oort 1 until the entire stockpile has been dismantled. We've got the scientists and commissars that remained behind pouring out of rat-holes and eager to show us where the nukes are hidden, ever since they were sure that he was on the Slowtrain.

From: SysGov Internal security report, declassified 3/12/2300

Abret watched as the aliens piled things in front of them. And then Derfel slipped back his helmet hood. Abret knew that Miran could breathe this air. Knew he'd have to, furthermore, if this went on much longer, or he would never have enough air to get back to the lander.

The thought still filled him with dread. He was already close enough to changeover to start having longing thoughts of the nesting territory he was from. The idea of alien air was terrifying. He did not want to breathe it. And then he saw something even more horrifying. Derfel was picking up some of the alien stuff up and putting it into his mouth.

"You'll die!" he said, horrified.

"We'll die if we don't eat," said Derfel. "Get used to it, Abret. We've had no more calls from the spacecraft. Something has gone wrong. And the two of us can't fly the spacecraft. You can do the navigation, yes. But I can't do the engineering. At least we are trapped in an environment where we can breathe the air, and hopefully eat the food, and where the natives are friendly."

Derfel was in one of his more rational periods. He'd been quite right: leaving immediately when they got the call had been impossible. Having Abret admit he'd been right did seem to soothe him.

"Well, yes. But are they going to stay friendly, Derfel? I mean, Zawn believed that the other ones were friendly, and they were attacked. We'd better get back to the spacecraft. We're closing on Miran. Maybe we can get instructions by laser-transmission."

"They'll worship us forever," said Derfel confidently. "While you've been moping, I've had Transcomp working on the language. They believe that we are the saviors from the West, finally come to free them from the oppressor. If we have a problem, it will be explaining what took us so long to get here, not when we're going to leave. They pray that we will stay forever. This will be home, I'm afraid. They will treat us well, at least."

Abret knew that, by using the hormone supplements on the lander he could put off changing sex for another

few years. There was also some food from the synthe-
sizers and protein vats on the spacecraft. But then . . .
well, no place would be like home, except some place
that had a lot of the scents of home. As a female one's
sense of smell became very keen. "We can't . . . "

"We can," said Derfel crossly.

Then his radio came to life. "Is anyone receiving me?"

It was a Miran voice. Abret would have thought any
voice but Derfel's would be welcome. However . . .

The pitch of the voice was that of a Miran in hormonal
shift, and well on the way to becoming female. The hormonal shifts caused extreme irritability and some degree
of irrational behavior. That was the reason Miran tended
to leave those in changeover to themselves. They were
dangerous—and very territorial.

"Selna?"

"Who do think it is, you idiot?"

## 11

Re Habitat 37.
Date: 2120-11-4 Time: 15:31 NMT
From: Chief Scientist S. Guthrie
(Environment Construction)
To: Chief Construction (Spacefitting) Officer M. Kabongo
Re: repair and maintenance robots.

Mike K, you're a cantankerous and ornery pain in the butt. Look, the Brethren are archaic agriculturalists. These guys actually kill pigs and chickens to eat. That's had the animal welfare groups on Earth in ferment and it's got the Brethren claiming they're victims of religious persecution. The habitat environment is set up on the lowest degree of mechanization we can contrive. They've even got synthetic soils instead of stable granule growing mediums. They're planning on growing trees! The microdrop set-up is supposed to be manually serviceable, which as you know from

A23 the others aren't. These guys plan to cart dung and fertilize their soils. It's primitive but it might just outlast those JB232 units you're fussing about. Where the hell is this lot going to get the knowhow to repair a JayBee? Our modeling analyses show that complex and varied agricultural units have a degree of plasticity and biofeedback that more mono-focus ones don't have. There will still be micro-monitoring and macro-consumables replacement while they're in Deep Space. They're way under carrying-capacity and as long as they restrict their population growth, they'll be probably be better off than some of the other habitats.

Now that Kretz was healing and talking, and had proved less demonic than Howard had secretly feared, Howard found that he was beginning to enjoy his houseguest. For starters, he never knew quite what Kretz would say next. For a second thing, Kretz liked talking about mechanical things. He liked to work out just how they worked. And he kept asking Howard. This gave Howard a great rationalized excuse to think about them. Of course there were some areas of confusion to clear up.

First, that pigs were not intelligent part owners of New Eden.

And, second, that humans were very different from Miran, despite the similarities.

"Transcomp wishes to know what the honorifics 'Brother and Sister' mean, since they seem to be more than simple family references."

"Who is Transcomp?" asked Howard.

"It is my mechanical translator. It works on the vocabulary I have established and also deduces other meanings and words and the way the speech should be structured.

Zawn is . . . was our expert on translation. He said that your language was old, because it was complex and had absorbed structure and words from several logical rule-pattern stems."

That didn't clarify very much. Well, Howard thought, it was his turn now. He blushed, just thinking about trying to explain sexual differences in humans to Kretz. Perhaps he could get Sister Thirsdaughter to do it. She was a midwife, and Kretz . . . was somewhere between the two of them. Hopefully . . . she'd do it when he wasn't around!

He heard her outside. She had a habit of singing choruses while she walked. Howard hastily found a reason to go and do some chores in his kitchen. Never had chores seemed so attractive.

But scrubbing his tabletop was interrupted by Sister Thirsdaughter calling. Reluctantly, but worried in case something was really wrong, he went.

"Explain to Brother Kretz that you are not female, Howard. He believes that because you are big and your skin is taut you might be."

Howard lost himself in a tangle of half-sentences. The only small comfort was that Kretz was obviously as embarrassed as he was. He was attempting to hide his face behind his hand.

Sister Thirsdaughter was taking all too much pleasure in it all. "He also labored under the delusion that because you were bigger than I was, you were much older. I gather that you were able to persuade him that pigs were not another form of human this morning?"

"Yes," said Howard, eager to change the direction of the conversation. "One of my shotes got out of the sty and looked in at the window this morning. Kretz had seen wild ones up near the core."

"You will be relieved to know that I can tell my fellow councilors that you did not undress a woman after all, Howard. Kretz is male, at the moment, and will be for some years, still. Then he'll change to having babies instead of fathering them. They keep growing throughout life, like trees. They have babies when their bodies are large enough. It makes good sense actually." She cocked her head and looked at him. "A penny for your thoughts, young man."

"I have just realized that 'looks like' does not mean 'is like,'" said Howard. "A door is still a door if it is made of wood or metal, but the stuff of it, and the making of it is not the same."

"You're too bright for your own good," she said with a smile. "Now, I have decided that it would do Kretz a bit of good to take a short walk outside. I've never believed in bed-rest unless absolutely necessary. The muscles become pulp, and the digestive system doesn't work properly. But he needs someone your size—even if you're not female—to catch him before he falls over. That arm needs protecting. Walk him around your garden. And then I shall sit with him while you go and irrigate your crops."

So Howard took Kretz out to look at the herbs and then—to Kretz's evident excitement—the chickens. Kretz stared at them for a long time, before Howard went and caught him a new hatched chick to hold.

Kretz shook his head. "They are so much stranger than you. We have nothing like this on Miran!"

The cow and the pigs and even the sheep, while plainly fascinating, failed to make as much of an impression as a single egg, and the flip-flop of rooster-flight.

"One thing I have been meaning to ask you," said Kretz, watching Howard laboriously shovel animal feces into a simple one-wheeled barrow with two handles. "Why do you do everything yourselves? A machine could do this in seconds. I have seen your repair machines . . ."

Howard lowered his spade and looked around in what seemed to be a wary manner. "Don't let anyone, even Sister Thirsdaughter, hear you say that word. I know you don't understand, Kretz, but it's sacrilege to even suggest doing such work by machine. They robbed mankind of their purpose and their dignity. Robots are an invention of Satan."

*Robots.* Kretz told Transcomp to file that word, and to use it only with prior notification. Personally he couldn't see what purpose and dignity had to do with shoveling animal manure, but then he wasn't human, for which he was deeply thankful. Increasingly, he was realizing that these humans were primitive—not because they'd lost their technological knowledge, but because they'd chosen to do so. That made for a simple life, but a rather tedious one at times. It also seemed rather counterintuitive to their long-term survival in space.

Today he had walked, with a pause to sit down, with Howard to the water reservoir in the nearby polar region.

He was still getting over the shock of that experience.

Besides watching Howard carrying buckets made of hard plant-matter, and rolling a barrel made of the same stuff, which was bad enough, he'd also seen something that made him despair.

It was a sight he'd longed for.

The airlock.

But it was not the right one.

Now it was finally clear to him just what he had done while his mind had been hazed with pain and blood-loss.

He had indeed escaped the stripe-faced humans—by leaving their space-habitat entirely. He'd crawled down the inside of the linking cable to another habitat. No wonder the locals didn't know what he was talking about. No wonder these "brethren" managed to live such peaceful lives. They had a gulf of space to protect them.

Of course, that also made getting back to his ship nearly impossible. Not only did he have hostiles to contend with but space too. If only he hadn't closed the door to the cable behind him.

He sat down on the bed in Howard's room and examined the rebreather and suit-tank—and his radio. It was only the high-gain antenna that taken a direct hit. And even that was a testimony either to the toughness of the antenna, or to the ineffectiveness of the weapons of the stripy-faces. It still hung by a thread of metal. It was still useless and unfixable without the proper tools. Howard watched, fascinated. When Kretz dropped it onto the bed in disgust, he said "I could mend it for you, Brother."

Kretz resisted the temptation to say *with what? Cow dung and spit*? It was kindly meant. "I think it is beyond your ability," he said.

"The solder we use for stained glass might work." Howard obviously had learned to recognize Miran bewilderment by now. He just walked out and came back with a little glass container, made up of multicolored fragments in a metal frame-matrix. It was a picture, Kretz realized, made by sticking fragments together. A delicate, intricate and very decorative item that would have been intensely desirable on Miran. He blinked. It was not what he'd expected of the aliens.

"Look," said Howard, "you join the cames like this." He pointed to a tiny spot of shiny metal, plainly melted into place.

"You did this?"

Howard nodded. "It is my hobby."

*Hobby* was a new word to Kretz. It seemed wrong that a man who could do this kind of work was shoveling animal excreta.

"I suppose you can try," he said. After all, what did he have to lose? The radio didn't work now. Howard's attempts could only leave him just as badly off. Besides he wanted to see how the alien did this feat of dexterity. Having a grasping finger—which they called a thumb—on the inner side of the hand made everything that Howard did seem either awkward or intensely miraculous to Kretz.

He found himself both amazed and aghast at just how Howard did the job. He didn't have a single real tool, just heat and some small steel rods. But he was very dexterous with them and very, very precise. At Kretz's direction he joined the antenna and soon had it appearing fixed.

Warily, Kretz switched it on. Flicked *send*. "This is Kretz for the Spacecraft or any other receivers. Respond."

He waited. It crackled. Well, it had been a forlorn hope anyway. The system seeded granule-sized passive repeaters at communication intervals, but they probably were of insufficient strength to carry across the distance needed, relaying into and out of the cable-tube.

He tabbed to search-beacon just in case. That would scan and ping off any radio source. It was a search and rescue device that had saved many a lost traveler. It would give strength, directional and distance data, if it picked up anything—if the alien's soldering hadn't wrecked more than it healed. If there wasn't other, less visible damage . . .

He got three pings.

For a brief instant he knew wild hope. Suit radios?

One was definitely not of any use. Distance suggested that it must be in the region of the fusion plant. Presumably alien.

The other two . . . one was forward on the bead-string, in the same direction as the ramscoop. The second was a powerful signal too—in the opposite direction. It must be the beacon on the spacecraft. The first must be beacon on the lifecraft.

Still forward. Abret and Derfel must have had a problem there too.

And then . . . a voice. A frantic voice speaking Miran. "Who is out there? Reply."

Along with the joy and the relief came shock and a degree of horror.

With sex-change came changes in vocal pitch. And Kretz had seen them shoot him . . . now, by the sounds of it, her. He'd seen Selna fall, and be kicked and spat at.

But this sounded like . . . Selna. A female Selna. Shock and trauma *could* bring on early sex change.

Female Miran needed certain things. First, they needed territory. And then, before they could start gathering a harem, they needed to have lots of space and only cautious people anywhere near them. The hormonal adjustment made them very snappy.

Selna was loaded with male hormone supplements. Readjustment was going to be dangerous—for anyone who couldn't run. And there wasn't a lot of space on the ship to run in. "Who is out there! Answer me! If you're some alien scum you might as well know I've got the airlock booby-trapped. If it is Abret again, I can't get to you. You'll have to get yourself free, idiot!" screamed the changed-over Selna, raw fury and anxiety mixed in equal quantities.

"Kretz calling in," he said, as speaking calmly as he could.

"Speak louder!"

He tried again. But, as Selna began a tirade about being alone, he realized that the problem was a simple one. The suit-radio just lacked the power to send far with clarity enough to transmit voice. He could receive, as the spacecraft's radio unit was far higher powered, with far greater range and signal clarity. He couldn't do anything to soothe her anxiety. He also couldn't ask for help, even if she was in a position to render it. The spacecraft's physician could manage the hydroponics, as a second skill, but she couldn't fly the ship alone. Navigationally, the return did not require as much skill as matching trajectories and landing had, but it still required more than Selna possessed. Kretz himself might have managed it, especially with laser-sent guidance from Miran. He would still have to get a braking orbit right, but there was a little more space for a margin of error . . .

The situation did leave him feeling comforted on one issue. Laser messages would have surely beamed back from her to Miran. Yes, it was too far-off to be of any help to Selna, but they would be warned of the impending attack.

Looking up, Kretz realized that Howard was staring into his face with that forehead wrinkling that signified worry in the aliens.

"What's wrong?" asked Howard. "It is working properly now? I heard voices issue from it. Is it possessed?" He had the Bible-thing in one hand . . . and a piece of heavy dried plant-material in the other. For a moment Kretz thought he was being threatened. Then he realized that Howard's gaze was now focused on the radio antenna.

"It is working. That is what it is supposed to do," he said soothingly. "That was the voice of one of my companions. She was injured but managed to get back on the ship. She is alone and very afraid. My transmitter —the part of this machine that can send my voice across the distance—is too weak to reach her with my voice. All she knows is that there is a signal from far away. Her sender is very much more powerful. I can hear her."

The alien proved much more empathetic than Kretz had expected. "You must go to her, then. She must be in a terrible state."

"She is. She was the expedition's healer. I hope she can help herself." Kretz paused. But he felt he had to tell someone. "I left Selna for dead. I ran and hid when Selna fell."

Howard tugged his face-mane. And then, awkwardly, he put a hand on Kretz's shoulder. "Don't blame yourself, brother."

"I can't help it. I should have stayed," said Kretz.

"By what you've told me both of you would have died. Maybe because they followed you, she got away."

For an alien he was very understanding.

"We must get you back there, brother. She'll need you."

Very understanding.

"She'll need a man's guidance."

Howard did not understand Miran at all. Even with Selna in an emotional and disordered state, Kretz felt in need of female guidance. They were bigger, older and wiser . . . Except, well, if he was logical about it, Selna wasn't much wiser.

But in one way Howard was right. Kretz had to get back to the ship. The trouble was that he was space and a hostile bead away from the spacecraft. The answer was simple—yet terrifying. He'd have to go out onto the surface, because he couldn't get back inside the cable-tube . . . somehow cross the gulf between the habitats, and then instead of going inside the bead full of stripe-faced murderers, cross the *outside* of it. Then he just had to climb the equatorial ridge, and walk to the Miran spacecraft.

Easy . . .

Compared perhaps to drinking an ocean or the alternatives. He'd need an army—not likely to be forthcoming from the Brethren—or fantastic luck to get through the hostile bead. The only further problem he could see was that even if he could get through, Selna might not let him in. Not surprisingly, she'd sounded a little paranoid.

The other alternative, if he could not get back in that way . . .

Then he could go on. The lifecraft was on the sixth bead. From what Selna had said, Abret and Derfel had run into trouble in that one too, and were captives, asking for help. Whether he could help them or not, the lifecraft held the key. That could go to its docking station and bypass the booby-trapped airlock.

There was, of course, one small problem. The sixth bead was four more habitats away. However, as this one proved, they need not all be full of hostile aliens. And as both this one and the last had proved, the aliens didn't expect visitors. That, he supposed, was hardly surprising. Still, having to go through it all over and over again was an even worse choice.

And there was also the small matter of his arm, and his physical weakness. Thank heavens Miran were evolved from a fairly small omnivorous species. There was little doubt that proto-Miran had lived principally by scavenging after the larger predators and the tall-stalk fructivores in winter. It had meant in his present predicament that alien food had only once made him feel very queasy, and did appear to be—in the short term at least, capable of sustaining life. In the long term, the matter might not resolve itself so happily. There were bound to be problems with the various fatty acids needed for nerve repair, for starters, and amino acids . . .

The question was, how long did he have? How long before a desperate Selna attempted to take the launch window alone? How long before the alien substances killed him? How long before the bone knitted without modern medicine, but just on its own? He struggled to recall the physiology he'd studied back as a new student. The human healer had said three weeks, minimum, which worked out as twenty-one of their day-night periods. He'd been meaning to time these periods and get a precise conversion to his own time-units, but hadn't got there yet. It was—to be awkward—going to be slightly longer than a Miran day. He was sure that it didn't take that long for Miran physiology to do these sort of internal repairs. Isolate, inject bone-matrix, and rest for three days was the modern norm. If he remembered it right, stilt-legged sathin—the high-stalk fructivores of the plains—often broke those thin legs. If they could survive for eight days they could walk and feed again. Of course that healed bone would still be fragile, but it gave him a vague figure. Counting the days he had been unconscious, he'd been here for five days now. That left him with plenty of time to the launch window. But the sooner that he got back to Selna the better.

He waited until Sister Thirsdaughter returned and then asked her opinion. "I need to go to her as soon as possible."

"As a possible alternative to driving Brother Stephensson insane while he tries to explain the Bible to you?" said the elderly female, smiling and then remembering hastily to hide her teeth.

"Perhaps you need to ask him to start me on this 'reading' instead," said Kretz. "Maybe with something with simpler words than in your Bible. He reads to me and I have to keep asking him what he means."

She shook her head. "Books—other than the holy book—are vainglory. The society of healers and midwives have three texts for teaching. The Elder keeps some printed texts in trust, on the workings of New Eden, for emergencies. He has been searching them for advice on you, by the way. He has decided that you are not a demon or an angel, but something called an alien. The book said that it was very improbable that you existed."

"Most of our scientists had decided the same about you. Then we detected your spacecraft."

"What is this 'spacecraft'?" asked Howard, curious as ever.

As he asked that question, Howard was still bubbling with curiosity about the books. He hadn't even known they existed! Perhaps they included information on how to fix the pipes taking water to the canal on the lower section of his holding. He was sure that the odd flanged device he'd taken a secretive look at was supposed to allow water to pass—but one way only. Instead it flooded the ground in that section.

"This is a spacecraft," said Kretz. "Or at least this is part of one, a very big one. It is a whole world to you, but it is a spacecraft, traveling across the emptiness between the stars. We came from our world to have look at it in a very much smaller craft."

Howard blinked. Some of that was probably being lost in translation. The rest didn't mean much. Howard knew there was an outside to New Eden. Being sent there was the ultimate sanction the council of New Eden could impose. The airlocks were shown to every youngster. The one near his own home had apparently been used long ago. But the adulterer Samsson had been pardoned by a sign from God, in that the door would not open when they tried to put him out. That episode was often used as an example of the miracle of redemption.

"New Eden is the promise that was made to our fore-fathers," said Sister Thirsdaughter. "If we forsook the paths of unrighteousness, we would have a world of our own, where only the Godly would be, and our sun will not shine on the unjust, and we will be safe and secure in his love, from henceforth."

Howard had heard that before too. It was part of the creed. But what, exactly, was the sun? Well, he had animals to feed, a cow to milk and chores to do. He could ask Kretz more that evening.

Sister Thirsdaughter got up. "You seem too well to need my attentions, Kretz. I'll pass on your request to the council. They don't really know what to do about you. Half of them wanted to throw you out of the airlock."

"But that is where I need to go," said Kretz.

Sister Thirsdaughter smiled. "The outer darkness is where they believe you belong, so that'll make things easy for them."

Of course, thought Howard, it wouldn't be quick and easy. The council would argue for weeks. Days if it was clear-cut. Brother Stephensson would want more time to read the Holy book to the heathen, for starters.

He was right about the time, anyway. In the meanwhile Kretz wanted to see the sludge traps. And the wildlands. The alien found the strangest things fascinating.

# 12

In 2050 there was the Alpha habitat. By 2070, there were seven habitats; by 2080, there were 23; by 2100, there were 1300, and size and volume had increased seventy-fold. It is estimated that by 2500 more surface area will occupied by humans in space than on Mars or the moon. At first, these provided a haven for miners. Then, gradually as they grew larger and more environmentally stable, they became havens for more out groups, people who were poorly adjusted to mainstream of Earth society.

> From: *Space and Sociology.* May-Mertins, J., 2230, Wirral and Co. (Pub.)

It was obviously all settled, thought Howard, looking at the procession of elderly brothers and sisters from the

council. If it had been anything but a good verdict they'd
have been accompanied by a couple of the sturdy young
men, at least.

One of the junior council members, a relatively young
man of sixty or so years of age, came to call them. "Peace
be with you, Brother Dansson," he said. "Will you and
the stranger come out now and hear the council's
decision?"

All fifteen of them could hardly have fitted into Howard's front room. He turned to Kretz, who was sitting in
the tensed up position that Howard had learned meant
"nervous, extremely nervous," in the alien's body language. Howard felt, not for the first time a combination
of sympathy and irritation. Sympathy because Kretz was
obviously scared. This was hardly surprising, if you considered the treatment he'd had from the stripe-faced
monsters, whom Howard had decided were probably
minor demons of some sort.

The alien was also obviously missing contact with his
own kind. But why had he chosen to collapse into Howard's tomatoes? Besides the damage to the plants, which
was considerable, Howard really hadn't needed more
trouble with the Elder and the council. It had all been
. . . interesting, no doubt, but he could use some peace
to get on with farming. Kretz's advice had worked with
the flooding pipe, and that area could be planted now.

Howard would miss the alien's unafraid-of-mechani-
cal-things attitude. He wouldn't mind getting his own
bed back, though.

They walked out. Kretz had insisted on wearing his
own alien clothes, even though Howard had told him it
was a bad idea. "They don't like different things,
brother."

The alien had just given him the narrow-lipped look that Howard had learned was his equivalent of a smile. Howard found he'd gotten used to the expression. He knew by now what Kretz meant by it, without thinking about the matter. "It is some sort of protection against weapons of attack. It may save me from being killed."

"I explained to you," said Howard stiffly. "We do not believe in violence. At worst the council would sentence someone to be taken to the airlock, which is what you've *asked* them to do to you."

"I see," said Kretz. He cocked his head sideways, a surprisingly human gesture. "And then what has happened to those who have been put out of the airlock?"

Howard had to admit privately the *and then?* part had occurred to him too. "They must go elsewhere," he said stiffly.

"But I have explained to you what is out there," said Kretz.

Howard shuddered. "Yes, but you say that *you* have to go there."

"Indeed," agreed Kretz. "Which is why I must wear my suit. There were human suits that our second party from our spacecraft discovered in the airlock of the first habitat, but they would not fit me."

"They won't do that to you," said Howard, suddenly feeling guilty. So what if he had had to give up his bed and had his life disturbed? They couldn't do this to Kretz. He was harmless. "You've done nothing wrong."

"But that is what I asked them to do. Must I go and find something wrong to do, then?" said the alien, with the expression that Howard had learned meant worry rather than amusement. "I do not like milk, and although the honey is palatable, I cannot stay here. I want to go back to my spacecraft. I want to go home."

Howard was at something of a loss. Being put out of New Eden was an inconceivable horror to him. From earliest childhood, it had been drilled into him that that was the worst thing that could happen to you.

"Let's just see what they have to say," he said lamely. Whatever happened, at least it would stop being his problem. He felt guilty all over again about the relief that knowing this brought to him.

They reached the semicircle of councilors. Elder Rooson cleared his throat. "Stranger," he said, refusing to acknowledge that Kretz might not be human. "You say that you come from a far-off place, outside of New Eden. You have asked our help in getting yourself back to this 'spacecraft' of yours. I have examined the Elder's texts, and they have borne what you say, although I don't pretend to understand all of it. Still, it is our God-given duty to help those in need and those in distress."

He paused and looked at Howard. "It seems very clear to me that our duty is to assist you, to send you home to your own people," said the elder firmly. "But we find ourselves on the horns of a dilemma. To go out through the airlock has always been our ultimate sanction. It does not seem to me, or to Sister Thirsdaughter, that you are ready and healthy enough to do this on your own strength. Therefore, we will send one of our number to be your assistant, to be a strong shoulder for you to lean on, and to guide you."

He pointed at the horrified Howard. "We have decided that Brother Dansson will accompany you. We will provide food, good honest clothes, and our blessing for your journey."

"I thank you," said the gaudily clad Kretz. "You are very different to the aliens we met in the first habitat.

As you know, I have much enjoyed seeing your animal life. What sort of animal is this 'Dilemma'?" he asked earnestly. "While my principal purpose is to return to my spacecraft, I am a scientist. I wish to learn as much as possible. There are many convergences between the life-forms on our worlds. We have a long, thin, legless creature which uses three long horns on its head to attack prey. It uses the long outer horns to trap the prey, while the inner mobile horn stabs them. Is this 'Dilemma' similar? I am curious."

For a moment they all looked at him in silence. Then Elder Rooson laughed. The others followed. "It would appear that we've chosen the right companion for you. Someone of equal curiosity."

Howard had stood numbed, up till now. Now, finally, he found his voice. "But, Elder . . . What have I done to deserve exile? Why do you send me out of New Eden?"

"You are free to return, brother," said the old man. "That is not exile. We know that it is a great deal to ask of one of our brethren. But to be fair, you are the best suited to do it. It is the opinion of a large number of my fellows that you are the right, and possibly only person for the task."

Kretz nodded eagerly. "I will send the . . . Brother back to you when I get back to the ship."

"But no one who has been sent out of the airlock has ever come back," protested Howard.

"No one in all the history of New Eden has been free to do so," answered the old man with a sigh. "I do wish God had not seen fit to make these things happen in my time, but doubtless he has his reasons."

"We pray that you do not bring some evil communication back with you," said Brother Galsson sourly. Howard was sure that he had pressed for them to make this a real exile. There was also no doubt in Howard's mind that Galsson was praying that he wouldn't make it back at all, never mind bring back some problem with him.

Howard's mouth was too dry to reply. Yes, he'd experimented with a few things to find out just how they worked. Fixed things which perhaps he shouldn't have. But did they have to exile him? Call it whatever they liked, that's what it was. From talking to Kretz, Howard was sure that the end result of exile was always death. And suddenly, life seemed very precious. It was more than mildly blasphemous to doubt your security in the hands of God. But life had handed him any number of doubts in the last while, shattering things he'd always known to be true. Maybe they were right to exile him. He couldn't have gone on, living in the closed box, now that he knew there was so much outside of it.

It still frightened him.

## 13

Transcript of meeting 37 of the Deepspace design and Engineering team (Slowtrain project), and Sysgov Administrator Belthazar Lowe (Accounts)

"One of the things you've got to accept, is that it isn't the habitat launch that we consider important. The gauss-rings are being set up to serve our future purposes of moving materials insystem—ice from the Oort rings, particularly —not sending a bunch of misfits outsystem or launching the Astronomy Commission's probes. Therefore the positioning and size of the gauss-rings must fit our principal purpose. You'll have to prove that to me if you want me to release the money."

Kretz had wanted the other airlock, the airlock closest to his spacecraft. But it had defied him too, and refused to open. So they had taken the long walk to the up-pole airlock. Howard had no idea why it was called that. It just was.

And God had not intervened to stop them going through it.

The airlock closed behind them with a hiss. Howard looked around the metal-walled room with some horror —for good reason. There were several skeletons lying there. The grey utilitarian clothes of the brethren remained but the flesh had gone the way of all flesh. A few strands of hair still clung to some of the skulls.

A voice spoke from the box on the far wall. "Depressurization will begin in ten minutes. Please don your suits and run through pre-vacuum-checks. Depressurization may be interrupted by pressing the red buttons, at any point. To reinitiate the sequence press the green button on the control console."

"There is someone here," said Howard, alarmed. "Perhaps one of the ones who was exiled? Are they actually in that little box?"

Kretz shook his head. "It will be a recording. Or a computer voice simulation."

The thing Kretz called Transcomp had no human words for either of those devices. Or maybe it did—it extrapolated words, but Howard recognized neither.

"We'd better look for a suit for you," said Kretz. "If this matches the design of the lock on the last habitat they should be on a rack inside that wall-plate there."

They were. The wall-plate slid open and revealed them. The suits were ranged in a large number of sizes, hung neatly above the boots, with helmets on the top shelf. "Dress," said Kretz.

"Do I have to put one of those on?" asked Howard doubtfully. "It is our belief that the simple garb of the brethren is far better protection than clothes which serve vainglory and folly."

Kretz felt the cloth of the homespun of Howard's sleeve. Then he lifted it to his mouth and drew breath through it. He shook his head. "It is not airtight, Brother Howard. Here. Try it on my sleeve." He held up an arm to Howard's mouth. "Breathe through it."

Embarrassed, but obedient, Howard did. It was like sucking on a sheet of glass.

The only reason that he could think of that such a fabric might be valuable was to keep one dry. "Is it going to be wet on the other side of that airlock?" he asked, being glad that he had learned to swim, on those frowned-on trips to the pole reservoir.

"No. Airless, as I said to you," said Kretz. "But like being underwater, in that you cannot breathe out there."

"Uh. Brother Kretz. I can't hold my breath for very long. I didn't actually like putting my head underwater," admitted Howard. How was something "airless"?

"There are tanks of air here. The same as the thing that you took to be a backpack on my suit," explained Kretz.

The idea fascinated Howard. He'd often dreamed of making a device that would have allowed him to go underwater in the end-seas. His idea had been to take a heavy bath that could be inverted and be pressed down into the water, taking the trapped air under with it. He'd even done a few simple experiments in his own bath in this direction. But it had been something that had never gone beyond the realms of speculation, really. He knew that the council would never have allowed it.

"I think that you will have to undress first," said Kretz.

Howard was shocked. A man did not undress before another person, unless it was his wife. Kretz was half-female, after all, even if he was not human. "I can't," he said.

"Howard," said Kretz.

He was learning to read the alien's expressions by now. That was irritation. "Yes?" he answered.

"Do you see these bones? That is what will happen to you if you do not put on a suit, helmet and boots and clip on the air tank."

It was a powerful argument, when put like that. Howard stripped. He allowed Kretz to help him dress, and they dealt with the unfamiliar fastenings together. Kretz also found a rack of cylinders. He took one and fitted it onto a box-device on the back of the suit. Howard was startled to see a plate on his wrist change color from red to green. He pointed it out.

Kretz pursed his lips into his smile. "Good. It must be an air-pressure indicator. I did not know if the cylinders would still retain pressure. The humans who built this were first-class engineers."

He didn't say that the Brethren weren't, but somehow Howard got the feeling that he was saying *and you carry water in wooden buckets*.

Kretz handed Howard a helmet. "Once that is on we will not be able to talk. I am going to attach you to me. If you need to say something, press your helmet against mine." Howard noticed, in the dissociated way of someone who is on the verge of panic, that Kretz had extended a hood from the suit that he was so fond of and that a transparent screen now covered his face. He noticed that Kretz had taken the little parcel of journey bread and preserves and soup and put it into a suit too. And then put boots and hood onto that, which was truly strange. Did the alien think that it had a life of its own?

"Depressurization sequence beginning," said the box voice, as Kretz clicked the helmet into place. Howard still wanted to know: how did they fit someone into a box that size? Anyway, he preferred thinking about that type of problem than about what he was about to see, outside of New Eden. Ideas on the subject kept troubling his mind as Kretz attached a rope onto a clip on his suit's belt. Would there be the corridors of Earth—the source of persecution and corruption—out there? Or would there be a way through to Kretz's "ship"?

Kretz had tried to explain. All that Howard had managed to understand was that it was big and empty and that the light out there did not come from light-tubes. And it was not easy to cross.

Then, after an eternity, a door at the far side of the room slid open, and Kretz pointed at it. Awkwardly, as his boots seemed to stick to the floor, Howard moved forward. Out onto a metal platform . . . and froze in the doorway.

He was looking out onto more emptiness than his mind could deal with. Tiny points of light turned in the blackness. And there was no end to it. He knew that he was screaming, but he couldn't help himself.

Eventually Kretz had to pull him inside. The door to the terrible nothingness closed. Howard just stood there. Even the bones looked familiar and safe compared to that.

"It is now safe to release the helmet seals," a voice said—the same voice that had spoken from the box.

Voices in your head! A sure sign of demonic possession! Brother Galsson had been right.

Kretz lifted the helmet off Howard's head. "I could not prepare you," he said.

Howard shook his head, slowly. "What was that?"

"That was what you would call 'the heavens,'" explained Kretz.

"Not heaven," said Howard, sitting down, slumping against the wall. "Not hell either. That is a place of hellfire. Out there it is just dark."

"It is, out here, far from the light of the sun."

"But it is so big. So open. Where is the end of it?" Howard was still stunned and fearful.

"We're not sure if there is one," answered Kretz.

Howard's next words surprised himself. But they were drawn from somewhere deep inside his mind. "We've been so small. How could we be so small in the face of something so great? We have hidden away from it."

The alien cocked his head in that oddly human gesture. "It *is* both frightening and magnificent."

"Yes. Both frightening and magnificent," said Howard. He'd never had the experience that others had described of a spiritual enlightenment. And now, in the midst of his fear and the smell that came from the suit . . . he knew that he had finally done so. "I have looked on the infinity of God," he said humbly. "And I was very afraid. What were the spots of light, Brother Kretz?"

"Suns. Very far off suns."

Was it not written "And the sun shall not smite thee by day . . . "? So that was what it referred to.

"The brightest one you saw is ours. Miran is the second world orbiting it."

Kretz had obviously learned to recognize Howard's blank look. "That is where I came from. My spacecraft crossed the heavens to come here."

Howard stared in awe at the alien. "How could anyone cross that?"

Kretz narrowed his lips in his smile. "Howard. As I said to you: This 'New Eden' of yours is a spacecraft. Or, rather, your whole world is part of a spacecraft. We saw you crossing the heavens and came to find out what you were."

Howard wrestled with this one. "New Eden is also definitely this thing you call a spacecraft?" Yes. He remembered that Kretz had said that before. But that was before it meant anything to him.

"Yes," Kretz nodded. "Much bigger than ours, intended for a far longer journey."

Howard looked at the metal floor. "I believed . . . in my heart of hearts that New Eden was all that really existed."

Kretz shook his head. "There are millions and millions of worlds out there. Orbiting around hundreds of millions of suns. They're many thousands of times bigger than New Eden," said the alien, cheerfully compounding Howard's turmoil. "I suppose in a way, you are naturally going to be frightened . . . "

"You don't understand," said Howard, interrupting, fierce feeling overwhelming politeness. He had to tell someone, and Kretz was the only person there was to tell. "I have been kept in a tiny little cage all my life. With limits. Limits on what I could think. Limits on what I could do. It chafed me. But I did not know why. I didn't even know that I was inside the cage. I feel as if I've been a chick growing inside an egg. I didn't know there was an outside to the egg. Why didn't you *tell* me?!"

Kretz smiled. "I was not sure that you could deal with a bigger universe. Your kind have lived in a very sheltered and protected environment for many generations, even if you did build this ship."

"I don't think some of us would deal with it too well," admitted Howard. "Someone like Brother Galsson, probably couldn't. It still frightens me, but another part of me wants to go out and see it. See all of it."

This definitely amused Kretz. "There is rather a lot of it. I will settle for seeing if we can get to my spacecraft. I must be honest with you, Howard. If we can go along the outer skin of the habitats I don't really need you, except perhaps as security. I wanted a human with me if I had to venture back inside. I am very afraid of your kind."

Howard was a little puzzled by this. But he'd heard what Kretz had said about the next space habitat. He was part way to understanding just what a habitat was, now. It would be a world such as his own New Eden. A tiny enclosed piece of greenness and light in an infinity of blackness. But that Eden had been taken over by striped-faced snakes.

He took a deep breath. "But if you cannot, you will need my help. So: let us go and find out."

"Very well. Put on your helmet again. It is important that we move quite fast out there."

Howard knew that it would be the most courageous thing he'd ever done. But somehow, he could not have resisted trying again. He took a deep breath. Held up a hand to stop Kretz. "Brother. I will try not to look other than at my feet as I may slow you down. Will you lead me?"

This time Howard kept his eyes on the metal floor of the hanging catwalk, trying not to be distracted by the vast panoply visible through the bars.

The headlights helped, making a narrow pool of light for his feet. He couldn't help but see some of space, and the vastness of New Eden above him, but at least it kept him from being too distracted.

They walked a long way. And then, when he was just daring to take a peek sideways, they stopped. Kretz was at a gate. Beyond it, Howard could see a metal-runged ladder. However, despite Kretz's efforts, the gate did not open. It appeared to have no form of catch. After some passage of time, they walked back to the airlock.

Howard had gotten far more used to looking around by then. He could see, across the blackness, the cable that linked New Eden to the next habitat. It was a good five cubits thick—still an incredibly frail link for something as vast as their world.

Once the airlock had cycled closed, Howard removed his helmet. Kretz sat down, next to the bones of the exiled brethren, and—even if he was alien—looked despairing. "I've lost the tool I need to open the gate," he said. "I used it to gain access to the tube I crawled down to reach your habitat. I thought we could go around, outside and over the equatorial ridge."

He sighed, again, an oddly human mannerism. "I cannot get back to my ship. The only possibility is the lander, and that is five habitats on from here."

Howard patted his arm awkwardly. "Then that is what we must do."

"I am afraid," said Kretz.

"So am I," admitted Howard. "Although, for me, these experiences have almost become dreamlike, they are so far beyond my understanding, Kretz. I think I would be rigid with terror if I wasn't . . . somehow detached." He paused. "I have one question . . . all of those spots of light?"

"Suns, yes. Very distant suns, as I told you."

"Why are the suns moving? Where are they going to?" asked Howard.

"The suns are not moving. Or at least they're not moving very fast. The space habitat—New Eden—spins, to provide a simulated gravity through centripetal force."

Howard looked blankly at him. "I don't understand it," he said, eventually. "But I want to. I want to understand it all."

Kretz drew his lips into his smile. "Like space, there is quite a lot of it. What I am going to suggest we do now is entirely insane. That was how I got my place on this expedition. Because I am a little mad."

"Mad?" asked Howard, warily.

"Yes. By the standards of my people. Of course there are many mad people, but not all of them are biologists and mechanical engineers." He paused. "We need to cross the gap between the two habitats. I crossed the gap by crawling down the hollow inside of the cable. It is plainly intended to be possible. There are other pipes in there, perhaps linking all the habitats, perhaps there to replenish ones that are in need. But we can't get in there. So we must go along the outside."

"It looked like a long way to climb," said Howard, doubtfully.

"It would be too far to climb. Besides I do not think we could. But I think we can fly," said Kretz.

Howard looked long and hard at him. "You have assured me you were not an angel, or a demon. I have seen your body, and I know you have no wings. How do you plan to fly? Even in the low gravity heart of New Eden, men cannot fly. Can you?"

"I'd forgotten that you would be familiar with low gravity. When we leave the ship and go along the cable, there will be virtually no gravity. And the slightest thrust would send us away into the heavens. There is nothing to push against to come back, either."

Howard digested this. "Then I think we must use this rope that they have seen fit to equip these suits with. If we tied it to one wrist and then passed it around the cable, and then tied it to the other wrist again . . . but how strong is that arm of yours?"

Kretz nodded. "I had thought about that. My arm will be strong enough. But I am surprised you thought of it, Howard. You have surprised me a great deal. You appear to be such primitive people, and yet you grasp things with speed."

"I've surprised myself," said Howard, standing just a little taller. "But all of this has left me very hungry. I saw you put the food into a suit. Were you planning to take it with us, or should we eat?"

Kretz shook his head and smiled. "Perhaps we Miranese need you humans. I had forgotten about it."

"Why did you put it in the suit?" asked Howard.

"Depressurization and cold would have ruined it," explained Kretz.

"There is still so much for me to learn," said Howard humbly.

He hadn't yet learned to work out quite what alien laughter sounded like, but he suspected that the gurgling noise Kretz made might just be that.

They ate, carefully sitting where the bones were not visible. Then Kretz rigged a sling from a safety rope to carry several extra bottles of air. Or tried to, at least. Once Howard had worked out what the alien was doing, he took over. Howard had made things with his hands all his life. Kretz plainly had not. Besides, if they could take cylinders he could take his clothes, even use them to make part of the carrier.

When it was time to go, Kretz turned to Howard. "We could be dead, shortly. Do you not wish to remain here?"

A part of Howard wanted to stay, very, very badly. Even staying here with the bones was better than what even the alien plainly regarded as a mad enterprise. But . . .

He'd lived through so many mad enterprises since he came through that airlock. The frequency of them had numbed him. He just stood up, and took the sling. They had no way of taking the rest of the provisions, sadly. It went against every grain of Howard's conservative soul to waste.

They went out again. By now Howard felt that he was becoming a seasoned explorer of space. He was quite blasé about it. Not even shaking that much.

But he was totally unprepared for what Kretz did, this time.

The alien climbed out between the bars of the catwalk where it met the airlock and was a little wider, and turned himself upside down so his boots came into contact with the white roof . . . well, not really the roof. The outside of New Eden itself. He hung upside down. Like a bee. And then he motioned for Howard to follow.

Doing so was the greatest leap of faith that the New Eden man had ever made.

His boots also stuck . . . and sank slightly into the white stuff. But to walk—having to pull loose each foot, hanging —was pure torture. Howard was sure that he was going to fly off into the endless void with each step

The strangest thing was that it got slowly better. By the time the base of the cable came in sight, Howard didn't feel as if he was walking upside down any more. Instead, the force tried to drag him backwards. But it decreased, step by step, until, at last, they stood at the cable.

There was a railing around the base of it, and it stretched up into the blackness, to the distant curve of another habitat, like a huge bead on a string. The cable was several feet thick, but it seemed very thin when it had the gulf of the void all around it. Without conscious thought, Howard began to pray, the simple prayers of his childhood.

They walked around the cable—it was more like a very thick pole in appearance—and put the ropes around it, then attached them to their belt snap-links. Then came the worst. Kretz reclaimed the sling-bag, and got up onto the rails, using the rope around the cable to keep his balance. Breathing hard, although Kretz had said he shouldn't, Howard got up too. He put a hand against the great cable to steady himself.

As he fell, he realized that the cable was turning—or perhaps New Eden was. But he was floating only secured by the thin cord on his belt. And his fall had pulled his partner too . . . Or perhaps Kretz had jumped.

They were free-floating a few yards above the turning railings. And then Kretz took out an air cylinder, opened the valve at the top, and pointed it back at the outside of New Eden. They began to move, not too fast, but steadily, toward the next space habitat.

Flight was something the bees could keep to themselves, so far as Howard was concerned.

Theirs was not a fast progression. As they crossed farther out into the gulf, Howard had a long time to consider how insignificant he was against the hugeness of God's creation. He even got detached enough to think that the experience would do the likes of Brother Galsson the world of good.

They were using the third and last cylinder when Howard noticed something faintly alarming. The disc on his arm that Kretz had said indicated air-pressure was no longer green. Instead a good two thirds of it was now red. And although Kretz was shaking the cylinder in his hand furiously . . . they weren't moving forward very fast.

The turning surface of the new habitat was still a good hundred yards below them. And if he was any judge of alien expression—Kretz was at edge of panic. Kretz threw the cylinder back toward New Eden. It produced a few yards of movement . . . They were still a long way from the next Habitat.

And plainly the alien was out of ideas as well as the air that had pushed them this far.

Howard took a deep breath—even if he shouldn't do so. And pulled himself closer to the cable. He was one of the Society of Brethren. He knew God had given man muscles to use, and the cable was thick, but not frictionless.

Wrapping his hands around the rope clipped to his belt, he pulled himself flush against it, and began shinning his way along the cable to a new world, towing his alien companion. After the briefest pause, Kretz pulled himself in and then, alien and human, they linked hands and pulled themselves towards what was slowly becoming down.

The Brethren believed in the virtue of hard work, and by the time they reached the railings of the habitat, Howard was glad of it. It was hard to judge through the view plate of Kretz's suit, but the alien's grip had weakened on the last part. Howard would bet he was tired too. Still—their feet were down on the outside of whole new habitat. A new world!

They un-clipped and began walking . . . Howard noticed that the disk on his sleeve now showed a thin band of green and was otherwise almost entirely red. If he understood it correctly that meant he had very little air left. He tried to walk a little faster. Then he noticed that Kretz—whose line had constantly pulled him forward on their walk to the cable, was lagging. Actually, the alien had stopped completely. Kretz staggered, almost pulling Howard from his upside-down stance. Now that he understood that the habitats spun on the cable, the feeling of being upside down was quite understandable. Logical, in fact. It was still uncomfortable, but he could see the railing of the catwalk ahead. It drew him like a magnet. Besides they were walking with the spin—it was less effort.

Something in his helmet flashed red just above his eyes. At the top edge of the visor, Howard saw text appear, as if by a miracle.

If it was a divine message, it was not a kindly one. It read:

WARNING. 10 MINUTES OF RESERVE.

And his alien companion was standing still, and leaning gently with the spin, his eyes closed.

The end of his ordeal was just so achingly close. And if he understood the message right he had very little air left. Well. He had no choice really. He could not just abandon the alien here. But carrying him, upside down like this, was going to be difficult. He went back. It took all the strength and courage he had, but there was enough. He pulled one of Kretz's feet away from the surface, and then the other . . . and then realized he should have held on to him . . . The alien was floating away. But they were tethered together. And towing him had to be easier than trying to carry him.

It worked. But the red text now said WARNING. 6 MINUTES OF RESERVE. Howard tried to keep calm, keep walking. It was a long way, towing his companion behind him. Was Kretz dead? He could never do that crossing back home without the alien. His blind faith in Kretz's knowledge and ability had carried them this far. But he was sure that it wouldn't carry him back. And the red text was ticking away the minutes of reserve air. It was reading seconds only when they got to the railing of the catwalk. He had to walk along the outside until he found a corner they could fit through. Howard squeezed between the bars, and hauled Kretz in and through. Now, the right way up again, Howard resolutely ignored the red text and picked up Kretz and began walking to the airlock. Breathing was difficult.

He knew how to open the airlock after having watched the last time . . . and he knew how to close it for repressurization . . . But he was not sure that he could manage the helmet, before he died here. He needed to breathe, his body shrieked. He forced himself to keep calm, to wait, as they had when Kretz had taken him out twice before. The "pressurization complete" light did not seem to be coming.

When it did, he was almost too weak to do the catch.

He sucked air. It smelled just like the air of New Eden. This airlock, however, had no old bones in it.

Kretz opened his eyes, feeling something patting his face. Vaguely he remembered beginning the walk to the habitat airlock. And then nothing, except for the alien prizing his feet off the metal of the habitat. Yet, plainly, he'd got here. He opened his eyes. The alien Howard was staring down at him, with the wrinkled expression he'd learned meant worry. Howard wore it a lot.

"Are you all right?" asked the alien.

A good question. He was feeling extremely exhausted, actually. But that was not surprising considering the physical exercise and the fact that he'd barely recovered from his last set of injuries. Also the human food hadn't killed him, yet, but his diet was probably short of a fair number of things. Miran were broadly omnivorous, and historically had adapted to living on everything from an almost pure vegetable diet to one which had been made up almost entirely of deep-water invertebrate creatures, but never alien food, even if some of it was very appetizing. "I think so." he said, moving his limbs experimentally. "What happened?"

Howard sat back and exhaled. "I thought you might have died. Or run out of air like I did."

"You did?" It had not occurred to Kretz that that was a possibility. His own suit rebreather system was good for at least another trek across the surface. He had of course no real idea what the oxygen requirement of these aliens was. Perhaps their metabolisms were much faster than a Miran's metabolism. Perhaps their rebreathers were less efficient. "So how did you get here? How did I get here?"

"I carried you," explained Howard.

Well. The metabolic requirement for that sort of load-carrying would have been high, no matter how fast the alien metabolism was. "Thank you."

It seemed that statement was as important to aliens as it was to Miran. The big human flushed. "It was nothing. I expect you'd have done the same for me."

Kretz had to feel somewhat guilty. Actually, what he had done was to risk the human's life for his own benefit. True, he had intended—if reasonably possible, to return

Howard to his habitat—well, if he could. But he'd wanted a human escort to protect him against humans. And he'd wanted a human escort to enable him to get back to his people and warn them that it was no probe coming through their system but a habitat full of settlers. Vicious, cruel, Miran-killing settlers. A plague that would have to be destroyed first before it killed Miranese. In that first habitat they had abused him and the other Miran explorers. It dawned on him now that he had in turn abused the hospitality and kindness of the New Eden "Brethren." True, they were primitive and their habitat was going to break down further as the technical support systems—which they plainly no longer under-stood—broke down. They needed help. And what had he done: take one of their people as a human shield. He suspected—by the speed that Howard had understood and adapted—that he had taken one of their best. One of those that offered some kind of hope of survival. It was still something of a wild guess as to how long this string of habitats had been streaming through space at one-third lightspeed, but it must have been a long time. Perhaps the habitat that he and the others had been ambushed in had once been peaceful and the occupants as hospitable as these "brethren" before their society collapsed. His own people had been quite savage in the distant past. Nowadays they were peaceful—but now—with shrinking populations and plentiful resources they could afford to be.

"Shall we see what this new habitat holds?" he asked, unlocking the switches to convert his pressure suit into something he could wear with more comfort.

"I should like to change first," said Howard stiffly.

Kretz had been somewhat puzzled by the the clothing taboos of the humans of New Eden. It probably came of having two distinct birth-to-death sexes. Every Miran knew after all that they were going to have intimate knowledge of male and female bodies sooner or later. There seemed to be a great deal of conflict and misunderstanding between the human sexes. It seemed to make for all sorts of behavioral and societal problems. He'd love to study it, if he had time. "I still have the sling," he said, handing it to Howard.

Howard didn't understand Kretz's feeling on clothing. Or on sexes for that matter. He just knew that he wasn't comfortable in the space suit, and longed for the familiarity of his own clothes.

Alas, he was poorly prepared for the effects of deep space on natural fabrics.

His woolen homespun trousers were shredded. He held them up in horror. "What happened!"

Kretz put his hand to his face. "I'm sorry, Howard. I think there must have been moisture in the fabric. Of course it froze out in the cold of space. And with the movement it must have needed to bend. Bent frozen fabrics crack."

Howard shook his head, looking at the tatters. "But what am I to wear?" he asked desperately. "I can't go out there naked! I . . . I'll have to stay in this clumsy thing. The people here can't see me undressed!"

"Then you will just have to remain in it," said Kretz. "Let us go on, Howard."

They walked to inner lock. It opened before they touched it, and Howard saw a startled looking local staring in at them—and Howard realized that they might not see him undressed . . . but *he* was going to see them in that state.

It seemed that Brother Galsson was right after all. This was one of the cities of the plain. Gomorrah, at a guess.

## 14

Transcript of Justice Adriaan Vosloo's reply to Inspector Mohataman Dhal of Sysgov Human Rights Inspectorate on his application for an injunction against the sysnet advertisements of the Women's Matriarchal Movement for men to accompany their outsystem journey.

"No, Inspector, what they're planning on doing is neither illegal nor a violation of human rights. It would be, if they stayed insystem. But out beyond Öpik-Oort limit they're also out beyond your and my jurisdiction. And I may tell you that even by the time they get to the Kuiper belt, they're effectively on their own. The Kuiper colonists like to think they're independent and they're only a year's fast travel from the House of Assembly. What are you going to do when this lot are light-minutes beyond that? The men going along on this trip are all adults. We drew the line at children.

In a whole system you're bound to have enough men with nudist dominatrix fantasies. They probably won't like it much when the reality gets home to them; but then it'll be their problem and they'll have to sort themselves out."

━━━━━━━━━

Lani LaGarda was irritated. And when Lani was irritated wise people stayed out of her way. It didn't seem that Station-Commander Juno Morgane had got that message. "It was plainly some kind of malfunction, Juno," she snapped. "I have better things to do with my time than trot off to look at a closed airlock for several hours."

"I'm not asking you, Lani. I'm telling you. According to the records, we haven't had a peep out of that alarm system for four hundred and three years. The system says that there are two warm bodies in there. It's probably runaway men. Go down there, and haul 'em out. And try not beat them too badly. I haven't forgotten last time."

Lani scowled at the communicator. "He got up my nose and itched."

"And he lived. Which is why you're still at liberty, Lani," said the matriarch's station-commander, grimly. "Now get your ass down to that airlock, open it up and haul them out of there, put them into the cells until someone claims them. In one piece. Get on with it. I've got enough problems on my hands with the elevators having stuck again."

"Again?"

"Except that this is bank three. They haven't got bank five working yet. At this rate people will have to walk up from skinside to the upper regions."

"That's going to be really popular."

"Tell me about it," said Juno sourly. "So I've got problems enough without you getting shirty with me. Get moving."

So Lani got. She took her scoot and headed down the ramps to the airlock. She was one of the nearest officers, fair enough. And catching a couple of runaways before they vented themselves into space would be fun. There might even be bounty, enough to make a down payment on a first for her harem. The thought was an interesting one, enough to spur her on.

She parked the scoot, illegally, but then who was going to come down here anyway, and, even if they did, who was going to give a captain a ticket?

She stepped up to the airlock and put in the opening sequence to the coding panel. How had they ever found that out? Well, there was a manual override . . .

The door swung open.

And Lani, the toughest graduate of Officer's academy of 395 AD, nearly screamed and ran.

But there was more steel to her than that.

"Okay. Very funny. Very clever. Now get out of them," she snapped.

The two of them just stared at her, their mouths open with surprise at being caught. "I said get those clothes off," she said, her temper flaring at having been given such a fright. "MOVE. And the mask! Pervert!"

"Painted Jezebel!" said the taller one. He was very tall, taller by half again than any man she'd ever seen. "Have you no shame! Cover your nakedness, woman!"

Despite what Juno had said to her, she took a swing at him. He didn't go down. He just stood there rubbing his cheek. "Have you no respect as well as no decency?" he demanded.

She really had no memory of how the nightstick came into her hand.

Howard saw the woman who had just hit him pull a long black club from the belt she was wearing. The belt that was all she was wearing, besides a layer of paint, and sandals. Her face was contorted with fury as she lifted her arm to hit him again. He couldn't actually bring himself to lay a hand on her, but the stick was another matter. He caught it. She was quite strong—for a woman—thought Howard, holding on to it as she struggled to pull it away from him. She swung a kick at him, screeching like a banshee. Fortunately, the suit was well padded and thick, because she didn't aim for his shins. Well, with a woman dressed, or rather undressed, like that what did you expect? Her eyes opened wide and she grabbed her stick with both hands, kicked both her heels into his stomach and wrenched.

It was enough to knock some breath out of Howard. But certainly not enough to make him let go. Before this he'd simply held the stick and held it and her out at full arm's length. It was an effort, but no worse than tossing a two-hundredweight bag of pignuts into the loft, which he'd done often enough. Now he shook her stick, and her.

"Put me down!" she screamed.

So he did. She landed hard enough—on her well-padded behind—to knock the breath out of her instead. She still clung weakly to the stick. He twitched it away from her.

"Huu . . . 'ive 't back," she gasped, fighting for breath. For the first time in her life Lani had encountered something that frightened her. She worked out for two hours every day. She was used to being stronger than any woman, lct alone male. Still, she wasn't about to let the experience stop her.

"Not until I am sure you are not going to try to hit me with it again," said the big male crossly.

The other male came forward, and . . . extended a hand. She was about to use it to throw him, when she focused on the shape of it. It had three long fingers, and a thumb . . . in the middle of the wrist. "Let me help you up," he said, or at least a mechanical voice said. "We mean you no harm. We are just passing through."

Lani spidered backwards, knocking her illegally parked scoot over. She hit the com button of the prone two-wheeler as they walked towards her. "Mayday. This is Delta 95 at the South airlock. Mayday. I say again. Mayday. This is Delta 95 at the South Airlock. Am under attack."

The big one looked at his monstrous companion. "Maybe we should just go back out of the airlock and return to New Eden. Or climb the equatorial ridge."

The monster shook his head "I think we should proceed as rapidly as we can, Howard," he said. "She has called for help, by some form of electronic communicator, at a guess. They are not as primitive here as either the first habitat or your one."

He looked down at Lani. "You didn't injure her, did you? If so we must render assistance."

The big man shook his head. "No. We do not believe in physical violence except for gentle chastisement of children. I just stopped her from hitting me again, and took the weapon away from her. Although," he said, looking down at her with a curl of lip, "This wanton harlot deserves to whipped on the cart's tail. Let's go then,

Kretz. If this is what you encountered before you came to us, I'm not surprised that you were so wary."

"But this is not the same species as you, surely," said the monster as they began to walk off, leaving her. "The patterning is very different. You have only small spots of darker skin below your eyes, very slight. This is more like the patterning on the striped faced ones, except theirs was in dull and drab colors."

"It's just paint," said the man before they disappeared around the next corner, walking away from the airlock. The disgust in his voice was almost palpable.

Lani sat up, eventually realizing that she was still pressing the send button on the scoot's communicator. She took her finger off. " . . . espond Delta 95. Lani, come in! Delta 95 are you receiving us? Respond . . . "

She pressed the send button. "Delta 95 receiving you. They're heading up corridor 9. Over."

"Lani! Are you all right! Uh, over."

Lani felt her bruised derriere. It wasn't as badly damaged as her ego. "I'm okay," she admitted gruffly. "Have you got someone going to the 9 H3 intersection? You should be able to stop them there. Over."

Another voice cut in. "Captain LaGarda. Give us details. How many and who are they? Over."

Lani felt her face start to redden. "Um. Two. One man and one . . . something else." She cringed. "The man is quite large and strong." Damn. Of course all of this would be recorded. She could just see them playing it back to her next time she was in the station. And the next. And the next. But he was exceptionally strong. She had to tell them. "Look, you'd better be careful. I think they came from outside. Outside the airlock. Over."

There was a moment's silence. "Captain, are you sure? Over."

"One of them is not human, ma'am. And they're wearing clothes. One of them has a pressure suit. The non-human has clothes in orange, lime green and purple. Over."

"How are they armed? Over."

Now the blush was positively fiery. They'd never let her forget this. "The man has my nightstick. Over."

There was a pause. "What other weapons, Officer?"

Oh, so she wasn't 'captain' any more. "None visible," she said hoping that sounded truly dispassionate and professional. Then she realized that she'd forgotten to say "over."

Someone had obviously guessed, however. "All right. Just stay there. Medical and back-up are on their way to you. Over."

Like she was a casualty. "Send a team here to watch that they don't double back," she said irritably. "I'm going after them. I don't think the scoot is damaged. Over and out."

"Captain LaGarda! You are not to attempt to engage them on your own again! That is an order. Do you understand me? Reply!"

"Yes," she said, lifting the scoot with the other hand. "I hear you. I won't. I'll keep back, and try to just keep in sight. I'll maintain communicator contact. They're on foot and I'm on a scoot. Over and out."

"Do that, Captain. Don't do anything stupid. Over and out."

Reluctantly, as she put her bruised butt onto the saddle, Lani had to admit to herself that it was a bit late for that instruction. She set off after the two of them, wondering whether she should just have stayed and pretended to be injured. But her pride was too deep for that. She'd like a second crack at them, and besides it just wasn't in her to lie, even if the truth had made her look pretty feeble. She was going to take her nightstick back from that big ape and shove it up his ass. Then she heard voices ahead, and slowed the scoot down. She wasn't quite in that much of a hurry, after all.

"I think we ought to take a cross-passage. Soon," said Howard. "I think I heard something behind us. I don't want to meet up with that painted Jezebel again." Well, that was what his mouth said. To his horror part of his mind disagreed. It wanted to take a closer look. He banished the thought, but it did keep creeping back as they walked. They took a branching corridor, which both impressed and irritated Howard. Their micro-irrigation was so much better. Their pruning—a sure sign of a good hard working farmer—was mediocre. A lot of pruning was a judgment call, and that seemed to be lacking.

And looking ahead as they rounded the curve it appeared that it wasn't only the pruners whose judgment had been poor. Theirs hadn't been too good either, Howard had to admit to himself. There were at least thirty people waiting for them, and, looking back, several more on the little two-wheeled things behind them, led by the naked painted Jezebel, grinning triumphantly.

The people with her—and in front of them—were just as naked and just as painted, or even more painted. Some of them definitely wouldn't have been even Brother Galsson's idea of Jezebel. It began to dawn on Howard that they probably just didn't wear clothes here.

"Surrender your arms," said an odd booming voice. "Allow yourselves to be peacefully arrested and you can expect lenient treatment. Any resistance and you will be exterminated."

Kretz looked puzzled. "They want us to take our arms off? Do human limbs detach?"

Despite being in obvious trouble, Howard had to smile. "No. They mean weapons. Do you have any?"

"No," said Kretz. "I lost my laser pistol when the stripe-faces attacked us."

"And I threw that odd stick away." Howard took a deep breath and shouted back, "We don't have any weapons. We're men of peace. Please let us pass. We intend no trespass and no harm. We are just passing through." Then his upbringing got the better of him. "Why do you not put some clothes on and cover your nakedness?" The guilty fantasies that every man had had of naked women had not prepared him for the fact that sometimes clothes could be doing you a favor.

There was a long pause. "Advance one at a time," said the booming voice. "The bigger one first."

Howard looked at the women, and felt that perhaps the terrors of space had not been that bad. But there seemed no help for it, so he advanced, trying not to look at them. "Peace be with you, sisters," he said, holding out his empty hands.

The Jezebel who had met them at the airlock came running up, and grabbed his arm, twisting it up behind his back. "You're under arrest, scumbag emseepee."

Howard blinked at the woman next to his left shoulder. "Why?" he asked. "What have we done wrong?"

"Indecent public appearance. And being out in public without a woman. That'll do for starters. And assaulting an officer!" she said, trying to force his arm upward.

All Howard could think was that she'd gone mad. Maybe they were all mad here. "It is you who have kicked and hit me, and are now trying to twist my arm!" he protested.

"Cuff him," she snapped. There was a red blush of fury to her features, that contrasted with the painstakingly painted picture pattern on her face. "You can tell your story to the judge."

They put metal links which clicked shut onto Howard's arms.

"Right. Let's get the other one," said the woman. "He could be just as dangerous."

Kretz had walked forward while they were talking. Now, suddenly, abruptly, he began to run headlong. Whether it was a dash for freedom or an attempt to rescue him, Howard never found out, as one of the women brought him down with a running tackle. He too was handcuffed. They were marched forward to a small trolleylike device which had a single wheel and a seat in front and a cage behind, balanced on two wheels. "Take them to central," said one of the the women—a plump one carrying an odd conelike device. "You'll have to go via 34th upramp. Elevator bank three is out."

"Still?" said the virago who had captured him.

"Still," said the plump woman. "And it is causing problems enough without your false alarms, Lani."

"It wasn't a false alarm!" she protested.

"Right," said the plump woman dryly. "Forty-five officers to deal with two . . . people. Unarmed people."

Jezebel-Lani put her hands on her hips. And took a deep breath. "He stole my nightstick! And you have to admit that the other one is not human!"

"He's a freak, I admit. I've never seen anything like him. Or the other one. But they didn't exactly put up a fight, did they?"

"You weren't there!"

"No," said the plump woman. "If I had been we wouldn't have all wasted our time. Now let's move out."

The cage trolley—driven by one of the underdressed women—she had a belt and sandals—which seemed to be the total uniform of these women, started moving. Its motivational power was something of little miracle to Howard. It just went. There was no horse. It squeaked. In Howard's opinion it needed oiling—but then maybe it was part of the unseen propulsion system.

"What are they doing with us?" asked Kretz.

"I don't know," said Howard. "Perhaps they'll take us to some men we can ask. These women don't seem quite sane, as well as being daughters of Magdalen."

"Oh. I am very afraid, Howard," said Kretz

Howard didn't want to admit that he was too. Instead he patted Kretz's shoulder—an awkward thing with the cuffs on his hands, but the act seemed to soothe the alien slightly. "I'm sure it will be all right. God will protect us. We'll be taken to see a man in charge, who will put a stop to these women's foolishness."

"I hope you are right," said Kretz despondently. He closed his eyes and lay back on the bars.

So Howard sat and looked at the passing world through the bars. In many ways it looked rather like home. There were a few dead areas—like home. Unlike home there were few homesteads. When they did occur they were in clusters. There were also a few people walking—all, Howard noted, naked. There were other wheeled vehicles—a few, rather than many, and not one horse. Then, as they went a little farther—Howard realized why there were so few homesteads. The people here all lived together. On top of each other! There was no greenery here at all! It made him feel claustrophobic just looking at it. And there were plenty of people here. Naked people. Women, mostly, but here and there a woman was trailed by what Howard realized to his shock were painted men. Men who were all smaller than the women they followed. Naked too.

Howard also noticed that it was warmer here. Well, it would have to be. He was perspiring in the heavy pressure suit, but he certainly didn't fancy the alternative.

It was thrust on him by force though.

The cage-trolley had taken them to the back of building, into an enclosed courtyard. From there they'd been taken to a small room, which was overfull of naked women.

"Strip," said the grim-looking female with a silvery baton who was obviously in charge.

Kretz began undoing the fastenings on his multicolored suit. Howard stood stock. "That means you too." She touched her baton to Howard's neck.

It bit him. Jolted him, savagely.

Howard had never felt anything quite like it. He wasn't keen to do so again. But still, there were some things a man had to stand up for! He folded his arms. "No. It is not decent."

"Taser him and strip him."

They did.

Behind the bars of his new cage Howard wished that he had cooperated. They might not then have cuffed his hands behind his back.

Kretz, naked but calm—which was more than you could say about the women looking at him—had asked to be allowed to keep his necklet—in which, it appeared, his "Transcomp" resided. The women were willing to accept that he needed it, and that he was alien—on the evidence before their eyes.

They had examined both of them with a shameless curiosity. "Who has been hiding you two?" one the women asked Howard, staring at him in what was—to put it mildly—a most embarrassing way.

"No one has hidden us. We're just travelers from outside your habitat. We would like to have our clothes back and go away. We will do you no harm."

"Darn tootin' you won't," said the grim-looking woman. "Not behind the bars."

"What are you going to do with us?" asked Kretz, plainly fearful. Howard felt he had to try to deal with his own fear and discomfort to help the poor fellow.

"You're due up before Judge Garanet in about half an hour. She'll decide," said the grim-looking woman. "Now, go on all of you. Show time's over. I'll call you when you're needed."

"Ah you just want to have fun with both of them, Sarge," said one of the women, cheerfully. "He's well hung, huh? And the other one is . . . different."

"You've got no mind above your belt, Ruby," said the sergeant, with a glance at Howard, who hastily turned around. There was no wall to face.

"Nope," said Ruby cheerfully. "What else are they any good for?"

"We must escape from here," whispered Howard, forgetting that he'd been doing his best to keep up a brave face for Kretz. "They're an evil people without decency or morals."

"They're still better than the ones in the first bead," said Kretz. "Try not to antagonize them further, Howard. You seem to be offending them."

Howard thought about it. They certainly offended him. But the council had imposed a stern duty on him to look after Kretz. Kretz felt that he needed help among humans . . . well, so far Howard had to admit he'd been absolutely useless at that aspect. He would just have to try to ignore his nakedness. It was a heavy cross to bear.

A little later Kretz was taken out of the cage and led through to an adjoining room. Howard had to stand there alone.

# 15

"The social dynamics of societies have never really been studied with a total absence of external influences. This presents a unique sociological research opportunity second to none. It will finally put real Science into future interventions."

—Dr. G. Zola, Chief Operating Officer
  Sysgov. Psychometrics and Sociological
  Monitoring and Adjustment.

"We need to go back to her, Derfel. She's in trouble and so is Kretz. He's out there somewhere," said Abret, trying for a semblance of calm amid the surge of aliens that cramped him. "Look, I'm sorry that I said to her that we needed rescuing, but we do. Unless, well, you haven't

155

given me your local language dataset, can you talk to them? Get them to let us get out of here. Or you can stay if you want to. But Kretz and Selna both need our help."

By the sour expression, neither of those were popular names. Well, that wasn't surprising. Derfel had had his attentions refused by the better part of the crew. It wasn't his fault, maybe. But it meant that he had a few extra grudges, as if he needed such excuses. "No," he said. "Let Kretz help Selna. You're not making things easier here. They expect you to behave like a leader."

Abret had made up his mind. He drew the laser pistol. "Tell them that they're to take me to the airlock. You're needed, Derfel. But you can stay here if that's what you want. Let's go. Now."

Derfel didn't move. "Check your charge meter," he said.

Abret looked down at it. It was blue. Empty.

"I expected trouble from you, Abret. You always treated me as if I was fecal matter. Now it is your turn." He spoke to the coterie of brown uniformed aliens in their language, and they advanced warily on him. Abret turned to run.

Later, in the cell, he realized that that had been a mistake.

But at least he was alone.

# 16

"A societal structure based on group dominance has an intrinsic problem: it needs an underclass. Without them it has no reason to exist. It needs to keep them down, and this provides cohesiveness and also usually structures the society. For instance, if the discrimination is on the basis of color, then the skin color of the upper echelon will be as far from the color of the repressed as possible. If it is based on religion, leaders will be high priests and the repressed or despised will be apostates, etc."

> From: *Elementary Societal Psychodynamics.*
> 2089. James R. Grey (ed). New Harvard
> Library (Pub.)

Alone in the cage, Howard prayed, hard, for redemption, for his companion, for guidance, and for a pair of shorts.

All he got, in the short term, was a prod with a shocks-tick to chase him into the courtroom. And without the insulation of his suit that really hurt. He was herded like a sheep into a box with railings on the top edge. For a blessing the solid part of that box was just over waist high.

The room was full. A woman stood up and said. "The pretrial hearing of the male found in the beta-airlock in the presence of the alien is now in session. All rise for Judge Garanet."

A courtroom full of painted bare breasts did. He was the only male in the place. The paint was as varied as the breasts, a part of Howard's mind noted dispassion-ately. The rest of him was too shocked, and frightened.

A middle-aged woman came in and took her seat behind a desk—a desk embossed with a woman—naked —holding a bow in pursuit of what looked rather like a badly drawn sheep, with upright horns.

"Sit down," she said, in a preoccupied tone. She looked at the papers in front of her. And then at Howard. And then again at Howard, with more interest. "What is your name and which woman is responsible for you?" She asked. "I've got you down as male, unaccompanied."

Perhaps at last he'd get the opportunity to set things straight. She looked to be a woman of some authority. "My name is Howard Dansson, ma'am," he said respect-fully.

Her expression warmed a little. "And which woman are you bound to, Howard? She needs to be brought before the court, as you know," she explained, as if she was being nice to a small and perhaps slightly mentally deficient child.

"I am not married, ma'am," replied Howard.

She blinked. "Married?"

"Bound to woman in matrimony, ma'am."

The judge shook her head incredulously. "Where did you get that from? The last time I came across that word I was reading some ancient history. So, you are still in the custody of your mother, Howard."

"My mother is dead, ma'am," said Howard stiffly.

She peered thoughtfully at him. Or at his physique. "So, who assumed responsibility for you then, Howard?"

"I was an adult, ma'am," said Howard wishing that she wouldn't stare so. "I have responsibility for myself, ma'am. As my companion might have said to you, we have come from another habitat. Our customs are a bit different from yours." He remembered that he was supposed to be talking their way out of this mess. "I do apologize for any offense we've caused. We're just passing through. If you could take us to a far airlock and put us out we'd be very grateful. It would be a charitable thing to do."

She seemed to have ignored most of his statements and focused on the first part. "A place he claimed you called New Helen."

"New Eden, Ma'am. The Society of Brethren live there." Remembering Kretz's story of the first head, he added. "We're a peaceful people. I was simply sent to try to help Brother Kretz get home."

"I have it here," she tapped the paper, "That you assaulted Captain LaGarda. Did you?"

"No ma'am," he said. "The Society of Brethren do not condone violence. She struck me. When she tried to attack us with her black stick I held onto it to prevent her doing so."

"I find that hard to believe. That you could hold her off without striking back."

Howard's patience was getting a little thin. "Ma'am. I can show you, if you like."

"I do like," said the judge. "Captain LaGarda has something of a reputation. Is she in the court?"

The painted Jezebel stood up from the front row. The judge had plainly known that she was there. "Ma'am Judge."

"Captain, take your nightstick and show us how the prisoner attacked you."

She looked distinctly sulky. "He stole my nightstick, ma'am."

"So you said," said the judge dryly. There was plainly no love lost between the two of them. "Borrow one from one of your fellow officers, and come and show us." So she did, amid the buzz from the crowded room.

"You'll have to come out of the dock, Howard," said the judge.

Blushing furiously, Howard realized that he'd set himself up to leave the comforting shield of wood and walk naked in front of all these women. Well, there was no help for it. Nervously he walked out. "I think you'll have to uncuff him, Sergeant," said the judge, looking him up and down. "It seems a bit unreasonable to expect him to assault anyone with his hands behind his back. Or even to defend himself."

So one of the women freed his hands. Instinct took over and he immediately put them in front of his privates, and then had to duck to avoid a vicious blow from the Jezebel. She swung again, and this time he caught the black stick, using his superior height to grab it before it had time to begin its acceleration. The stick still smacked audibly against his flesh. And—just as he had the last time, Howard lifted her off her feet. He felt his muscles stand out with the effort.

"Nice body," said the judge. "Stop trying to kick him, Captain. He's only doing what I told him to do."

"Put me down!" yelled the captain.

So once again Howard did—just a little more gently than last time. She wasn't a quick learner—this Jezebel—or maybe the idea was just too alien for her to grasp. She landed on her derriere again on the courtroom floor. Howard didn't know if it was the landing or the laughter that hurt her most. She was gritting her teeth and looked ready to kill him. "That's what I did, ma'am. Can I let go of this stick now?"

"I think you've made your point," said the judge. "You can go back to the stand now."

Howard did, gratefully. Yes, it wasn't the same as being naked before the Brethren. He was almost able to switch it out, pretend that they weren't real women. Almost. But being sheltered behind the wood made it easier.

"Not you, Captain," said the judge, as the painted Jezebel stood up, rubbing one cheek. "Now. You've claimed in your statement you were assaulted. Will you show me the injuries you sustained?"

"There aren't any," said the young woman, looking as surly as a Jersey bull-calf.

"Oh?" said the judge. "In the violent assault on an officer, known for her combat skills, the male who has just proved he is capable of lifting your considerable bulk, inflicted not one bruise? The idea behind pretrials is to stop the court wasting its time on the mendacious and malicious rubbish. I think that it has just proved its worth as a process, don't you?"

You don't tease Jersey bulls, thought Howard.

The captain stood her ground, chin lifted. "There is still the matter of the indecent public appearance. Being out without a woman. And the theft of a weapon."

"Which was conspicuous by absence when Howie here was taken into custody. Like the assault, more petty malice, eh, Howard," The judge said archly.

Howard flushed. Even coming from the sheltered environment of New Eden there was no mistaking that look. "No . . . uh Ma'am. I *did* take it away from her. I dropped it in some bushes a little distance away."

"Why?"

Howard shrugged. "I didn't want Kretz and me to be attacked again, I suppose."

"That does seem a fair probability. I must tell you, Captain LaGarda, that I have listened to the recording of your Mayday call." She gave a little snort. "It was apparent even then that these two came from outside the Matriarchal Republic of Diana. Of course we expect them to comply with our rules here, but you hardly helped to explain the law to them by assaulting them. I consider it to be unworthwhile to pursue these charges in a formal court, as extenuating circumstances, mostly caused by you, would have any penalties set at such a level to be not worthwhile. The alien comes from a Matriarchy too, and is deserving of better treatment."

She stood up. "These charges are dismissed. Out of here all of you." She pointed to Howard. "Except you. We have to sort out your future."

So a few minutes later, Howard found himself alone with a woman. He tried not to look at her nakedness. Maybe jail would have been a better option. She looked hungrily at him. "You're very big and muscular, aren't you," said the judge.

"We do a lot of physical work, farming," said Howard. "I don't understand why your men are all so small?"

"A little genetic engineering after the oh-33 revolt," said the Judge. "History. Some crazy men decided to start a revolution, claiming that they were stronger. So we made sure that future generations would not have the problem again. I suspect that I'll get several petitions to sterilize you."

Desperate to move the conversation elsewhere—preferably toward getting the two of out of this Gomorrah. "And clothes? I don't wish to offend, but we . . . I am very uncomfortable without clothes."

"They're a source of vanity," said the judge, stretching and displaying a complex pattern of flames and leaves painted on her body. "They were banned by our original charter. Besides they're a place to conceal weapons. And, for you men in particular, to hide your intentions."

Howard decided not to even venture onto the vanity of the body-paint. Or the fact more clothes could only improve some people's physical attractiveness. Instead he tried another tack. "My companion. The alien Kretz," asked Howard. "What are you going to do with him? He needs to get back to his own kind, Ma'am Judge."

"Ah." She scowled. "He's a problem. As a male he can't just be allowed to wander around. There are a few women with exotic tastes in what they choose to add to their harems. But it would be very awkward for someone to enter into such a contract, as he says that soon he will become female. Anyway, as a male, the disposition of another male is not your problem."

"But I need to know, Ma'am," persisted Howard. "I promised to look after him."

"Well, as a male in the Matriarchy of Diana, your promises to another male have no standing. If whichever woman wins the bidding for you wants you to know, then she can make enquiries," said the judge firmly.

"You are going to sell me into slavery?" said Howard in horror.

"It's not slavery, dear. Like a child, a man has to belong to somebody," the judge said kindly. "You men can't help yourselves. You're creatures of base and uncontrolled instincts, weaker in mind and body than women. You instinctively turn to women for wiser counsel. It's all that testosterone. It interferes with your thinking. You need a woman to take care of the rational side. It is the natural human pattern, you know. Matriarchal societies predated patriarchal societies, and humankind moved from bestiality to civilization. Then along came patriarchal societies and patriarchal rule, and it was all downhill from there. It led to conflict and psychological trauma, especially for men. Men are much happier when they have women to tell them what to do. To take responsibility for their actions for them and see they don't get into trouble."

"The Society of Brethren believe that all men are created equal in the eyes of God," said Howard stiffly.

"My dear young man." She smiled patronizingly at him, her eyes roaming over his body a lot more than was comfortable. "Of course all *men* are, if not . . . physically. It's women who have the edge, mentally." She looked at her desk. "Now. I have a number of bids for you. Normally this would be arranged by your mother, but as you've so eloquently pointed out—your mother is not here. It's been agreed that, as in the case of orphans, the court will stand *in loco parentis* for you. And I must say—" she beamed—"you've attracted some very good bids, in spite of being so big. Some of these are women of power, wealth and influence, with wonderful harems. I'll arrange for the meetings this afternoon, shall I?" she said. She got up from her desk and sat down next to him. "We've got an hour or two to spend together in the meanwhile. I need to be able to give a testimony as your . . . ability," she said, putting her hand on his inner thigh.

Howard backed away uneasily. "Uh. Please don't," he said nervously. "We . . . don't believe in relations before . . . or," he said hastily, a horrible thought occurring to him, "outside of marriage."

"I wish that not believing in my relations would make them go away, honey," said the judge throatily.

"I mean, uh, physical relations. Sex," he said desperately as she advanced on him.

That stopped her. She put her head on one side. Shook her head in amazement. "You mean you've never . . . Oh honey, you need me. I can teach you all sorts of things you need to know. Give you the pleasure that only comes with experience." She was advancing again.

Howard hastily turned his back and pressed against the wooden edge of the box. "No." he said firmly. "I am keeping myself pure for my marriage."

"You'd better not take that attitude with me," she said sharply. "I can make things very difficult for you, young man."

"I'm sorry, but no." Howard looked resolutely at the wall, and pressed himself into the security—poor security—of the corner.

"If that's the way you feel, so be it. You're going to regret this." She walked away back to her desk. She leafed through a pile of papers and pulled one out. "This'll teach you a lesson," she said grimly. She flicked a switch on her desk. "Find Captain Lani LaGarda. Tell her that her bid has been accepted."

Howard looked at her.

She smiled with an unpleasant satisfaction at Howard. "You'll have the joy of living with a nonentity with no status, who can't even afford a place in the city, instead of a good catch with age and experience on her side. LaGarda will beat you too. She has a reputation for aggression."

Miserably, Howard had to believe her about the last part anyway. He'd experienced it firsthand.

The speaker on the judge's desk crackled. "Have located Captain LaGarda, ma'am. Shall I send her to your chambers?"

"No. Send her to the clerk of the court, to have her deed of acceptance written up. And send someone to escort this male from my chambers, to his new mistress."

So it was that Howard found himself marched off to the painted Jezebel who had got him into this situation in the first place. Now he had an extra problem, as well as being indecent and having somehow to find and rescue Kretz, and get on with Kretz's mission. Life out here was anything but pleasant and simple. Even being shot at might be easier to cope with.

She was waiting in the foyer—a large room with more of the hunting scenes with the naked woman and her bow. And the sheep with branched horns. They must have a lot of these wild mutant sheep here.

He felt a bit like lamb to the slaughter himself.

# 17

Extract from the Transcript of the Slowtrain funding debate of Lower House, SysGov.

"Tolerance breeds tolerance. The only thing a tolerant society should not tolerate are things which impact on the lives, liberty and happiness of its citizens, such as, for example, bigots. Personally I think shipping them out of the system is a wonderful idea."

—Carmen Albert,
Representative for Ceres-West

Kretz found some comfort in a female-dominated society. Mind you, so far he'd seen little or no evidence of it being any more rational. In his world, Miran females were older, and once they'd got over the hormonal riot

167

of changeover, more stable. These females didn't have that advantage.

The room full of women gave him his first chance to really study human female form. Fascinating convergence! He'd had a talk with Sister Thirsdaughter about child-rearing and had wanted to see human mammary glands. It was a bit that odd they only had two, and they were larger than the Miran ones. That was natural enough as they only had two, he supposed.

"What are you staring at?" asked the large woman that they'd all had to stand up for. She'd sat herself down behind the desk, and everyone else in the room had sat too.

"You," answered Kretz. "You're quite different from us, but quite alike. I have not had a chance to examine you without clothing. I am sorry if I am offending some taboo."

She gave him no reply, but instead asked: "What are you?"

"We call ourselves Miran. I believe your term for us is 'alien.' "

There was sudden buzz from the watchers on the seats. "Silence," said the woman firmly. Then she turned to Kretz. "I can see that you aren't human. But what I want to know is whether you are male or female. Looking at you, you could be either or both."

Something about the way she asked made Kretz suspect that this was a trick question. But he had no real idea what the trick was. All he could do was answer and hope he'd be lucky. "I am, at the moment, male. I should become female in about two of our years time. This is how Miran are. We begin as male and then become female. All animal life on our world that doesn't reproduce by binary fission follows this pattern."

The woman at the desk made a note on her page. "It's a lesser charge, I suppose. As a male yourself you can't be held responsible for another male. So, where are you from? What are you doing here, in the Matriarchal Republic of Diana?"

For a brief moment Kretz toyed with trying a lie, for instance that there were several thousand other Miran males armed to the teeth coming to fetch him. He decided to stick to the truth. These aliens were definitely more technologically advanced than Howard's people had been, although there were small signs of breakdown to be seen.

"I am from the second planet of a sun some 1.8 light-years away. We saw this ship and came to investigate. We mean you no harm. My companions were attacked in the first habitat, by primitives with weapons that flung projectiles at us. Most of my friends were killed. I was separated from my companion. She is now back on our ship. I was hurt, fled down the central cable and reached the habitat of my companion. They are primitive humans, having regressed from technology, or for some reason turned their backs on it. They tried to help me, and sent one of their number with me, as an escort, helper and guide. I could not get back, but there is a lifecraft from our ship some four habitats on. We are trying to reach it."

He paused. "The human who is with me has saved my life. I apologize if we have broken your taboos. I plead for you to understand. You are an advanced people. He is very primitive."

The woman at the desk made a note on her pad, then steepled her fingers. "Nonetheless, you broke our laws about clothing. And while I am sympathetic about you trying to reach your mistress, and being separated from her, you were still moving in the wrong direction, without a woman to escort you."

"We did not know of your law," said Kretz.

"Ignorance of the law is no excuse," said the woman, firmly, in the manner of one using an accepted truism to clinch an argument.

That struck Kretz as an excuse itself. After all, what kind of legitimacy did a regime have that did not inform its citizens (or visitors) of the rules it expected them to follow? That surely was its responsibility? The law-setter had failed, not the citizen.

But there was no point in fighting with her about it. "I have no objection to being without clothes. The clothes that I wore were simply to protect me from space. It is cold and airless out there."

"I know that," she said dismissively. "You could have taken them off once you were in."

A thought struck Kretz. "These laws of yours apply to your people? You are humans?"

The large woman nodded. "In full, alien, to human females. Males are considered as minors under law."

Kretz nodded back, pleased to found a loophole. "I am not human. Therefore surely I don't fall under your law. My wearing clothes then is no worse than . . . " What was that animal Howard had found so amusing that he'd thought was another intelligent species called? "A pig wearing clothes."

The woman frowned slightly. "You're very well informed about the animal-life on old Earth. Very well. It'll do away with a tricky case. I suppose, as you're not human, you belong to those who handle animal tissue."

She turned to the woman who had escorted him in. "Have him shipped off to Dr. Geriant at the protein vat research unit at the university. Make him her problem, at least until he changes sex."

Kretz wondered if he'd been cataclysmically stupid. They'd made no attempt to take the cuffs off his wrists and had transported him in the same cage-vehicle, and left him sitting in it for long enough for curious faces to peer from windows.

Then two people came down with the woman who had brought him here. Howard would have approved. They wore clothing. From head to foot—some sort of overall garb in bright orange. They were both scowling. This looked like trouble. And then the shorter one—the one with the red head filaments peered at Kretz, and stopped scowling.

"I do believe the silly bitch is right this time! I suppose statistically that was inevitable," she said, sticking her head forward like an attacking tunnelworm. Kretz had to remind himself, pointedly, that exposed teeth were not always a sign of aggression. She could just be smiling. He wasn't that good at alien expressions on these unfamiliar faces yet.

The red-head-filamented one turned to the woman who had brought him there. "Well, what are you waiting for, woman? Get him out of there. Hurry up."

"First you insult me, then you argue with me, then you tell me to hurry up," said the woman who had driven the cage, moving with exaggerated slowness.

"Yes. And if you don't hurry up I'll see that you get transferred to driving sludge. Now move it."

The driver's pace accelerated dramatically, and Kretz found himself stumbling out. No attempt was made to remove the handcuffs, but the women led him inside the building.

He was put into an empty room, an empty store, by the looks of it. "I'll be back down and have a look at him properly when I've adjusted the lysine levels in the batch in A17," said the woman, and left Kretz to himself and his fears. There was not much else in the enclosed space to distract him from them. The walls throbbed faintly with machinery-vibration. And no one came. The door was securely locked and there were no windows. Eventually —cold, tired, hungry and thirsty, Kretz lay down on the hard floor and slept.

He awoke, aware that he was being stared at. It was the woman with the red head-filaments. "Hmm. I suppose I'll have to start with communication. Sign and point," she said. "And organizing food and drink and something for you to sleep on."

Kretz sat up. "I can speak your language. Please, I am very thirsty."

"Holy Susan!" the woman blinked. "Naturally that idiot from the court didn't tell me you could talk our language. Let's get you some water."

She led him to another room, down the passage, gave him a container with water in it. At least his handcuffs were in front of him, unlike Howard's. He wondered what had become of the young man.

"Now, where are you from?" she asked when he drunk his fill.

Kretz gave his standard answers, told the same story. The only difference was that she seemed to understand it.

"So what have you been eating?" she asked.

Kretz did his humble best to name the foods that Howard and Sister Thirsdaughter had fed him. She took notes on a small pad with a tiny stylus—both taken from the pocket of her orange overall. She stopped him and got descriptions from time to time. When he'd finished, she closed the pad, which was not the "paper" that Howard's people or the court had used but some kind of thin hard substance—probably a computer, Kretz realized.

"Right, we'll analyze that lot and see what we can come up with on the ones that made you feel sick. In the longer term, you're almost certainly missing some dietary requirements. We'll have to see what we can synthesize. I'll need a tissue sample."

"Tissue sample?" Kretz repeated.

"A small piece of your flesh," explained the woman. "To grow you some food that will match your dietary needs. I could do it with other food material from your world but we don't have any. And the one thing that material taken from a species has: it has all the dietary requirements for that species, if not in the right concentrations and format. Looking at your teeth, you're probably omnivores." She scowled. "And if you even offer me that ridiculous cannibalism argument, I'll be tempted to let you starve."

"I wouldn't think of doing so," he paused. "I presume you mean cell-culture. We do that on shipboard, as well some degree of other food synthesis." He paused again. "Transcomp needs information. What does 'cannibalism' mean, actually?"

"A word to describe what politicians do," she said.

"Could you clarify 'politician'?"

"No," she said, showing her teeth in what could be humor. "I haven't understood them myself. They're a kind of parasite. An animal that looks superficially like us, but has no brain and lives only to breed and devour our food. Now, tell me, why is your fur in constant motion? It looks as if waves are running down it. Or is that just a light-property?"

"Fur?" Another new term. Transcomp had deduced that it was probably another word for the long and apparently permanent filamentous manes which grew on the face and heads of the aliens.

She confirmed that. "Hair." She touched her own. "You've got a layer all over."

"Oh. That is not the same as your hair. It is an extruded cilia to try to help my body thermo-regulate. The motion is a relic of our evolution when it helped to keep us dry."

"I see. Are you too hot or too cold?"

"Too cold. If I am too hot, the cilia stand out to increase the cooling surface. If I was the right temperature then the cilia would resorb. It is an energy expensive process with high metabolic demands. My suit helped me to thermo-regulate."

"What happened to your suit?" she asked, walking to a locker and measuring him with her eyes.

"I was made to remove it by the people who brought me here. There is some taboo here against the wearing of clothing. My companion and I were not aware of it and we got into difficulty with your authorities."

She snorted. "They're not terribly bright. What have they done with your companion? Is he also one of you aliens?" She tossed him an orange overall. "Here, put this on. I'll get this suit of yours back from them."

"No. Howard is human. He was sent to help me get back to my spacecraft."

The red-head-filamented one lost interest in Howard. Kretz held up his cuffed wrists. "I cannot put this on with these. And . . . will I not get into trouble again for wearing it anyway?"

She laughed. "You would, out of this building. But unlike the rest of the environment of Diana, this area has coldrooms. There are also various things you wouldn't want to have exposed to the skin, and there are cultures we need to keep dead skin cells out of." She looked at the cuffs and sighed. "It would take them a month of Sundays to get up here with the keys. I'll need to get some bolt-cutters."

She pointed at a chair. "Sit down. I'll be back in few minutes."

She came back, not much later, with an enormous clipper-device, with which she cut the links between the cuffs. Kretz had got himself into the lower half of the overall and now he was able to pull it on. It was thick and soft.

"Don't go wandering beyond the courtyard in that," she said. "The matriarchy are obsessed about nudity. It's an overreaction to a piece of ancient history. The reason is lost to them, but they've become obsessed with the form of the thing."

"It is a little odd," admitted Kretz. "Clothing is worn for protection from weather or to help with temperature-regulation in our society."

"Oh, it's all about sex with us. You aliens will find that we humans are crazy. After all, what sane species could believe that covering someone from head to toe would lessen their sexual attractiveness?" She laughed, patting her own rounded midriff. "Mind you, in a lot of cases seeing someone naked will do that. Covering it up just feeds the imagination. And the imagination is always better than reality."

# 18

The populations of space habitats differ, as does their societal structure. Take for instance the low-tech environment of the Society of Brethren. The initial nine thousand occupants, scattered in individual holdings, farming their land, was very different from the habitat of their neighbors, the Matriarchy of Diana. Diana, with a high degree of technical sophistication and mechanization, had some 70,000 occupants, and still had room to grow. That's the difference between urbanization with mechanization and a primitive lifestyle.

> From: *Basic Sociological Engineering,* Herne,
> G. & Weaver, A. Oxbridge VoxPress, New
> Britain, 2307

The painted Jezebel who had assaulted and arrested him had a rather puzzled expression on her face. "I didn't expect to even have my bid considered." she said. "I don't know how I am going to afford this. I wish I hadn't done it, to be honest."

She looked . . . well, less of a virago now, and quite troubled. That found a chink in Howard's armor which her aggression had failed to.

"I think she did it to punish me," he said humbly.

His new mistress looked at him in puzzlement. "Why? She just let you off scot-free. She's been drooling all over you for the whole hearing. I thought she was going to take you right there on her desk at one stage."

Howard blushed to roots of his hair.

"Oh," she said, scowling. "That's it. She's punishing me, not you. You can't get it up, can you?"

Howard's mouth fell open as he grasped what she was saying. He shook his head furiously. "No. It's just that I would not lie with a woman I was not married to. It is a sin!"

It was her turn to gape at him. "You mean you turned Judge Garanet down? You wouldn't let her have it?"

Howard nodded, almost dying of embarrassment. "I'm afraid that it is true. Hell hath no fury like a woman scorned."

His new mistress shook her head incredulously. And then began to giggle. And then to laugh until the tears ran down her face. She had to hold onto the wall for support. "So, I am supposed to make your life a misery?"

"I would guess that that is correct," said Howard uncomfortably.

Lani bared her teeth in a savage grin. "She really is forcing me to be nice to you. Let's take a walk up past her office. You can put your arm around me," she said with the air of someone giving him an enormous privilege.

"It would not be seemly," he said, folding his arms hastily.

She turned her basilisk look on him, muscles tensing . . . and then shook her head at him. "Now I really do believe you turned her down. It must be a weird place, this New Eden of yours. I'll just have to remember that. Keeping my temper with you is going to be hard, but worth it, just to get up her nose. Look, it's a big privilege for a man to be allowed to touch a woman in the street. You should walk a little behind me."

"But you all take such short steps," said Howard, desperate to talk about anything else.

"That's because you're too big," she said with her normal scowl. "Now, take my hand at least. Look, I'm not going to bite you! I just want to make the old bat turn green. She made me look like a fool in that hearing."

Howard had to admit, with the vision of hindsight, that the judge had gone out of her way to make the young woman look foolish. He extended a nervous hand. His palm sweated as he took her hand gently in his. "The path to redemption lies in forgiveness. It is better to forgive than to seek revenge."

She closed her eyes briefly. Took a deep breath. "Good. So we're giving old Judge Garanet a chance to take the path to redemption. Isn't that kind of us? Now walk, and try not to look like you think I'm going to bite you. I won't, not yet, anyway."

That was almost more worrying.

They did a little promenade and then walked to her odd two-wheeled vehicle. Howard eyed it with trepidation. "What pulls it?" he asked, as she swung herself onto the saddle.

She shrugged. "It's electrically powered. Get onto the pillion."

"What is a pillion?" he asked.

She looked at him, and shook her head. "You really don't know anything do you? I'll have to try to remember that. This bit." She patted a narrow pad behind her.

It looked very small and very close. "Er. Can't I just run behind? I'm afraid my weight might break it," he added ingeniously.

She snorted. "Don't be ridiculous. Get on."

So he did, painfully aware of his nakedness and her closeness.

It got worse. "Hold onto my waist," she said.

Riding back to her home Lani had time to wonder what sort of a mess her impulsive behavior had gotten her into this time. The one thing she was determined to do was prove that old harridan wrong. Still, there was an exotic fascination to her man. She just had to accept that he really didn't know anything.

And then, within sight of home, they hit a bump. There was an alarming *crack*, a high-pitched squeal, and the scoot stopped dead.

They didn't. The two of them landed—at some speed—in a heap in the wall-growth. Lani was totally winded by the steering bar being crunched into her midriff, not only by her own forward momentum but by the weight of Howard as well. She lay there struggling for breath, with a warm wetness trickling down from her hair, feeling shocked and stunned.

The next part was even more shocking. Her new man got up off her, looked down at her and said, "Are you all right?"

She had too little breath to spare to reply. So he picked her up and carried her at a run, to her own door.

He managed to knock thunderously, and hold her—without quite dropping her. Of course there was no reply. "It's my house. You can put me down," she said. She seemed to be in the habit of saying that.

This time he didn't drop her hard, but set her down as if she were porcelain. Fragile porcelain, at that. It didn't help. She still swayed and he caught her just before she fell. Somehow, he managed to open her door, while supporting her, and then picked her up again and carried her inside. He took her to the couch and put her down. "How do I call someone to help?"

"I'll be fine. Really. Just let me lie back for a bit."

"I need to stop that bleeding," he said firmly. "And then we need to get a healer to you. I was foolish and a little shocked. I shouldn't have moved you. It was just seeing all the blood . . . I panicked a little. Anyway, head injuries can be serious. You need to get it checked. Here. Press your hand to it, gently. Now, I need to find water, boiling and cooled, and clean cloth to staunch this cut."

"Head wounds bleed," she said. "There's a first-aid kit in the cupboard down the passage. Get it for me."

He looked at her, and went. A little later he came back with a bowl, warm water and her first-aid kit. "I will need to wash it and see. If needs be I must carry you back to the last house we passed."

He washed and cleaned the area around the wound, and then with care snipped away the hair with scissors from the box. "It appears superficial," he said, his relief obvious. "It should still be looked at by a healer. Shall I walk to the last house?"

"And get yourself arrested for wandering around without a woman, stupid." Lani frowned at him, and then wishing she hadn't. It pulled at the cut.

"Stay still," he said firmly. "I am going to put a dressing on it, but I want to clean the wound itself. I have read the instructions on this bottle and it says I should add two drops to the water before cleaning it."

"You can read?" Men couldn't read. It wasn't permitted.

"Can't you?" he asked, adding the disinfectant to the water. "Every child learns how to read in New Eden. It is beautiful script you have here. As neat and uniform as the oldest holy writ."

"Of course I can read!" she said. "It's just men that can't . . . uh, usually."

"You mean you have kept them from doing so," he said grimly. "We are all, men and women, made in God's image, and equal in his sight. Hold still! I need to work very carefully here."

"You need to learn to be careful with your big mouth too," she said, "You're an intolerant bigot talking about our culture like that. It could get you into serious trouble."

He worked in silence. For someone with big hands he was very precise.

"I had not thought of it as being intolerant of your culture," he said quietly, as he put a dressing over the wound. "I had just seen it as right to proclaim against you. Forgive me."

Having just gotten herself angry, Lani felt wrong-footed again. She bit her lip. Pulled herself together and tried to make amends. "You're wrong, but you can't help it, I suppose." She said it sulkily, knowing that she was behaving a bit like a very ungenerous spoiled brat, knowing that she'd made no allowance for his background. He was a man, after all, and from the weaker sex. You had to make allowances. She knew that was part of her problem with them. She kept forgetting you had to.

He smiled. "Yes. I'm only used to my own culture, lady. Now, I am going to put a bandage around this dressing. Sister Thirsdaughter would be very rude about it, but it will serve. I still do not see that what you people do is right in the eyes of man or God, but I will try to keep my opinion to myself. To keep my mouth shut." He began winding the bandage around her head.

Lani sighed. "You're going make me old before my time. I suppose you can talk. To me only. When we're alone. I won't beat you, even if I should. Now just let me lie here with my eyes closed for five minutes, and then I'll contact someone to do something about the scoot."

He nodded and took the bloody water away, and Lani closed her eyes. She now had bruises to show. And a few grazes too. And quite a headache.

When she next opened her eyes there he was. Sitting, watching her, a worried expression on his big open face. He smiled warily when he saw her eyes open. "How are you feeling now?" he asked.

She felt her head. "A bit sore, but I'm all right. How long was I asleep for?"

"Perhaps half an hour."

"Hell. I'd better do something about reporting that scoot. It's blocking the roadway. The harvesters use the road a lot." She started to sit up, wincing.

He put up a quelling hand. "Don't worry. I went and fetched it. I carried it back here."

"On your own?" she demanded.

He nodded. "It wasn't that heavy."

She raised her eyes to the ceiling. "Get this into your dumb head. You can't walk around here without a woman to escort you. It's not that I don't appreciate your doing it. It's just that you have to work within the rules here. Our rules, or you'll get both of us into trouble. I'm liable for your actions, you know."

She sighed. "Look. I know you didn't mean any harm. But the next time you end up in front of a judge here, it might not be one with more lust on her mind than justice. Or you might get old Garanet again. She'll throw the book at you next time. And it wouldn't just be at you, it would be at me too. You're my responsibility." She sighed again. "I wish I knew what went wrong with the scoot. There are a couple of women who've started doing repairs. They don't know much about it, but apparently they know how to charge . . . "

"This." He held out a metal shaft. "This is half of the rear axle. As you can see it is badly worn along here. It fractured, with the extra weight, as you went over the bump. I'm sorry. I should have run behind."

She sniffed and dabbed the corner of her eye, irritably. Crying like a man! "I need it for my job. I'm afraid it'll have to be fixed, no matter what they decide to charge me."

"I think I could fix it if I can find a suitable shaft," he said diffidently. "Fixing mechanical things is permitted here?"

"Oh, by Susan, yes. Can you imagine if it wasn't!?"

"It isn't encouraged in New Eden," he admitted. "But I'm a fair artificer."

She scowled. "I thought about going in that direction myself. There is money in it. But the trouble is, according to my history teacher, everything worked beautifully in Diana . . . for the first seventy-five years. By the time that things started breaking down, we'd lost a generation's worth of minds that were used to dealing with technical repairs. Anyway, they were used to being part of a technical society, that had robots and factories. We were cut off from those. Now we're even losing an increasing number of maintenance robots, and no one has the sort of skill required to fix those. The matriarch set up a rota for training, but we're short on experience."

"I will happily try to fix your vehicle. It would work better if I could talk to Brother Kretz," said Howard hopefully. "He is a very good engineer. That woman would not tell me what she'd done with him. He's alone and scared."

He had a way of putting obligations on her. "Oh, hell. He'll be treated all right, Howard. We're not barbarians. Look, I'll call a few people and ask."

"Thank you," he said humbly. "I promised the council I would look after him. So far I have done a poor job. I will try to fix this 'scoot.' The bearings appear to still be sealed."

Bearings? "Is that good or bad?"

"Good," said Howard. "They failed in the corn-grinder at home. Getting it to work at all after that was difficult. But I contrived."

It sounded promising. "You've fixed things lots of things before?"

Howard nodded guiltily. "I enjoy it," he admitted. "I like to understand things. They're easier than people."

She had to have that scoot. Without it, she would be on desk-duties, at best. "If there is a part number on it I can order it from stores. It'll cost, but if you think you could put it in it'll be a lot cheaper than getting it fixed by someone else."

He looked at the piece of metal. "There is a number on it. But explain how this works, please, woman? There is a store of such parts, prepared like the granaries Joseph had made in Egypt?"

"Yeah . . . well there is a store of them," she said, amused. "I've never heard of the Joseph and Egypt part. And call me Lani, not woman." She thought a bit. "Look, I should be able to access the onscreen manual . . . Just don't ever tell anyone I let you look at it. I'm not supposed to let a man learn to read, but you already know how to read. You've read all sorts of things in this New Eden place I suppose."

He shook his head. "Only the Holy Book. The Elder has some others, and the healers have some too. But I have never even heard of a book called 'Onscreen Manual.' "

"Book . . . like a thing made of paper and printed on? Like court papers?"

Howard nodded. "Yes. Written, with ink, and bound."

Lani shook her head. "I've seen one in the museum. An original Susan Sontag! Anyway, let me show you the screen. Most things can be accessed by vox, but reading is a lot faster. I'm lucky, in a way, being out here. The Matriarch ordered all the town computers still in working order to be put into the computer room, and you get access by time allocation. But out here . . . Well, no one wants to live out of town, so there are some perks for a lousy social life."

She got up and took the arm he offered. The offer was done in such a way that she was pretty sure it was because he regarded her as walking wounded. He certainly had no idea about the duties a man owed to his mistress! Teaching him was going to be quite a lot of fun, although right now her head and ribs were still sore, which rather limited the appeal of sex. She stole a look at his profile. Okay, so some women might regard the first addition to her harem as a freak, but there was some odd primitive appeal to his body. She leaned on the arm. It was solidly muscled.

"Right—here is my work cubicle. Normally men should keep out of this area, except to clean it." She sat down gingerly. Winced. It was from the graze on her side, but he reached the wrong conclusion.

He blushed. "I didn't mean to drop you so hard." He bit his lip. "That is a lie. What I mean is, I am sorry I dropped you so hard. It was un-Christian of me. I didn't think about how much I would hurt you."

"I'd just kicked you in the belly and in the balls," she said. "And I did mean to hurt you."

He shrugged. "I should have turned the other cheek."

She swatted him. Playfully, across the behind. "Right. Consider the other cheek hit."

He backed off, looking very fearful.

"Oh, for goodness sake! I didn't hurt you."

"No." He bit his lip. "But it is not right that you should touch me, flesh on flesh, exposing me to the temptations of the flesh. I . . . the Society of Brethren do not believe a man should have . . . uh, knowledge of a woman unless they are man and wife."

He was turning her down? It wasn't exactly something he had any choice about! The court, acting as his mother, had accepted her bid. It was a woman's right! She'd noticed that he wasn't entirely disinterested. That did add a certain . . . piquancy to it all. She was used to young men physically desiring her. She'd bitterly come to accept that they regarded her as fine for a bit of experience, just not old enough, or wealthy and powerful enough, to really tempt them or their mothers into signing a bond.

She decided on a direct approach. "Don't you find me attractive?" she asked.

He blushed to the roots of his hair. "It's not the same thing," he mumbled, and looked terribly embarrassed. "It's not right, and nothing will ever change my mind."

"Really?" said Lani, feeling something of a challenge here. "We'll just have to see."

She gave him her best smile. This was something entirely new. It gave her a rather perverted little frisson of excitement. This sort of chase . . . was different. Diana the huntress would approve. She doubted if the rest of the society of the Matriarchal Republic would, but they didn't have to know what she was doing inside the walls of her own home.

"Anyway," she pointed to the screen, activated it with the other hand. "We don't still have books. We have this. There are several hundred thousand texts available. Let's see if I can find a manual for the scoot." She flicked to search. "Ah. Here."

"The letters are so clear! They're . . . wonderful!" Looking up at him she realized that she might have serious trouble seducing him from these bizarre ideas of his . . . as long as he could have something to read. His face was rapt, and he was plainly entranced by the dull technical text. He looked like a child with the most wonderful toy.

Rather cute, really. She didn't bother to ask if he wanted vox. He, like her, obviously read faster than the machine could say the words.

"There is more?" he asked hopefully.

"Millions of pages. Oh, you mean of this document? Just hit this button to scroll down."

He did, almost devouring the words with hungry eyes.

At length he shook himself. "It is strange to read something that isn't holy writ. The letters are so regular! How do they do this?"

"I've never really thought about it. There'll be a book on it somewhere. Or I can ask someone at the university for you. My mother didn't have the money to send me, but I know a few people."

He sighed. "It is very wonderful. I have seen so much today that my mind is almost numb with wonder. But this . . . this is one of the most wonderful. I don't understand all the words, but it is like a door opening. Thank you."

It was so obviously heartfelt that she could hardly refuse to show him how to use the dictionary by highlighting the word. She was, she admitted to herself, totally unprepared for his delight at that. It was rather sweet, really.

They found the numbered part together and ordered it. It was surprisingly cheap.

Eventually, she looked at her wall-clock. "So late already. We'd better eat." She jerked a thumb at the kitchen. Howard looked blank. Lani started to get angry and then . . . checked. "Can you cook?" she asked warily. "I suppose that's something else you might not have learned to do."

Howard beamed, straightening up from leaning over the chair, and almost bumping his head on her ceiling. "I'm a good cook," he said. "Well, that's what Sister Thirsdaughter said. I can't cook anything like as well as my mother could, of course. But for a man, I can cook well." He looked faintly embarrassed. "It comes of being a bachelor still at nine-and-twenty. Most men marry much younger—often straight from living with their parents, and have never touched a skillet."

Lani looked at him suspiciously. "Your mother cooked?"

Howard nodded, his blue eyes innocent. "Didn't yours?"

"I'm damn sure she never touched the inside of a kitchen. Next thing you'd be suggesting that she washed plates or changed diapers." She caught the look on Howard's face. "I suppose your mother did?"

Howard nodded. "My father did help. He cooked on Sundays, and took his turn in the chores list with the dish-washing. But many people in New Eden consider cooking and housekeeping to be women's work. I did it because I lived alone, of course. But I would have expected my wife to do the bulk of it if I married."

Lani pushed open the kitchen door. "Things are very much the same here. Except that it is *you* who are expected to do the cooking. And, as a woman living alone, I've been looking forward to it. I can burn nearly anything. I suppose I should show you where things are."

She was a little embarrassed by the state of the kitchen. But then she hadn't expected to be bringing home a man when she started her day. "It's a bit primitive," she said, gruffly. "But we can improve it one day when I have a bit more money."

Howard was unprepared for the kitchen she propelled him into. He didn't really mind the cooking part, that she seemed to expect him to do. It was abnormal, but then, so was their society. And he wasn't planning to spend very long here. Just long enough to find Kretz and get out of this piece of Gomorrah. It could have been worse, he supposed. It could have been Sodom.

But how was he expected to cook without a methane-burner? What were these glass-fronted cupboards with dials? And where were the essentials of a good kitchen: the sides of bacon, the hams, the strings of onions and bunches of garlic? He didn't even see a single crock or any preserves, let alone wicker baskets full of fresh produce hung where they would catch the cool tunnel-breeze. Perhaps there was a pantry? The only thing he felt familiar with was the sink.

She was obviously watching his face. "We could get food from a take-out, but we're too far from town for anyone to deliver, and the scoot still needs fixing," she said, her voice defensive. "I've got a fair number of instant meal-for-ones in the freezer, but I haven't got around to doing much food-shopping lately."

"I don't understand all these things," he said humbly. He seemed to spend a lot of time being humbled. "In New Eden almost everyone grows their own food and barters with their neighbors. I have never bought any food."

It was her turn to gape at him. "Grow your own? Do you each have your own harvesters and plant-tender robots then?"

"I'm not sure what this 'robot' you mention is. If it is a machine, we have no machines. God gave us hands to work with. I plant, tend and harvest my crops. I tend, feed, milk and slaughter my animals."

Her mouth hung open. "Really? With your own hands? Doesn't it take a lot of time?"

"Yes. But we have no machines. It is good honest work."

"Well," said Lani, obviously trying to take something positive out of this, "I guess they can't break down then. I suppose I'll have to show you how to work all this stuff." She sighed. "I'm not really very good at men's work, you know."

She opened a chest full of coldness, and took out two square packs. Took a look at Howard and took out a third. "You're going to be expensive to feed."

"I'm sorry," he said. He supposed that he would be, compared to the tiny little men he'd seen.

"Don't be so damned humble!" she snapped. "You make me feel guilty, always apologizing like that."

"I'm sorry," he said again, before he realized what he was doing, and felt foolish. "It's a habit. I am always in trouble back . . . among my people."

She laughed. "Probably for picking up women and breaking things."

Howard was acutely uncomfortable. "No. I've never even touched a woman before, well, except my own mother and my aunt, and Sister Thirsdaughter. I mostly got into trouble for fixing things. For taking apart mechanical devices too. And for going to places I wasn't supposed to."

"Who is this 'Sister Thirsdaughter'?" she asked, head tilted.

"The healer and midwife for our community. We are blessed indeed to have such a wonderful woman with us," he explained.

"Pretty, is she?" asked Lani.

Howard blinked, suddenly getting the drift of the woman's questions. "She brought me into this world. And my father and mother before me," he said.

She had the grace to look a little embarrassed. "Oh. Well, look you put these into the micro. Here. You set it on three minutes thaw and one reheat for each. Have you got that? To think I'd be teaching cooking!"

It wasn't much like any kind of cooking Howard had encountered. He had it fixed in his memory, but he also had no idea what it meant. And he wished that the kitchen was a bigger room and that she wouldn't lean on him like that. He wished that he could get a bit farther away from the temptations of her body. He had found himself reciting psalms to keep his thoughts from straying. There weren't enough psalms. And by the look on her face, she'd noticed.

The light went off in the square glass-fronted box she'd put the icy blocks into.

She opened the door of the device, and took them out. Slightly fragrant steam curled up from them. She put the now obviously hot blocks onto plates she took down from a cupboard. At last—something familiar, although these were not made of wood.

"I normally just eat out of the container," she said guiltily. "It saves on washing up. But I suppose we'll get used to using plates now."

The knives and forks were just knives and forks. The food, revealed once the cover was pulled back, was like nothing Howard had ever seen. It had been cut to fit the shape of the container. Square meat. Square-ended vegetables.

It wasn't like anything he'd ever tasted, either.

He prodded the square of meat. "What sort of animal does this come from?" he asked, trying hard not to sound critical.

"It's vat-protein beef."

"Ah." Howard desperately struggled for something polite to say about it. "It's . . . very tender. They don't run about much, these beasts."

"It's not really an animal. It's a cell-culture. We don't actually have any animals in the Matriarchy, although I've read about them and seen pictures." She looked a little wary. "You actually have them running around? And then you kill them?"

Howard nodded. "It is the normal thing, yes. Of course we keep cows for milk, butter and cheese too, and chickens for eggs and meat."

She shuddered. "It sounds barbaric."

Howard, fresh from his new meeting with technology, felt a bit embarrassed. "It . . . tastes good. There is a certain satisfaction to it too, raising and providing your own food. Of course it isn't as quick as this."

"Well, you can buy unprocessed stuff. It's very cheap. I have no idea what to do with it, though. I'll get you some and you can try."

Howard wasn't planning to stay here that long. But, although it was not quite honest, he had a feeling that he'd better not tell her that. At least the food filled the gaping hole in his belly.

She yawned. "Leave the dishes for the morning," she said. "Let's go to bed. You'd probably like to wash first. I would."

It was the kind of invitation that part of Howard thought would be worth a fall from grace. And he wasn't thinking of the opportunity to wash.

"Can I draw and heat the water?" he said. A cold bath would help him anyway. "Where do I find the buckets?" Maybe here they would not frown on his bucket-yoke.

She looked at him very oddly. He held his head up high. Some were born to be hewers of wood and drawers of water. There was no shame in that. "I still have working faucets, Howard. And hot water," she said, leading him into another room, overfull of bath.

He found the idea that hot water could come out of a tap fascinating, and a little threatening too. What was a man to do if machines did all the work? Still, the bath was convenient and a welcome thing after the sort of day he'd had. The bubbles were . . . odd, but fragrant. Howard felt he ought to disapprove of them because of their frivolity, but then he wasn't too sure that they were frivolous. Maybe they served some purpose that he knew nothing about. He got that feeling about half the things in this world.

He climbed into the warm fragrant water, sat back, relaxed, and closing his eyes, let the troubles and complexities of this new world ebb away.

"Move up," she said. "You occupy a wholly indecent amount of a bath, you know."

Howard sat up hastily, as she stepped into the bath. He tried to get out, slipped and nearly submerged. Fortunately, it was quite a large bath without that much water in it.

She laughed, and, while sitting down into the water, pushed him back with a hand on his shoulder. "Don't be sillier than you have to be," she said calmly.

"It's not . . . decent. Not right," he spluttered, reverting to trying to avert his eyes.

"I don't have a problem with it, and it's my world. Nobody wears clothes here. Now relax. You still need to wash. And I want you to do my back. And open your eyes. It's not as if you hadn't seen me already."

"You are making it very hard for me," he pleaded. "I had never even seen a naked woman until today."

She smiled at him in a very alarming way. It reminded him of a cat, stalking a chick when the hen wasn't watching. "I intend to make things very hard for you. You'll just have get used to it."

"I feel I have seen too many naked women today," he said gloomily.

"That wasn't quite what I meant. Anyway. I need my back washed."

"Yes, mistress."

"I told you to call me Lani. It's a privilege, you know."

"The mistress's privilege and slave's view of the same thing are not alike."

"You're not a slave."

"You paid for me. That's slavery."

"Actually, the money is held in trust for your care if I throw you out, and also to pay for your children's maintenance. I pay it in installments every month."

"It still feels like slavery," said Howard, taking the loofah.

Lani looked at him sleeping. On the floor on a rug, the big lunk. He'd point blank balked at sharing the bed. This was proving to be quite a challenge. Not something she'd ever experienced before. But he was so innocent and helplessly naive that she felt rather maternal about him. She'd have to stop him getting locked up and gelded with his crazy ideas and behavior, though. And, she thought, practically, he might actually be quite useful at some things. She wasn't one of those immoral cows that made money out of their men, making them work while claiming the income and sitting on their broad behinds, but . . . he did say that he liked fixing things. At least he could save her money, to make up for feeding him.

A laughable bid put in as a sour joke with the others in the station, saying that if she got him, she'd teach him how to behave, had backfired in her face. Maybe, she thought, as she looked at him breathing slowly and rhythmically, his big chest rising and falling easily, for once she'd done the right thing, out of malice.

It was going to be rather nice, finding out. She was still smiling when sleep took her.

Her waking was not peaceful.

A crash . . . and then, "There he is! Kill him!"

The sound of breaking things, and yells. The sound of flesh being struck. Lani lunged out of her bedroom and plunged into her small lounge. Right at her door, Howard was down, being viciously attacked by three of her fellow officers.

Lani used her velocity to kick one over him, and a straight arm to knock the turning one so hard into the wall, that the picture above her fell down. The corner of it hit her head and picture-glass sprayed.

Lani stood over her fallen man, hands at the ready. "What in hell are you playing at?" she demanded of the sole standing officer.

"L . . . Lani?" the nightstick tip dropped along with her jaw.

"Who the hell did you think it was, Madeline? The Matriarch? This is my house, damn it! You know that. Why are you beating him up? What the hell is going on here?"

Captain Madeline Rodgers looked in horror at the smashed door, the broken chair, the picture, and her colleague, looking very ready to kill someone, standing over the man she'd just hit. "We . . . we have been hunting for you. You're m . . . missing."

Howard groaned and tried to sit up. Slumped again.

"We thought we were rescuing you," said Lieutenant Rubia, from where she sat against the wall amongst the glass-shards. Lani was already on her knees, checking for a pulse, making sure his airway was open.

"Where did you get that idiotic idea?" she snapped. "Get me my first-aid kit from the cupboard in the hall, Madeline, instead of standing there like an idiot."

"Your scoot was reported wrecked, by one of the harvester crews," explained the captain. "She said there was lots of blood on the scene—and you didn't call in. Major Nalzac assumed . . . Well, we've been searching the upper levels for you. We thought he might have carried you off to the runaways in the dead sections. Then early this morning we got a report in that someone had seen a large unaccompanied male near here. We stalked the place and heard a male speak, so we hit the place hard and fast. He's big and we didn't take any chances. I'm sorry."

"The scoot broke down. Axle broke. I cut my head in the accident and Howard carried me home. He's big but he's just a baby, and the gentlest thing alive, damn you, Madeline." Lani realized that she was crying, but right now she didn't care. "We'd better get him to hospital. And if he dies I'll kill all three of you."

Howard sat up. Saw her and saw Madeline—still with her nightstick. He staggered to his feet, and Lani found herself pushed back by a hamlike hand. "Get out the back, lass," he said muzzily. "I'll hold them off."

"Don't be an idiot, Howard," said Lani pulling him towards the chair. "Sit down before you fall down."

"They're attacking you . . . "

"It was a mistake. Now sit down before *I* attack you. And I'm a lot more dangerous than these clowns." It sounded tough, but her chin wobbled slightly as she said it, looking at her lunkhead. He was big, but barely able to stand right now. She pulled him down into a chair.

"He just threatened us," said Madeline, with an edge in her voice.

Maybe calling her a clown had not been so bright. Captain Rodgers had a high opinion of herself. "He's concussed," said Lani. "He tried to protect me, and he can't even protect himself. Now will you fetch the first aid-kit and call an ambulance?"

"No," said Rodgers. "You can do it yourself. And I'm going to charge him with threatening to assault officers. Come on, girls. Let's get out of here."

The other two had picked themselves up, and followed their captain out of the kicked-in door. Looking at their backs, Lani knew that she would have a problem there. The three of them had broken a whole lot of procedural rules. The only way out was to claim hot pursuit . . .

Howard might or might not need medical help, but unless she did something pretty sharply he'd need legal help. She picked up the communicator and called the station. Get it in fast, before they did. "Captain LaGarda here. I need to report a breaking and entry and an assault on the person of my man."

"Lani, there is a search out on you!" said the desk officer.

"I'm home," Lani said. "I had a scoot accident last night, but I'm fine otherwise. You can't say the same about my man. I have just had my home broken into and my man attacked. I'll need an ambulance."

"Requested. Any idea by whom?" asked the desk-officer.

"I can provide positive ID on the three, yes. Looks like a bit of blood on the glass they broke and I have one nightstick. I'm afraid this is going to be an ICD affair, Sarah. It was Captain Rodgers, Lieutenant Rubia and CO Lewis. Howard was just making my morning coffee when they broke in and attacked him."

There was a silence from the other end of the communicator. Then the desk-officer asked: "Where are they now?"

"They left when I told them they were under arrest," said Lani, lying smoothly. "I was trying to do emergency first aid on their victim so I couldn't stop them."

It was contestable. But it was a long way better than leaving Howard accused—as he no doubt would be—of fleeing arrest and running into her home. The problem was that there were three of them, and one of her. Howard, as a minor in the eyes of the court, could not provide the same quality of testimony. In the meantime she'd better check on him. And spill a mug of coffee on the floor. She put the communicator down and looked at him.

Howard smiled weakly up at her. "I didn't know what do, Lani. I was in the kitchen trying make breakfast."

"Hush." Then she thought. "Who did you speak to? They say they heard you speak?" another witness would resolve the matter.

"Myself. God. I was praying for guidance."

Religion. She'd read about it. If anyone had been listening, they weren't going to let her into the witness stand to testify.

# 19

e-vox to: Marlene Tzu-Lee
From: Jean Mbuli, GAL Centre
Subject: Recruiting among our members to join the
Women's Matriarchal Movement habitat.

The answer is 'no.' They're not a real woman's liberation movement. They're just a bunch of man-haters led by a woman with too much money and a chip on her shoulder. Have you read her take on gay rights? You know why they're taking men at all? To be second-class citizens and get her rocks off. And you know who'll be next once she's finished kicking male butt? There has to be a dominant woman in control of any relationship in their eyes. You know what that'll make the other partner?

Dr. Amber Geriant, chief microbiologist for the Matriarchy of Diana's protein vats, had had two major turning points in her life. When she was sixteen she'd suddenly realized that, unlike her peers, she did not find men sexually attractive—and that no amount of trying was going to change the situation. That one had been dealt with easily enough. She'd channeled herself into her work—again, unlike her peers. It wasn't an entirely satisfactory alternative, but it did speed up her academic progress, a progress only interrupted by a brief and exploitative relationship that did at least clarify her sexuality if not help the situation.

Like her mother before her, she'd been heading up the ladder of the administration. When you're a retired deputy-matriarch's daughter things were smooth for you, in this direction.

The second turning point had been the result of attending, as an observer, a governing council meeting. The infighting had been vicious and the level of intellectual debate had been . . . absent. That came at a point in her life when Amber had been studying ancient Earth history, and had increasingly come to the conclusion that the social pendulum had swung to an extreme in Diana, and remained stuck there by its isolation. The move, sideways, into the science faculty and microbiology, the only area of real substance there, had been accompanied by the shouting-match to end all shouting-matches at home. An only daughter should follow her mother! Amber knew she probably shouldn't have pointed out that she was an only daughter by design, and that her mother could have had a permitted second daughter if she'd chosen to.

Still, living on her own had suited her, without the constant stream of "boys from good families." And science had suited her far better than politics.

She'd been taken aback to inherit her mother's estate, and even more taken aback at the size of it. In retrospect she knew that she shouldn't have been. Political success took money.

Now, she realized, she'd reached another turning point. It had taken another shattering argument to do it, and the grim realization that every single day she was going to have to work with and see someone indispensable to the protein-culture unit, and, until the argument, indispensable to her.

Now, with nothing to turn to but work, where daily contact with Jean kept the wounds raw, she realized just how bored with her work she had become. It had been the better alternative to be at the top of protein culture, rather than to take orders. She'd inherited her mother's political skill as well as her money. That, her relationship with Jean, and some research had kept her relatively happy for some years.

She hadn't realized how stale it had become until the alien arrived.

Amber had never agonized over her decisions. She made them and moved on. She hated having them made for her by circumstances.

Only there was no place to move on to. Not here in Diana. Not in Science. No, "On" was elsewhere. To see a universe she'd never seen before. A universe that didn't greet her with Jean's face every day. All she had to do now was persuade Kretz. And, of course, to prepare things. One of the joys of money was that she could afford to do that.

In relative terms, Kretz could almost say that he was happy. At last he'd fallen among his own kind, in a mental if not a physical sense. Even alien scientists were still scientists. And these were nearly his own kind of scientist. True, they were microbiologists rather than focused on macroscopic things. But there was, despite the differences in discipline and species, some convergence of world view. Amber Geriant was sensible enough to be a woman of his own kind. Perhaps it was because she was well-rounded like a Miran female. He knew that he'd been away from his own kind too long when he found aliens arousing.

It could also be the food. It was, now that she'd explained the term, a form of auto-cannibalism. He could only regret that he wasn't a sociologist. The idea of Miran eating other Miran for ritual reasons was . . . disturbing. But the cultured protein had definitely helped.

"You need me to open other file-accesses for you?" asked Amber, bustling in. She walked too fast for a female.

Kretz shook his head. "It takes a long time with having to use the audio output. I am still busy with the one about the setting up of the 'Slowtrain.' Fascinating! It is what we came so far to find out about. I only regret that my colleagues could not hear it, too. We're so alike . . . and yet so different. Miran do not remain in space. We go there, but we return to Miran. To the place of our birth, to breed."

"Always to the same place?" she asked, eyebrows raised.

Kretz shrugged. "As close as possible. A female must have a reasonable territory, so it is not necessarily the exact spot. When we colonized the second continent, the first generation females always needed some tons of earth from home. There are laments written of the misery they suffered, nonetheless. For males it is easy, but for females, once the nesting instinct begins, they must be at home. If I live that long, it will happen to me too."

"So, although I'm tempted to keep you here, I think you'd better get on your way back there." Amber sighed. "You wouldn't like a passenger, would you?" There was a tentativeness in that voice.

Kretz struggled to grasp what she'd just said. "On a one-way trip with aliens? Never to return to your birth-nest area to breed?"

"I'm not going to breed," she said.

As soon as you started to get used to these aliens, they showed you, again, how alien they were. To admit this to a stranger! It was distinctly perverted.

"I do not know if there is still anyone to return to," he said. "Only Selna survived, that I know of. And the injuries and the stress he had sustained caused sex-changeover. The hormonal imbalance is hard, normally. Loaded as she was with administered male-hormones, she's, uh . . . unstable. Difficult to speak logically to, when I briefly managed to contact her. Females are usu-ally the cautious, logical sex, being older and more expe-rienced. But not during changeover."

Amber nodded. "She's having the PMS of a lifetime loaded into one session. It can make for interesting times with humans and it's not of that magnitude. So when were you last able to contact her?"

Kretz explained.

Amber bit her lip and tugged at her chin, social signs of thought in this odd species. "I think I can get you to a high-gain antenna, which would allow you to retrans-mit," she said. "Electronics isn't a discipline that has survived well, whereas microbiology is reasonably healthy. There is some gear left over from the original

construction team, in the museum, though. There's stuff
in the orbital hub, too, but that is unreachable until we
detach from the slowship string. It's intended to provide
the solar-panel and some elementary construction equipment for starting a new habitat construction in whatever
solar system we fetch up at."

The truth dawned on Kretz then, with the brightness
of a starburst. "Your species does not colonize planets.
You colonize space."

She nodded. "We colonize suns. Or, rather the life-
envelope around suns. That was the idea, anyway. Most
suns are unlikely to have suitable planets, and terraform-
ing of the ones that do have would take centuries. We're
not interested. We stopped being a planet-bound species
two centuries before we left our own solar system. Why
should we want to climb back down the gravity-well?
There was no evidence of other intelligent life out there,
and the habitat inhabitants wanted away from the restric-
tions of system government." She smiled wryly. "A few
writers have speculated that the SysGov wanted to get
rid of us as badly as we wanted to see the back of them."

The vastness and sheer grandeur of the undertaking
was almost overwhelming. Kretz shook his head. "Miran
stayed on Miran. There was once talk of colonizing other
planets around other stars, but when we failed to exceed
the speed of light and discovered that the nearest
star—our sun's companion—had no planets of suitable
size and potential habitability, interest turned back to
the Miran system. Even the ideas about making other
insystem planets habitable to Miran were abandoned
many years ago. The farthest—beside this expedition
—that we've been was an automated probe to the com-
panion-star. Less than one in forty thousand Miran ven-
tures into space, at all. Our few industries struggle to

find personnel. If the people of your last habitat were friendly, and prepared to work up there, they could have been welcomed."

"We nearly had the same thing happen, apparently," said Amber, "if ancient history is to be believed. Humankind nearly turned inwards. Space was too big, too expensive, too remote from the problems we had on our own world. Then the space habitat and the ideas of increasing the surface area within them changed the equation."

She stood up. "Anyway, I have to get back to work. The old systems are creaking, and the administration is too busy spending money on themselves to allocate real resources to refurbishment, let alone the vat replacement we ought to do. Besides, we'd have trouble with the electronics and heavy engineering. I'll see if I can finagle some bits out of the museum for you later."

Kretz had fairly little hope of his being able to patch alien components onto his suit radio . . . but, she'd gotten the suit back for him, after all. He had to keep trying. Trying and hoping. And later he realized that he'd underestimated her grasp of the situation. What she brought back was a powerful transmitter—with a frequency scanner. "We'll just use it as a repeater," she said. "I found out that you can still hook this lot up to an old external antenna. There is a jack in the main lab. I'll set it up there, and you can stay here."

When she came back, Kretz switched on the suit-set. Tabbed send. "This is Kretz calling the Spacecraft or any other receivers. Respond."

He waited and repeated. "This is Kretz calling the Spacecraft or any other receivers. Respond."

An incredulous Miran voice came from the speaker. "Kretz! Kretz, come and get me! Come armed. Come quickly."

It was a male Miran voice. Abret. Abret on the edge of hysteria.

"Abret, give me a full situation report." Kretz tried to keep his voice calm, his own emotions under control. He knew that he was probably failing. Fear and hope mingled. Hope because at least he and Abret could fly the spacecraft, together. Fear because Abret might be unreachable. He braced himself mentally for the worst. He still didn't expect what he got.

"It's Derfel. He's gone mad. The locals have made him their ruler. I think . . . I think they're going to kill me. I'm a prisoner."

A voice cut in. A female voice. Selna. "Kretz? Kretz, where in the name of the first mother are you? Are you safe? Are you injured?" She sounded rational, and scared.

"I am safe. I am alive and reasonably well," he said reassuringly.

Abret spoke. "Kretz. Selna's alternating between fury and screaming and suicidal despair. I've been receiving her, but I haven't been able to talk to her. The hormonal imbalances and the situation has been very hard for her. Be careful. She's not stable."

"I want to come and get you. Kretz, I need to get back to my birth-nest area, NOW," said Selna. "Tell me how to find you?"

"You can't get here, Selna. I am two beads away. I am in touch with Abret. I'll be trying to reach him, and we'll get back to you as soon as we can," Kretz said soothingly.

"No! You must come NOW!" She shouted. "Don't you understand, you stupid male? I need my nest territory. I need it NOW."

"Calm down, Selna. I'll come as soon as possible, I promise. I just need to rescue Abret," said Kretz.

The name sent her snarling "Abret? Abret has the lifecraft. Tell him to come back here NOW!" she screamed.

"He's a prisoner, Selna. I've just got to free him," And cross two more of these alien habitats, which could be occupied by . . . almost anything, thought Kretz, but he didn't say that. She was frightened enough.

It was difficult, talking to Abret, with Selna constantly butting in and alternately being reasonable, shouting at them and then pleading, but Kretz felt better for it all the same. There was nothing quite like feeling that you were not totally alone. The awkward part was going to be explaining to his hosts that he had to leave soon. Preferably as Selna put it, NOW.

There was also the question of Howard.

## 20

"Engineering and Robotics—especially with microbots doing maintenance—have increased mechanical safety beyond the real need for redundancy. We still build it in. What we haven't been able to do much about is the fragility of bio-systems, and the ability of humans to mess with them. We need multiple redundancy here. We can get that partly with size and species diversity, and party by simply having a number of habitats, strung together. This will also give us a crack at avoiding the other area of which is never considered for redundancy—social systems. Humans are even more likely to destroy their own habitat than engineering disasters are."

Transcript of Dr. W. Andrea Asiago's address to the new-formed Interstellar Colonization and Exploration society, considered by many to be the germinal point of the Slowtrain Project. From: *A Concise History of Human Space Colonization.* P233, Chipattari, H, and Shah, G.D. (Ed)

———

Howard was relieved to be discharged from the hospital, even if Lani still had that Jersey-bull look in her eye. "The local elevator banks are out. I'd forgotten that," she said, as they came to the closed doors a few yards from the hospital gates. "We'll have to take a taxi down to the public transport-system and those cost . . . "

"I want to walk," he said, firmly. "I would like to walk, and I feel in need of it."

"But you've just been to the hospital," protested Lani.

"My legs were in no way injured," he said with a smile. He had enough on his conscience without impoverishing her further. Besides, the pill they'd given him had left him feeling as if he was on top of Eden. A bit muzzy headed, but fine.

She sighed. "We don't have a lot of choice, anyway. There isn't a vehicle in sight. They're all driving people up at this time of day, with the elevators out. This place is falling apart."

"At least we are walking down," he soothed.

Lani spent the walk feeling guilty. She'd only agreed to do it because the bank balance was perilously low. As a single young woman she'd lived pretty fast and freely. It was now becoming rapidly apparent that she'd spent more on beer and boys than was wise. At least he'd taken her arm for the walk. They stopped to rest at the next elevator station. A dispirited-looking crew were emerging from a door next to the shaft. She and Howard got several wolf-whistles. Well, Howard did. Still, it made a girl walk tall. "You watch it. He's mine," she said.

One of the repair-crew raised an eyebrow. "I did watch it! It's gruesome. And if you play with it it'll grew some more. Hello, Lani. Big piece of beefcake you got yourself."

Lani recognized the blond under the helmet . . . funny how it changed someone's face. "Hello, Dee. So this is where you got to after school?"

The woman came and flopped down on the bench next to them. "It's a dirty job, but someone has to do it. And the pay's good even if it doesn't have the glamour of the force."

"Besides you never could fight your way out of a brown paper bag," said Lani, grinning. "Hey, leave him alone. He's mine. Besides he doesn't like it, see."

"He's yours? Entirely? Not just trial? Wow! Bid sealed, the lot?"

Lani nodded proudly. "Paid for, too. I'm settling down."

"I'm still playing the field," said Dee with a chuckle. "I heard about this one. I heard that the other one has a tentacle instead. They've got him up at the Vats and they're charging the girls a dollar a look, or ten a time. I reckon you could get twenty . . . "

"Stop it. You're making him cringe and he's all mine. You haven't gotten any less coarse, have you, Dee? You've got a mind like a sewer."

The repair-crew worker shook her head, cheerfully. "Nope, just as coarse. Not much else to think about on the job except fried electronics, and sex is more fun."

"So what's up with the elevator bank?" asked Lani, more to stop Howard actually getting up and running away than out of any real interest.

The blond repair-worker shrugged. "Search me. It's none of the electronics modules. We've tried pulling and replacing all of them in case it was something that wasn't showing up on the tell-tales. We had a job getting out the people who were stuck, I'll tell you. Took about four hours, and the car stinks like hell. It stuck just here, where the control module is too, so we have to work with the pong in the background. At least all the others came to a stop at the nearest floor."

"Could we have a look?" asked Howard, for once pressing against Lani, as a defense, presumably to the predatory Dee. Well, you could understand that.

"Sure," said Dee, getting up. "Lovely bouquet in there, mind you. I'll just take him in there for a little while, Lani. You have a nice rest."

You couldn't help laughing at Dee. She hadn't changed an iota. "Holy Susan. You never give up, do you? Put another hand on him and I'll take it off at the wrist, you maneater."

"Huh. Just selfish, that's all you are," said Dee, her lips quirking and eyes full of mischief. "Come and have a look."

Howard's eyes took in the mechanical guts of the elevator with fascination. It was safer than looking at that scarlet woman anyway. His ears were still burning. And now she'd assumed a posture which no decent woman would put herself into, not even in private! His nose told him about other things besides distressed trapped passengers. It told him of hot metal. It reminded him of a bearing that had seized in the corn-mill.

Surely this couldn't be as simple? The "car," as she'd called it, ran on rails. The central ratcheted rail in between the rails was obviously what provided movement. It was quite worn, he noticed. He sniffed at each of the wheels . . . and then realized that his nose wasn't even necessary. There were little pieces of metal—fragments of roller, on the rim of the third wheel.

He coughed diffidently. "I think you should look at this."

"I am, big boy," said the lewd woman.

"I mean at this wheel. The bearing has gone."

The scarlet woman got up and came across to where he stood. "That stuff is tough, big boy. It's the electronics that doesn't last forever. Oh."

"Nothing actually lasts forever, except God's love," said Howard stiffly, but she was too busy looking at the wheel in the light of her helmet headlamp to notice, and giggling to herself. She turned around and punched him on the arm. "You could just be right, beefcake! Heh. And we've spent days testing the electronics! I reckon I could just get a bonus out of you two."

"Well, I think you owe us a ride down in the cargo elevator, if that's still working," said Lani. "And keep your hands off him, Dee."

"Tch. He's big enough for both of us, aren't you, big boy?"

"No!" protested Howard, backing off and nearly falling down an elevator shaft.

They got their ride down to the transport system, which took them close to Lani's home. It would appear that no one walked any distance here. If Howard was any judge, they'd have to start soon. Things were plainly beginning to break down. Anything will, eventually. Maybe that was what that scarlet woman had had in mind with his morals.

When they got home, the part for Lani's scoot awaited them.

He had a knife in his hand, and a look of triumph in his eyes. However, the most censorious woman in the Matriarchy might have forgiven him. Howard's knife was an old rounded buttering knife—and the reason for his triumph was finding that its tip fitted the slot on the top of the shaft. They had the part. What they didn't have was any tools. The little ring of metal the online manual had described as a circlip had been hell to remove. It had taken the near destruction of her tweezers to finally send it whizzing across the yard. Then they'd had to hunt for it.

She'd hugged him when he spotted it. He'd gone bright red and hastily backed off.

"What's wrong?" she asked.

"I forget myself. I . . . wish you were wearing clothes," he said slowly.

She considered him, standing there looking awkward. Looking at anything but her. "I could wear clothes if it would make things easier for you." It was perverted, she knew. And unnatural. But, if it would help to free him of his inhibitions . . . excite him and arouse him . . . Well, if rumor was to be believed quite a few women did it in the privacy of their own homes anyway. Was a piece of cloth really that bad? A guilty part of her subconscious said "yes."

He looked at her face with those adoring-puppy eyes. "It would be much easier. I must be honest, your body is a temptation, and as much as I try to resist, I find my eyes drawn to it. It would help me greatly to resist the temptations of the flesh that are set in my way by the evil one. Thank you."

It wasn't quite what she'd meant to achieve, but the very idea had somehow made him more at ease, able to hunt a makeshift tool in her kitchen with her, without him leaping like a startled child if they touched. He was very good with those big hands, she thought clinically.

He spun the scoot's wheel, beaming with pleasure at the achievement. "I really believe," he said earnestly, "that if God hadn't meant us to do such things he would scarcely have made it such a wholesome pleasure to succeed."

*I wonder if I could stretch your mind as far thinking that about sex*, thought Lani, far from clinically. But she held her tongue, and took the scoot for a brief test ride.

It alarmed her with its sudden, easy acceleration, and the smoothness of its ride. The back wheel had always had a bit of a shake at speed. That was gone. It seemed quite obvious now that problem had been developing for a while. Well, if it was going to be this simple, maybe they *should* start repairing scoots. After all, there was nothing wrong with your man helping you, working as a team with you, on a job. The idea of being in the force was giving her a sour taste in the mouth, now.

She came back to her yard, smiling. The smile didn't last long. Not when she saw two officers standing waiting, with what was obviously a writ.

"Captain Lani LaGarda, you've been charged with neglect, improper man-care, and common assault," said the belted woman. "Accordingly, I must ask you to proceed to the station with me until your pretrial hearing. Your man will be held in protective custody until the matter is resolved."

Howard stood stock still, waiting to see what would happen next.

It obviously worried the arresting officer too. "It's a technicality, Captain. But it is the letter of the law. I'm sorry. I can't see why you won't be released on your own recognizance . . ."

Lani scowled: "Chapter three, paragraph 7. They'd be breaking the law themselves if they tried to do otherwise, as the people who laid these charges are themselves facing charges placed by me. I assume these charges come from Captain Rodgers and her patrol, and are unsubstantiated except by their accusations?"

"Er. Yes," admitted the officer.

Lani shrugged. "Well, we'd be playing into their hands if we didn't cooperate. I'm sorry, Howard. First they beat you up then they want to jail you. Let's go."

But they discovered that it wasn't quite so simple when they got to the police station. Lani could go, yes, and just come to her pretrial. But Howard . . .

"I'm afraid he'll have to stay in, Captain. I've got a gelding-order here for him. If he is found to have been beyond your control, well, they'll cut. Of course charges of irresponsibility on your part would be diminished by that."

"*What?*" she demanded.

"He's too big," explained the desk-officer. "The attached affidavit reads that they do not want any aggressive tendencies linked to high testosterone levels and large size to enter the male population again."

"That's ridiculous!" snapped Lani.

"If you sign the disclaimer," said the desk-officer holding out the form, "the medical officer can do it quickly now and we can release him into your custody, while your restitution claim goes through."

Howard listened in horror. If he hadn't been in the cage, he'd have been running. He was relieved to hear Lani say "No," firmly.

The desk-officer shrugged. "I've heard that they're easier to manage and far less inclined to stray after they've had the chop. And they still do the housework well, even if they don't father children any more." She was talking about him as if he was a troublesome dog. "Well, then, he'll just have to stay locked up. I'm sorry."

"But you can't do that!" said Lani, hitting the desk hard enough to make it vibrate.

The desk-officer folded her arms. "I'm sorry, Captain. I have to. You know the rules about visiting times."

Howard found the loneliness and fear even worse this time. Lani was a naked painted Jezebel from a Godless culture. But she had her good points too. When she'd reached through the bars and squeezed his arm, her eyes wet . . .

There'd been a shift in the foundation rock of his beliefs. The edifices of the life he'd built on it, trembled.

In the meanwhile he had to get out of here. There are some male fears, Howard discovered, that are shared beyond religion or culture. As soon as he was left alone, he began exploring his cell for a way out. The walls seemed solid. The bars too. The roof . . .

They hadn't thought of anyone easily reaching that, he'd bet. The ceiling was low. With his arms straight up Howard had to bend his knees. Ideal. He pushed. *Hard.* Howard had done enough labor to know that human strength was principally in the legs.

Nothing happened.

So he tried again. He was about to try a third time when he heard voices. Two of the little local men were herded into his cell. They were tiny, Howard realized, seeing them close up for the first time. He was tall, large and muscular from farm work. These men were half his size, with little muscle tone. The two plainly found him intimidating, too, by their posture.

Well, they could hardly help being painted and pallid; and, like him, they were in trouble. "Peace be with you, strangers," he said, smiling and holding out his hand.

Their hands were very small in his. By the way they trembled, they were expecting him to do terrible things to them. Still, the one with scar on his head called him closer. "We are from the Men's Liberation Movement. We want you to join us. Escape and flee to wildlands near the core, to join our liberating army. Men must be free!"

Howard had to agree with the philosophy. Men here certainly needed liberating!

"When we march," said the other, "all the men are going to rebel. We will capture all the elevator banks, seize city hall, behead the Matriarch and declare male rule."

It would have been even more shocking if the poor little mite had sounded more convincing. He sounded as if he were reciting timetables.

"And these women with the belts and clubs?" asked Howard. "Won't they stop you?"

"They'll have to be killed if they try," said the first one. "Of course, we'll keep some. Every man will have as many women as he pleases to take whenever he wants. Male rule!"

The smaller, more miserable looking one took him by the arm, just as he was about to reply. In his hand was a small piece of paper. It read: DON'T. LISTENING. He put the piece of paper in his mouth and ate it.

As Howard had been about to disagree—at least to ends and means—this made things easier. Men weren't supposed to read, but inevitably some would learn. "You are wrong, brothers," he said calmly. "Violence and killing will not achieve anything. We must be gentle."

"But they beat us!" protested the first man.

"And then we must turn the other cheek," said Howard.

Howard actually had a very enjoyable half hour repeating sermons and scripture to the two. The smaller one, who had originally been so frightened, was now plainly hard-pressed not to laugh. Howard was shocked to notice that the two had their fingers entwined. But then perhaps men did that here.

The two belted women who came to fetch them soon after that looked decidedly sour. It had undoubtedly been a trap. Was there such bitterness here? Or was there really a men's liberation movement to fear, to fuel this?

## 21

"Surface area, not volume, is the key to many biological processes. By layering the inside of a habitat we increase—at approximately four meters per layer—the surface area from roughly 5500 hectares to near on twenty thousand square kilometers. By using vertical surfaces too—by growing plants on the growth medium on the walls we increase that growing area—assuming tightest possible corridors—at about 3 meters to roughly double that. Now that's just not practical and you lose too much space to interstitial support and piping and so on. So the optimum corridor width is about ten meters. Of course that's optimum for materials use. For practicalities and aesthetics—which may be even more important than we realize on longer trips—we need some wider and higher areas. It's a series of trade-offs. It's going to make the inside of these structures into a maze. The biggest maze ever built. More easy

to get lost in than any jungle. Capable of carrying—
physically—if not sustaining, several million people."

Transcript of Professor Lucas Teich's presentation
to the Interstellar Colonization and Exploration Society, on the bioenvironmental factors in the proposed
habitats for the Slowtrain Project. From: *A Concise
History of Human Space Colonization.* P233, Chipattari, H, and Shah, G.D. (Ed)

───────

"He's in jail. I have heard that they want to castrate him.
Neuter him," explained Amber.

The idea didn't seem to horrify her the way it did
Kretz. Sterility seemed to be more or less acceptable
to these aliens. To a Miran it was social ostracism. To
humans—well, to some humans—it seemed a mere fact
of life. But then . . . the species didn't need nesting territory, either.

They were odd, there was no getting away from it, no
matter how used to them you thought you were getting.
"I have to save him!"

"You're very loyal," said Amber. "I thought they tried
to kill you?"

Kretz shook his head. "Those were the humans in the
first habitat. Howard saved my life. He cared for
me—and I brought him here. To face a fate worse than
death." He shuddered.

Amber smiled wryly. "A male might see it like that, I
suppose. Well, we'd better spring him then. He's good
at making friends. I had a call from his mistress a few
minutes ago, which is why I knew where he was. She
wanted me to intervene because he has unique genetic
material. It's true enough. But she didn't like it when I

pointed out that all I could justify was a few cc of cell-sample. Her comments on my suggestion that she collect a sperm sample and freeze it were an education to me. That girl can swear!" she said admiringly.

Kretz doubted that he'd ever get the hang of this language. Transcomp gave him the words, and several subtext guesses as to what they might possibly mean. "I will have to try to get him out," he repeated. "And then I must try to move as fast as possible to rescue Abret and then we can return to our spacecraft and Selna. Are you still determined to accompanying me?"

"Into a life of crime, and strange places . . . " she said flippantly.

Kretz was getting used to alien expressions. She didn't look as if she objected to the idea. Well, some humans were probably insane too. By the sounds of it they'd not selected the most normal parts of their society for this colonial expedition, just as the Miranese expedition had required odd individuals to chase down this alien target. "We just need to go quietly, if we can just get to Howard."

Someone pounded on the door and Amber went to open it. A disheveled looking female human stood there, bleeding slightly from a cut above one eye. "Dr. Geriant. You haven't seen Howard have you?" To Kretz's ear she sounded on the edge of panic, the words rushing out, high pitched.

His human host tugged her chin. "You'd better come inside, Lani."

"He's here?" The hope in Lani's voice transcended species barriers.

"No. We were just about to go and try to see what could be done for him. But you need help right now.

Come. Then let's see what can be done about him and you."

Lani hovered on the doorstep . . . and then came inside, and allowed Amber to lead her to the bathroom.

She sat there, letting Amber stitch the cut.

"They claimed he'd escaped. I . . . I didn't believe them. I beat a couple of people up trying to find out where they'd taken him. I think he really has run. He's got no more sense than a child." She wrung her hands. "He'll be killed."

Water leaked from her eyes, which Kretz gathered was a sign of extreme distress. "He's just a big fool. I've got to find him."

"We were just planning to go and break him out of the cell. We'll try looking for him with you," said Amber crisply, "If you'll just hold still and let me finish stitching first."

Lani looked at the head of Protein Production and Research, incredulously. "*You* were going to help him escape? I thought about it, but I decided that they couldn't possibly convict me. I haven't done anything wrong. Well, I hadn't, before I went in and found he was missing. I'm afraid they're looking for me too now."

"And they will doubtless think of looking here soon," said Dr. Geriant. "Which means we'd better move out." She got up from where she'd knelt to sew up Lani's temple. "Do you still have your scoot?"

Lani nodded. "Yes. Howard fixed it."

"I have a small personal car. I can hide Kretz in that. I need to change your appearance, and then I think we can search in reasonable safety." She pushed Lani ahead of her to the bathroom. "If we listen in on the police channel on your communicator we may get some idea where he is, or if he's been caught or killed."

A hasty hair-dyeing followed. "I thought I'd try blond, once upon a time. Fortunately, I'm terrible at throwing stuff away." Double braids, and a quick down-and-dirty paint job and they were on way, Lani eavesdropping on the police channel. Howard was just too big to go unspotted for too long.

Yet it would seem that he had. He'd vanished. Lani even heard someone getting instructions to search the protein production unit.

The ceiling had lifted. It had taken Howard thirty-two tries, before something moved, with a sound of tearing metal. A little stud popped and the roof rose three inches, tearing the next stud. Looking up, Howard could see that the room above was dark. He dropped the ceiling boards down and waited. No one came to investigate the noise, so he lifted again. Another stud tore free. The assembly method was tongue-and-groove, quick to assemble and impervious to rot. Very useful, light and easy. It was similar to the old barn, a relic that had collapsed under too much hay, but was made of something that wasn't wood.

And now that he'd lifted it, it was possible to get the tongue out of the groove. It wouldn't go back down, leaving a finger-wide gap. With a lever, he'd be out of here in thirty seconds. Unfortunately, he didn't have a lever. All he had was himself. It took him quite some time to get the next boards to part, giving him a hand-width gap. Then he managed to haul himself up and feel into the room above. His hand hit a chair leg. He grabbed it, pulled it into the crack. A lever . . .

. . . And the sound of footsteps coming down the passage to his cell. Hastily Howard dropped down and went to a far corner of the cell. There was a piece of chair leg sticking through the corner of the roof. Howard sat down on the floor. Maybe they'd look down at him.

It was a little male with two bowls. The man was graying, and his face was lined and tired.

And he did not just look down.

All he said, very quietly, as he passed the bowls through the bars: "Run to the badlands near the core."

He turned and walked away, leaving Howard with water, a sort of stew, and some idea of direction. The food was not particularly tasty, but it seemed wholesome. They weren't cruel to prisoners in that way, at least. The water was even more welcome after all the effort. But the hope that there was somewhere to go to was sweeter. He set the empty bowls down and took hold of the chair-leg with vigor.

A minute later he was standing in a dark room—the only light coming from his cell below.

Howard was a tidy worker by nature. He slipped the tongues into the grooves and put the floor-ceiling back, before even thinking of trying the door he'd spotted in the light from his cell. It was not locked and led onto a passage, lit with dim-set glow-lights. He walked quietly down the passage until he found a door marked "Fire Exit. Emergencies only."

Under the circumstances, using it seemed reasonable. He walked out, closed it, and walked down a fire-escape to freedom. A freedom he intended to keep, along with his testicles. He'd had time to think of strategy. These women had everything done by machine. They lived in a different world to the society of Brethren, but the basic

design of the habitat was close to identical. Howard would
bet that they did no crawling along the water-arterials to
check for leaks, like the Brethren did. He'd spotted one of
the belled arterial walls when they came in. It was a bare
hundred yards off. Of course, he'd have to find an access
door, but there was usually one every few hundred meters.
He simply had to wait for a lull in the passing people and
vehicles—not hard, even here in this town, as it was plainly
after the working day and things were slowing down.

He reached the water arterial unobserved, and found
an access door. For a horrible moment he thought that
it was locked in some way, but it was simply stiff from
lack of use. He crouched down and got inside, pulled it
behind him, and began crawling. He wished, briefly, that
he was as small as the local men. He crept onwards. He
wanted to rescue Kretz. He wanted the sheer joy of
wearing clothing, but first he wanted to be as far from
these women and sharp knives as possible.

Then, in the sheltering darkness, there was something
else. Something with green and red eyes that flickered.
Howard nearly knocked himself unconscious, trying to
turn and flee, before realizing that it was a machine. It
flashed lights at him—and then began to reverse, far
faster than he had been able to crawl. So Howard
crawled on. True to his memory of the water system of
home, this too came to a larger belled tunnel—with a
larger pipe system and just as little space for a man.

It was no place for a man. Only, there were men here.
Men, and light.

They had weapons. Knives. They were smiling, though.


"We're not going to find him, if the force can't," said
Lani, dispirited, when they paused in a quiet corridor.

"I think we need to split up. At least that way we can cover more ground, and if I'm caught, you won't be implicated."

"That might be true," admitted Dr. Geriant. "But I was planning on using you, and your ability to look and act the part to get Kretz and me to the airlock."

"It won't work," said Lani. "They've stationed officers at my home, and at the airlock he came in. They're expecting him to head there."

"That wasn't the airlock I had in mind," explained Amber. "There is the forward one. You could take us to that."

"I'm sorry," Lani said with genuine guilt. This woman had helped her, after all. "I've got to find Howard first. I'd gladly help you if I could. I'd even gladly go with you, but it wouldn't work. There are alarms on the airlocks. It's part of the original system."

The Chief Microbiologist slapped her own cheek. "Of course! I didn't think of that. Don't worry about the alarm. I have the system codes . . . but, aha! We can ask the system if this Howard of yours been detected by any of the machines in the system."

Lani blinked. "You can do that?"

"Oh, yes," the scientist said casually. "It's quite possible. All I need is an approximate weight—you say that he's very large?" she said, opening up a portable computer and linking with the web.

Lani gaped at her. "Do you know how easy that would make police work, Dr. Geriant?"

The woman scientist raised her eyebrows and smiled wryly. "Call me Amber. Yes. That's why I never pointed the idea out to anyone. Now, how much would you guess he weighs? Approximately?"

"About . . . I don't know, two hundred and fifty pounds?" said Lani.

"We'll try that. There are a few women in that bracket, but it does make the search narrower." She looked at the screen. "Ah. Two hundred and eighty-three pounds, moving here, at a speed of fifteen miles per hour. Let's get some more detail. . . . Good grief. There are four of them, on a pipe-maintenance machine, heading inward to the core, toward sector Zed Alpha 32. That's one of the damaged sections."

"Four? He's been captured?"

She looked at the screen and tapped something in. "The other three weigh less than one hundred pounds each. Males, at a guess. No, I would say that he's with some of the runaways."

"We need to rescue him!" said Lani, starting the scoot. "They're dangerous!"

Amber looked at her, very squarely. "To us, yes. To him, no. He's quite safe, except from being caught by one of the patrols that the force periodically sweep those areas with. We aren't."

Lani shook her head. "We don't know that he's safe. Look, there are only three. I can deal with three easily enough."

"And then?" asked Amber.

"And then I'll help you get to the airlock, and out of here. I think . . . we might have to go too," said Lani, quietly. "It doesn't sound too bad, back where he came from. Let's go."

Amber had to smile at the child. She was pretty, but really not her type. Too large and Juno-esque by half. Lani had absolutely no idea what anything outside her own environment was like, but she was plainly so cockstruck that she was ready to leave Diana. Well, it suited the rest of them. Amber wasn't going to point out, just yet, that "back" to her Howard's habitat was not going to be possible.

Instead she engaged the transmission of her car, and they went up, corewards, heading into lower G and areas that showed definite signs of breakdown. The lighting had gone in a number of places, and so too had the irrigation network and with it the plant life.

It made sense to concentrate the system's resources on the working areas, she supposed, but this was alarming. In downtown Diana one forgot that there was a problem. This was not an area that anyone lived in these days, but it had been very popular up to a hundred years back as a retirement haven for the elderly. Less strain on the heart, and on old joints. Now it was the sort of environment where only the brave or the fool-hardy went without a police escort. And not just one policeman, either. Preferably about twenty.

Well, she had a few surprises for any troublemakers, if the worst came to the worst. They possibly wouldn't be enough to help. Unlike that young woman, she was not a fighter.

She continued to track the pipe-maintenance engine, until it stopped. A door to the arterial opened . . . and Amber then realized she should have watched the surrounding area more carefully before coming to a stop.

There were a good number of people in the shadows. People and the gleam of steel.

It was amazing how much less attractive a life of adventure suddenly seemed.

Howard had found the ride on the back of the pipe-checking machine an education, not only in how the work might be done mechanically but also in how men—runaways—had adapted their lives around the system. They used what the women running Diana ignored. It appeared that they'd learned the schedules of these machines, and used them rather like Lani used the trolley-bus system out in the open. The runaways also plainly had more contact with the kept males than the women rulers realized. They knew who he was, and that he'd escaped—and that he was being searched for.

"We get traitors and spies, sometimes," said the leader of the three men, a swarthy-skinned fellow with a gap between his teeth. It was hard to see more in the dim light that shone from the instrument panel. "But you're probably all right. How did you know about the hidden ways?"

It took Howard a while to figure this one out. The doors to arterials weren't obvious—unless you know what you were looking for. "Among the Brethren they are not a secret," he explained.

Apparently his explanation was less than clear. "Who are the 'Brethren'? Have they told any women?" asked the scar-faced one, worriedly.

"You are quite safe," reassured Howard. "The Brethren are the people of New Eden. My habitat." He was proud of that word. "I am the first man to come from there to here. Women do not rule there. God does."

"Is he a man?"

Howard was spared having to answer this one by the pipe-checker slowing down. "Time for us to get off," said the gap-toothed leader.

They jumped, and, with a small flashlight, gap-tooth led them to the door. "Welcome to the kingdom of men," he said sardonically, opening it.

Outside was dim. A number of the light-emitters were missing and the place was full of shadows and . . . people. Mostly short men—but there was a surprise too. A strange woman and Kretz in a car, with a woman beside it, swinging her nightstick in a defensive arc.

"Howard!" she yelled. There was no mistaking the relief in her voice, even though, until he heard it, he hadn't recognized the blond-braided woman.

He waded through the armed men to them, holding up his hands in a pacifying gesture. "Peace be with you," he said. Lani dropped her nightstick and hugged him, fiercely. One of the men decided this was a good opportunity to grab her. Howard caught him by the hair. "Now. There is no need to fight," he said, trying to calm the men and cope with being hugged at the same time. Holding off the small attacker was easier. "No one needs to do anyone any harm."

"She's a cop! We kill them if we catch them on their own," said gap-tooth, "after we've had our fun with them."

"Yeah. You want to try your luck?" said Lani, snatching up her nightstick again, trying to push Howard aside.

"Calm down," said the woman from the car. "Or I'll have to shoot some of you." Her voice quivered. She sounded far from calm herself. She had some device in her hand that Howard failed to recognize, but several of the men obviously did. A frightened keening echoed around them.

"We're runaways too. And Lani is a wanted woman, I believe. Not a 'cop.' "

"What?" The shocked exclamation came from Lani.

"I don't think that you can still be part of the force, Lani. Not after beating up several officers in your attempt to find Howard."

"Uh. I suppose not," said Lani, looking shamefaced. "Look, we just came to fetch Howard. We're out of here."

"No," said gap-tooth firmly. "You—and him especially, know too much. And also, this stinks. How did you get here at the same time as him? How did you know where to come to, to find him?"

"A computer system I have never bothered to show the police," the other woman said. "It is possible . . . "

She never got any further because someone snatched the weapon out of her hands and the little men swarmed over them.

Howard was totally unprepared for the ferocity of it, or the suddenness. They were trussed up before he could even start to struggle. Howard had to admit that he'd done more to get in Lani's way than anything else.

"What are you doing this for?" he demanded.

"They're women and you're a traitor," snarled gap-tooth.

"I'm not," protested Howard. "I hardly know who you are. All we want is go to where we need to. We're not intending any harm to you."

"Yeah?" said gap-tooth sardonically. "Well you're not going to have a chance. Spread their legs, boys. Captains get first share. Those of you who like a bit of bum can have him."

They'd tied Howard up well, by their standards, but not by the standards of the furious disgust and rage that went through his thews right then. As Lani screamed furiously, the cord they'd used snapped at the same time as his temper did.

"Have you no decency!" he roared, snatching up the fallen nightstick and laying about him as if he were threshing corn.

They were small, and he was in such a rage that he had forgotten that he was a man of peace. But there were still too many of them.

Then there were a sharp series of bangs.

"Stand still or I will shoot all of you!" said Kretz. He emerged from behind the car with a smoking metal pipe in his hands. Thinking back now, Howard realized that he must have fled in the first attack. At least he'd come back!

Gap-tooth had the device that someone had struck from Amber's hand. He pointed it at Howard. "I'll shoot him first." Howard stalked towards him.

Gap-tooth was standing just above Lani, where he'd been about to exercise his "rights" as a captain of this filth.

The device went flying. Lani's second kick sent him sprawling.

Howard helped her to her feet. "Get the gun," she said urgently. "And then untie us."

"Gun?" Sister Thirsdaughter had said that a "gun" was what had inflicted those wounds on Kretz. That metal device was a gun? He picked it up, and a fallen knife.

"Don't get between me and them, Howard," said Kretz. Too late—several darted away up the passage.

"They'll call the others," said gap-tooth savagely, as Howard cut Lani free.

Her first act with her hands free was to snatch the gun-thing from his hand. Click something. "Damn safety

was still on." She pointed it at gap-tooth. "It won't help
you if they call anyone. I'm gonna blow your stupid balls
off first." She took a stance, both legs apart, and the gun-
thing held in both hands.

Howard paused in cutting free the other woman, suddenly realizing what was going to happen here. He
stepped in front of her.

"Get out of the way, Howard." Lani's eyes had a dangerous glint to them.

His temper had cooled now, and with the cooling his
conscience had returned. He'd hit . . . and hurt those
men. Some of them were still lying on the ground. "No,"
he said calmly. "I cannot let you do this. It is a sin."

"That's what they were going to do to us, you idiot!"
she snapped.

The defiance was not all out of gap-tooth either. "You
treat us like that, why shouldn't we do the same or worse
to you, bitch?"

It was an awkward question, but for once Howard had
an easy answer. "Do unto others as ye would have them
do unto you."

"Yeah? And if they turn around and kick you in the
teeth?" said the gap-toothed one. "What you do then?
Give them the rest of your teeth?"

That was less easy to answer. "Rape is not right. Neither is violence."

"We were just doing what they do to us. A woman's
got to know her place up here," said gap-tooth sullenly.
"And we share and share alike here when we get one.
Not fair that you keep her to yourself, big one. Two is
greedy, anyway!"

Howard hadn't thought of it quite like that. "She's not
mine. None of them are."

"Correctly speaking, he's mine," said Lani crossly. "Although it doesn't seem to have gotten through to him."

"Can we get out of here, and you can argue about who belongs to whom somewhere less dangerous?" said the other woman.

Lani nodded. "You've got a point. And now we've got these jerks to avoid as well as the force."

"I've thought about it. I can get the computer to simply give me all warm bodies, not just those over a certain weight. We should be able to avoid any more charming incidents. I do begin to understand why Diana came into being."

Lani had picked up her scoot, with one hand, and kicked the stand down. She moved towards the remaining men. "Don't worry, I won't shoot anyone—as long as they cooperate. We'll keep this one as a hostage." She grabbed gap-tooth, twisting his arm up behind him. He squealed. "I'm not hurting you, yet. But I will if you don't shut up. I'll let you go as soon as we're in the clear, idiot. All right, the rest of you lot. Move out and we'll move out too . . . In opposite directions. Those of you who can walk take those who can't. And don't try anything stupid. I was top of my marksmanship class."

They backed off. Lani slipped the weapon into her belt, took a pair of cuffs off it, and handcuffed the gap-toothed man. "Open the back. I'll put him in there," she said to the woman in the car.

A minute later and Howard was again holding onto her waist as they followed the little car down the passages, and into a cross-passage. They stopped in a wide chamber, where a mechanical-shredder asthmatically chewed plant-matter.

Lani pulled up next to the car-window. "What are we stopping for?" she asked.

For an answer the woman pointed to the screen of the little black box next to her. "A group of people in our way. A force patrol by the looks of it, judging by the individual weights."

Howard got off the scoot and looked at them. "It's me they're looking for, isn't it?" he asked. "If they catch me they'll leave you alone. I'll go."

Lani looked at her gentle giant. He was an idiot, besides being confused about his status as her man. He'd also waded into a pack of wild ones for her. And then stopped her blowing one of them away. She might just understand him, one day. She was beginning to think it might just be worth waiting for, aside from the physical gratification.

"I can't go back either, Howard. I . . . I thought they'd, uh, done something to you. So I'm afraid I beat up three of the station-cops to try to get them to tell me where they'd taken you. Your cell was empty, no sign of a forced exit."

"I went out through the ceiling," said Howard, sounding as humble as ever. "I put the planks back. I thought they might put me back in the same cell, or perhaps some other poor person. I'm sorry. I just was afraid they'd . . . " He blushed. Bit his lip. "I'm sorry. I think I have ruined your life."

She shrugged. "It was just a matter of time, I guess. I've been heading for trouble with everything I do." She paused. "Howard, will you take me to this New Eden of yours?"

She bit her lip nervously, and tried something unfamiliar. "Please?"

Howard cringed internally, looking at her. It was amazing just how fast you forgot about being naked. Well, with her body, it was impossible to forget entirely, but you did become accustomed to anything, to some degree. However, his now-broadened mind admitted, New Eden would *not* get used to her. Brother Galsson and his ilk would have fits. It had taken Howard—while out of his home environment—a lot of time to acknowledge that she wasn't just a painted Jezebel. If he'd been at home in New Eden, it would never have happened.

And that, as far as he could see was just the smaller part of the problem. He simply couldn't see her becoming Goodwife Lani, wearing clothes and obeying her husband in all things. That would kill her. Anyway, besides the undeniable physical attraction, she was a long way from the ideal wife he'd dreamed of. There was no getting away from the fact that she was bad-tempered, violent at times, and used to ruling the roost.

His long silence plainly worried her. "Don't you like me?" she asked quietly.

Howard tugged at his beard, trying to find the right words. He *did* like her, in spite of his better judgment. He'd been raised to speak the truth. But . . . she would be much happier here, his conscience said. Even if they punished her for her wayward actions, they accepted violence here—and reaped the bitter fruit of it, too, of course.

He saw the tears starting to form in her eyes, and tried for compromise, which, as he knew, usually ended up pleasing no one. "It's not that I don't like you. It's just . . . New Eden would kill you, Lani."

She looked doubtful. "I thought you said that they were gentle people who never killed anyone."

"Well, yes," said Howard, diffidently. "But they do put people out of the airlock. You can make people's lives a misery too, without actually killing or imprisoning them. That's not what I meant, Lani. It's . . . well, we don't have any machines. We wear clothes all the time. We work, every day—except Sundays—for our food. We eat meat. Real meat, not this vat stuff. A wife promises to honor and obey her husband. She doesn't have as many men as she likes. You would have to give up everything."

She cocked her head on one side, and looked at him with eyes full of uncertainty. "So you do like me, a little? Do you love me? If you do . . . I think I could do that."

Howard swallowed, hard. "I don't think it would be right for me to ask that of anyone."

"So do you love me?" she asked directly.

Love? Did this place even know the difference between love and lust? He'd always thought of love as some remote ideal flower, not . . . well a rather earthy bad-tempered woman. "I . . . I like you. I didn't *mean* to like you. It is too early to speak of loving." He sighed. "We come from different worlds, Lani. Yours would kill me, I think. And mine would kill you."

She sighed. "We need a world of our own, I guess."

"You two lovebirds can mount up again," said the woman in the car. "They're past. And I have to break this to you, Lani. There is no way he can take you back where he comes from. To do that you'd need to go out of the other airlock. This one—will take us on, not back. And I don't think we've really got any choices. They'll have been looking for Kretz here. Some of those injured men will also be caught and talk, probably. I've taken

things from the office and museum that are not supposed
to be removed—that I doubt if I could get back into
place anyway. Lani would sit in jail for half her life.
Howard here would be gelded. Kretz would die when
he changed sex. His companions will die if he doesn't
get to them. We haven't really got many choices. And
who knows, the next habitat on might be that world of
your own? Now. I've plotted a clear path. Shall we go?"

So they went.

Kretz clutched the alien weapon, keeping it carefully
pointed at the window. He had very little idea of what
it could do. He'd only learned to work it quite by accident, after his panicky flight. At least he'd found the
resolve to turn back. And the alien weapon had worked
when it had to. He had no idea if it would again, or if
he'd exhausted its charges. But it gave courage to beat
back the fear. He wasn't going anywhere without it again.

This area of the habitat was in bad repair. Yet, on
the biological side, they were far more advanced than
Howard's people. So: What was going wrong? Kretz
didn't know, but he was beginning to get an inkling.
However, his main worry right now was that the next
bead might turn out to be as inimical as this one had
turned out to be.

Amber pulled her vehicle to a halt. The female with
Howard on the second seat of her two-wheeled vehicle
pulled up next to the window. "There is one person at
the airlock. We'll have to wait," said Amber.

"It's probably a guard," she added. "We can't
wait—the police channel tells me they're starting a systematic sweep. We might be able to hide ourselves, but
not the vehicles. We can't get far enough from them not

to be found by the kind of search they'd start then. I'll leave Howard with you. Let me go and deal with it."

She grimaced and tugged at her braided hair. "Even my mother wouldn't recognize me with this."

Riding on alone, Lani had to ask herself why she was doing this. It was crazy. But . . . having gone this far, how did you get out? A mercenary part of her mind said: *by turning the others in.*

Could she? She'd get a plea-bargain deal, probably. Amber was too valuable for them to punish very severely. Besides . . . what was the scientist or the alien to her?

The answer was clear enough: People who'd helped her, with hair dye and a pump-action shotgun. And then there was Howard. Taking on thirty men to stop her being raped . . .

And then stopping her dealing with their leader, the loon!

She'd forgotten all about that worm lying quietly on the back seat. The others could let him go now—except that she had the keys to his cuffs. And she couldn't turn around now. There was the airlock, and someone looking at her.

She pulled the scoot up at the airlock, and, as she'd correctly surmised, a police guard.

"You're late. As usual," said the woman, scowling. "Oh. Sorry. I thought it was Marianne."

"She called in sick," said Lani, scowling right back. "No sign of anyone here, is there?"

"Nah. A waste of time." The woman got on her own scoot, and, to Lani's horror took off up the same passage she'd just come out of. The passage the others were waiting down.

After an instant's hesitation, Lani leapt onto her own scoot and set off after her.

She caught up as the policewoman was radioing in " . . . backup. Have encountered armed—"

She slumped as Lani hit her. "We'd better move!" yelled Lani. "Why did you apes let her call in?"

"Because we're less good at violence than you are," said Amber, engaging the vehicle's transmission.

They raced onward to the airlock.

It opened in front of them. "I put the access code in," said Amber, holding up her portable. "Let's get the stuff out of the back and get in there. The cops will be here any moment."

They leapt out.

Their unwilling passenger chose this moment to squall. "What about me?"

Lani unlocked the cuffs hastily. "Run, you little rat. Be lucky you're still alive."

He darted down the passage, and Lani turned back to the vehicle.

Amber had three large bags. Did she think she was going on holiday and needed a ton of body paint? Lani grabbed one, and Howard the other two.

"What the hell is in here?" she asked, struggling forward.

"Dehydrated cell culture for Kretz," said Amber, grabbing the other handle. "Spare ammunition. Clothes from the museum. Some tools. I hear sirens. Let's try to run."

The lock was only yards off, but the siren sound showed that the Diana police force was coming in fast. Lani could almost be proud of them.

Then, suddenly, running as if his butt was on fire, their former hostage ran straight past them and into the airlock.

As soon as they were in, Kretz activated the closing switch. Glacially, the door began closing. The sirens were really on top of them now. The door closed just as tires screeched outside. Lani breathed a sigh of relief.

And then the door began to open.

Frantically Amber opened her portable and entered numbers.

The door began to close again.

Someone shoved a nightstick into the crack.

The stick crushed. Lani sat down, tension easing.

"*Seal cannot be achieved*," said a mechanical voice. "*Inner airlock seal must be achieved to commence lock sequence.*"

"What does that mean?" asked Lani.

"It means that the airlock is inoperable," said the alien. "If it is like ours, one door won't open if the other is not closed. We are trapped here."

Lani looked around at the chamber. Including a small alcove it was about ten meters long. "Can't we break open the outer door? Or . . . isn't there a manual override?"

"Probably," said Amber. "But that will kill everyone in Diana, even if it's only a slow leak. I'm not prepared to do that. I've altered the access codes, and made this an entry-code required door. We're safe enough for now. But we can't go anywhere."

Lani felt remarkably foolish. She knew what space was, after all. She'd seen pictures and read about it. Living inside the habitat, she had just forgotten.

Howard was on his hands and knees, studying the end of the nightstick. He tugged at it. The high-impact plastic had not broken, just crushed down into filaments. You could vaguely hear hammering on the door.

"Can they possibly break it down?" he asked.

"I doubt it," Amber replied. "Eventually lack of food and water will force us to go back, though."

"If it were opened a fraction I could remove this," Howard said.

Lani shook her head. "If we open it a fraction, they'll put more in. And then, if they can get it to open more than a bullet-diameter, they'll just call in a weapons team and let the ricochets take care of all of us." It was grim, Lani found, being on the wrong side of her own profession. "In fact, I'll bet the firearms squads are on their way right now."

"Hmm." Amber looked thoughtfully at the door. "If we could get them to back off, we could snatch the obstruction in and close it."

"And how will we do that?" asked Lani. "We can't even talk to them—not that they'd listen to us telling them to back off."

"Even though they know we're armed? If we said we were coming out, shooting, and they'd better get out the way . . . " The scientist started typing in to her portable again. "I can access a speaker outside the airlock door. And we can count and position them onscreen."

Lani pursed her lips and nodded. "You're going to have to do some tricks with that thing to get it all done fast enough."

Amber pulled a face. "I'll set up the opening and closing sequence to one key-stroke macros. You want to talk to them."

"Okay. When you're ready," Lani said. "Howard, will you pull it in? Kneel next to the door. We won't get more than one chance."

He nodded, took up his position and a grip on the end of the stick.

"Ready," said Amber.

"Let's just move back from a direct line of fire." Lani pointed to the wall. "Right. What do you want me to say? Will we be able to hear them too?"

"Can set that up. Hang on . . . Okay. Say whatever you think will get them to back off. Speak to the portable's pickup. You're live . . . *now*."

Lani cleared her throat. "Hear this! We're coming out! We will come out shooting! Back off!"

A pause and then someone yelled. "Let the hostages out and you men will be well treated. No harm will come to you if you lay down your arms."

Hostages? The only "hostage" they had the police were welcome to. They wouldn't consider him one anyway. They must assume Amber, at least, was a hostage. There was no sign of movement from the screen. "Back off and we'll let the hostages out!" said Lani. "We don't trust you. Back off first."

"We are," replied the officer on far side of the airlock door, a statement belied by the screen. They were bunching to rush the door. It was exactly what she would have done, had she been on the other side of that door. There must be mechanical pick-ups in more places than she'd ever dreamed of.

"I can see you," said Lani. "Move away from the door."

"Speak up. Sorry, we can't hear you clearly." Negotiating technique. Keep them talking . . .

Lani saw how a sudden brightness leapt into Amber's eyes. "Heh! Thank you!" She hastily opened a screen window. "Wav. File generator. Block your ears, all. They say they can't hear us. Let them hear us. At *full* volume."

Even on the other side of a meter-thick door, the shriek was penetrating. By the scattering of people indicators on-screen, on the other side of the door, it was intolerable.

"Now!" The door began opening.

Howard twitched the nightstick inside. And the door . . . closed.

*"Seal achieved,"* said the mechanical voce from the speaker-box. *"Depressurization will begin in ten minutes. Please don your suits and run through pre-vacuum checks. Depressurization may be interrupted by pressing the red buttons, at any point. To reinitiate the sequence press the green button on the control console."*

Behind them, the burned bridges fell.

Howard sighed with relief. Yes, it meant going out into the vastness of space again. But that was a less frightening place to him now, compared to coping with a female-dominated world. He breathed a little prayer of thanks. Why God saw fit to send not one, but two, of these women with them, he did not know. Part of him admitted he was glad Lani was here. Another part rejoiced because he was going to don clothes again, even if they were heavy, bulky spacesuits.

He smiled at the two women. It was a minor pleasure to feel that for once he knew more than they did. "The suits, helmets and boots are in alcove-cupboards. Let me show you."

"Clothes?" said Lani warily.

The other woman—the one Lani referred to as Amber, laughed. It was a little tinged with hysteria, but it was still laughter. "Skin may be beautiful and natural, dear, but it doesn't deal well with vacuum. We're going into space, remember."

"How do we get out of here?" asked a scared voice from the huddle in the corner.

Howard had forgotten the man. "What do we do with him?" It was rather their fault that he was here, he supposed.

Lani had also obviously forgotten his existence. "Damnation, what the hell did you run in here for, Perp?" she snapped.

"It was you or the cops," he said defiantly. "And if they catch me, I'm dead meat. Or I might as well be."

"You might as well be dead as here too," said the Amber woman. "We're going to have to get him out there."

"Can't. I'll bet they have ear-muffs and are just about solid at the door. If we open it, we'll never get it closed again," said Lani decisively.

Howard remembered the bones in the airlock on New Eden. "We can't leave him here," he said with equal firmness. "He will die."

Lani scowled. "And the world would be a better place without one perp. What else can we do with him?"

"At least help him into a suit," said Kretz "Vacuum will kill him."

Howard nodded. "He can wait here and go out when the hue and cry has died down."

"That could be difficult," said Amber. "I have reset the doors so they will not open without a pass-code input direct to the computer. We don't dare change that. I wouldn't put it past the Matriarchy to try to follow us. I could maybe set a time delay and he could sneak out later, I suppose. Long after we've gone."

"After this, there'll be guards on the airlock doors until doomsday, I reckon." Lani scowled. "You're going down, you little perp scumbag."

He stared in defiance at her, but said nothing.

# 22

"While I consider it extremely likely that the isolated societies will develop a high level of inward focus, I suspect
that—because of the gene-pool we're selecting from—
there will always be explorers, visionaries and dreamers.
People who revel in pushing the boundaries."

> Transcript of testimony given by George
> Walsingham, Professor of Psychology,
> University of New Colorado, to the Senate
> Select Committee of SysGov. on the mental
> health stability of the Slowtrain colonists.

Nothing, Amber Geraint realized, prepared you for deep
space. You could look at a million pictures but it wasn't
the same as being there. The darkness and vastness of it

all crushed her. Paralyzed her. How could the others be so casual about it? She thought that she'd prepared so well. Old vacuum-tight bags, relics of the initial founders, and everything from food to tools. The part that wasn't ready was her mind. She'd wanted to do this. Believed it would be a whole new world, away from the frustration of her life in Diana . . . but you always took yourself with you. It was a difficult time to discover she was agoraphobic.

She struggled forward, trying not curl into a tight little ball and die there. Voices crackled over the suit radio.

Lani: "Fantastic! I was born to do this!"

Then Howard—her big lover. "It is magnificent, isn't it? It's a very spiritual place." His deep voice was calm and sincere. Trying desperately to think of anything but the billions of miles of nothing out there, Amber wondered if anyone apart from herself knew that male average weight in Diana had been climbing slowly for the last three hundred years. Sexual selection was triumphing over genetic engineering. Female humans—at least a fairly high proportion of them—must have hardwired somewhere into their mate selection criteria "bigger is better." Oh Holy Susan. How did they walk so casually! She tried just looking at her feet.

"Howard, that little rat has followed us. What we do with him?" Lani demanded.

Amber managed a glance back. Sure enough, toddling along after them was a diminutive space-suited figure. She wished that she hadn't looked. There was a vast blackness lightly salted with stars out there, trying to devour her. She gave a low moan, despite her best intentions. She was the scientist. She'd wanted to see this!

"Are you all right, lady?" asked Howard.

Who was "lady"? Oh, yes, it was an extinct term for woman. "No," she admitted. "I think I may throw up. This is horrible!"

She knew she was slipping into hysteria. This was no place to panic! She couldn't help herself, though.

"Lani and I will walk either side of you," he said. "Put your arms around us and close your eyes." His voice, deep and calm, helped. So did the steadying presence of an arm, someone there holding her, someone close in all this nothingness.

With her eyes tight shut, they walked. She tried to tell herself it was all just a horrible dream. She would wake up in her own bed, with the alarm shrilling, her running late for another boring day at the protein vats. . . .

"He's still tagging along, Howard," Lani said again.

"I don't think we can stop him, Lani. He will go back of his own accord. You can't do the cable-flight alone."

"I'm not going back there," said a defiant male voice. "Not alone. This place frightens me."

At least Amber wasn't alone in that. As a scientist she knew that being sick in this suit would possibly be lethal. That didn't stop her feeling nauseated.

"I think I'd better go back," She decided that she'd been incredibly stupid. Being bored and frustrated didn't kill you.

"Too late," said Lani heartlessly. "I'm not going back with either of you, and you won't get there by yourselves or with each other. Is this where we tie them together, Howard?"

"Yes. Together with these bags we've been pulling. We have more air this time, fortunately. I wish we could also talk to Kretz about these two. I would take them back if I could explain. But we can't just leave them here."

"It's nearly as far back as it is on, anyway," said Lani. "That is, if we're talking about the walking part. I can't wait for this 'flying' bit! Here. Hook this onto the little perp, if you insist on taking him along. I think we'd do better just to leave him here though."

"Please don't." That was genuine fear in his voice. "Please."

"Hell's teeth. Howard, you should have let me shoot him. Okay. He's attached."

It wasn't just a bad dream. It was a nightmare.

And shrieking with glee, in someone else's nightmare, should not be allowed!

# 23

Internal e-vox:

It's a nix on that, Mike-O. The reason that there are no external amplifier antennas in the shipment is that we're not supposed to fit them. They don't want the crazies to talk to each other, I guess.

Samantha Browne (stores)

PS. When do I see you again, darlin' man?

Out here without the interference of a thick sphere of metal between him and the ship, Kretz's reception was reasonable. What he was hearing, wasn't.

"Selna, I *can't*," he said. "It's not that I don't want to." Kretz was worried by the tirade. Normally changeover tantrums and instability were unpleasant . . . but not as

255

bad as this. They normally only lasted about fifteen days, dropping in intensity as the more conservative, rational female side of the Miran personality kicked in. Of course nest-territory deprivation and the huge male hormone supplement load would make things worse. But she seemed almost entirely out of it.

And the news from Abret seemed to be worse.

None.

Of course it could just be that the retransmission granule unit's power was exhausted. The suit radio just wasn't intended for long-range transmission.

# 24

"History proves that misfits in a stable static society often prove to be leaders and desirable citizens in a pioneer one. Of course this is not universally true."

From: *Elementary Societal Psychodynamics.* 2089. James R. Grey (ed). New Harvard Library (Pub.)

Lani found that entry to the second airlock bordered on the tragic. She'd spent her life not knowing what she wanted to do. Not in the short-term sense but in the "what do you want to do with your life" sense. She felt that she'd just found it. It was as if she'd been caged all her life—without knowing it—and had suddenly had been allowed to get out. To think that she'd been mildly worried about the unfamiliar environment. Now, the walls seemed to close in around her.

Not so, by the looks of it, for Amber Geriant. You could hear her breathing in faint gasps through the suit radios. The woman's face was as pale as a sheet, her facepaint stark against it. And she was clawing ineffectually at her helmet already. She had it off the moment the repressurization light came on. She leaned against the wall and slid down it to sit, still panting.

"That was the worst thing I have ever, ever, ever experienced. Never again. Never, ever again," she said. "I thought I was going to die. And then I thought I might not, and that was far worse. It's so good to be inside."

"I can't wait to go outside again," blurted Lani, despite meaning to keep quiet. "This just seems to be so small now."

Howard beamed. "I must admit that once I got used to it, it had something of the same effect on me. It did frighten me at first, though."

"Well, your species were plainly quite used to working in space, once," said Howard's alien, Kretz, folding back his hoodlike helmet. "And now we need to prepare ourselves for crossing this habitat. I hope it is not dangerous. Can you instruct me, properly, in the use of this weapon?"

Amber made a face. "I think Lani had better do that for all of us—before we go out. I was under the mistaken impression that just having a gun was enough. Was I ever wrong!"

"Sure," said Lani. "I'll give lessons just as soon as I'm out of this suit. How do your people wear clothes all of the time, Howard? They itch. It's the one bad thing about space. So confining!"

Amber was looking at a screen display on one of the cases. "I have some bad news for you, Lani. The air temperature in here is a good three degrees cooler than it is at home. I think we can reasonably conclude that the people of this habitat wear some clothes."

"Clothes?" Lani looked at the suit she had half off. "You mean I have to wear this thing? How do you . . . have a pee?"

Amber laughed. "I looted the museum and brought several sets of clothes along. I assumed that we might have to try to pass as locals. They're in the other bag."

"Can you help me out of this thing?" said a plaintive voice they'd all forgotten about, the small gap-toothed Male Liberation Movement captain. He was still struggling with his helmet.

Howard helped him to snap the catches. "What are we going to do with him?" asked Lani. She felt that popping him outside the airlock—without the helmet—was an attractive idea. Unfortunately, she was pretty sure that Howard wouldn't like it.

"We will help you to find a safe place. After that you are free to go," said Howard, confirming her suspicions. This was one little perp who had succeeded in evading the Diana law. It suddenly struck her that they all had. Well, not many criminals would flee justice this far. Not many would have the skill and the knowledge, even if they weren't afflicted by the open spaces. There was a lot of open space out there. Enough, if you had air, to live a life of your own, in your own way. It was an attractive thought.

Amber had opened the space-bag and was now busy laying out cloth items from it. "There was a limited choice. A lot of the fabric had not survived, even in museum conditions. I brought along a set of overalls from the protein vats . . . but they are bright orange."

"Brown and green are the best colors, if we are going to have to avoid attack," said Kretz.

The idea of putting on clothing that wasn't absolutely necessary to cope with the vacuum of space in front of other people was distinctly discomforting. It was bad enough being perverted in private. "Can we perhaps see on your computer, how many people there are around here? We can then avoid them and avoid the clothing."

Amber shook her head. "I don't know if I'll be able to access their network. I hadn't thought of that. I suppose I can search for frequencies. There must be a way."

Howard was inspecting the clothing. First with eagerness, and then with horror. "These are all women's clothes!"

Amber looked from her screen and nodded. "Yes. I didn't anticipate needing men's clothes. They're from the female repression display in the closed access section of the museum. I planned this and got the clothes before we knew about your coming with us. I hope—as you come from a clothed society—you can tell us what some of them are. Some appear more lace than covering."

Howard blushed fiercely. "They are woman's underclothes. Uh. I think. I have never seen anything like them."

"And that's your story, and you're sticking to it," said Lani, picking up a red lacy item. It could fit around your breasts, she supposed, although it must have been designed for a woman with enormous breasts. "One thing about wearing your skin: it doesn't come in different sizes."

She held up a long sort of black sacklike thing, dropped it with distaste, and then picked up a semitransparent metallic-sheen strip of material. At least it was a pretty color. "How do people put these things on, Howard? Is this what you wear in New Eden?"

His eyes seemed to bulge. "No! We wear good homespun, in the natural colors of our animals or the plants that it comes from. It is vanity to wear such a thing. And that's not so much intended to cover your nakedness as to . . . to flaunt it."

She could wear something like this without feeling so perverted, she thought. "So how do you wear it?" She held it up to her breasts.

"It's . . . it's a skirt. It's not really decent."

"I'm not wearing that black sack," said Lani. "So does it go around the waist?"

"Uh, yes."

It was quite obvious, when you knew what to look for. There was a little belt with a tiny label attached, which read: *microskirt, circa 2030*. She stepped into it and fastened it. "How does that look?"

"You need underwear. And a blouse. It's really not decent," repeated Howard, as red as a beetroot salad.

It was fun watching the effect semi-clothing herself had on him. And with another woman around, especially one at the top of the social hierarchy, she needed to make sure that his attention was well and truly fixed on her. "Underwear? Oh, that lacy thing." Presumably to be worn under the skirt. Then why so lacy? "What's the point of underwear? You can't see it."

Howard swallowed. "In that skirt, you can."

Howard realized that he'd gotten used to coping with nudity. It had not occurred to him that anyone could be even more alluring in clothing. It wasn't fair. And what could he wear? Women's clothes? He wasn't sure if nudity wasn't almost better! None of them would fit him anyway.

"I can't raise it!"

The woman with her screen looked as if she might just burst into tears. "Scan says there is no connection available. I've always had a connection. How am I going to cope without one? Holy Susan! I feel . . . dressed."

The black sack—labeled *Hijab, circa 2010*—was at least made of honest sturdy cloth, Howard had to admit. Of course, he wouldn't have fitted into it in a million years. But, by wrapping it around his waist, it made quite a respectable skirt, just over knee length. A man in a skirt was ludicrous, but it did beat nudity, and at least it was in a decent color. He was less fortunate in what was available for a top. The only item that would remotely fit was glowingly pink, had tassels, and wouldn't close in front. Still, it was better than the only item left for the little wild man—he must find out his name. That tutu-thing was ludicrous. He would have preferred to stay in a pressure suit to wearing that. Lani hadn't thought it practical, though, and Howard had to agree with her, even if it did have trousers.

He sat, contriving carrying straps for the bags. Some of the things, like the unwanted clothes, they would abandon here. But the food for Kretz, and the tools, had to be taken along. The others—except for Howard himself and the little fellow with the gap-tooth—were getting a lesson in how to use firearms. On principle, Howard had refused. And the women had refused to let the little man participate. He was keen, though, and sat staring at the drill Lani was putting them through. On impulse Howard touched him on the shoulder. "What's your name?"

The little gap-toothed man blinked. "John," he answered warily. "John Bhangella."

John Bhangella looked at the big fellow. There seemed no sign of malice there. He was as weird as they came, even if he hadn't been the size of three normal men. Imagine turning down the chance to learn how to use a gun! Still, the big guy had stopped that cop-bitch from killing him . . . a couple of times. He said things and she listened to him. Weird. Weirder than that other guy who looked like a mixture between something from a bad dream and a cross between a man and a woman. He definitely had an extra hole and no balls. But he also had quite a piece.

Bhangella smiled tentatively at the big guy. John hadn't survived being a womanless man, and then worked his way up to being one of the Men's Liberation Army captains by not knowing when to kiss a few butts. "So it's just us two men," he said.

"Yes. We will have a hard time protecting these ladies. I am sorry we dragged you into this. It was not my intention."

*Yeah*, thought John, *protect them? It was your girl-friend's intention to blow my balls off though.* But what he said was: "These things happen."

"I believe that it is all part of God's plan," said the big man, tying knots dexterously. "I did not wish to go out of New Eden with Brother Kretz, but if I had not gone, well, my world would have been much smaller. I would not have seen the glory of the heavens and seen how infinite His majesty is."

That didn't mean much to Johnny Bhangella. The best he managed was, "Uh. Yes."

"I cannot promise anything, but this habitat might be a sweeter place, where men and women live in harmony under God, as equals like in my own," said Howard hopefully.

The words made sense, but the substance of them didn't. But if the big guy wanted it like that, he'd agree. John nodded. He'd heard some talk of other worlds from some of the runaways who'd learned to read. He'd never felt a need for reading himself. He was already quite clever enough. He noticed that the big guy seemed hooked up on clothes. He used some of his words back at him. "Hopefully they will have the decency to wear clothing."

He knew he'd struck well when Howard beamed at him. "At least we men understand the need for clothing."

John nodded. His old mistress had made him dress up sometimes. It was a pity that she hadn't had Howard to beat for her pleasure instead. "Oh, yes," he agreed.

A few minutes later they opened the inner-airlock door, and stepped out into a new world.

# 25

"Let's face it, Henry, primitive cultures have no place in a modern world. We can't keep them in the damn reserve. They won't stay there, and they're damaging the biosphere anyway. They need, in that ancient military parlance you like so much, to either shape up or ship out. The trust fund is awash with UN guilt money. So we buy them a habitat. So what if they barely understand it? Let them take their dirt, their disease, their stupid culture and die somewhere a long way from me."

> Transcript of secretly recorded discussion between Assistant Commissioner H. Obisando and Commissioner of Indigenous Rights (South American subregion) Phaedra Van Pensdorm.

Within the constraints that the surface area must be vastly increased, and that the shaping of this must also assist the

water and air circulation—as the main vehicles for thermo-
regulation—there is tremendous scope for variation and
imagination in habitat architecture.

> Extract from notes: Space Architecture 101,
> University of Beijing, South Campus.

———

A red and blue bird greeted them with a raucous cry as
it flew up into the vegetation. It was an odd looking
chicken, Howard had to admit, but there was no call for
Lani to shoot it.

Howard picked himself up off the ground. There
wasn't much left of the chicken. Just some red and blue
feathers. Here they were barely ten yards into this
place—and she'd killed someone's livestock!

"Do you mind," he said trying to keep his temper,
"telling me next time you're going to shoot at something?
You gave me a terrible fright, and now we've got a dead
chicken to explain to some householder, and there's not
enough left of it for dinner."

She stood there looking shaken. "What the hell was
that thing?"

"A funny colored chicken," he said.

"What?"

"An animal we grow for eggs and meat," he explained,
realizing that she really meant it. When she still looked
blank he went on. "A domestic animal. Harmless. Where
have the others gone?"

"I think they ran away," said Lani. "It . . . do they
always make that noise?"

Howard shook his head. "Not the ones at home. But
this is a different place. Warmer. They would have chickens that were suited to their environment, I imagine. I

suppose we'd better look for the others. I hope the owner is not too upset about his chicken."

They found Kretz, Amber and John in his tutu peering around the door of the airlock. "It's all right. It was just a chicken."

"More mobile than most chicken-vat culture," said Amber, grinning. She appeared, despite the fright she'd just had, to be recovering her tone of mind now that they were inside again. Howard wondered if it had occurred to her that the whole purpose of being inside . . . was to get to the far side and go out again. What would they do then. Would she stay behind?

"You mean that's the same as the chicken we eat?" said Lani. "Oh, how gross. I just killed it. I think I'm going to be sick."

Every time he thought he was getting to understand these people, they mystified him afresh. Chicken had to be killed before you could eat it. Even the squares of dull meat they ate had to have been killed, didn't they? But they could contemplate killing people with no qualms.

Well, best not to make an issue out of it right now. "We need to move on," he said, practically. "Please don't kill any more chickens or other livestock. The owners might get very angry."

"It's pretty wild and unprocessed looking greenery. Maybe it was a runaway . . . chicken," ventured Lani.

There was something in what she'd said, thought Howard, looking at the plants carefully now, instead of just looking for naked women wanting to attack them. "I'm not sure I recognize the plants, but, as you say, none of them look farmed, do they?" he admitted.

"No. No signs of any cutting," agreed Lani.

"Some of the leaves do look familiar, but not too familiar," said John, plucking and sniffing one. He chewed a piece and spat it out, making a face.

Amber spoke up. "It's cooler than Diana. The plants would need to be adapted to that. And they might come from different geographical areas. I read somewhere once that the vegetation of old Earth's continents was quite different."

Howard nodded. "It is warmer, and more humid, than New Eden. I suppose different plants would flourish here. Still, it's not as warm as your Diana was, and I recognized those plants. There was less variety in your place than at home, and yours appeared to be all soft-plants. I don't think I saw any trees. We have trees—many different fruit trees. This place here is quite different from both my home and yours. The passages are taller than those of home, and much taller than yours. There is far more plant variety. Those are trees, back in the undergrowth."

He looked around, frowning. "Very untidy," he said, disapprovingly. "It's worse than the upper core sections of New Eden that have gone wild."

"Has this place gone wild?" asked Amber. "Have all the people died off?"

"It could have happened," said Kretz thoughtfully. "You're a very robust and adaptable species, but biohabitats are relatively fragile, although it is obvious that they're less fragile once they get to this size. We had several experimental ones on Miran. They all failed. But they were all small and very micromanaged."

"It's wrong to hope that all the inhabitants have died," said Howard, knowing he sounded self-righteous, but unable to help himself. "Even if it would make things easier for us. But we need to get you through to the other side of it, Kretz. Shall we go? And, Lani . . . please don't just shoot things."

"Sorry. Just a nervous overreaction," she said apologetically. "I think you'd better lead this time, Howard. Not," she said fiercely, "because of that stupid argument of yours that men ought to lead into danger, but because you at least know what chickens look like."

She paused. "And this other 'livestock,' whatever that is. I'm too inclined to shoot first and ask questions later. It was why they wouldn't have me on the firearms squad, in spite my graduating top of marksmanship." She scowled at John in his pink tutu. "Or we could send the perp first to be a target for any trouble."

So Howard led them off into the corridors. It was much harder than he'd thought it would be. There was a path, but unlike the practical ones of New Eden this one was not straight. It was narrow, and wound around the trees.

"It does seem very wild. I don't see any signs of farming or harvesting," said Howard after a while.

"The tops are trimmed," said Amber.

It was true enough. The tops were trimmed, cut short of the actual roof. Howard walked forward cautiously. Several more flying things exploded out of the underbrush and flew up the trail, shrieking.

"More chickens?" said Lani as Howard got up. "They gave *you* a fright this time. They certainly come in a range of colors, don't they?"

Howard felt as if he was on far less certain ground than he had believed he was. "Um. I don't think those ones were chickens. They could fly—like chickens do—but they didn't look at all like chickens. They didn't even fly in the same sort of way as chickens, or sound like them. They must be some other creature."

"Not dangerous?" asked little John, peering around him.

The sheer unfamiliarity of the environment injected a bit of caution into Howard's reply. "I don't think so. Chickens aren't."

They walked on. "I really do think you're right, Lani. This environment has gone wild," said Howard, as they had to push through a section where the branches overhung the the path.

She gave him a half-smile. "Well, anyway, there's no shortage of these chickens of yours. In all sorts of sizes and colors . . . urgh. What is *that* thing?"

Her gun was in hand again, menacing a small green creature with bright black eyes on the branch next to the path. It had a tail, four legs, clawed feet and was covered—by the looks of it—in tiny scales, rather like a bird's legs. Howard looked warily at it. It looked back at him . . . and abruptly turned and scurried off. "I don't know," admitted Howard. If Kretz had looked like that, instead of human-ish, the people of New Eden would have killed him. Was it some kind of small demon?

"Maybe it has gone to call its friends," said John.

Howard nodded. "Let's move along."

They did—but not for long. The trail led into water. A stream ran down the path. "Pipe burst somewhere."

There was nowhere to walk but in the water, and, like dense vegetation, that was full of life. Things that darted off in the water, shoals of tiny fish, and a sucker-footed croaking thing that jumped on prodigiously large back legs.

The "path" got deeper and then ahead . . . Water spread out into an expanse, covered by splotches of floating flat round leaves. One of the tree-edges of the trail continued, going off into the water.

"Pipe burst," repeated Howard, gloomily. "A huge, long-ago pipe-burst. Look how the grass-stuff is growing out of it. We'll have to start wading."

"Do we have to?" asked Kretz. "It looks as if it could be quite deep."

Howard had to admit that he didn't like the look of it himself. "I suppose if we went up to the higher levels, closer to the core. But that'll mean going back."

"Back is better than on, by the looks of it," said Amber. "I'm tired. I'm not used to all this walking. But we can't even sit down here."

"You would be dead-beat," said Lani, waspishly, holding on to Howard's shoulder.

Howard blinked. All this walking? They'd hardly done any. But looking at them, he could see that all three of the Diana people were tired. He supposed that they weren't used to using their legs much, what with scoots and cars and trolley-busses. And Amber had probably wasted a lot of energy on fear.

"We'll go back, at least until we find a cross-trail or a riser." He remembered seeing one back just before water started running down the track.

They walked back, and across into another passage. Fortunately Lani spotted a riser—a steep curve of path that took them up one more level. There was a small clearing, a grassy patch. "Rest time," said Amber, panting, and sitting down. The others followed suit with obvious degrees of relief.

Howard wasn't tired. He'd passed from nervousness to fascination with this environment. His mind had already been fixing it, mending the broken pipes, thinning the trees, and planting crops. Kretz was peering intently at something on a leaf, but the others looked nearly comatose. The alien gave him his odd smile. "This place is a biologist's paradise. I enjoyed seeing your domesticated animals, Howard, but I think this place must be a conservation area. A place to preserve the wild ones. We have many of them on Miran, outside of the hunting areas. Fascinating. Look at the tiny little animals on this leaf."

Howard looked. They had six legs, like bees. Definitely the New Eden council would have killed Kretz if he'd looked like _that_. Kretz continued. "We have tried to set up conservation areas on Miran that are just like the planet must have been before we became intelligent. This is like that."

"Eden," said Howard. "So you think this is our paradise?"

"Paradise," announced Lani firmly, "has scoots."

It was a little too warm here, but otherwise it did look like an untamed paradise, ripe for a farmer. Howard walked over to the trees a little beyond the glade. Out of the corner of his eye he saw that John had got to his feet and was walking across to him, looking around. Howard wondered what he wanted. Perhaps he was looking for a place in Eden to call his own. Mind you, this Eden didn't seem in very good repair. He thought he heard more water . . .

He wasn't wrong. There was another stream of it. Was all the piping in this habitat rotten? The stream of water ran into a hole. It must be a deliberate drain of some sort. It was too square to just be water-worn. Come to think of it, he hadn't actually seen any of the ubiquitous drains of New Eden. He knelt to have a closer look. As he did so, he heard a sort of half-gurgling-scream. Turning, he saw that the small man from Diana was looped in the thick, sinuous coils of some creature. Howard ran to help, and found himself in the creature's coils too. As he yelled in surprise, a second and a third horrid length looped around him, trapping one arm.

It squeezed.

As he tried to draw breath the creature—as thick as a feeder-pipe—contracted around him again. A forked tongue flickered at him.

With his free hand he grabbed the creature's neck just below its head and tried to pull it away from him, to throttle it, as it was throttling him. The creature was winning, when Lani came running up. She calmly put her weapon against his clutching hand and fired upwards through its skull.

The cracking coils spasmed briefly and painfully, and she helped him to push it away. He sat down, drawing air into his lungs, hauling the heavy scaled creature away from his body. John squirmed out of the coils, panting, and sat next to him.

"Now, what sort of livestock is this?" asked Lani, kicking it. "Beef? Lamb? If you ask me, growing them in a nutrient vat is much safer, even if you don't like the taste as much."

"It's a huge snake. A serpent." He was shocked and shaken by all of this, but even if he'd never seen it, he knew that much from the holy book. "Don't eat any apples it offers you. Maybe this is Eden."

"I don't think so," said Amber. She had her portable computer out. "Look. I can't hook up to the dataweb here, but I have found that there is an onboard encyclopedia. Looks as if that thing was an anaconda. From South America. Not Eden."

"Perhaps South America was in Eden, then? Or Eden was in South America? It was lost, you know, when man was driven out of it." Howard was reluctant to abandon the idea. It would be something to return home and tell them he'd found Eden. He stood up.

"Come and sit down over there for a bit, you two. We still need some rest, and I really get the feeling that you shouldn't wander off on your own here," said Lani, kicking the snake again. "Or do you think its owner is going to come demanding compensation? I'll give him compensation . . . " She pointed the gun. "That thing could have hurt you."

Even if he didn't approve of violence, it was hard to disagree entirely with her. Howard went to sit on the grass. Looking carefully, he could see something had been cropping it.

"What are these black things?" Lani held them up to him.

"Goat droppings. Well," he corrected himself, in the light of his recent experience, "droppings from an animal possibly something like a goat." That was obviously what had been doing the cropping.

"Droppings?" She looked at him in puzzlement and sniffed the black ovoid objects. "Poo." She wrinkled her nose.

"Uh, yes. Dung."

That was plainly another word that had been lost from Diana's vocabulary. "What?" Lani peered at them, wrinkling her nose.

"He means excretion. Shit," supplied Amber.

Lani dropped the droppings as if they were burning hot. Looked around and raced to the stream, ignoring the dead snake, and washed her hands frantically.

"Can't they be taught to use bathrooms?" she said crossly to Howard. "If that's what they do all over the place they deserve to be eaten!"

The problem was that they just couldn't keep going in the same direction. There was water everywhere. A few hundred yards on from where Howard had proved that, if this was Eden, it still had its serpent, they came to a lake—again. This was quite a narrow one, barely thirty yards wide. "We can't just keep going back. We've got to cross it," said Howard. "I'll go first. I can swim."

He stepped into the water. A black drifting log in the middle . . . submerged suddenly. Amber grabbed his shoulder and hauled him back. "Don't." She said. "I looked up dangerous South American animals . . . " Part of the black log came up, much closer to them. It had eyes. Curiously flecked eyes—about six inches apart. Evil eyes. Hungry.

"I think we need to back away from the water," Howard said in a steady voice. "Don't run." Running was the worst thing you could do with Jersey bulls . . . and this creature looked even nastier.

They retreated. Gradually the whole "log" surfaced too. It must have been four or more yards long, ridged and spiked. Amber pointed to her portable. "I think it is a black cayman. See."

The onscreen picture included teeth.

"I think we have to avoid the water," said Kretz thoughtfully.

"That's not all." She flicked to a picture of a fish. A fish? It looked like a fish . . .

"Those are its teeth below," she said, pointing. They were triangular, interlocking. "They're not very big fish, but they move in large schools. It says here they can skeletonize large mammals very quickly, although they do not often attack man."

"Do they have those here too?" asked John fearfully, dancing his feet out of the water.

"Who knows, Perp?" said Lani. "Shall we send you ahead to find out?"

"What other animals are listed as dangerous?" asked Howard, to keep the peace.

So Amber showed them. They made mere Jersey bulls seem attractive, good tempered and friendly. "Of course they won't all be here," she said.

Lani put an arm around Howard. "We've already met two of them. I don't think we need to take any chances."

That seemed like common sense. . . . The only trouble was that they were thoroughly lost as a result. Howard was still sure of up and down—but which direction to go on, was another matter. And they seemed hemmed in by interconnected waterways. There was no help for it but to wade in the very shallow ones.

The Diana people were finding it very hard going. Walking was an unfamiliar exercise, the creatures they encountered in the water and the vegetation were quite terrifying to people who had never seen any animal except a live human before. Not only did the color of their clothing make them very visible but the progression of screams and shrieks made it seem certain that the entire habitat must know of their passing. Yet they had seen no signs of people, and no certain signs that humans had ever lived here at all. The cuts on the trees could be the teeth of some big animal. They were rather straight for tooth marks, but until today Howard hadn't known half these things existed.

*"Whaa whhaa whaa woooo-huh."*

"What's that noise?" asked Howard.

It came again. *"Whaa whhaa whaa woooo-huh."*

"Fortunately, it sounds far off." Amber was too tired to be frightened by anything that wasn't within biting range.

"Good. I don't think I can run," said the younger woman, sitting down on a low bank and rubbing her feet.

Amber sat down too. "I'm glad I'm not the only one. I don't know how much farther I can walk, to be honest." She sighed. "You know, I calculated the distance to your lifecraft, Kretz. At top speed I could have driven there in two hours. I thought of walking. I thought I was so good with my calculations. I worked on the speed one can walk in Diana. On the flat, on a nice open walkway. I'm beginning to realize that the only sure way past the water is to head for the core. That's uphill. About a mile straight up."

"And it's not straight or flat underfoot either. Our sandals are not really made for this sort of thing," said Lani, looking at hers.

"Not to mention all of these dangerous creatures," said little John. He was staying right in the middle of the group, now.

"I'm tired, I'm hungry and I'm thirsty. And I can't believe there are no bathrooms," said Lani. "If this is paradise, there ought to be bathrooms."

"Well, we're not in jail," said Howard, trying to look on the bright side. "And we are closer to Brother Kretz's lifecraft. There is plenty of clean water in the streams—"

"Please!" Lani cocked her nose up. "We've been walking in that. Not to mention those goat-drippings that have probably ended up in the water too."

"Droppings, not drippings," corrected Howard.

"Droppings *and* drippings, probably," said Lani, looking at the water in distaste. "It's bad enough that we have to walk in it. And it's full of slimy swimming things."

The more everyone talked about it, the more Amber wished that she was home. It was one thing to dream of the wonders of space travel. Another entirely to find that space was big and empty and that your decision had brought you to sore legs and feet and a shortage of water and food. She'd brought plenty of food. For Kretz. The idea of needing water hadn't crossed her mind. Like it or not, goat drippings and feet, and slimy things too, she was going to have to drink some, soon.

Then Kretz pointed out something even more unwelcome. "Is it just me, or does the light intensity seem to be dimming?"

It wasn't just him, and the idea was terrifying. "We can't be out here in the dark," said Amber hastily. "Let's get back to the airlock! At least it is clean and dry."

Howard shook his head. "To be honest I don't know if I could find my way there. At least, not in a hurry. I'm sorry. I think it is back that way, but we have changed direction so often . . . "

That was accurate enough, thought Amber, and not based on imagined problems—unlike Lani's attempt to always put herself between Amber and Howard. That came from living in a society where wealth and position had major pulling power, Amber supposed. She must find a way to reassure her soon, although Howard seemed oblivious to the matter.

"We'd better find a place we can wait out the darkness then," said Kretz. "Or do you think we should travel on in the dark? Perhaps these creatures sleep then."

Amber shrugged tiredly. "Not according to the encyclopedia," she said. "We need to beware of vampire bats and jaguars and . . . "

"And find a spot, soon, where we can fort up for the night," interrupted Howard. "I do not wish to have one of those drop on me during the night. Nor do I think that a black cayman is a pleasant thing to meet in the dark, let alone all these other horrors. We need a place that is high enough for us to fend them off and which has no trees overhead. We need to find it before the lights go off."

The spot was not ideal, Howard admitted to himself. Still, as the light had faded far more quickly than at home, they were lucky to have found something this good. They had a patch of interstitial wall that had no trees against it, and where the ground was a little higher. The little mound was covered in grass.

"Something's been cutting this vegetation," said Lani suspiciously.

Howard looked. "I think it is some kind of grazing animal. Like those ones that fled from us two levels down, perhaps."

She sighed tiredly. "Well, we'd better look for something else then."

"Grazers would be food for caymans and jaguars. If they come here it's probably fairly safe," said Amber. "Besides, I don't think I can go on."

"At least there are no trees for that serpent thing," said little John, sitting down on the grass. "Do we have any food?"

Amber scowled at him. "Freeze-dried protein for Kretz. Analysis says it wouldn't be good for us to eat."

"You brought me here to starve," whined the little man.

"Oh, for Holy Susan's sake!" snapped Lani. "We didn't bring you here at all. You brought yourself and you're welcome to leave as soon as possible. In fact I think you should go now."

John looked into the gathering gloom. "With those serpent things? No way."

"Then stop complaining. I'm hungry and thirsty too. I might even have to drink some dripping-water at this rate."

Howard sought to pour some oil on the water. He was, to some extent, responsible for keeping Kretz alive —which had dragged all of them into this. "I believe that is a pumpkin climbing up the edge of that bit of underbrush," he said, pointing. "The fruit is not quite the same as the ones at home, but the leaves are right, and so are the flowers. You can eat the young leaves and the flowers too. And I am sure there is other food here."

"Is *that* what a pumpkin looks like in the raw? It had to be my least favorite vegetable, didn't it?" said Lani, eyeing it. "Well, it's better than nothing, I guess. So how do we nuke it?"

Howard picked the large knobbled fruit, thinking about this and the other problems of provisioning the party. The water system in New Eden had been a bucket that you let down into an arterial canal. The faucets of Diana seemed like a recipe for things to wear out and get broken, to Howard. They were convenient, true. Right now he'd be glad of a bucket to haul clean New Eden water for Lani. She still hadn't brought herself to drink. Mind you, then he might as well wish for a sparker, and a nice flow of methane from the slurry-digesters to cook the pumpkin on. What was it going to be like raw? He'd heard you could grate it, raw, to make a salad out of it. . . . Well, they didn't have a grater. They'd have to find out what it was like just chewed. He picked flowers, some leaf-tips and two immature fruit for good measure.

"We need to cut this thing." The skin was thick and hard.

"I could shoot it, I suppose," volunteered Lani. "We should have brought that snake. Snake steak."

The idea made Howard shudder. Raw snake! How could she be so casual about a creature like that and yet worry about chickens or drinking the water? The thing was, he supposed, that the snake was just so alien to her that it had no meaning. He tried dropping the pumpkin, hard. It cracked.

There are better things than raw pumpkin. Raw pumpkin seeds for instance—they ate those when they'd finished with the pumpkin. But at least it was food. It was sweetish, and provided a good, long chew. The cracked seeds were delicious, but took a lot of cracking for very little meat. Lani eventually braved drinking the water, too.

She sat down next to him, and started laughing.

"What is so funny?" asked Amber. Howard hadn't dared ask.

"I was just thinking," said Lani. "We went through all of this to escape from the Diana police force. And right now a nice clean cell sounds pretty safe and pretty good."

"And they feed prisoners," said Amber.

"Yeah," agreed Lani. "I was just thinking if the force turned up here, now, I'd be pretty hard-pressed not to kiss them."

Howard didn't think this place was *that* bad. But he kept his opinion to himself. "I wonder how they would do with the cayman and the serpent?"

"Oh, hell, they'd all be back in the airlock, any that were still alive," said Lani. "This place is not what we trained for, but it was a fun thought. And I guess I don't really want to be in a cell. I wouldn't say 'no' to a hot bath and a cup of coffee, though."

"I'd like a strong drink," said Amber. "Strong enough to knock me out."

Then there was just the darkness to wait out. They sat together, listening to the noises that came out of the dark. Howard had to admit that "Silent Night" was not something you would ever sing here. There were croaks and whistles and odd hollow calls, and strange deep grunts out in the darkness. Instinctively, they huddled closer together. No one slept. They just sat there, waiting for the light. Gradually, things got quieter. Little snores came from at least two members of the group. Howard was tired himself, but he felt that sleep might be the last thing that they did. He'd sleep when they could see. Lani nodded against his shoulder. Snuggled into him. He sighed. It was all a heavy cross to bear.

Sitting in the darkness John Bhangella pondered his next move. This place frightened him. It was too strange and too alien. He wasn't planning to go off on his own either, especially not unarmed. The scientist woman was a better target than the cop. He could snatch that semi-automatic shotgun out of her hands before she knew what he was doing . . .

And then? He wasn't going to run off into this darkness. He might have been tempted, before the snake incident. But he also wanted to keep at least one woman. He wasn't too sure, yet, where this place actually was. The whole experience hadn't made a lot of sense to him. His mind still struggled with what he'd seen out there in that funny suit. It didn't make a clear, understandable picture. What was clear was that the others regarded this place as beyond the reach of the cops. If he could bring the other Men's Liberation Army members here, they could raid, loot and capture women—and never be followed. That had appeal.

# 26

e-vox to: Sarah Printemps
From: H. Obisando
Subject: uThani

Sarah, their language doesn't even have words for any number above four. That bitch is sending them out there to get killed. I've given you the tapes. Can't you stop it?

Henry

e-vox to: H. Obisando
From: Sarah Printemps
Subject: uThani

Van Pensdorm is history, Henry. But we can't stop them going. This came as a bit of shock to me too, but they're as keen to see the back of us as she was to see the back of them. We flooded their valley, and they haven't forgiven

285

us. They're not stupid. A deal is a deal, and just because they're a primitive Pacaraima culture, doesn't mean we can break the law. Besides, there are some real heavyweights in SysGov social psychology branch sitting on this one. I don't know why, but they want the uThani to go. Look, they'll have the best of everything, and the place will be stocked with livestock and plants from the area that they came from. There are only two hundred and thirty-nine of them. Yes, they have a unique language. Yes, they have been cut off from most of the rest of the human race for several hundred years. At low population densities . . . well, the habitat will be about twenty times as big as their valley. Maybe they'll evolve a civilization. Learn to count. With the repair bots and low pop. density, they'll have a thousand years (at least) to do it in.

Sarah

It was a long night, in which nothing happened. Nothing . . . other than buzzing things biting them, and, at least in Howard's case, not much sleep. The noises —from the slightest splash of water or crack of twigs, to echoing, yarring cries—fed the imagination. The truth was that the things they probably needed to be afraid of, they wouldn't hear. But that didn't stop Howard straining his ears. Before the lights began to warm up again, Howard had had a lot of time to think as well as time to worry. He thought about home. About his confused feelings for the woman next to him. About the vastness of space.

He had to acknowledge that Kretz's sudden arrival in their midst had changed his perspective somewhat. Perhaps Lani had been right. What he needed was a world of his own, where they took the good out of New Eden, and added it to the good in her world, had a place like this to develop, and where "outside" was not a place to fear, but to go out into, to explore.

Lani stirred against his shoulder. He patted her arm, awkwardly. She woke. He felt her tense against him. "Is everything all right?" she whispered.

"Fine. I'm sorry if I disturbed you," he said quietly.

"It's okay. I didn't mean to go to sleep. Did I sleep for long?"

"A century, I think."

She snorted. "Doesn't feel like it. Must have been one of the short centuries. Have you slept at all?"

"No," he said. "I thought someone had better stay awake."

"Yeah. Right. True. Well, I will now. It's time you slept. You can't do without any rest at all either," she said gruffly.

"I will try," said Howard. "But have you had enough sleep to stay awake?"

She chuckled. "I need the bathroom badly enough to keep me awake. And no, I will not go out there in the dark. You close those eyes. I'll shoot and scream if anything comes too close."

"Thank you," said Howard. Tiredness washed over him in a huge wave, with handing his responsibility over to someone else. Lani might be a woman, but she was more dangerous—and probably more reliable—than any of the male Brethren he could think of.

As he was drifting off, in that zone where he was between sleep and wakefulness, when the guard on his tongue and mind are less than alert, He said: "Lani

. . . do you think this place could actually be made into a world of our own? It's good farmland."

If she answered, it was in his dreams.

Lani sat in the dark, thinking about that last sleepy statement. It had . . . interesting implications, not least about how he saw her.

The place did change your perspective. True, it was pretty vile right now. But you had to start thinking about what it could be, rather than what it was. Diana was having trouble with food production. A few tons of these pumpkins, say, and there was the possibility of trading for some of life's little essentials, like a scoot and a fitted bathroom and a food-nuke. True, there were some minor problems, like some difficulties with Diana's law. And a gulf of space to transport the stuff across. She knew a few other girls who were fairly peeved with life at the bottom of the ladder. And if Howard knew a few other New Eden farmers . . .

It was a pleasant daydream, anyway. They still had to survive at least until morning, but there was a faint glow in the lights. Dawn was always a lovely time of day. The breeze that picked up from the air recirculation system was always gentle then. Someone had once explained it that it was a question of temperature differential. It was hotter during the light-period and by dawn the differential between air temperature and the cooling and moisture scrubbing loops was less. That took the magic out of it somehow.

The different chickens of this place had started their calling. That was quite magical too. She almost woke Howard to listen to it, but he was sleeping so peacefully. She was getting hungry enough to think of those chickens with some interest.

Unfortunately, breakfast was more pumpkin, washed down with more of this free-running water. It was all very well for Amber to point out that the dilution factor for the goat and any other animal dropping was huge. It was still there, which eroded her desire to look at this place positively down to a nub. There had to be a way around that aspect!

They moved on, upwards, skirting water, avoiding a small herd of animals and later another group with coarse short hair that squeaked at them before plunging into the water. None of this seemed to give Howard pause. "It's in bad repair, but it can be fixed," he'd said at least half a dozen times that morning.

And then on a small spit of sand, they came to something that did halt him in his tracks.

Ashes. A few bits of burned twigs. One still smoldered.

"There are people here." Howard's voice was full of the death of his hopes.

"But there is room for us, surely? I mean, we haven't even seen them," said Lani.

"Maybe. But this is their place, and will always be their place."

The big guy looked absolutely shattered by that spot of ash. Johnny Bhangella didn't see it the same way. It did away with one of his worst worries. Food. The Men's Liberation Army had always survived by eating food gathered from the plants of the upper corridors, by stealing from the women, and, principally, from "donations" from sympathizers. If they didn't give willingly, they would under pressure. He was within reach of two automatic shotguns, and a pistol. Power beyond the dreams of the MLA. If there were people here, well, their men could be pressured the same way. This place was wild enough to lose an army in.

To Howard and Lani, the fire seemed to spell disappointment. Kretz puzzled over that, especially the young female's reaction. Then it came to him. She was looking for a mating territory!

He decided that Miran were much more sensitive to behavioral cues than humans. He'd noticed the way she was looking at Howard, even if Howard hadn't. Her posture changed subtly when she addressed him, and, if Kretz was any judge, her tone. The food Amber had made for him—a little odd to think of eating a cell culture of himself—was plainly helping his own metabolism. He was thinking about sex again. That was more like a normal Miranese male. Females only thought about it—and nothing else—when they were in heat. Popular belief held that that was how they managed to get work done . . . unlike most males, who had half their brain otherwise occupied all the time. The other popular theory was that they'd gotten it out of their systems by the time they changed.

Kretz found himself now thinking about sex with aliens, even though the fire ash spelled danger to him. To Miran a relationship with another male was perfectly normal. One way or the other, it was an exploration of a possible future, and recreational too. Kretz wondered how the little male would feel if he told him he looked appealing? Judging by Howard, male humans did not make these approaches. It was all very confusing and frustrating. He must ask Howard what the polite way to seduce a human was.

That distracted him from studying the undergrowth.

And that would possibly have saved Howard from a little arrow in his shoulder.

Lani shot in the direction of the trees. Maybe she'd seen something. She was rewarded by a scream. She didn't follow it up, as Kretz and then Amber did. The young female caught the swaying Howard and did her best to stop him falling. As a result the two crashed down together into a patch of creepers.

Amber had never fired a weapon before, and nothing had prepared her for the reality of it. Her shots were not of much use, unless you counted blowing the top off a tree. Kretz might have been more accurate, but she didn't wait to see. Lani was yelling for help. Howard lay loglike. Lani held a little arrow in her hand.

"It barely cut him! He can't be dead."

If he wasn't already, he was going to be pretty soon, if Amber was any judge. She opened the pack he'd fashioned from her spacebag, spread out the medical kit, and gave the anti-shock-cortico steroid injection with shaking hands. Then she put the little med-diagnostics unit onto his arm. It was useful for viruses and bacteria, running blood analysis. She didn't know if it would be in the least useful for this kind of injury.

"It must be poisoned. Just keep away from it," she said, pointing to the arrow.

"I'll kill the son of a bitch. I hit him." Lani turned and stood up in one fluid movement, and ran into the brush. She emerged moments later, dragging a bleeding man. She hauled him up to Howard, grabbed the arrow and held to his face. "I need an antidote, asshole, or I'll shove this down your throat."

The plainly terrified man said something incomprehensible. Lani slapped him. "Speak English, you son of a bitch."

"It's possible that he can't," said Amber, staring at the small readout screen on the med-diagnostics unit. "Induces paralysis of heart muscle, and stops nerve function. Heart massage time, Lani. The med-diagnostics is administering countertreatment. It says standby for CPR *now*. His heart hasn't stopped yet."

"Kretz," snapped Lani, taking up position. "Shoot this bastard if he tries to run."

For the next ten minutes they worked on Howard. Amber watched the med-diagnostic anxiously.

It bleeped suddenly.

"Dear Holy Susan," said Amber. "Stop, Lani."

"He's not dead! I won't let him die!" said Lani desperately. "We go on, damn you!"

Amber patted her shoulder. "He's breathing and his heart is beating on its own, Lani."

Amber almost needed the service of the little med-diagnostics unit herself. The hug nearly cracked her ribs. Tears were streaming down the young woman's face. "He's too big and dumb to die," she said gruffly.

"Yep. The heartbeat's strengthening slowly. But I don't know what other damage may have been done, Lani. Fortunately—by what the diagnostic unit is saying—the poison must be something like what is used for surgical operations. Med-diagnostics thinks we must have botched the dose! It's giving us a stern warning!" The laughter was like heady wine.

"I suppose I'd better deal with the new perp," said Lani. "I'd rather sit here and watch Howard, but he might try something with you."

Amber was intensely grateful not to have to deal with the man. "Just be careful, Lani."

"Trust me. He's not getting any of that muck into me. I'm just not sure whether I should shoot him or patch him up and keep him as a hostage too. But this one does not come with us to the next place!"

Amber was in no mood to be merciful either. "See how badly hurt he is."

From the moment he'd seen the strangers in their strange clothes, Dandanidi-ti-dala-po-rado had known that his life, having been complicated, had got worse beyond his most lurid imaginings. He was a good hunter. By uThani standards, too good. Too good to be unmarried anyway. It was fun being chased by several women, but sometimes the consequences of letting more than one catch you . . .

Caught up with you. Especially if your name meant *hunter-whose-balls-are-bigger-than-his-brains*. So he'd gone off on a hunting trip, a long hunting trip. The longer the better, right now.

And instead of getting him out of trouble, it had brought him this.

He'd known what his duty was the moment he'd seen the strangers.

Kill them.

So he'd put an arrow in the back of the scary looking one. He did not miss. Not at this sort of range. Not a target in those bright colors.

The target had winced slightly, and kept right on walking. So Dandani put another arrow in him.

He still kept on walking.

Dandani was really, really scared now. One of those arrows had enough vine-poison on to drop a jaguar. He lost his head and shot the big man in front.

He'd fallen, all right.

And somehow that woman had shot him. The stories told about those weapons. "Guns," they were called. What they never told you was just how painful it was and how much of shock it gave you. Or how loud and sudden it was.

He knew that now. And how stupid a hunter could be to choose a hide too thick to run from. He had chosen it with care. The *carpincho* were very spooky these days. There were too few of them to shoot easily any more.

Dandani was used to women wanting to hit him. He just wasn't used to one that could do it with such ease. If this was what the women were like, what would the man who could take two doses of poison and still walk do to you?

She spoke one of tongues of the enemies-of-the-people. He wasn't supposed to know any, but with Nama-ti-spaniti-goro-y-timi as his hunting companion and childhood friend, he'd learned a few words. Enough to know that he was very close to death, even if her tone of voice hadn't told him that.

Lani didn't explain to Amber that chances were that it wouldn't matter how badly hurt he was. She needed something to hit back at after her fright. And if the new perp moved a muscle wrong it was going to be him that got whacked.

Her first act was to rip the wicker arrow-quiver off his shoulders. "I'll have that." He was a stocky man, brown-faced and brown-skinned, smaller than Howard—almost anyone was, of course. But slightly bigger than she was. Still, it was fair to say that right now he looked frightened out of his wits, and in shock too.

His wound wasn't going to kill him . . . unfortunately. He'd stopped the bleeding with the cloak he had knotted around his neck. She pulled it aside roughly. He'd been lucky. Another few inches left and her instinctive shot would have taken this perp out of this world and into the next without messing around with airlocks.

She went back to the first-aid kit and hauled out some antiseptic and local anesthetic. Then, by training rather than any sense of kindness, she slapped it on the wound before putting a piece of gauze and a dressing over it.

He winced as she tightened the bandage. "Stop that. You nearly killed him." She gestured at Howard. "You're just lucky I didn't kill you. And that's 'yet.' If he dies, you are dead meat."

He answered her with some gabble. All that was recognizable was the hand-gesture. Throwing out your hands is pretty universal.

Howard groaned. It was a very quiet sound, but audible nevertheless. That seemed to frighten the man even more. He gabbled again.

"Shut up," said Lani, and handcuffed him. "Sit down."

He looked blank. She pointed at the ground, and he hastily lay down. Well, that was probably even better. "You," she said to the little runaway male, "go and collect the rest of his kit. He dropped a basket and a sort of big knife up there. Kretz, will you keep watching him?"

She ran back to Howard. His eyes were open. Well, that was a start. His lips moved faintly. She knelt and listened. He was trying to say something. . . . She hugged him fiercely. "At least you can't push me away right now, you big lunk. You're going to be all right. I promise."

His lips moved very slightly. He was trying to smile. Would the poison wear off or had it damaged his nerves forever? If jungle boy talked anything but jungle-gabble, she'd have an answer out of him. But by the looks of it, he thought Howard ought to be dead.

Amber got up and smiled at her. "His heartbeat is reasonably strong, and he's breathing. Now that that's over, can I go and be sick?"

"You were just wonderful." Lani felt the tears prick in her eyes. "I'd have lost him without you. I'm sorry I moaned about the weight of that stuff. And I'm sorry that I was catty . . . Jealous, I guess."

"Honey. I don't do men. I thought you knew that. Everyone else in Diana seems to."

Lani blushed fiercely. "Uh. I suppose I was the one who didn't." She was a little uncomfortable. Gay-bashing was . . . sort of force standard. Someone who was a fake man was really a weak sister . . . She tried hard to remember if she'd made any comments.

"So now can I go and be sick?" asked Amber, with a slightly impish smile.

"Hell, no, you can pick up your shotgun and go and see what happened to that little runaway male. You're too tough to be sick," said Lani with a return smile, stroking the big hand she was holding. "The perp had a basket. Maybe it has coffee in it. I'd kill for coffee— anyone but this idiot, that is."

"I'd kill for a cream donut," Amber said wistfully. "Simply to replace the extra calories I've sweated off in this place, not just because I'm hopelessly addicted to them. Ah. Here he comes."

"Taking his own sweet time as per usual," scowled Lani. "Let's see what's in the basket, Perp."

"My name's Bhangella," he said, smiling his best smile. "John."

He still made her flesh crawl. She grabbed the basket. It had a variety of plant-fruits in it, none of which she recognized, three dead chickens and some mysterious smelly dry stuff. A little bow and a piece of dry punk, several lengths of line, some with bone hooks on the end. All in all, what someone who was out hunting and gathering might have with them. "The knife. Where is it?" she said flatly.

Sullenly, he dug it out of the back of his tutu top. It must have barely fitted. "I'm the only one who hasn't got a weapon."

"Good. Let's keep it that way."

"But there are dangerous things here," he said, not parting with it.

"You included," she said, snatching it out of his hand.

"You don't trust me."

"Nope."

"I didn't do anything to you," he protested.

"You were going to. And that's enough for me. You don't have to stay here. You can walk off on your own right now. I won't miss you." That, she thought to herself, was very true.

He shut up and went and sat down in the shade. Lani went back to the other prisoner. He'd gotten over some of his shock and was now just looking sullen and angry. How the hell could she communicate with him? As far as he knew they were going to kill him or enslave him, whereas, if Howard was going to be all right, she'd just as soon kick his butt, hard, smash his arrows and send him about his business. But she really didn't need him calling all his friends and having all of them shoot at them. Maybe Howard had been right. If they'd stuck with the space suits . . .

She had to tell the suspicious-faced prisoner, somehow, that they were just passing through and meant him no harm. She started by giving him the basket. He blinked uncomprehendingly at it. She had to press it into his hand. He gabbled at her again. And held it out to her. Pointed with his eyes at the cuffs.

She shook her head. Pointed at Howard.

He shrugged. Put the basket down. Held out his hands, palms up. And then indicated with a finger drawn across the throat. Eyes closed.

She shook her head, and as if to confirm what she was saying, Howard groaned again, softly. He stood up and walked toward Howard, plainly incredulous. She stood ready to kill him if he made one false move. He bent over Howard and listened. Slowly, carefully, he took Howard's wrist. Shook his head as felt the pulse. And smiled tentatively at her. Gabble gabble.

Now it was Lani's turn to throw up her hands in a lack of understanding.

So he mimed. Lani could follow that. But how in the hell could they carry Howard? She was the strongest of them, and there was no way that she could manage more than a few yards. Howard was just too big.

He did some more miming. Cutting something? He pointed at some saplings, and she had it. A stretcher. On sudden impulse she handed him his overgrown cheese-cutter and pointed at the saplings. After watching him make two ineffectual strokes she came over to him and, scowling, unlocked the cuffs. She stepped back and stood watching him, one hand on the pistol-butt. She saw that Kretz had taken a flanking position too, and had the automatic shotgun at the ready. But all the new perp did was cut two thick saplings, and trim them into poles. He put the overgrown knife down, untied the cloak from around his neck, and started tying the corners to a pole. She came to join him, tying opposite corners.

He slowly picked up the knife again when they'd done. Reversed his grip on it, taking it by the blade, and offered it back to her.

Lani narrowed her eyes. Thought hard. Took it, reversed it, and handed it back to him.

It was his turn to look thoughtful. He nodded, took it and tucked it into his sash. Parole offered . . . and accepted.

They walked back to Howard with the makeshift stretcher. "You let *him* have that knife," complained Bhangella.

"Yep. And I'll let him keep it just as long as he behaves himself," she said. If he was faking it, best that he got the message. "He's going to be carrying the stretcher in front of me. If he wants to try his knife against my gun, he'll die. But he might just need it here. Now fetch that basket of his for him while we try to get Howard onto the stretcher. I hope it'll hold him."

The material creaked and cracked. But it did hold. Still, even the five of them weren't going to be able to carry Howard very far. He was a heavy lump. And Lani wasn't too sure where they were trying to carry him to. But the man she'd winged did have ideas on that, apparently. He pointed with his injured arm. They walked along the stream-path until it widened out. There was the usual small lake . . . and a four-log raft.

So that was how they got around here. The local stopped, looked around very carefully and then walked them into the water until they could off-load Howard onto the raft.

"It's not as good as a scoot, but it beats walking, hands down," said Lani to Kretz, as she sat next to Howard, holding his hand.

Kretz nodded. "It is better than walking hands up too. When I first came to human habitats, we assumed that it was a greeting. Walking like that is very tiring for a nonarboreal species. Is Howard going to recover?"

"I wish I knew. I wish I knew where we were going, too," said Lani.

On the bank, two of the brown-furred creatures they'd seen earlier appeared in a clearing. By mime the local explained that that was what he'd been hunting. "Do you want me to shoot it?" asked Lani . . . and then played it again in mime. It was hard to tell if he got it, but when she mimicked shooting it with a bow, and pointed at herself, he nodded.

Skeptically.

That was enough for her. Besides, it might just give him a message.

"Lend me the shotgun for a moment, Amber."

She took careful aim. No point in showing off . . . and failing.

Once they'd hauled their local guide back onto the raft, they poled to the edge of the water, and collected the dead creature. The man was all smiles now—and very respectful.

A little while later, Howard managed to tilt his head over and be sick. Never had someone throwing up looked so good to Lani. He'd moved to do it.

They rounded a bend and there were huts. Well, roofs. Roofs that went down to the ground without any walls.

And a fire. All of Lani's instincts from her training said "Put it out," but the locals didn't seem much worried.

They were very worried about the strangers, though. There were an awful lot of bowmen hiding behind those odd wall-less dead grass roofs. Their guide's gabble didn't do much to relax them. But an old man came out of one of the huts and spoke a string of slightly different sounding gibberish.

Lani looked at Amber. They both shrugged. Howard tried to look at the man.

The old man spoke again. "You are spikking Engrish?"

"Yes."

"I am spikker-for-uThani. You sign paper. This is our place for always. You not welcome. Go."

"We don't want to stay. We want to go." Amber pointed to Howard. "He is hurt and needs help. Help us and then are very happy to go and never come back. We do not want your place."

The local who had shot Howard gabbled to the old man.

"What's he saying?"

"He says not possible. Man dead. Shot with poison for *carpincho*. Man not dead. Therefore: not man. Demon," explained the old man. He seemed to find demons more acceptable. "Healer come look," he said. "Then you go. Never come back or we kill. Our place."

Amber wrinkled her nose at him. "Trust me, old boy. I can't wait to get to the airlock, even though I don't know how I will face what lies beyond it. Maybe, I'll just sit there and rot, but at least it'll be clean and dry."

The strangest thing about all of this, thought Howard, as the chanting and drumming rang in his ears, was that he remembered all of it, perfectly. He could hear Lani talking. He just couldn't answer her. Or move. Things had all gone a little dim, for a while, after he'd been shot.

"This is just mumbo-jumbo rubbish," said Amber. "A waste of time. Either we take him back to the Matriarchy, and take what they hand out, or we try to find help farther on."

Howard couldn't tell her how much he agreed with her. This was not just mumbo jumbo, but pagan mumbo jumbo—and he was determined not feel any better because of it. Even if he did.

"We'll try this first," said Lani, firmly. "It's their damn poison. The woman seemed to have some idea of what was wrong."

Howard could tell her what was wrong. His muscles didn't want to work. He was used to being strong. Right now he felt like a weak little newborn.

"He's crying," said Lani. "Have we got anything for pain, Amber?"

Her distress was so palpable that somehow he made the effort. Bigger muscles were responding a little . . . He could lift his legs. It was finer movements like smiling and talking that were impossible. He managed to make a noise. He'd tried earlier when he'd been sure he was dying. Telling her then that he did love her seemed the right thing to do, even if she hadn't been able to hear him. She knelt over him, intent, listening. Unfortunately, talking was out. So was smiling reassuringly. He managed to shake his head.

"What are you trying to say, Howard? Do you need water or something?"

Now that she mentioned it, he was devilishly thirsty and his mouth tasted vile. He nodded.

Lani on a mission to get water became the queen of mime. And a few moments later he was lifted and given a trickle of fluid.

It very nearly killed him. His swallowing reflex was still not right. And the stuff they gave him . . . burned.

"It's not water, Lani," said Amber, sniffing the gourd, as Lani patted his back. Howard saw how Amber lifted it to taste it, but the healer-woman pushed it away from her mouth. Pointed at Howard. Not more!

More. And this time at least none of it went into his lungs. But it, or the poison, was making him feel woozy. Very woozy. With interesting visions . . .

Amber was doing her best to be soothing. "Med-diagnostics says his pulse has strengthened and slowed. His color is better too, Lani."

"Yeah. I suppose so, but did they have to feed him that stuff? I thought she was giving him water. It's alcohol and some drug—that crushed-up seed she showed us. From what I can work out it's some kind of hallucinogen."

She scowled. "It's given him a hell of an erection."

"Well, that's one muscle that's working, Lani."

Amber put a hand on her shoulder. Lani fought off an irrational desire to shrug it off. By now she'd come to accept that most of the stories about gay women were ignorant BS, but it took a while to shake the reaction completely. "I don't know how best to say this so I guess I should just say it. We don't know what damage that poison did. He could never recover. Or he could be brain damaged. He stopped breathing."

Lani felt her nails cutting into her palms. "I know. But I've got to try. Thanks. You've been great and I've been a bitch. A stupid bitch, at that."

"We both made judgment mistakes, I guess."

"Yeah. Look, sorry," said Lani, awkwardly.

The little perp—Bhangella—came into the long, thatched hut. "They're calling us to eat," he said.

"I can't leave Howard here." She wasn't leaving him unwatched, that was for sure.

Amber stood up. "I'll get some help to carry him out there with us."

A few minutes later, Lani was wishing desperately that they'd left Howard where he was and stayed to sit vigil over him. They wouldn't have had to sit here around the fire and eat pieces of not very well charred animal. The cooked roots and vegetables were one thing, but meat that had squealed when she shot it?

By the looks of her, Amber wasn't any happier about it. "We have to look like we're enjoying it," said Amber, *sotto voce*.

"Next time I ask to borrow your shotgun, see that you shove it up . . . Don't give it to me," said Lani, looking warily at the "feast."

"I can see the appeal of vat-protein again. I never thought I wanted to see another vat," said Amber. She drank some of the stuff in the gourd. "Holy Susan. That's . . . strong. Enough of that stuff and you won't care that you're eating half raw dead meat. Here, have some."

Lani did. And some more. Whatever it was, it loosened the tongue a bit. A little later, having eaten some of the meat without gagging too much, she said "I've been meaning to ask you . . . "

"Ask. Whatever that stuff is, I don't think I should drink any more of it."

"Why did you do this? I mean, come with us. Uh. You had everything."

"Except a life," said Amber, pulling a face. "The old story I suppose. I broke up with my girlfriend. After five years. She works . . . worked with me. No way I could avoid seeing her every day, and nowhere else that either of us could work. Kretz came along and, well, I could get out of there. Really get out there. Right out of the whole world. I'd . . . I'd been thinking of taking myself out of it completely before. You can only put on a brave face for just so long." She laughed. "I suppose that whatever else comes out of this I haven't really thought about Jean for days."

"There have to be easier cures, though."

Amber shrugged. "Maybe. Maybe not. We never really did develop a cure for broken hearts. At least not a cure that leaves no scar tissue to stop the thing working properly."

"Why isn't it simple?" asked Lani, feeling as if she was going to burst into tears.

"Yeah. I thought we weren't going to drink any more of this stuff?" said Amber, who just had.

Lani looked blurrily at the gourd. "I can't drink any more. I finished it. If this is what they gave Howard no wonder he's unconscious."

"You know I read somewhere that before the Slow-train left, before Diana, that all men regarded women as inflatable sex dolls that could cook and clean house."

Lani blinked owlishly at her. "I had an inflatable mattress once."

"So?" said Amber, looking almost equally owlish.

"So they must have needed a lot of puncture repair kits," said Lani after deep cogitation. She looked at Howard. "I'd have less problems with an inflatable man."

Amber agreed. "Or me with an inflatable woman, but they'd be less fun."

"We could get a bulk order of puncture kits."

"And comp-installed 'cause misery' units, so they'd feel real."

"And buy a dishwasher."

It seemed very funny at the time.

Dandani judged that Chief Fripara-wa-reepal was a worried man. Too worried to be thinking too much about what his youngest daughter had said about a hunter called Dandani. "I put not one, but two arrows in him, Chief. He should be dead. But the other one may not be dead, but he's pretty sick," he explained.

"But he's getting better," said the chief sourly. "I think we should change your name to 'hunter-who-could-not-hit-a-jaguar-from-the-inside.' I think you saw women and shot skew."

He wasn't serious. Except maybe about the women. However, Dandani knew it was obligatory to look affronted. "I always hit what I aim at."

"With arrows for small birds," said the chief. "Anyway, we need to talk about what we do now, not your lousy marksmanship."

"We do what uThani always do," said he-who-talks-to-strangers. "We behave like good little ignorant savages. 'We don't understand what you say,' while we listen and learn."

"And then we cut their throats and hope more don't come looking," said the chief. He sighed. "But maybe their throats don't cut any easier than they poison, old man. Dandani fools around with too many women, but he doesn't miss."

He-who-talks-to-strangers shook his head. "We don't cut their throats. We don't let them go home either. We see if they can solve our other problem."

"Hmm. It's nine warriors so far. Who are we going to send?"

"Him." He-who-talks-to-strangers-pointed at Dandani. "And Nama-ti-spaniti-goro-y-timi."

"Good," said the chief. "Even if they get killed, it will get him away from my youngest daughter."

So he hadn't been that distracted, Dandani thought. But like a good uThani he misled. It was how the small tribe had survived.

Kretz was increasingly convinced that Miran in general were better observers of behavior than humans. Maybe it came of having to survive tempers at sex-changeover. Sitting on the far side of the circle he'd noticed that the local humans took tiny sips from the gourd they passed around. By the time he tried to warn the others it was too late. Well, for the females, anyway. The little male appeared to be behaving with circumspection.

Their spokesman came and sat down next to him. "So, demon," he said conversationally, "why does the other demon try look like people and you don't? Him better demon?"

Transcomp had given Kretz a number of approximations on "demon." None of them had been flattering. Obviously it was one of those words that depended on your viewpoint. He thought about his reply, carefully. "If I change my appearance too much, I cannot talk across the distances to all the other demons, and they will have to come and look for us. One of us had look as we do."

"Hmm. Teeth very small for Jaguar-demon," said the speaker.

How did you answer that? He did recall the picture Amber had showed them. Best to head off the question with another. "How come you speak the language of hu—the women."

The speaker pulled a face. "One man learn. In case outsiders come back. Clever. O-Mike Computer teach." He looked at the two women, lolling against each other. Giggling. "Be very sick tomorrow," he said clinically.

Interesting. So there was some kind of live computer network, even in this primitive environment. Well, miniaturization could take computing power and robots to the microscopic. Big machines were still more efficient for doing tasks of scale, a fact the miniaturization lobby eventually learned.

The speaker shifted his attention to the little human male. "You demon's child?" He said conversationally. "Which one your mother?"

## 27

There is a life zone around every sun. Around some suns
it is huge, and lasts for billions of years. So what sort of
lease do you think a settler needs? What do you think we
can do if anyone breaches the agreement?
—Johnson Defarge, Slowtrain Legal committee, SysGov.

Bhangella took the automatic shotgun from the hand of
the sleeping woman, before she was carried to the boats.
Kretz made no move to stop him. It seemed wiser that
they were all armed.

The hollowed-log boats slid through the water, close,
but never too close to the overhanging trees. Inside them
Howard and the two women slept, oblivious to the
brightly colored fliers that darted between the branches,

or the troops of reddish furred creatures that scattered, roaring, swinging through the tree-tops. Kretz watched all this, and attempted to fathom out if there was any evil motive on the part of their hosts. He couldn't see one.

It was a long journey, involving many portages, but eventually the locals hauled up the boats and lifted out the two women. A hundred paces away you could just see the airlock door.

Lani woke as they put her down. She groaned, blinked, and said: "Where are we?"

"At the airlock," explained Kretz.

She tried to sit up, but plainly found the exercise too much. "Oh, Holy Susan, let me sleep again." She collapsed.

Kretz waved at the departing canoes. His study of human behavior seemed to indicate that it was an innocuous gesture. Hardly a reason for the small male human to be pointing a weapon at his head. "What is wrong?" he asked puzzled and suddenly afraid.

"You are. Put the gun down slowly."

Kretz complied. "But what are you doing?"

"Taking over for the Men's Liberation Army. Lie down on your stomach, freak."

Kretz found himself being tied up and then gagged.

"I guess I'll just deal with the scientist before I get to the cop. The bitch is lying on her gun," said the small male. "By what those savages said, they should be waking up soon."

Moments later, Kretz heard a brief scream.

The scream pierced Lani's uneasy sleep. She hadn't meant to sleep! Had she been poisoned? It felt like the mother of all hangovers. Never—not even after the force academy graduation—had she felt like this. She tried to get up. It was a question of whether she threw up or stood up.

Standing up won. Narrowly. But she only remained standing by holding onto the vegetation.

The adrenaline rush that came from realizing that she had a shotgun pointed at her helped. But not even that would get across the ten yards between her and the perp. It wasn't going to be easy to draw and fire, either.

Then she realized she wasn't even going to have that opportunity. Now he wasn't pointing the shotgun at her. He was pointing it at Howard.

"The gun, cop," he said. "Take it out of your belt with your left hand and throw it down."

She looked at the shotgun, evaluating her chances. They weren't good and she knew it.

"You've got to the count of three. I'll blow him away if you don't cooperate."

She did. Alive he had a chance. Dead, none. You learned after dealing with many perps and situations just which ones were for real. Who meant it when they threatened. This one wanted the chance. The weapon landed on the floor a foot or two from Howard. His eyes were open, she noticed. She hadn't even had a chance to ask how he was doing. What the hell had happened? How had they arrived here? All she remembered was that burned dead animal and having to eat it. The thought was too much for her. She leaned over and started being sick. And then fell to her knees and did some more of the same.

At least that stopped the perp from shooting her. He watched, grinning nastily.

"They said you'd feel like death when you woke up," he said with malicious glee. "You drank more than ten people do normally, you and that other bitch. Come on. There is nothing left inside you now. I need you to tie her up."

She managed to get up. She felt weak and drained but at least that muck was out of her. He pointed to where Amber lay holding her head. She wasn't just hungover. She was bleeding.

"I need to see to that," she said.

"Let her bleed," said the perp callously. "It's not that serious, and it's her own fault. Tie her up. Here." He tossed some cords at her. She recognized them as being from the basket of the local who shot Howard. She knelt next to Amber.

"Do a proper job. I'll check it and it'll be worse for both of you, if you don't," said the little creep.

So she did. And tried to follow force training: keep them talking. Talking people don't act. "What are you going to do, Perp, uh, Bhangella? The locals will kill you."

He laughed. "Not likely. They're not getting close enough to put any arrows into me. They scare easy. This place is wide open for us. The Men's Liberation Army is gonna have a hideout that the women will never find, and anyway you can't do nothin'. We'll take this lot's women. Shoot any men that won't join us."

"You're crazy. They'll shoot you full of those little arrows. They nearly killed Howard."

"Yeah," said the Perp, nastily. "And now they don't believe that the poison works on us. And you better believe they know how well shotguns kill. They're good and scared, thanks to you. And we know where they live. Now shut up, or I'll blow a foot off you. You'll still be good for what I plan to use you for. Take those handcuffs from your belt and put them on your own wrists. Then throw the keys down and back off, and lie down next to the others. I'm going to tie your feet together."

Howard's muscles still felt as if they belonged to some far smaller, weaker person. But he couldn't just lie there. John Bhangella had ignored him, assuming that he was still unable to move. Whether he was capable of wrestling the shotgun from the small man was another matter. But he definitely could move. And Lani's weapon still lay on the ground a few yards off. He'd refused to let her teach him, but he'd learned all the same, by watching. Safety catch. Squeeze the trigger . . .

He pulled himself out of the stretcher, slowly. Bhangella was busy rifling through the bags. The gun lay on the ground, temporarily forgotten. He edged himself closer. He actually felt a little better once he was moving.

After an eternity, he reached it. Felt the weight of it in his hand. He pushed the safety catch over.

Now . . . could he use it? To kill a man was a sin. Yet, in inexpert hands, this was a much less deadly weapon than the one which Bhangella had in his hand. If Bhangella put it down, Howard could threaten him.

It wasn't going to work like that.

The small man walked over to Kretz and put the shotgun under his chin.

"Leave him be," said Howard. "He's done nothing to you."

Bhangella looked at Howard. "So you're back with us. You're talking a little oddly," he said matter-of-factly, swinging the shotgun to cover Howard instead.

"My muscles aren't quite right. I feel very weak. Leave Kretz. As I said, he has done you no harm. If you want to blame anyone, blame me."

"You? I wouldn't give you that much credit." The muzzle of the shotgun had dipped, as Bhangella realized that there was no immediate danger from his victim.

"We've all helped to keep you alive," said Howard carefully. "Perhaps you resent the way Lani treated you . . ."

"Silly bitch," said the small man disdainfully. He pointed the shotgun vaguely at her. "She let you stop her. And she didn't kill the guy who shot you. I'm gonna have fun teaching her some manners."

Howard took a deep breath, and kept calm, resolutely. The man was baiting him, enjoying making his victim suffer. He also seemed quite serious about it all. So Howard said, calmly, "You asked me once what a man had to do, if he turned the other cheek and the offender kicked him in the teeth."

Bhangella smiled nastily. "Yeah, I remember that, you stupid big soft dick. You never did answer it. You've got a last chance before I shoot the alien and you. I thought it over. I don't need him and I'm pretty sure I don't need you." The gun barrel was now pointed somewhere between them.

"I've thought about turning the other cheek again," said Howard. "The Brethren believe that all people have a better nature to appeal to. But I have decided it is not always possible to reach it."

He raised Lani's pistol and shot Bhangella.

As Bhangella crumpled, Howard said sadly, "This is not the right answer, but it is the best one I could think of."

The Men's Liberation Army captain lay on the ground. He was obviously dying. Howard stood up, as fast as he could, despite protesting muscles. He walked over and picked up the automatic shotgun Bhangella had dropped. "May God have mercy on your soul," he said. "And forgive me, Lord. I did what I believed I had to do."

Howard shot him again, between the eyes. The Brethren killed livestock. They killed them as mercifully and quickly as possible. Who was he to deny even a man like this, what he'd give to a hog?

Whether it was the right answer or not, Howard didn't know. But a man had to make decisions sometimes, and leave the final judgment of his deeds to a higher authority. He staggered across to Kretz and the bound women.

Lani held up the cuffs. "He's got the keys on a thong around his neck." She looked at his pale face. "Do my feet and I'll get them."

He touched her cheek, gently. She'd held his hand, talked to him through the paralysis and through the fear. "I am strong enough."

"You're stronger than I ever guessed. And I don't just mean in muscles."

Howard walked back to the corpse. Bhangella looked very small, now. Howard took the thong off his neck. He carefully ignored the condition of the dead man's face.

He went back and freed Lani, and then the others. "They're still watching us," he said quietly.

"Who? The locals?" She took the pistol he gave her. Then took out the magazine and reloaded it from the pouch on her belt. Clicked it back in—and handed it to Howard. "I think you'd better keep it."

"No, thank you." He took a deep breath. Even that hurt. He turned to the undergrowth. "It's time for us to talk," he said loudly. "What do you want?"

There was a silence. Then someone came out of the bushes. Just one person. Howard was certain there were others. The local held up an empty hand. "No weapon," he said.

Howard held up his empty hands. "And no weapons in my hands, either."

Lani looked at the local, suspiciously, with narrowed eyes. "I thought only one of you spoke any English?"

The local shrugged. "Others of us learn."

"But don't tell the foreigners," said Amber, holding a gauze pad against her head wound. "He was sitting next to us when we drank that stuff, Lani."

"You strong woman. No uThani drink half so much," he said admiringly.

Amber cocked her head on one side. "Pretend you don't speak the language. Ply the visitors with strong, drugged liquor and listen to what they say between themselves?"

He nodded.

"So . . . what do you want?" asked Howard, sticking to the point.

"We make sure you not go. You bring others. We take you to the opposite airlock," said the local with a disarming smile.

"Which is actually where we wanted to go," said Amber. "So why didn't you just kill us?"

The man pointed at Howard. "He did not die. Hunter shoot him too." He pointed at Kretz. "He did not even get sick."

"My suit," explained Kretz, "is quite tough. I probably didn't notice. Besides I am not sure how it would affect my metabolism."

"So . . . we're demons you can't kill. Accept it," said Lani.

"We really don't want your land," said Howard calmly. "I promise."

"But we want yours," said the uThani, smiling cheerfully. "Not enough here for us any more. Fights in subclans over place. So our chief say: follow. Find. See. Also get iron things. Knives and guns. We know about guns."

"But . . . How many of you are there, here? We never saw anyone."

"Need a lot of jungle to hunt and to gather. Comp say one hundred hectare for one. Too many persons. Food short. Now we fish a lot. But there still too many of our people. We need place. We send others to airlock. They have not come back." He pointed to the group. "You know how to go to another place."

"So how come you are telling us this?" asked Lani.

The uThani shrugged and smiled slightly. "Because chief could not tell me how to look through the door. And here we can still kill you. Or try."

"It makes a lot more sense than a sudden outbreak of truthfulness," said Lani sourly.

Howard bowed his head. "Let us go and talk among ourselves."

"Without any help from your long ears," said Lani.

The coffee-skinned uThani gave a flash of sudden white teeth, and put his fingers in his ears.

The four of them walked off into a clear area.

"We cannot do this," said Howard, his face stiff. "They want to make war."

Amber held up her hand. "Look. First, not everything here is what it seems at all. One of the things I did find out on the portable encyclopedia—once I got the tribe name—is that the uThani were a tiny Colombian tribe. They were something of a *cause célèbre* when they were discovered—only after their valley was being flooded for a hydroelectric scheme. They were barely two hundred odd members strong. They claimed never to have seen outsiders, which was called into doubt over some steel tools. Anyway—there has been intervention here. Their gene pool was too small to start with for them to have survived without that intervention. They plainly talk to this 'comp.' Beside any of these Conquistador dreams they may have—which are wildly impractical given the number of suits available in the airlocks—within the next hundred years they're going to be on their own, positioned around a sun, with the potential of a million space-habitats—or extinction. So what do we do? I think we bite the bullet and start teaching them. And the best way we can do that is take at least one of them and show him."

"Yeah? So why hasn't this 'comp' helped them with this airlock dream?" asked Lani. "I'm not saying that I think we shouldn't do this, just that it still smells a bit."

"Maybe 'comp' wants them to stay primitive," said Amber slowly. "To keep them in a conservation state, as Kretz suggested. In the time elapsed they could have moved from primitive to machine culture, if it and they wanted to change."

That obviously got through to Lani. "What the hell. I don't like the idea of a machine keeping them eating burned meat. If that's the case . . . Let's take the country boy to the bright lights. Who knows, we might want to turn this lot loose on the next lot."

"It wouldn't work," said Amber. "Too few suits."

"Besides, it would be immoral," said Howard. "After all, Kretz wishes to get back to warn his people of incipient invasion by evildoers himself."

Lani lifted her eyebrows at him. "Even if the next lot are like the guys that attacked Kretz and his friends? I think that would be pretty fair."

"They do need help, Howard," said Amber.

Now that Howard had seen space, seen technology, and was beginning to understand what Kretz had said to him about this being an enormous colony-ship, a ship that was beginning to need repair, he could see that also. "It is our bounden duty to try to help those less fortunate than ourselves. But not to attack others. And by that token the people of New Eden will need help soon too."

"You might say that they are training you for the job," said Amber.

Howard pursed his lips. Shook his head. "I don't think I could go back. But yes. I agree."

"Well, that's all of us," said Lani, practically. "Unless Kretz has some objection, or wants to ask something?"

Kretz nodded. "Yes. Why does one bite this bullet? Is it edible? And which bright lights?"


"Very well. We have conferred. We will take one of your people with us."

"You will need to leave a hostage," said the uThani warrior. "They will be well treated." He obviously saw the hesitation. "Eat meat nearly every day."

"That does it. I'm *not* staying," said Amber firmly.

"Obviously Kretz needs to go. I don't think I can stay," said Lani, equally firmly. "Howard needs a proper medical check . . . and I won't stay without him." She paused, looking thoughtful. "Why do you want a hostage?"

"To make sure that you do not kill me."

Lani gave him a wry smile. "We will need to cross your land to go back home. Your friends can stop us if we don't bring you back on our return. You don't need a hostage and we need all of us to succeed in crossing."

He looked thoughtful. "Let me confer."

He melted back into the bushes.

He returned a little later. With a familiar face—the local who had shot Howard. "We say yes. If you take two of us."

"Yeah, but why him?" asked Lani.

The local translator grinned. "He says you are very much of a woman. He wishes to marry you."

When she stared at him, open-mouthed, he added. "He is good hunter. Shoot much meat."

"If I'm going to teach you anything, I need names," said Lani.

So they introduced themselves. "Me Nama-ti-spaniti-goro-y-timi. Him Dandanidi-ti-dala-po-rado. Names very important thing to us," explained the translator. "Mine means *he-who-stalks-jaguar-without-bow-and-falls-over-root.*"

"They're certainly a very long thing," Lani said. "Anyway, I refuse to bend my tongue around that much of a mouthful. Perp-One and Perp-Two will do for you two."

The hunter looked at the translator. Said something that made the other crack up. The translator turned back to Lani. "Perp-one is good for me. But my friend he say you not call him name that sounds like bad smell. Not respectful for future wife."

"I suppose 'My-Lord-and-Master' would suit him?" said Lani with a dangerous level of sarcasm.

Translator gabbled. His shoulders shook at his friend's reply. A sense of humor was obviously an uThani trait. "He say you too strong a woman for that. Call him Dandani."

"I'll call him 'Uppity,' " she said with a nasty grin. "It's shorter than 'Delusions-of-Grandeur.' "

So Uppity and Perp-one cheerfully continued with their lessons in elementary space safety and the basics of what a vacuum actually was, either in happy unconcern about the meanings of their new titles, or just humoring this woman who could shoot. When it came down it, they were quick learners, and their smiles were quite infectious.

So, according to med-diagnostics, were they.

"You're all next," said Amber. "It appears that population control here is via disease. And Med-diagnostics picked up plasmodium in my blood. First, I don't want anyone getting sick, and second, we don't need to pass our new germs and parasites on to the next bead. I should have thought of it before we came here."

The space-bags were packed—with everything from the strange clothes to the bows and poisoned arrows. And two of the brightly colored flying creatures, recently deceased.

"Do you have to take chickens?" asked Amber, looking dubiously at them.

"Not chickens. Parrots," said Perp-one. "Why you want to put our bows in here?" he asked. "What if we meet dangerous animals or good food?"

"Trust me. You won't meet either. I should let you leave those things out. Hard vacuum would sort them out, PDQ. Now, close up those helmets. And do what you're told and *don't* panic. Breathe slowly and calmly. Decompression sequence is beginning. And I'm just popping a few tranquillizers . . . "

# 28

"We can put in every fail-safe known to man and build in as much computer backup and redundancy as possible. We still won't stop really determined, really stupid humans from wrecking everything. Looking back at history it only takes one ass to destroy millions of lives. Give them a Stalin, a Hitler, a Mugabe or a Pol Pot and they'll destroy their own habitat. That's something we can't engineer out of the system."

—Senator Lin Te Kauni: Transcript of the Debate in the SysGov Upper House on the Slowtrain funding bill.

Outside again, Kretz listened hopefully. He began receiving Selna. She was plainly simply repeat broadcasting. Well, that was a sign of rationality at least, even if her voice was full of fear.

"—has been large explosion from the alien habitat. Enough to rock the ship. Things have been violently thrown around here, but the electromagnets held. I do not know what they are doing. I am making preparations as best I can to lift the ship at any sign of attack. I repeat, Kretz or Abret, there has been . . . "

It was worrying enough to have distracted him from another, nearer alarm. The rebreather system was bleeping at him. He'd just started using his reserve.

Abret was trying to do what he knew he should have done a long time ago—learn the language of his captors. His jailors were less cooperative than they'd been with Derfel, of course. He was, apparently, an evil usurper. Only the one would speak to him at all, and he appeared to hate his prisoner. Abret was also wondering whether the alien food would kill him before hormonal changes did.

And, of course, he was devoting a great deal of time to thinking about escape. It wouldn't be easy. The bars were rusted, but it was a very thin layer of rust. That must have been a very good corrosion resistant alloy that they'd used many hundreds of years back. Selna's repeat broadcast was a bit more rational—sudden fear had plainly forced her back to her senses. Abret hoped that it would last, but her attempt to fly the ship would probably be disastrous. She had neither the engineering nor the navigational skills it would need.

He'd given some thought to this explosion, and the violent throwing things about. The only thing that he could think of that could possibly do something like that would be some kind of explosive decompression.

# 29

"There is really no place for danger-sports in a modern society. We cannot allow people to willfully risk their lives for no gain whatsoever."

> —Senator Achmed Selbourne, on the passage of the law outlawing participation in non-computer-override vehicular racing, paragliding, rock-climbing and skydiving.

The two uThani had been remarkably unperturbed, out in space. They'd even helped Howard guide Amber along and across.

When repressurization was complete, and their helmets were undogged again, Lani said:. "I'm impressed. You were very calm."

Perp-One sat down. "That, strong woman, is because anything that bad has to be a dream." His voice was shaking a little.

"Well, another successful crossing," said Howard, tiredly. "Just one more, Kretz."

The alien shook his head. "The bad news is that my suit's rebreather system's indicators say I have insufficient air for another crossing. And I have heard strange things happening at my spacecraft."

They stood there, silenced by this matter-of-fact announcement. "So what do we do now?" asked Lani, finally.

"What can we do, except to go on into the habitat?" said the alien. "We cannot sit here in the airlock forever. Perhaps I can somehow be fitted into a human suit."

He didn't sound very optimistic.

"Is not as heavy as home," said Perp-One, putting into words what Howard had felt, but was not sure if was just light-headedness. The air felt heavy, though, a little like breathing soup.

"It actually looked bigger than the last one from outside," said Lani. "Is that possible?"

Amber looked doubtful. "It could be. The real cost apparently wasn't sheer size but fitting the insides."

"Well," said Howard, "bigger or not, whatever lies inside this bubble surely can't be as hard to cross as the watery jungle. Shall we go?"

Everyone nodded. Howard noticed that the two uThanis' knuckles were white on their bows.

The door swung open, to show Howard just how wrong he could be. They looked across five kilometers of distance to the far airlock-platform. That was a lot of open space, even if it was broken up by many pinnacles and vertical ridges. The air was full of flying things. Things that, except for their wings, looked very human.

Had he come from Eden to Heaven? And—to judge by the blackness of the wings of the creature spiraling in towards them—was Lucifer back in Heaven?

The face-paint reminded Kretz of unpleasant encounters, even if he'd never seen anything like the rakish array of head plumes. However, the flier appeared more curious than threatening. "Who are you guys?" she asked, folding her wings and pulling her very human arms free. "Interesting clothes, dudes."

Her garment came under that heading too. It was tight and yet plainly flexible. Kretz envied it.

"We're just passing through. No intention of being any trouble to anyone," said Howard.

The flying-woman looked incredulously at him, taking in his size. "How do you ever get off the ground, big guy? And don't you get a breeze up your skirt? You sure aren't from Icarus."

A second flier came swooping in and landed. He had a longer blue wing and head plumes of similar shade, just tipped in red.

"Neat landing, chick," he said, grinning at her.

Behind him two more wings were dropping in. Rapidly any numerical advantage the travelers had had was being overwhelmed. There were others dropping towards them too.

The first one lifted her chin. "All my landings are neat, Andy. Not like yours."

"It's a pity your stalls-spins are so lousy," he said.

Looking at this new place, Dandani knew that Chief Fripara-wa-reepa would be disappointed. They'd learned just how to get the people here, not that it was easy—nor was bringing game home going to be easy either. It was green enough. But he could see no water. And what did a hunter do on land that went straight up and down? And how did you fight an enemy who could fly?

Nama-ti said: "Nice tits. Shame about the wings, eh Dandani?"

Dandani nodded. "Make them chasing you afterwards a lot harder to avoid. Neat trick, though, the flying. We could shoot more *carpincho* that way."

Nama-ti turned to the woman who shot straight and said, in their language: "We go home now?"

"I'm not stopping you. The airlock is back there," she pointed.

"You go back too?" he asked.

"We've still got business ahead," she said. "We're going have to cross this place."

"How you do that? You fly like them?" Nama-ti asked.

"Nope. And before you say 'so how you do it?', Perp-One, I have no idea."

"We'll try asking them," said Howard. Dandani had decided a while back that he too was a dangerous individual. Not because he had shot a man, or lived through *cigale* vine poison, but because he always seemed to actually get things done. You had to watch people like that, especially the quiet ones. Besides, if he did get angry, he was as big as two men.

So Howard asked. He interrupted the cheerful bickering with a loud clearing of his throat.

"Peace be with you, brothers and sisters. Can you help us? We need to know how we can get to the far side of this habitat. Unfortunately, we cannot fly."

You could cut the sudden silence, it was so tangible. Howard wondered if he'd said the wrong thing again.

They all looked at him. Finally, the man with red tips to his headdress said: "You've got to be having us on, haven't you?"

Howard shook his head. "We can't fly."

"That is *so* weird," said the girl who had landed first. "You come from the habitat next along, don't you?" There seemed no animosity in this question. And it would seem that they had a good understanding of other habitats.

Howard pointed at the two uThani in their woven cloaks and loincloths, holding their bows and looking wary. "They do. We come from two and three along. Kretz doesn't come from Earth at all. But he is a good being. We are trying to help him to return to his home."

"Three different habitats?" exclaimed red feather-tips. "And none of you fly? Wow. It's really bizarre when you find out that old legends are true."

He didn't sound upset about it. Howard persisted. "So, can you tell us which way to go to reach the far side of your habitat? We mean no harm to anyone."

"Without flying?" asked the man.

Howard nodded.

The flyer shook his head. "A bit tricky for you to get there, if you don't fly. I don't rightly know if it can be done."

"Right now it would be tricky to get there even if you did fly," said one of the others. "The Goshawks are not cool on other people in their air-space. And in case you forget they're on top right now."

"Hey, the Goshawks are just not cool," said red-tipped head feathers to her. He turned back to them. "So. What are the opportunities like for flight out there? In space I mean, outside Icarus."

"Why don't you go and have a look?" said Lani, her voice brittle.

The flier shook his head. "We've got a prohibition on it. We've got nearly eighty years to go before we get to Signy. We'll need suits then. We can't have trashed all of them playing."

"Signy?" said Amber in an enquiring tone.

"What we've decided to call our star," said the flier. "After the founder of our habitat cooperative. It's got a gas giant approximately three times the size of Earth but without the heavy elements. There is a reasonable chance of an upper atmosphere life-zone, besides the habitats we'll build."

Howard swallowed. What did all this mean? Lani looked equally mystified, as did the uThani. Amber was beaming though, and Kretz looked—as well as Howard could judge by the alien's face—fascinated.

At first Amber had taken them for a bunch of playboys. Well, playgirls too. The first one in had been distinctly sexy. But this conversation suggested that not only did they still know why they were going, but they also knew a lot about where. You couldn't really say that about the average citizen of the Matriarchy of Diana. For them Diana had effectively become all of reality, and the purpose of the journey or even the existence of the journey, little more than something touched on in school. Slightly less interesting than Founder Susan—who could bore any girl to tears by the third time they had to study her life. "You're already in planning against arrival?"

Red feather-tips grinned. "Sure. I might even live to see it."

"Not likely," said one of the women. "You'll deck it before you're thirty, Andy."

"A fine flier like me? Ha," he said loftily.

"There is just one question I have to ask," said a flier at the back. She was small but her wings and outfit were jet black, and she commanded instant silence. With black hair and little golden chevrons on her cheeks she was an arresting sight, but still not someone you'd have thought called for the sudden respectful silence in this rowdy, cheerful crowd. Maybe it was the single black feather with gold trim in her hair.

"Yes?" said Amber.

"Are you prepared to learn to fly?" she asked.

There are times in your life to be bold as well as hopeful. She was gorgeous. And slightly smaller than Amber was herself. "Are you prepared to teach me?"

The woman in black raised her eyebrows. Looked thoughtful. "I'll try. You might do better with someone like Maryna, who has young children, but I'll try."

"Shee-it," said the flashy red-tipped head-dress. "Can't I pretend I don't know how to fly either?"

"Andy, in your case, there is no need to pretend," said the woman cheerfully. "And most of you are going to be late for work. I'm off shift. I'll take this lot along to the kindergarten. Fortunately, we can walk there."

"That'll be a first for you, Zoë," said one of the women, launching into space, and unfurling her wings as she fell.

The tiny raven-haired woman shook her head disapprovingly. "She'll kill herself doing stupid things like that. The first thing you need to learn about flying is that it isn't about showing off."

"The air is thicker and gravity is lower than on old Earth. This makes flying a lot easier. It's still not easy," explained the slim, raven-haired woman. She was minuscule, Kretz realized. Long boned, but with very little body-weight. It must be awkward maintaining bone density without a rigorous exercise program, here. In the habitat where the women had ruled he'd seen a good few rounded humans. His friend Amber had been heading in that direction—although her weight had come off fairly fast across the primitive habitat. "Rounded" wasn't something you could say about any of these fliers.

"In addition we heat the air near to the outer skin, and this makes for thermals toward the core. There is also wind-funneling in the shaping of the valleys. Despite the small area there are several thousand edge-rotors." She pointed. "This is Kindergarten Slope, where parents teach their toddlers."

"Children fly?" said Lani.

She nodded. "As soon as possible. Learning the interface and building the musculature takes a lot of time, and the younger they start the better they are. In another hour you'll have hundreds of them here. I come here early because it is a safe place to try out new stunts, and test new wings. For my sins I am also the test pilot for Osprey-wings. We have some adult-size trainers in storage here, intended for injured fliers relearning."

She looked at Howard. "Nothing with a big enough span for you, though. I'll ask work . . . it could be expensive."

"What can we pay you in?" asked Lani.

"That's going to be interesting. The Goshawks hold high wing right now, and unless I manage something spectacular, they will continue to. One of their reps will have to put a value to your labor. The trainers . . . well, temporarily they're not a problem. This is something of a coup for the Osprey, and we need it."

She'd led them to a wide door. "In here."

Inside were racks and racks of wings. "We'll need to size you, and weigh you."

Kretz wondered how the humans would respond if he said it was too dangerous. But it was fascinating nonetheless.

Howard found the wings were actually a pair of wings with a body strip and a broad, flare-able tail, which fitted onto the human body. Flight was a dream. Here humanity had reached out and made a reality of Icarus. Each wing had about one hundred and fifty neural inputs, interfacing to the nerves in the hands and arms. You had to learn to read and respond to those inputs without conscious thought, just as the body adjusted to the less complex task of walking, explained the fascinating woman in her black lycra.

"The first wings were quite simple. About twenty inputs and most people only started to fly as adults. Apparently there was a lot of legislation preventing minors from trying it."

"The truth is you don't need neural inputs. It's just been the fashion to chase that area of development. Now, there are force-multipliers in the wing mechanical structure, and fail-safes to stop the air dislocating your arms, but it is still hard work. You need to flap your arms for lift, and rotate your wrists for forward movement."

"You mean you fly by flapping your arms?"

She nodded. "Unless you're using a thermal, or a rotor on a cliff edge, which in reality is what most people do. The multipliers add a further twenty-five percent to your efforts. With these trainers the wings are helium filled too. Right, let's start fitting."

Twenty minutes later, all of them except Howard stood uneasily trying their wings' neural interfaces at the edge of a twenty-foot cliff, which had a stiff breeze rising up it. In actuality the wing-interface felt like tiny sensations of pain, temperature, or pressure. "In time you'll learn, or rather, your reflexes will learn what those feelings mean. Basically, the only way to learn is to jump over the edge. Often."

She stepped over the cliff edge . . . and seemed to stand on air. With the tiniest occasional flick of the wingtip, Zoë hung there.

"When you can do this you are ready to move on," she said.

Dandani shrugged. He obviously thought that if she could do it . . . he now had wings. He launched himself casually. Spun, and managed to nosedive earthwards. The landing-pad was thick and soft, for which he was very grateful.

"Again," said their instructress. "And try to lift your wings clear when you crash."

She was merciless. Only Howard failed to try crash landing, and that was only because of a lack of wings. They kept it up time after time, until little two-year-olds started arriving and doing it too—almost inevitably better than they did.

She'd done some talking on a wrist communicator while this was happening. "The head of Osprey has said that the co-op will sponsor your wings, big one. Also after breakfast you'll all get some decent flying lycra—also with our compliments. The boss says we can make some publicity out of you. And now it is time to eat."

"No fish? No meat?" asked a dismayed Perp-One, voicing Lani's thoughts. Well, it was sort of payback for the half-raw, half-burned experience they'd had with the uThani. She'd have liked to get *them* pissed as newts and have them babble the family secrets, and wake up with the mother of all hangovers. However, they'd probably babble in their own language. And they probably had heads like rocks, knowing her luck.

"We're having a little trouble with our protein vats," admitted their host. "At least we think that's where the problem is. All the instruments read normally, we're just not getting results. Two of our cultures have died. There is more in cryo, but we don't want to break in on the stores until we work out what the problem is. And we're not having much joy, with people trying to make sense out of four-hundred-year-old manuals."

She grimaced. "It's the Osprey's part of the cooperative. So what production we do have goes to the other flight co-ops. Everyone is a little sour with us, but we've been having seriously worsening problems for twenty-odd years. One of the vats has been out for over a hundred years."

Amber got up. "Lead me to it," she said. "Flight may not be my field of expertise, but protein-culture vats are. Is it the equipment that's getting tired, like ours?"

"We don't think so," said Zoë. "You must realize that I just work in fabrication. We've rebuilt from scratch one of the smaller vats for them. I believe they've taken each one of the majors out of service, and refurbished them."

"Wow," Amber was plainly impressed. "We don't have the basic engineering skills to do that. Right. It looks like a biochem problem, then, unless there's some form of contamination getting in. Can I have a look?"

"I think they'd welcome you with open arms," said Zoë. She bit her lip. "I'm just trying to think how to get you there without flying. Um. Would you survive the indignity of being hauled around like cargo? There is a winch that we use for bringing up raw feedstock to the plant."

"No problem at all," said Amber cheerfully. "Indignity I can live with."

Lani worried about them splitting up the party. True, the local flyboys and girls seemed friendly, but . . . "I think we'd all better go."

Amber shook her head. "No insult intended, Lani, but you'd be as much use in a lab as I am in a fight."

"I'll take good care of her," said Zoë.

If Amber had been a male that tone would have made any good mama suspicious. Lani wondered if Zoë was . . . that way. Oh, well, not her problem. Her problem was examining the mechanics of the wings. Any minute now Howard would take them apart to see what made them work.

"How about if we went for a walk to help to settle the meal," she said artlessly. The thoughts about having designs on someone had stirred something within her too. And if they were going to split up the party they might as well split up properly.

He brightened. "I'll ask Brother Kretz and the uThani."

"Kretz is tired. You need to work the muscles more. And Perp-One and Uppity are trying it on with those girls."

"I don't think 'You want to make out' is a very polite thing for Dandani to be saying. Is it?" asked Howard doubtfully.

"Perp-One says he told him it means 'How do you do?'" said Lani. "They're terrible practical jokers, those two."

"So what does it mean?" he asked.

She linked her fingers with his. "Come for a walk. I'll show you."

"We'd better not go too far," said Howard, looking at the others.

"I'll do my best to stop before we do," said Lani, looking at him with half-lidded eyes.

He might not be following her meaning. But with Howard, you never quite knew.

They walked to where they could look out into the green folds of the fliers' habitat. Lani, casting a sideways glance at him, decided he looked tired. Hopefully the poison was still leaching out of his system and hadn't done any long-term damage. Except maybe to his brain, she decided. He hadn't removed his hand from hers. It was a sort of brain damage that she decided she could live with. "Let's sit a bit," she said.

They did. She leaned against him . . . and he didn't shy away. Instead he put a very tentative arm around her shoulder. "You know," he said. "I'm realizing that it doesn't have to be flat and fertile to be beautiful. For a New Eden farmer that's quite a mind-leap."

There seemed to be more than the superficial behind that statement, especially combined with the arm around her shoulder. She thought about her reply quite carefully for once. He had that sort of effect on her. "Are you ready to consider that maybe a naked cop could actually be a nice girl? Or is that too much of a stretch for your New Eden imagination?"

He smiled at her, his innocent, big blue eyes warm. "I decided on that a while back. There are lots of kinds of beauty, and there is more than one kind of nice girl, and it doesn't depend on the clothes that they're wearing, or not wearing."

"Oh, so there are lots, are there? Some wearing lycra?" she asked, getting a firm grip on his biceps. Torture time!

"But only one for me. And it doesn't matter what she's wearing."

Lani sniffed, blinked and smiled, feeling as if maybe she'd caught some of the brain damage. "In this straight-laced stupid culture of yours, when is a man allowed to kiss a woman?" She raised her chin, tilting her head towards him.

His eyes twinkled. "When they're betrothed, a man may kiss his intended."

She pushed him over backwards, gently. "Well, I'm intending to kiss you. 'Cause you see as far as I'm concerned you're not just betrothed. You're married. To me."

"Not in the eyes of God," he said seriously.

"We can sort that out," she said firmly. "You know her well; have a word with her. In the meanwhile we're both learning and adapting around each other's culture, right?"

"Right," he agreed after the briefest pause.

She put her arm across him and rolled onto her knees above him. "Now I've got to show you some aspects of my culture too."

"Oh?" he said, looking innocently up at her.

"Yeah," she said, touching the curve of his cheek. "Take a deep breath, honey, because I need to start explaining 'making out' to you. It's a long explanation and I think I've only got time for the very first part."

Kretz was fascinated by the culture change. These humans were far more diverse than Miran ever would be. Sort of sociological experiments in miniature, each of these habitats. If he hadn't been in a hurry to get through them, to get to Abret, and to get back to Selna, he would have been content to spend many days just observing. And, of course, taking notes.

Right now he was employing his skills in rather a different way. The treachery of the small male from Amber and Lani's world had frightened him. Partly he supposed it was size. To Miranese someone that size was a juvenile. To be humored because they were too young to really know better. Of course Bhangella had not been young —but it was hard to rid your mind of such ingrained ideas. He'd decided a long while back that Howard was as trustable as any human ever could be. Amber, as a fellow scientist, he had a bond with. And Lani plainly would stand by Howard. But he was wary about these new two males. So he was watching them. And listening to them. Transcomp was making fast work of learning their language, as there was a fair amount of translation going on. He'd already established that the one who claimed to speak no English certainly understood quite a lot. He'd also established that there was a fairly large amount of mockery going on. They liked to see how much they could get their hosts to swallow.

It was quite amusing to think that he was fooling them as much as they thought they were fooling everyone. And they were quite happy to say derogatory things in their own language, which Nama-ti did not translate. It let him keep a very careful watch over their plans without them realizing. After Bhangella, that was a good idea. Besides it made the waiting game easier, having such work to do.

He was so busy listening that he didn't notice that one of the fliers had sat herself down next to him. She put a hand on his inner thigh. "So how different from humans are you?" she asked curiously. "You are male, aren't you?"

It would appear that physical curiosity went both ways, and that he wouldn't need to ask Howard about human seduction after all.


"It's actually quite a simple matter," explained Amber. "You weren't looking at biochemistry high enough up your supply chain. With this readout malfunctioning you were getting too few lysines. It's obviously a problem that relates to this instrument batch, and it broke down first on the more popular protein lines. We haven't had the problem because we haven't automated that stage on Diana."

She smiled at all of them, saving her best for Zoë. She was getting a definite feeling of attraction there . . . but how did this culture feel about gay relationships? "You should be back on stream and up to full production in a week," she said. "Sometimes it pays to outsource an expert."

They sat together and had a coffee before heading back down to kindergarten. Zoë, Amber decided, was not just physically attractive. She was bright too.

"Everyone works," the flier explained. "Look, we were heading into four hundred and ninety years of journey in a very small environment. The problems we were going to face were pretty obviously social as well as merely environmental. Work . . . well, work keeps people occupied. It's a little artificial but there are jobs for everybody, even just making things we'll need when we get to Signy. Top skills get top dollar—worth trying for. We can—and do—automate the really dumb jobs. Well, we keep a few for nonachievers. . . . Anyway, naturally we were into flight-technology. A fair number of our original people worked or ran the sport-industry. Sure, we could have automated it. But we set up the cooperatives instead, each making and refining low-G wings, and taking a part of the physical environmental maintenance equipment under our wing. We're protein production, and of course, Osprey wings. We hold a biannual comp at which our latest wing flies. It's a complex judging—but pretty fair really. And whichever wing cooperative wins, becomes top wing, and handle general administrivia."

"After all these years your wing design must be fairly refined," said Amber doubtfully.

Zoë scowled. "Yep. It's always been a skills contest too. Chief test fliers' skills have been more of the deciding factor the last hundred years or so. There is a limit to what you can really do with remote neural input, and there is a ban on surgical implants. Actual wing shape and response Waldos haven't had major changes for at least two hundred years, although we're still experimenting. And the bad news is the Goshawks pipped me by one point last year. And they'll do anything to make life awkward for your group, as our protégés." She smiled wryly. "I had hopes that you'd give us a new design leap from outside. It's not likely, is it?"

She was wrong. The idea came from the most unlikely source too.

Dandani sat down hard, for the maybe the four hundredth time. He'd learned—very rapidly, that you needed to avoid going down head first. Unfortunately he hadn't managed to stop bending his tail pinions.

"He looks like a quetzal. They fly faster. Dandani only fly faster down," said Nama-ti.

"What is a 'quetzal'?" asked Amber.

"Is bird. You no have birds here? Is bird fly very very fast." He showed a pantomime of fast zippy movements. "Got fork tail like Dandani make for himself."

Amber looked thoughtful, then left the little cliff for her portable. A few minutes later she called Zoë. "Have you actually looked at real bird tails?"

The dark-haired woman shook her head. "No, we don't have any livestock, not even birds. I do remember studying them as a child."

"I had the opportunity to see some live ones. Look at this pic. Look at the tails of these 'swifts.' "

Zoë was already dialing on her wrist-mobile. "I need Aaron and Lee here. Kindergarten. Now. We've still got two days."

The two arrived posthaste, as Zoë was still talking to Amber about tails and their purpose. "Tails are there to act as air-brakes and to fix yaw and pitch. But look at the aspect changes in this tail." She pointed to the screen for the benefit of the new arrivals. "Look at this thing. Look at the potential for steerage, look at the amount of variation in this sequence. It opens some new doors in design, guys. I want a test-ready prototype by tonight."

It was apparent that she was used to being obeyed. And by the look on their faces . . . they were getting ideas. Icarus had the same computer net-resources as Diana did. Amber had found her portable quite happy to hook into their system. Obviously the habitat designers had used the same framework. Lee noted the address, and flicked herself over the edge of the nursery slope. "We'll pick up the pictures in the office. Come on, Aaron."

He departed in a similar fashion, with a broad smile.

"First time I've seen him smile in about a month. He's been battling . . . anyway this should give us top marks for innovation, even if it doesn't work that well. That's worth a cool fifty points by itself."

"I think we need to start pointing your design team at the wonderful world of chickens," said Howard, who had wandered up to them, with his new extra-huge wings. "Chickens like to spend their time on the ground. They only fly if they're very frightened. I think I am ready to try."

"I don't know about chickens, but you do need to look at birds."

"I'm beginning to understand the expression: 'this is for the birds,' " said Howard. He stood on the cliff edge and positioned his arms carefully. Then he kicked off with his big powerful legs.

And did not fall.

He didn't hang in the air the way their instructor did either, but sort of glided off at a gentle angle. Zoë took one look and leapt into flight after him. She caught one wingtip with her feet, and turned him. He landed, running.

"The point," his instructor said, going back to her hover-place, "is to learn to respond to your neural inputs, not to go gliding. Still, I'm impressed. I didn't think a big thing like you could do anything but fall. How—or rather, why—did you do that?"

"I watched. And it seems that the place where you hung was farther out than where the others were getting to. I got the wing angle wrong, didn't I?"

"You did. And you spotted by observation what I have been trying to get people to learn by feel. I'm sorry, most of this is simply unknown to us. Everybody here *knows* how to fly. Mothers take their babies out in tandem rigs. Even the injured, relearning to fly with disabilities, have done it before. Instructing at this level is . . . different."

"Boring, you mean?" said Howard, smiling.

"Actually, very funny. I don't think I'd find it that day after day, but the novelty has charm. Next. Try getting yourself a bit farther out and if you start to glide alter the pitch of your wing. It's very difficult to do, but once you can do it you have the exact difference between 'fly' and 'stall.' After that it's easy. Come on. I've got another hour before bed. I want you all onto the first glide slope by then."

# 30

Why doesn't the asshole get himself a life instead of messing around with mine? He doesn't know jack-shit about the gain you get from sticking your neck out. Screw him.
—Jean-Marie Signy, World Champion 2544,
   distance paragliding, in reply to Senator
   Selbourne's comments on the new
   legislation on danger-sports.

---

The wing folded and crumpled behind Amber. And her feet . . . were not the last thing that passed through her mind, after all.

"I did it. I lived!" Her knees buckled a little.

Zoë had landed, featherlike, next to her, supporting her with an arm around her.

It took Amber some time to realize that the kiss had moved from a sisterly congratulations to something else entirely. And that she hadn't thought about responding, just did it. And that if lycra wasn't as good as being naked, it wasn't that far off.

"Uh. I think everyone is watching," she said, when they paused for breath.

"Let them," said Zoë.

"Jealousy makes them nasty." The placement of her hand showed that Amber had every intention of making them jealous.

Zoë licked her upper lip. "Later, huh?"

"Yes. But not much later . . . please."

"A-okay," said her instructor, with a gleam in her eyes. "I think class is nearly over for today."

Zoë shrugged. "It's not easy to form real relationships, being the champion. About half the girls out there would have sex with me, just because I am the champion. I'm not a person, Amber. I'm . . . I'm a position. A trophy scalp or maybe some special, private training. Not a person."

"I think I understand. My first girlfriend wasn't even gay. I was just a stepping stone."

"Yeah. Exactly . . . I mean, experimentally, it was fun for a bit, but, well, anyway . . . " she sighed. "The only people you can really get close to are other top-rank fliers, and only the very top . . . otherwise they're using you again."

"And heaven help the relationship if one's career takes off and the other one's doesn't," said Amber, smiling in wry reminiscence.

Zoë looked sideways at her. "Been there, have we?"

Amber nodded. "Been there. So have you, I suppose. You do know I'll never be a champion flier, don't you?"

Zoë kissed her. "You started too late in life. I mean most kids start serious flying about when they start to walk."

"I loved doing it. I mean, space . . . space scared me silly. But this wasn't half so bad, there was a roof . . . I won't hold you back, will I? I couldn't bear that."

"No. Anyway, the truth is I won't be able to hold onto the title for too much longer. I'm getting a little old for high-G turns." She smiled wryly. "I don't know what it'll be like to see someone else take the gold feather."

"Like Lani and her Howard, I think we need a world of our own," said Amber, sighing a little.

"They're a very odd couple."

"Honey, you don't know how odd. He's from some religious pacifist group and she's . . . our Lani tends to hit first and think later. She's got some brains behind it, but she's got a Diana cop mentality to fight through first. He's from a patriarchal society that doesn't believe in sex outside of marriage. She's climbing walls. I think he is too, but it is sort of his fault."

"It sounds doomed," said Zoë, amused.

"Not really. I think they may be what each partner actually needs. He thinks and she acts. But they have a real problem as to a future. Lani sure as hell won't fit into his habitat, and neither of them can go back to Diana. They were getting starry-eyed about farming on uThani—until we met the owners."

"Those uThani are a pair of rogues. That guy with a scar on his cheek has propositioned just about every female flier in Osprey airspace already. He does it with such a smile on his face that he'll probably get lucky too. He even tried me."

"They were kissing. And they were holding hands when they left!" said Howard, shocked and obviously troubled.

Lani nodded. "I'm very happy for her, if it works out."

Howard gaped at her. "But . . . they are both women. It's unnatural."

"So is riding a scoot, and eating cooked food," said Lani. "Look, you got to know Amber. Did you like her? Did you trust her?"

"Yes, but not—"

Lani interrupted. "And you like Zoë, don't you?"

"Yes. But it's not—"

"Are they any different because they don't want to sleep with *you*? Any less likable as people, not because of their sexual preferences? Wouldn't you trust them now?"

Howard smiled reluctantly. "You've got a point, I suppose. It's just among the Brethren—"

"The universe is a bigger place than 'among the Brethren,' Howard," said Lani, putting her arm around him. "It's bigger than Diana too. I've started to come to terms with that. Can you? Or is all just about God and she only looks at and approves of the way things are in New Eden."

He stiffened up. "God sees everything. And it's God the Father, not the Mother," he said.

Lani looked at him with that challenging smile she'd been practicing. "You told me only God knew everything. So, how do you know? I thought you said God was everything. That would make him . . . her too. And being omni-cognizant would mean that he or she would know all about both sides." She fluttered her eyelashes at his serious face. She thought that was a valuable addition to a theological debate.

"I hadn't thought of it like that," he admitted with a rueful grin. "You'll have me labeled as a heretic, yet."

"I guess that's another decision humans ought to be taking. Anyway, Howard, all I'm saying is I've decided Amber saved your life, and I'm damned if I'm going to criticize the way she lives hers. And I'm not really prepared to let you do it either."

He sighed. "It's a lot to get used to."

"Yeah. But you'll cope," she said, smiling at him. "It shocked me too, at first, by the way. But I thought about it, and decided that what I wanted was for her to be happy. I think she is."

Howard nodded reluctantly. "And who am I to cast the first stone?" he said, taking her hand.

Lying on the big bed, a leg over Zoë, Amber found herself getting philosophical. It made a change from being physical. "Something is becoming quite plain to me. First, the population in each bead—even at high density like Diana and here—is just too low to sustain a broad technological base. You guys—with the aerodynamics to spur you on—are fairly good engineers—on the computer design side especially. Biologically and even biochemically speaking, on the other hand, you've lost the skills. From what Lani said, Howard's people are very good at straight 'hands-on' doing things. They're good artisans. And I get the feeling the uThani are probably better people manipulators than all of us."

Zoë laughed. "They overdo the 'we primitives' stuff. They know a computer screen when they see one. And they don't shock easily enough."

"Yet, they really are primitive in some ways. Clever and quick to catch on, though."

"But everyone should know what a harvester looks like."

"Maybe not, Zoë. You should see their habitat—it's uncultivated. And in Howard's habitat they do all of it by hand. The uThani have some computer access—their computer, damn the thing, pillaged my files, but wouldn't let me access it. They must have a computer net second to none."

Zoë grinned. "Don't you guys know about that? The microbots all data-feed to central computing."

"Which explains how I was able to read such quality information about the warm bodies in Diana," said Amber thoughtfully.

"Yep. Centcomp is compiling a digest of recorded information about everything. Huge files of the stuff. It's stored in the probe-units on the surface."

"You mean *everything*?" Amber said uneasily.

"Yep. Even the noises you make in bed," said Zoë, sticking her tongue out.

Despite knowing that microbots would be invisible to the naked eye, Amber couldn't help looking around. "Holy Susan. Haven't they any respect for privacy?"

Zoë tickled her.

Amber didn't respond as she would have a few moments earlier. "I don't feel quite comfortable knowing that I'm being watched."

"It's impossible to access onboard," said Zoë. "Believe me, some hackers tried. And why should we care about what some Terran sociologist two hundred light-years away—four hundred years from now, at least—thinks of us? We'll be long, long dead before they even see the stuff. And there are terabytes of it. It'll have to be machine analyzed."

That gave Amber pause. She thought about it with increasingly unholy amusement. "True. Shall we give them a show that'll burn their circuits out?"

"Ooh, sounds good to me."

Dandani picked his teeth thoughtfully. "Do you know there isn't one single bit of game in this place? The chief would be delighted if we expanded the hunting grounds here. No fish in the water either. Man, this place is in a terrible state."

"You seemed to find a bit of game."

"Yeah, but she's hardly worth pulling the feathers off, really. And she made me wash. Now I stink." Dandani wrinkled his nose.

"She said you did before," said Nama-ti.

"Maybe to her. But now every animal will smell me."

"There are no animals here. Just a lot of people. And I suppose if you're going to hunt them you've got make sure your smell doesn't make them run away."

"I suppose so. So what do we do now, Nama-ti?"

"They make good stuff with iron," said the translator, thoughtfully.

"Yeah. Not practical, though. Haven't seen one good machete or knife. And like the flying, I don't think it would work at home."

Nama-ti grinned evilly at him. "But those fake feathers they wear are not worth having. We don't want their place, but . . . we have something to barter."

"Knives and arrowheads? Isn't this like what comp said about the beads, whiskey and cheap junk they traded?"

"Except this time it's us trading the throw-away junk for things that have value to us, yes."

"They're not bad people, Nama-ti. We don't have to cheat them."

"We have to keep in practice. Besides, if they want feathers, it's what it is worth to the buyer, not us."

"You might have said that about the beads too," said Dandani.

Nama-ti grinned. "I won't, if you don't. Have you figured that our hosts lied to us?"

"About the flying? Yes. But I don't know that they meant to. They don't think of those ambulance balloons as anything except for sick people. I think they just assume people fly, like we assume they use canoes. It took a day—and then it was me, by accident—to find the strangers, in spite of the fact that Pili-cha-taaka spotted them not fifty yards from the airlock, because they were crazy enough to walk everywhere."

"You're going soft, Dandani," said Nama-ti with a grin. "I think they wanted to frighten the shit out of us."

"Nearly worked too, by the way you screamed," said Dandani, yawning. "Me, I think it was some kind of initiation. I think it would have been very hard if we'd said that we didn't want to fly. If we said it was too dangerous."

"You could be right," agreed Nama-ti. "They don't think much of people who don't fly."

"So what do we do now? Go on with outsiders? Stay here? Or try to go back home alone?"

The translator sat down. "It's a tricky question, Dandani."

"That's why I asked you. You are tricky."

"It's still not easy to answer. I think we go on. For one, we may find more hunting grounds. I don't think so, but maybe. For seconds, we are hunters. Hunters always like to see a new place."

"Besides that, Howard leaves me feeling like maybe I should," said Dandani grumpily. "Now go away. That little bird has left me exhausted."

"You shouldn't have chased her so hard."

"It wasn't the chasing part that tired me out."


The human artificer looked at Kretz's rebreather system and frowned. "The truth is, we can do it. Probably.

But it's quite an engineering challenge. We need to make sure that we don't wreck the mechanism in the process. It could take us a few days."

Kretz didn't know if he had a few extra days. He bit his paw-hand nervously.

"I have another idea," said Howard, tentatively. "We could go on without you."

Kretz shook his head. "I don't think you can fly a Miranese craft."

"I'm sure we couldn't," said Howard. "But could we fetch another unit back for you? Surely there must be spares on your ship."

Kretz nodded. He was naturally reluctant to contemplate the idea of letting them into the lifecraft without him. But Howard was as trustable a human as you could find.

It was a lot to ask, though. Still, coming this far had been a lot to ask too.

"Please," he said, humbly. "But I cannot ask you to take such a risk. To undertake this for me."

Howard smiled. Kretz found the big human's smiles reassuring by now, even if he sometimes showed teeth. "It is my idea, Kretz. It'll be easier than worrying about you running out of air out there."

"One other thing," said Kretz diffidently. "We used a radio system from the museum on Diana to enable me to talk to my spacecraft and to Abret—who is trapped in the next habitat. Unfortunately, it was obviously discovered and switched off quite soon. I have been able to pick up transmissions from the spacecraft, but I am uncertain as to whether they have received me. Do you also have such relics?"

The artificer grinned. Kretz had got used to its social meaning by now. "No," he said. "But we've got new ones in stock for colonization. And we've assembled a high-gain antenna to be put outside when the habitat arrives in the Signy system. If everything goes according to plan, we'll be a satellite retransmission system for many years. Even without external installation it would be worth running it as a relay station. We'd get to test it and you'd get to talk."

Within the cell, Abret paced. There wasn't much else to do except to look at the bizarre alien preparations out in the square. Pacing was a more cheerful exercise. Pacing and hoping for radio comms that weren't just Selna sounding off. Derfel had placed repeater stations. Obviously the madman wanted to be able to hear what she was doing. It occurred to Abret, belatedly, that meant that he had also received news of Kretz's progress. Pinging his source had told him that the biologist-engineer had made progress. Whether he could get here was another matter, but that hope was all that kept him sane.

When Kretz's voice came over the ether it was sweeter than a mating cry. It was loud and clear too.

"Receiving," Abret said. "Are you transmitting from the lifecraft?"

"No. I am still one bead away. But we have secured alien help. They've been more than kind."

"They're evil murdering monsters, Kretz. Listen. *Everyone* can hear you. I think you must go back to Selna. Just like you did when Zawn chose us to explore the alien airlock."

He just hoped Kretz understood what he *wasn't* saying. He hoped mad Derfel didn't understand.

Selna cut in. "You must come back, Kretz."

Abret chewed his lip. She wasn't too stable yet. And the word of a female carried more weight. Would he be abandoned here?

"I'll do what I can," said Kretz, tactfully. "I am dependent on help from the various aliens. They have kept me alive and helped me."

Was there a hidden message there?

A little later Abret knew that Derfel had been listening in. And that the little hope he'd had was dead.

Derfel came to see him with his human guards. "I've moved the lander," he said. "It is at the engine-ward airlock. And I have ensured that the tail-direction airlock won't open, in a manner these superstitious natives won't interfere with. The equatorial ridge will prevent Kretz from ever getting there, I would think. My guards will be waiting if he does come, and now you will get out of that suit. You have behaved with treachery to my great leadership."

It took a fight, but Abret was no match for that number of human guards. Now he was sans radio, and also without a suit to leave the airlock, even if rescue should ever come.

Despair.

# 31

Societies are dynamic things, feeding on inputs from outside. There is no such thing as a stable society any more than there is perpetual motion.

From: *Elementary Societal Psychodynamics.* 2089. James R. Grey (ed). New Harvard Library (Pub.)

There was a knock on the door. Zoë went to open it. "We have some people who wish to meet your guest," said the elderly flier who was standing there. "Zoë, you know flight cooperative chief Gersholm of the Goshawks and flight cooperative deputy chief Karasoff of the Falcons."

Amber saw how Zoë's eye's widened. "Come in," she said. "What brings the heads of the two other biggest flight co-ops into Osprey sky?"

"I think you know the answer, test pilot," said Kara-soff, waving a hand at Amber. "The Matriarchy of Diana wants her back. And we're not too sure we want any of them here in Icarus."

"That's too bad. You know they've fulfilled the basic requisites for citizenship, don't you?" said Zoë, putting a hand on Amber's shoulder. "They volunteered, in the presence of witnesses, to fly. No one has yet said it was 'too dangerous'?"

"Yes," said the older man who was plainly the senior Osprey. "I told them. But we're talking a lot more about practicalities than four-hundred-year-old idealism here, Zoë. The status quo isn't that bad."

Zoë exploded. "Like hell, Cremer! You know as well as the rest of us that the Icarus cooperative was formed to get out from under the 'status quo.' We're heading into our dream—dangerous and unpredictable times—they're less than eighty years off and suddenly you want to start living safe. Get out of here. I'm calling an Osprey general meeting and we'll vote ourselves a new MD."

"Calm down," said the third man. "I'm with you. And if Chief Cremer doesn't like it, I am formally mandated to give you and your guests entry to the Goshawks. I'm of the firm belief that your visitors should be shared among all the flight cooperatives, and not just Osprey."

The Osprey chief gaped at him.

He held up his hand soothingly. "Anyway. Just hear us out, please. Diana says they've got vat problems. You don't want people to starve, do you?"

"How do you know all this?" asked Amber suspiciously.

"There are comm lines in the cable," explained the Goshawk. "We have occasionally spoken to other habitats in the past, although we are not intended to. They were meant for major disasters affecting the whole train. We suspect that computer records of current status of all the beads are also sent to the last habitat, to be returned to Earth. They get their data on all of us serially, that way. Anyway, the Matriarchy picked up a radio broadcast on a frequency set onto a transmitter in your lab. They worked out that it could come from here. They're begging."

Amber bit a knuckle. "I'll tell you bluntly, there are at least five others in the Matriarchy that could do my actual job from the biochem or the micro side. If—and this is a big if—they have a real problem, it is likely to be engineering or computer support. I'm better with computers than most. I'm no engineer. I think they want me back for political reasons. *But*—I've got biochemical expertise that you need, and they are in no position to make you hand me over."

"We know that," said the Falcon. "They claim that you were kidnapped and that the others of your party are criminals. Is this true?"

Amber looked at the three: two men and a woman, and knew her future and her happiness hung in the balance. "No," she said. "If anyone was kidnapped by anyone, I kidnapped them. The others aren't criminals either—or at least they wouldn't be, here, by your laws. Howard—the big guy—his crime was wearing clothes and being out in public without a woman." That produced a stunned chuckle. "If you'll sit down, I'll tell you as much of the story as I know. Then you can decide for yourselves. To my mind, the best thing you could do would be help this poor alien to reach his ship."

They listened.

"These uThani—they want to invade? And you brought them here?" asked Karasoff.

"Be reasonable," said Amber. "What else could we do? And how practical would an invasion be? But they're going to be alone in space soon. At least this way . . . well, they have *some* idea what they'll face, and how to face it. Sending them out here was little more than genocide, actually. We ought to help them."

The trio looked at each other. "Actually, that seems to be the weakness of the whole Slowtrain," admitted the Osprey leader. "We *all* need some kind of help by now. Humans were designed to cross-pollinate, not to be self-fertile. Look, Dr. Geriant, I would be lying if I said the Osprey wouldn't like you to stay here, at least for some teaching-time. And as for the rest of your group, well, I'd say that if this is all true, the best we can do is, as you say, export them to the next bead. That might just be terminal, though. They've been lucky so far . . . but the next bead is another matter."

He grimaced. "Do you know that it was planned that the bead-societies would provide isolation buffers? The next bead is supposed to be a militant one. We're supposed to be untraversable. That's why the co-op got a reduced rate for our passage on the Slowtrain. We apparently couldn't afford anything nearer the tail. It has meant a long wait." He rubbed his chin. "Will you at least talk to the Matriarch? She genuinely seemed to be close to panic. Talked of sending a force out to fetch you if need be."

"The uThani would kill them . . . if they ever got that far."

"It does sound like it," said the Goshawk chief. "I might tell you that I envy you, Dr. Geraint. I'd like to see that place."

"You might be able to organize it. Going in uninvited would be fatal. I wish I could talk the Matriarchy out of this stupidity. I don't even know—without Kretz's ship —if we *can* get back. Going through the uThani habitat without their say-so would be impossible."

"We could organize comms right here," said the Osprey chief.

Amber nodded. "I suppose I'd better."

"You don't have to do anything for them," said Zoë firmly.

"I know. But a bit of talking might save some lives."

It didn't take very long. Nor did the Matriarch beat about the bush.

"Dr. Geriant, the Matriarchy needs you. We want you back. We're happy to let bygones be bygones. We're prepared to offer Matriarchal pardons to you and to all your associates, with any guarantees you want. Or name your terms." The woman cleared her throat. "I also have to tell you that Jean says she'd be prepared to try again."

A week ago that would have been all Amber Geriant needed to hear. Now all it said was that huge pressure had been brought to bear. She could—now—look at that last argument—and the ones that led up to it, and be dispassionate. It had all been about dominance, really. A relationship between two equals—both masters of separate fields and not competing—might just work better.

"Tell her she can sleep easy and alone. And then let me have a technical report on the problem. It sounds to me as if it's an engineering one, and we may just have a solution for you here. A real, long-term solution. One that actually doesn't involve me."

When the full report came through, Amber was pleased to see that her guess was right. The temporary answer Melanie had come up with was not a bad solution, really. But manual mixing of nutrients just wasn't going to work as well or in the long term. She showed it to Zoë who giggled a lot, and not just because she was being tickled. She couldn't show it to the Osprey, Goshawk and Falcon chiefs, because they had gone to meet the other travelers. Probably to see how their stories corroborated with Amber's. It certainly looked like the others would have their free passage soon.

"We will have to see what we can charge for fabrication and fitting," said Zoë.

"We should get the uThani to bargain for us about it. They're selling off feathers from some dead birds—that they would have thrown away—for a fortune."

Zoë winning the championship with her new tail mods, while sweet, was almost anticlimactic.

# 32

The trouble with a nanny state is that in the long run you're only going to have people who need a nanny. When you're pushing the frontiers you need attitude. Space is not for wimps. People who like danger-sports are not fools, nor, despite the risks we take, do we die often. That's because we learn PDQ what a nanny deprives humans of. Personal assessment. Learn it, learn it fast, or deck it.

> —Jean-Marie Signy, from her address to the
> Icarus cooperative founding meeting.

There were just four of them this time. Howard, Lani and two flier "apprentices"—no one who was in the least agoraphobic. From an early age, the fliers had all visited a lock that allowed a deep-space view, so a billion miles of nothingness was no shock to them. They also had a simple jet-pack—much less wasteful than venting oxygen —to "fly" the gap, and a reel of thin but strong cord and several powerful magnets with loops of cord. The fliers wanted to set up a Tyrolean traverse, whatever that was, and save fuel. They had major expansion projects that were just seventy-nine years off, and they weren't planning on being prodigal about their resources.

That was something Howard could admire about the Icarans. Actually, he found quite a lot to admire in them. Four hundred years was a long time to nurture a dream, to keep it fresh and strong. And their fabrication works were a place he could have been happy to fiddle in every day.

Crossing the gap, even while unspooling the line, was much faster this time. And they could all shriek with glee without offending anyone.

There was just one problem when they got to the next habitat. The craft Kretz had so painstakingly described to him . . .

Was conspicuous by its absence.

"And now?" asked Lani. "There is definitely nothing but standard walkways here."

Kretz's worried voice came over the radio. "It is possible that Derfel may have moved it. I suspect he may have been listening in . . . I suppose he could have dumped it into space. I do not believe that it could be taken into a habitat airlock."

"So what do we do now?" asked Lani. "Kretz's companion is stuck inside there. His ship isn't here and he hasn't got the air to come himself. Do we go in and deal with the perps, just the four of us? Howard is an army by himself, but he's a pacifist, you know. And, meaning no offense, but a stiff breeze will blow you flyboys away."

Howard's eyes narrowed. "We go on to the airlock, Lani. I need to see if I'm right."

They did—and found that the airlock would not open. Howard nodded thoughtfully. "I think we need to stop broadcasting on this radio device. Little pitchers have big ears. I believe that we can touch helmets and talk."

Lani knew him well enough to trust him implicitly. She toggled the radio off and touched helmets. "I don't suppose you wanted to tell me you loved me, privately," she said.

Talking through the helmets wasn't that effective. It was more like lip-reading. But she understood "other airlock."

It did make sense, she supposed. Unless the alien had left his "kingdom" completely, he had to have gotten back in. He could have still blocked the airlock after he did that, though. There was a trifling matter of a hundred-and-fifty-meter-high equatorial ridge between them and the next airlock. On the other hand, they had a long cable and some folk who liked to fly, even if they couldn't get into the ladder access. With all of them doing the trip at that speed—without having to lead Amber or any other panicky people—they had the air reserve to try.

It was a long way up and out, still. And there wouldn't be many reserves if they got it wrong. They began to climb up the bars enclosing the outside of the ladder. After a brief while the flyboy motioned that he wanted to turn on the radios. "Too slow," he said. "Give me the jetpack and you anchor here and feed cord."

Minutes later they had a line to the top. And the flyboy said cheerfully—obviously understanding the need to talk in riddles on the radio—"Jackpot!"

They "flew" over the ridge. That was scary, when you considered the fragility of that line. It was all very well knowing that the fabricators claimed that it had a ton and half breaking strain and that they needed the stretch-factor. Lani even understood why, but still, it was a thin cord between her and nothingness. She was glad to get back inside the bars of the walkways and back on her feet.

She was even more pleased to find out that the far airlock could be opened. They stopped there, to change air cylinders for fresh ones and also to talk—without the possibility of eavesdroppers.

"There is a chance he's booby-trapped the lifecraft, you know," said Lani, worriedly. "It's what I'd have done."

"We'll just have to look carefully," said Howard.

"That's all very well," said Lani skeptically. "Of course we can look for wires or such things . . . but electronic traps?"

Howard shrugged. "We will just have to trust in God. However we must also prevent this airlock resealing when we go."

"Why? I mean . . . that's dangerous to the people inside," said one of the fliers.

Howard nodded. "On the other hand, we don't want this one sealed against us too, and we don't want Kretz's craft lost, before we can get him here. The mad Miran may just decide to finally dispose of it. I know from prior experience that even a small obstacle will prevent the other door from being opened. Air leakage—if it happened—would be very slow. And we are planning to return, soon."

"But what would make the nutbag do anything like that?"

"We may need radio comms with Kretz when we get there, and we'll have to return to him with a rebreather unit—if this Derfel has not removed them."

"Okay. I don't like it," said the birdie-woman. "It's not space-safe. But I see your logic, I suppose."

"I don't like it either," admitted Howard. "But I have learned, in the course of this journey, that we have to do some things that we don't want to. The Miran who is in there is mad, and when he changes sex he will become homicidally mad. Kretz will die if we don't take these steps. His friends trapped in here and on the other ship need him. There are risks. But . . . Kretz has kept the faith with them. Our species has tried to kill him, imprisoned him, placed every obstacle in his path. He still has kept trying. Can we do less for him? This is a simple, relatively low risk act, if bad practice. It's a pragmatic step to make sure that his lifecraft is here, undamaged, when he gets here."

"You're a hopeless idealist, not a pragmatist," said the birdie-woman, grinning and shaking her head. "What do you intend to use?"

"This wire?"

She shook her head. "Might damage the seal."

"What about a piece of cloth?" offered Lani.

"That would be ideal if you've got something that you feel you can spare."

Thus it was that access was secured by a pair of panties Lani hadn't seen much point in anyway.

They approached the squat angular shape of the alien lander with trepidation. It did nothing, which they found quite worrying enough. Careful examination found a thin cable across the gangway. Lani cracked radio silence. "Kretz. Talk to us about Miran booby traps."

His voice came across the ether. "I have considered this since the ship was moved. The best answer is that there is an emergency exit on the upper surface, just behind the forward window. I think you could gain access there. It has a slitlike handle you turn clockwise. It is quite small."

"Out," said Lani.

They had to use Howard as a ladder. Fortunately, he made a good one, sturdy and very obliging about using his hands as rungs. Unfortunately, he also had delusions that he would go into Kretz's ship, just in case there were traps. It was a good thing that the emergency exit was just too small for him, or the argument might have wasted more air.

Lani felt very isolated when the little door closed above her; a few moments later she became the first human to walk inside an alien ship. It was remarkably like a dark, metal-walled human-built corridor might have been. Mindful of Kretz's irritating *don't-touch-anything* lecture—What did he think they were? Primitives?—she resisted the very human desire to explore and just concentrated on getting back down to the inner main door, where Kretz said the spare air cylinders for his rebreather were stored. With two of them in hand—just in case—she set off back, carefully not disturbing the tripod and possible weapon arrangement just inside the door. Howard was waiting anxiously to haul her out.

Then it was just a long spacewalk back.

By the time they returned, Kretz was in a ferment of worry and guilt. Indecisive worry and guilt. What should he do? Had he sent a being—who had become a friend—to his death? Would he be able to help those who depended on him? Should he have tried a human suit, even if his feet would never have fitted into the boots? It was difficult to imagine getting anything remotely close to a fit, but should he have tried? Should he have let the engineers in this place loose on his existing tank to see if they could refill it?

He was almost furious to see them back, smiling and laughing. With this came a realization. They were no longer friendly aliens. They'd become the same as any other Miran in the way he perceived them—and it was apparent that Howard and Lani viewed him in much the same way. They put their arms around him.

Howard suddenly realized what he was doing. Holding a woman, and an alien thing—as if it was the most natural thing to do.

And then he realized that it was. "It's nearly over," he said regretfully. "We have your air tanks, and we'll have you back to your lifecraft in a short time."

He squeezed Kretz's shoulder "And you know what? I am going to miss you, Brother Kretz." He smiled. "To think that I was devastated to be chosen to go with you. Now . . . I don't know that I can go back. At least, not to stay. I'd like to go and open a few blind eyes. But it would be strange to worry about tomato-yields after this. I have seen space, I have read other books, which are not about religion. I have seen that other people work metals and make things without being cast into exile or worrying about hellfire."

"You are a rather different human than the man who worried about this female," said Kretz, looking at Lani. "What was it that you called her again, when you first met?"

"A painted Jezebel," admitted Howard. "I behaved like a narrow-minded fool, looking back, and got us into a lot of unnecessary trouble. Mind you, I still worry about her. And about myself. But I am beginning to accept that the Brethren have tried to make God into a very narrow image of man, instead of man being created in the image of God. Man was created in the image of someone loving, omnipotent and omni-cognizant, that understands human frailty and differences better than we can. We must try to include, not to exclude."

"He talks like this from time to time," said Lani, giving Kretz's opposite shoulder a squeeze. "I don't understand him either, Kretz. I think I'm in love with an alien too."

At least she sounded very happy about it.

"I think I do understand him . . . at least in part, Lani," said Kretz. "And I did promise that I would return Howard to his home habitat. I should be able to do that, easily, if you want me to?"

"We hadn't really decided," admitted Howard. "I . . . wish to stay with Lani. To marry her. Marriage in the eyes of the church is important to me."

"We're staying together," said Lani firmly, "it's just a matter of where. We can't go back to the Matriarchy, even if we wanted to. We can't go to the uThani's habitat, really. They don't want us. And Howard is too heavy to ever really be a flier, so that leaves New Eden."

"Which would not be kind to Lani," admitted Howard. "And I do not know how they would deal with a man who had used a weapon to commit the sin of Cain."

"You had to shoot him, Howard," said Lani.

"I could live with not being able to fly," said Howard, smiling.

"Well, the truth is, we don't know if we are welcome here. Amber, uh . . . is. But what do we do here? Everyone works, everyone trains from very young to be something. They don't really have much use for an ex-cop and farmer. So . . . we're still thinking. I think it'll have to be New Eden for us two. And the uThani obviously want to go home."

Amber came over to them, hand in hand with her partner. "There is food ready. What are you lot plotting? How to get Kretz's other companion out of the next habitat? I've been giving that some thought."

"Uh, no. Howard and I were talking about . . . where we would live, after we got Kretz to his spacecraft," said Lani.

"Forgive me, Brother Kretz," said Howard. "I had forgotten about your companion."

He'd been with them for long enough to know the signs that Kretz was discomforted too. "I . . . do not see how we can rescue him."

"We cannot just abandon him," said Howard. "He is alone and desperate, as you were, Kretz."

Kretz nodded slowly. "But there is Selna too. I am torn. And . . . well, I have learned in traveling through these habitats that humans are quite capable of stopping me, even if I were armed with more than this automatic shotgun. I don't think I can rescue him. I do not see how."

"It's a good thing that I do, then," said Amber. She tapped her portable. "I think I can log into their computer system. The uThani's system did me a favor with their data-theft. They left some signs, and talking with the computer geeks here, we've got a very good idea of the access codes for the basic programming level. I think we should be able to get access to theirs. We should be able to work out routes to get there in secret. We might even be able to get in, in secret."

"She's too clever for her own good," said Zoë, smugly.

Amber blushed. "I got tired of the idea of Earth's computer systems spying on us," she said. "Now come and eat. It's lovely fresh vat protein." She grinned. "The uThani are even less flattering about it than you were, Howard."

Howard made a face. "That is impossible."

"Oh, yeah? They say it tastes likes something a bird sicked up to feed to its chicks. They're talking serious export opportunity from their habitat. And they've burned some birds that they call parrots that they had with them."

Howard brightened perceptibly. "Those funny chickens! I wonder if they have any left. I would love to taste real food again."

"Meals are going to be interesting in this relationship," said Lani wryly.

# 33

When the enemy believes himself utterly invincible, then he is at his most vulnerable.

> —uThani proverb, attributed to Chief Abasaque-do-rinti, the leader of the tribe when they left Earth.

Who did he think he was kidding?

> —Dandani

"The first step will be to get Kretz to his lifecraft," said Lani. She didn't know how she'd ended up organizing and leading this operation, except that her police experience was the nearest thing any one had to a military background. "Would you be able to disable any booby traps from inside, Kretz?"

373

He nodded. "I hope so."

"Right. At this point you will radio your spacecraft. Tell them that you have a few technical problems, but that you will be returning very shortly. Then you hop back and fetch Amber. It'll save her a walk in space."

"And me," said Zoë, "Although I rather fancy the walk. I never thought I'd say I fancied a walk."

"Fine," said Lani cheerfully. "Anything to avoid domestic problems. You take these two to the airlock I . . . um . . . secured. Once inside the airlock you probably make contact with the computer system of the habitat. At this point Kretz says that he is returning to the main spacecraft. If the perp inside is listening he assumes that his only threat has gone, at least for now. If Amber is correct we can establish where the enemy, um, the people inside are. Then we take the plan from there. Okay?"

"So who is going on this expedition?" asked Howard. "I volunteer, of course."

"I'll have to go. Nobody else drives a computer system well enough," said Amber.

"We go," said Nama-ti. "Food here terrible. Go look for game and new hunting grounds. Besides, want to see new place."

"People may try to kill us."

Uppity gabbled something.

His companion broke into laughter. "Dandani he say: is just like home. All women here give trouble. Need to get away."

"Yeah, but he understood what I was saying without you translating it, Perp-One."

Nama-ti grinned. "He understand more than he tell. But too shy to speak."

"Shy. Him?" Lani raised her eyebrows. "You're a sneaky bunch of rogues."

Nama-ti beamed. "Thank you for compliment. We small tribe. Stay alive. Stay tribe by being sneaky. Chief Abasaque-do-rinti say that. He say lots of clever things, like never argue with woman, she talk long after head sore."

"I appreciate this, brothers," said Howard. "But it will be dangerous. We have no right to ask this."

They looked at each other. "Without danger, what for is life?" said Dandani, venturing on his first English.

Zoë shook her head. "With that attitude you'll have half of Icarus going along. We have more in common than I realized."

"If I've learned one thing on this journey," said Howard quietly, "It is that men and women of goodwill have far more in common than I had realized."

Dandani looked at Nama-ti. Said something. Nama-ti shook his head, laughed.

"What's he saying?" asked Lani, suspicious because they definitely looked at her.

"He say: This 'In common,' does mean Howard no get cross when Dandani run off with strong woman?"

She raised an eyebrow at him. "You'd be so lucky. The one you have to worry about getting cross is me, Uppity," she said, shaking a fist at him. She had to smile at the two of them. And then again, she had to be glad that they wanted to come along. Those bows of theirs were silent and lethal. And the two of them could move like ghosts when they wanted to. Hunting had honed them into being very deadly. She wondered, suddenly, if it was this deadliness that made them so confident, if that had been what she'd been seeking with weapons and martial arts training? She also noticed that Howard was looking just a little protective. That was . . . very satisfying too.

"We might as well save oxygen. Taking Kretz across is not exactly a dangerous and stressful thing," said the flyboy. "And it gives us an excuse to do it again," he said with an impish grin. "We'll do it. Let your lot rest."

It made sense. But Lani discovered afresh just how much she hated anxious waiting.

Kretz slipped back down in through the emergency exit of the lifecraft and into a familiar world. The light—a slightly different color to that of the alien light-system —was almost like the familiar caress of an old lover. He walked through to the control room and sank into a chair that had actually been designed to fit Miran form, and started powering up, running system diagnostics at the same time. It took him a few moments to find the little preventative measures that Derfel had set up. The comforting thing was that they all seemed designed to disable rather than to actually destroy. Derfel obviously had plans for the lander. He was not the engineer Kretz was, and it was easy to disable the internal traps, even the one attached to the debarkation ramp. Next came the crucial phase. He hoped that the two humans had moved back to the walkways as instructed, because he took the lifecraft straight up, in a four G take off. Anything that went wrong or exploded would either be harmless on the surface, or at least have the lifecraft well clear of the habitat if it was destroyed.

He breathed again . . . he was still here. He began to set the craft down despite a voice in his head screaming "go back to the spacecraft *now*." And then he realized that it was not just his desire to be back there . . . but Selna's voice in his ears.

"I can't just yet, Selna. I have to set down and remove a few booby traps and clear up some damage," Kretz said. "But I will, shortly. I am afraid there is no way to rescue Abret."

"Don't delay," she said crossly. "I can't wait much longer. There is nothing that Derfel could do that you couldn't undo very fast. But I don't suppose you'll listen to me. You never do."

Kretz set the craft down again awash with guilt. What she wanted was self-centered. He knew that he'd done all he could . . . but had he really? Could he have been more effective? Should he take the further risks that had to be involved in trying to free Abret? Deep instinct said *no*. The females of the species had to be preserved. There were always more males, but to have survived to sex-change age, you were a rarer being. Instinct, and the culture built on it, still said this . . . even if male mortality was no longer the huge proportion it had been during Miran evolution. Logic had a hard time winning, over this. It had been a different matter before he'd had a real way of returning to her.


"But he could be anyone," Abret said to the guard, the only one that seemed to want to talk to him.

"He Great Leader," replied that individual, scratching. "Give much food. And also fulfill prophecy: Foreign devils come to free us."

"And are you free?" asked Abret.

The jailor thought about this one. Jangled a bunch of keys. "Me free. You prisoner."

Abret sat on the middle of the floor. "Has Derfel made anything better? Really better?"

"Killed president-for-life's guard. That good thing. They murder many."

"*I* killed them. And, I tell you, truly I did not mean to."

"Great leader say he kill with holy force."

"Ask someone who was there," said Abret.

The jailor looked thoughtful. Nodded. "I will."

Apparently he did, during his off-time, because he came back a very troubled man. "Is true. Why are you in jail?"

Abret sighed. "Because I want to go home. And Derfel enjoys being important here. He likes being your Great Leader."

"But we need a Great Leader," said the jailor.

"Why?"

"Because . . . someone must lead. We ordinary people are too stupid," said the jailor, with the air of someone who has been told this often enough to assume that it is true.

"I can promise you this: Derfel—the Miranese that you now call your Great Leader—is not very clever. At least he is clever enough, just not very sensible. Within the next few years he will go completely mad, when he becomes female."

The jailor blinked. "Foreign devils change sex?"

That might make the rule of Derfel a little more awkward. "Yes," said Abret. "He will become a she. Just like you."

"But now he is male?"

Abret nodded. The jailor said nothing, just got up and walked away.

A little later he came back with another human. One whose mouth was set in a thin, hard line. "This is my brother, Ji. The Great Leader he take his daughter."

"We are logged in," said Amber. "I'm initiating the search." She raised her eyebrows. "Can you please tell that guy on your radio to shut up."

"That is Selna. I'm afraid our main spacecraft detected the movement, and now she is insisting I return, immediately, to the ship."

"Oh. I suppose the voice being deeper makes sense with females being bigger," said Amber, adding parameters to the search.

"Yes. It confused me with your species at first," said Kretz. "The idea that the gender which would have to have the physiological strain of child-bearing would be smaller seems entirely bizarre to us."

"Hmm. I can see the argument, but different selective pressures got our males bigger than our females. And now please go and tell that female to shut up. So far I'm not having a lot of joy here. I'll need to think. Your body temperatures are higher than ours, right?"

So Kretz hit the transmit button on his suit radio. He couldn't tell her to shut up, since such rudeness to a female was just not to be considered. But he'd try reason. Otherwise he would just have to do without comms. "Selna. I have problems here."

"You have problems!" she shouted. "It is always about you, isn't it? Well, I have problems too. I'm working through the manuals. If you don't hurry I'll launch anyway."

"I promise I am doing my best, Selna. I will be back at the ship very soon. At the moment I need to recalibrate some instruments that Derfel sabotaged. If I tried right now I might fail to reach you. It's very complicated." He gambled on the fact that Selna was not particularly good with instrumentation, and fairly ignorant about it as a result.

"You've got sixteen TU's," snarled Selna. "Or I'll either leave you behind or come and fetch you."

And that was the best Kretz could do. Translating Miran time to human time, Kretz calculated Selna had decided on about eleven hours. He hoped that he had that calculated right. This base ten of the aliens was awkward.

He walked back to where Amber was calmly prying deeper into the computer system of the habitat. "There is a high population density," she said. "I've got to warm body scan. Our problem is not so much that we can't see where they are, but that they're everywhere. Especially here, watching this airlock. I think I have found your Miran. I'm hoping that we can get live vid images. In the meanwhile if any of you have any ideas—beyond just loud noise—how we get through this airlock, I'd like to hear it."

Kretz was hardly surprised when Howard asked diffidently. "You locked airlocks with the computer on Diana. Can you do things like that here?"

She nodded. "I have done so. This lock is shut until we decide to open it."

"Could you establish how the other lock is being prevented from sealing?"

"If I get vid-feed . . . Ah."

Images began appearing on the small screen. Most of them seemed to have people working on crops. Then they showed the other airlock.

The door was held ajar by a simple orb of metal.

"That won't damage seals," said Zoë.

"Ah, but it lacks the elegance of a pair of panties," said Andy, grinning.

"It is a pity we can't force the door and move it," said Howard. "I would have suggested that if it was an obstruction of the tiniest size. There are people there too, but at least they would not be prepared for us."

"Maybe we can get a maintenance 'bot to do it," said Amber, thoughtfully. "Let's see. In the meanwhile . . . here are your Miran." The screen split and produced two images, in circumstances of contrast. In one the individual was sitting in a stark cage, sitting on the floor, naked, arms wrapped around himself. Plainly he was cold as his body was covered in soft rippling cilia. He was speaking to someone.

"Abret."

The other Miran was also naked—but probably by choice. The human in the vast bed with him looked terrified, to Kretz's now accustomed eyes. "Well, at least he's not paying much attention to us," said Lani. "Although that picture makes it easier to understand where the Matriarchy of Diana came from."

"It is an abomination," said Howard stiffly.

"I don't have any trouble agreeing with you, for once," said Lani. "She looks in more need of rescue than your Abret, Kretz."

It left Kretz with feelings of guilt. Would they have regarded his own encounter of mutual curiosity with the same disgust? The flier-girl had said it made her feel a bit like a zoophilist, which, if Transcomp interpreted it rightly, had rather echoed his own feelings. It had been . . . interesting. Most male Miran would take any sort of willing partner. But one such as Derfel had trouble finding those. Now, it appeared, he was finding satisfaction among the humans of this habitat. It didn't look like he provided much of it.

Amber flicked off the scene, and showed a small 'bot crawling down off the roof, to move the doorstop of metal aside. As it rolled they could see that it was a human head, cast in bronze.

The little 'bot pushed the door, which clicked shut. Amber hastily typed something into her portable. "Airlock secure," she said. "Now let's see if we can map a route that will get us to the Miran from there instead."

It was rapidly apparent that it was not going to be that easy.

"It's very heavily populated. Much more so than New Eden or Diana or Icarus," said Lani looking at the corridors of diggers and careful pruners.

"Much more than uThani too," said Nama-ti in a melancholy tone. "Is even worse hunting grounds."

To Howard it was frighteningly crowded, yet painfully nostalgic. These were farmers. Hard-working farmers too, to eke a living out of such tiny, precise little fields. To live off so little land you had to make each inch count.

"They plainly have no birth control," said Zoë.

It was a delicate subject that Howard had not seen open discussion of. Among the Brethren the limit of two children was something most families insured by passive means. Howard's father had blushingly explained days of abstinence to him. Occasionally a family had an extra babe—but that was well countered by occasional accidental deaths, and those who failed to have children at all. He'd never thought about the effects of an absence of limits on this in a closed environment before. It was a terrifying one, reflected in the slight build and thin faces of the populace.

"They're never going to make the hundred or more years until they get to their sun. And it doesn't look as if, when they get there, they'll have the technological ability to build the habitats they need," said Amber, grimly. "They're worse off than anyone else, so far."

Howard shook his head. "The amazing part is that they've survived this long without famine."

"They may not have. There are states in the history of old Earth that had serial famines," said Amber. "I wish I hadn't remembered that."

"Our priority now is to rescue Kretz's imprisoned companion," said Howard, "but I cannot just leave these people in such wretchedness. When that is done we need to do something for them."

"Yeah, well, how do you intend to get to that first priority?"

Howard shrugged. "They are farmers. They work hard. Tonight they will sleep. It is not like your automated civilizations. People are tired. While they sleep we can walk through their midst."

The thinkers of high strategy blinked at him.

"It's so simple that it could just work," said Lani.

"Just like me," said Howard with a quiet smile.

"Huh," she said tucking her arm in his. "Dead simple."

"And how will we find our way in the dark?"

"We could take a shuttered lantern," said Howard, doubtfully.

"Or better still, use the gear we used for night-traps for perps," said Lani. "If the flyboys have anything like that. Infrared and special goggles."

"We do have some portable emergency lights," said Kretz. "Hand-held lights."

"What about programming your computer to guide us like . . . you know . . . one of those games? Beep if we go off track," said Lani.

"That's . . . within the realms of possibility," said Amber.

"Could you not just have a maintenance 'bot guide us? Or carry us, as the wild men in Diana had them do?" asked Howard.

"Yes!" said Amber, brightening. "And that way I don't have to walk. Let's see if there are any water arterials."

There were. A short walk would take them to one that led right through the grounds of the huge complex that housed both the prisoner and the alien who had—according to Kretz—gone mad. The exits might be secured, but Kretz had found a tool in the ship that he said had dealt with the other human electronic locks. It had dealt with the one on the hollow central cable, anyway. Now all they had to do was prepare and wait. It was never easy. Not even when Lani offered to distract him with further lessons in this "making out."

When the lights were dimmed in the habitat, they were ready. Despite not having master-flier status, they all had black lycra—even Kretz had an outsize set pulled over his suit, and they had all blackened their faces.

"I saw it in a picture of old-time soldiers, " said Lani, when Howard protested. "And it makes sense. Your faces would show up."

Howard had learned one thing of great value in his relationship already. When she used that tone, he just did what she wanted. Besides, all over black hardly counted as "painted." He was sure that that was not what they'd meant in the Bible anyway. As for weapons . . .

Kretz offered laser pistols. While the alien put one on his belt, he kept hold of the automatic shotgun. Lani settled for extra clips for the pistol. Amber accepted a strap for her shotgun, Zoë had a short broad-barreled weapon from a secure stockpile in Icarus, as did the other two fliers. The uThani, after consideration, kept to bows and machetes. Howard stuck to his hands. "You either have enough weapons—or far too few," he said quietly. "At need I will carry and kill. But I think my hands are going to be needed. So let me keep them free."

Zoë grinned. "Not so, big 'un. We want you to take this pry-bar. We may need it, and it's heavy."

It probably was to light-boned fliers. And, in need, it made a weapon.

An hour after full darkness had fallen in the habitat, the portable showed only one person anywhere near the airlock. So they cracked it and went in. If the person was a guard, apparently he had settled down some distance away. They didn't even have to disturb him on their way to the arterial tunnel . . . although it was a close thing. Howard stumbled over something in the dark. He managed not to fall, and felt for the object to move it before anyone else fell. It was roundish and heavy and he ended up taking it with him, as they crept on through the dark.

The door to the arterial was securely locked. And it did not respond to Kretz's electronic tickling either. Kretz used his laser-pistol on the lock eventually, and Howard finished the job with the pry-bar. He set the round object down to do it, but being a neat worker by habit, he picked up again. It was only later, hunching down on the running board behind the pipe-checker that he took a proper look at it. And screamed before he could help himself. It leered at him. For a brief irrational moment he had thought that it was a real human head, instead of one severed from a statue.

"What did you bring that for?" asked Lani, looking at it. "That was what was used to jam the airlock."

"I tripped over it," explained Howard. "Then I picked it up before anyone else fell over it. What should I do with it?"

Lani shrugged. "Bring it along. You can always throw it at someone. If you leave it here it'll fall off and block the pipe-checker's tracks, probably."

So, when the pipe-checker was inside the sprawling complex that they were to discover was the beloved leader's palace, Howard had a head under his arm. Following Amber's instructions they walked through the vast place, avoiding people, moving closer to Abret.

The patrolling guard's torch was an unwelcome surprise. They were halfway across the square and there was nowhere to run to. Howard and the rest stood dead still. Howard hunched his shoulders and tried to pretend that he wasn't there. The torch-light swung across them . . . and stopped. On the head. The patrolling guard gasped. And the torch toppled to the floor.

"Howard, you nearly frightened *me* to death with that thing," said Dandani quietly, lowering the guard's body. "How you stop this light?"

"Put it under him," said Howard, not wanting to ask if the man was dead.

"Hokay. We go on?"

So they did. In the shadows between two buildings on the far side of the square they stopped to consult the portable again.

Amber pointed to the screen. "He's moving. Somehow he must have gotten out that cell."

"Where is he going?" asked Kretz.

In the dim glow from the screen Amber's frown was ferocious. "Towards the other alien."

"We have trouble. Serious trouble," said Lani.

# 34

The spark of revolution is more likely to come from ordinary things, like family or food, than it is to come from deep philosophical thought. That is the tinder, not the spark.

> From: *Elementary Societal Psychodynamics.*
> 2089. James R. Grey (ed). New Harvard
> Library (Pub.)

---

It was dark, and Ji was dressed all in black. He'd moved so quietly that Abret hardly heard him. It was obvious that the night jailor hadn't heard him at all. Ji had his keys. He opened the cell as quietly as possible.

"Are you ready, foreign devil?" he asked quietly.

Abret stood up. "As I'll ever be."

Abret knew he'd agreed to this. Now he was determined to try. How close they might get to Derfel was another matter. At least Abret knew he could die free and fighting.

Naked and cold, he walked out of his cell and down the passage, stepping over the fallen body of the jailor, and following his human guide up the passages. Ji at least knew where they had to go. Abret knew what he had to do if they got there. He played all the possibilities in his mind. Escape after that might not be possible, but at least he would not go mad behind the bars. After all, death was inevitable. It might as well be quick. And what had these humans—be they ever so vile at times—done to deserve Derfel?

They rounded the corner. There, coming towards them, were a group of the brown-uniformed guards. Already, it seemed, they had lost! He half-turned, only to hear voices behind him. And then he realized that the brown-uniformed ones were not aiming those weapons at him. They had stepped aside and were standing rigidly, weapons shouldered, a hand across the weapon in what was plainly some ritual gesture.

Feeling as if his legs might suddenly fail him, Abret walked on past, waving vaguely at them.

"What happened?" he asked, once they were around the next corner.

"They believe you to be the Great Leader," said Ji. "I did when I first saw you. The Great Leader does as he wishes."

For a moment Abret was insulted. He didn't look a bit like Derfel! Did all aliens look alike to them? Well, he'd struggled with telling the humans apart at first. On the positive side, they were still free. There was a remote—very remote—chance, that he could recover his suit and win free to the lifecraft. It could only go better . . . if he took brave steps.

"Where are those who command?" he said, amazing himself with own audacity.

Ji looked him in puzzlement. "Those who command?"

"Those who command the ones in brown," explained Abret.

"The officers? General Su-Jin commands the night-staff of the presidential guard."

"Let us go and see him."

"Are you mad too?"

"No. I want us to succeed. I will tell him to put his guards on the outside."

The black-clad Ji smiled. It was the first smile that Abret had ever seen from the grim-faced man. "You must say 'send all the guards to defensive positions in Perimeter One.' The Great Leader speaks our language better."

It suddenly occurred to Abret to be suspicious. "How do you know all of this? How do you do all of this?"

Ji shrugged. "Because I am a senior agent in the secret police. I have worked for the Great Leader for many years . . . until I brought my daughter to see the new Great Leader. She begged."

His face set hard again. "They are used to seeing me in these clothes here. I come to report my work at night."

The general, in his brown uniform spattered with red braid, did not seem surprised at the instruction, or Abret's company, or his state of undress. "It will be done immediately, Beloved Leader," he said holding his one hand rigidly, flat palm out from his odd headgear.

Abret did not risk saying any more. He just nodded and turned and left. He allowed Ji to lead him to an empty room a little farther up the passage. "We will give them five minutes," said Ji.

In the narrow gap between the two buildings Lani watched as the briskly trotting squads of brown uniformed soldiery headed past. "Something has stirred them up," she said.

"Us, I imagine," said Howard quietly, at her shoulder.

Lani smiled. "If it is us, they're going the wrong way."

"Lucky that," said one of the uThani with a flash of teeth in the darkness. "We would never get through all of this lot. Not without a whole tribe."

"Many. Lot of beads and trinkets to sell," said the other with a chuckle.

They moved out, a little later, down deserted passages, until they came to an ornate, heavily carved door . . . with two dead men beside it.

Ji and Abret had proceeded down the empty corridors to the guarded double door. The guards blinked at Abret, one stopping in mid-salute. Ji kept walking and then, just as the guard on the left started to raise his weapon, lashed out.

To Abret it seemed impossible. You could not kick one man in the throat and knock the weapon from the other's hand that fast. And the blow that Ji followed that up with—an upward strike with the heel of his hand at the man's nose, dropped him. Ji leapt on the fallen throat-kick victim. The gasping man gave a half strangled shriek.

Abret tugged at the door handle, and the huge doors swung open. He and Ji bundled inside.

But they had not been quick or quiet enough.

Derfel was on the far side of the room. He held a terrified looking little human in front of him, his arm around her throat. He held a laser-pistol in the other hand. "You! How did you get here?" he demanded. "My guards will be here any moment."

The small human squirmed, "Papa?" Her voice was full of fear . . . and hope.

"Yes, little flower. It is me," said Ji. "Let her go, foreign devil."

"Come any closer and I'll shoot her."

The door pushed open. "Just in time," said Derfel.

"Actually," said the black-faced entrant, in Miran: "a little late."

Others came in behind him. Humans. Black from head to toe, except that one carried a bronze head under his arm. A head that Derfel had so boldly severed.

"Kretz?" said Abret, incredulously.

The blackened face smiled. "Nice to see Miran faces, even if it is not good to see you pointing weapons at each other. I've come to take you back to our spacecraft. Selna is getting a little anxious to go home."

Kretz took in the scene, and read the situation as best as he could. Derfel could still kill them. By the look in his eyes he was definitely off the edge of sanity.

He stepped forward as confidently as he could.

"Keep back or I'll shoot!" said Derfel. "I mean it."

Kretz looked at Derfel. Then at the wide-eyed little human female he held and the other humans. "He is threatening to kill."

"Can he?" asked Howard.

For an answer Kretz said: "Spread out."

"Stand still!" snarled Derfel—in Miranese, which no one but Abret and Kretz understood.

"I mean you no harm," said Kretz, as calmly as he could, while slowly raising the barrel of the automatic shotgun. "If you don't want to go, we'll just take Abret."

"And the human you're holding, and my suit," said Abret.

Derfel showed no sign of moving or cooperation. "My people will be here soon. You are right in the middle of my kingdom. You can't get away."

"I sent them away. They thought I was you," said Abret. "Now, let that little human go, Derfel. She's done you no harm."

The man who had been there with Abret said something in a foreign language.

Derfel looked at him and answered in the same tongue.

"What did he say?" asked Kretz, warily, wondering if he should be covering this man as well.

"Ji told him to let his child go. Derfel said he'd let the child go if Ji dealt with us," said Abret.

While Derfel's attention had been on the black-clad Ji, Nama-ti had been sidling farther around the room. He was very close to Derfel and the girl now. He said, very quietly in uThani, "Distract him, Dandani. I'll get the girl-child."

Kretz found it an odd way for learning their language to pay dividends. A quick glance showed him the scar-faced uThani had an arrow on the string and was nearly at the opposite flank. "Hey, you with ugly face," said Dandani loudly—in English—"why you no come fight me, one-one? You have face like *Carpincho's* ass." It was a huge pity that Derfel's translator couldn't do English, thought Kretz.

As Derfel turned, Nama-ti dived, grabbing the girl and wrenching her down. Forewarned, Kretz fired first. He barely beat Lani.

An arrow . . . A flung bronze head, and a screaming man called Ji.

It happened fast.

But not fast enough for Nama-ti. The brief dying convulsion of Derfel's hand sent a lightbolt to strike his forearm. The uThani's hand was half severed. He screamed.

One of the flyboys, slow to react to the violence, was quick enough now. He had a tourniquet on Nama-ti's arm, and a syringe in his hand, while the others were still almost stock still.

Ji held his daughter. The child stared not at him, but at the bronze head. She kept saying something over and over.

Lani was the first to come to terms with the situation. They were all a bit shocked. Amber looked as if she'd faint any moment and that flygirl of hers was not looking much better. Someone had to take charge.

"We need to move out," she said. "I can hear them coming."

"No," said Kretz, decisively. "We need to buy more time. Hide. Pull the bodies in from outside too. There is a room in there. Cover Derfel with that bedding." He turned to the other Miran and said something in a foreign language.

The other alien gaped at him.

Abret was shocked by the suddenness, by the violence. By Kretz. Mild mannered Kretz, what he'd done and what he now said. "Abret, you will meet them at the door and tell them to leave you alone. I hope that your Transcomp has that much of the language."

"Me?" Abret knew that was a stupid thing to say. But right now, with aliens pulling dead bodies past him in the aftermath of the killing, he felt stupid.

Kretz shook him. Hard. "Others thought that you were him earlier. To them we probably all look alike," said Kretz, hauling bedclothes over the dead Miran. "I found humans hard to tell apart at first. You owe them, Abret. They've risked their lives to rescue you."

Ji had sat up, still holding his daughter to his chest. She was still saying over and over again that the ancestor himself had come to save her. "What is happening?" he asked. "Who are these people?"

"These are friends who have come to rescue me. I am going to pretend to be the Great Leader." Without knowing why he did so, Abret patted the man on his shoulder. "We will get you and your daughter away too, if we can."

Ji nodded, spoke in the rapid-fire local language to the girl child, and gave her the bronze head. "Lie down, child. The ancestor is with you. Hide him under the bedclothes too." He turned to Abret. "She must be here. Tell them they interrupt your pleasure. Tell them to go back to the first perimeter."

The palatial bathroom was big but it had never been intended for this many people. Nama-ti was in the huge empty bath itself, having his partially severed hand attended to. He was not really conscious, after whatever it was that they'd injected him with. Amber had her head between her knees and was being patted by her flygirl. Lani stood with the others, including the grim-faced local, at the door. Waiting.

Then she heard the sound of the doors being opened. The other alien said something. The girl said something that sounded hysterical. The alien kept repeating himself.

There was the sound of the door closing.

The local man, Ji, was first out. It was just as well, because the girl was trying to brain Kretz's alien friend with the bronze head, and screaming at him.

Ji managed to take it from her and hold her. "Have you guys got a tranquilizer?" asked Lani, looking at the remaining flyboy with his as yet unused burp-gun.

He nodded. "Better check it out with the local man first though. He's scary."

Lani turned to Kretz. "Get your buddy to sling the language for us, Kretz. We've got something to tranquilize the kid. We can't have her screaming while we're getting away. Although her screams probably convinced the guards."

Kretz routed the message through Abret, and to the black-clad local.

Abret couldn't blame the little alien for her attack. If he had grasped it right she was an adolescent human female. Whatever else was different between the two species, the concept of adolescence was similar. He would cheerfully have killed Derfel for that alone. Ji still apologized to him. "She is distraught, foreign devil."

Abret pointed to Kretz. "My friend say they have something to help. Like the thing they give to wounded man. Can they give?"

Ji nodded. "I would be glad. So would she, if she was herself. She does not seem too rational, telling the guards that the ancestor would come and save her." He pointed at the head. "It is an object of great reverence here."

"Good. I will tell them to give it to her. Then we can see about escaping."

Ji sighed. "I do not think that is possible. There is nowhere in the Workers Paradise to hide. But I have done what I needed to do. Thank you. You are a creature of honor, even if you are a foreign devil."

As the young human was injected, Abret conveyed the gist of this to Kretz. "He got me out of jail. And . . . I feel a debt, Kretz. A debt of honor. One of us did this to his daughter. He says nowhere here is safe for them. Is there anywhere else we can take them?"

Kretz nodded. "I'll ask Howard. He is a good human. The people of his habitat are odd, but they were very kind to a stranger in their midst."

Kretz turned to the huge human and spoke.

Howard nodded, and replied.

Kretz turned to Abret. "He says yes. He has quoted his holy book at me. They take the belief in a noncorporeal being quite seriously."

Abret nodded thankfully. "I gather around here they would become noncorporeal beings quite quickly, if they stayed. The only problem is that we have still have is just how to get out of there."

"Leave it to them. Especially the big human and the one with the reddish head filaments . . . oh, they're black right now. That one." He pointed. "They are even more ingenious than Miran, Abret. And I know you were badly frightened and treated by these aliens, but some of them have been very good to me. They have kept me alive and helped me to reach you, at great risk and hardship to themselves."

Abret nodded. "I'm beginning to accept that it depends on which one you meet, Kretz."

Kretz looked thoughtful. "In these microcosms things are more concentrated, but maybe that applies to Miran too," he said. "I mean, look at Derfel. Anyway, I'd better do a Transcomp transfer of their language to your unit. I warn you, the language is quite bizarre."

"This one is too. I suppose," Abret said, his face working with distaste, "we should see if Derfel's unit is intact. He did one thing right. He started to learn the language and immerse himself in their culture right away."

"And we'd better look for your suit," said Kretz. "Or you'll stay immersed in it forever. And you need some Miran food, soon, by the looks of you."

"And hormone supplements. But there are some packs on the lifecraft."

"The best I think we can do, is to leave quietly and neatly and take the body with us," said Lani.

Amber shuddered. "Why, Lani?"

"Remember what happened when Howard disappeared?" said Lani.

Amber nodded.

"If I read this lot right, they're going to get very upset when they find a dead 'Great Leader.' One of these brown uniforms will call himself boss and kill a fair number of people. But if the Great Leader just disappears . . . Well, he might come back. I think that will slow them down in their response, if nothing else."

"There is quite a bit of blood and damage, Lani," said Zoë.

Lani smiled. This was her element. "For a forensic team, yes. For this lot—nothing we can't deal with. Turn that mattress over. We'll wrap the body in the sheet."

"It seems a crazy lot of hard work to me," said Amber. "And you'll have to deal with the other bodies too."

"I think we should do it. It won't be our problem, but why should we leave a purge behind us?"

"You're getting a bit more sensitive about this sort of thing than you used to be," said Amber with a smile.

Lani shrugged. "A side effect of living with Howard."

Amber grimaced. "I can believe that. He was on at me about the morality of vat-protein which we vivisect and never allow the joy of a full life and the respect of a quick merciful death. Look, why don't we ask the local boy?" She jerked a thumb at Ji, who was sitting with arm around his child. "We can get Kretz and his friend to translate."

As it turned out Kretz was by now capable of doing the translation alone. And the austere-faced Ji smiled. Pointed at the head.

"He says it is very good idea. And if you do it right, with that thing, then everyone will be too frightened to do anything. His daughter was screaming to the ancestor to save her from the foreign devil—and people here believe in the ancestors. He says that the people believe the foreign devils will come to free them. Yet they also believe that the ancestor will protect them from foreign devils. On their holiday—the Great Leader's birthday —the Ancestor would speak, and urge them to greater endeavor to build the workers' paradise."

Amber looked at the head. There were a couple of severed wires hanging out of the neck. She pulled on them and produced a speaker.

Zoë plainly recognized the device too. "I'll be damned . . ."

"No. They have been," said Amber grimly.

Kretz continued. "He also wants to know: How can we get out of the palace of the Great Leader? He says Abret must give orders."

"I think we can just leave by hitching a ride on the pipe-checkers on the main arterial. Hell. Tell him there is a secret passage." She pointed at the screen. "Here."

Ji listened—and replied.

"He says we must go quickly before the changing of the guard at midnight. And he says can we let him out of the passage to collect his family, once he is beyond the walls?"

"His family?" asked Lani, puzzled.

"Howard has promised them sanctuary," explained Kretz. "They'd want to ask him and his daughter questions, if they just suddenly reappeared."

Amber nodded. "Besides, I think that she needs counseling. I think I probably do too! But isn't it going to be a bit obvious if they just disappear? Isn't someone going to give the alarm if they hear anything? This lot must live in crowded quarters."

Kretz translated. Ji shook his head and replied. "People disappear. At night always. No one will say anything or look in case they are taken too."

Amber pulled a face. "I thought Diana was in trouble, politically."

Zoë said quietly. "Yes. We're going to have to intervene, somehow. Or do we just leave them to starve and kill each other? It goes against Icaran philosophy to have anyone 'nanny' anyone else, but without some help these guys are . . . " She shook her head. "We need to point them in the right direction at least, not rule their lives."

"I would say that it was their accepting that someone could rule their lives that got them into this trouble in the first place," said Lani grimly. "Come on. Let's do a quick and dirty clean up and move out. We can leave them that piece of brass as a souvenir." She pointed at the head.

"How about putting it on that throne that we saw on the vid? It's on our way."

"Sure. And I've a pretty evil idea. We'll put a radio unit in it. They're used to listening to the talking head . . . "

The head and its radio unit were left on the golden throne.

Howard had enough to carry, what with Nama-ti on his back, and one end of the bed-clothes shroud that had three bodies in it.

Half an hour later, Ji brought a frightened looking woman and three children to the door of the arterial. With him came Abret's former jailor with his own wife and child. The woman saw the tranquilized girl, and gave an inarticulate cry and ran to hug her. She turned from her child to look at all of them, the tears streaming down her beaming face and said something that needed no translation.

Ji said something and pointed to Howard. She bowed reverentially to him. Howard wondered just what was being said, and just quite how he was going to explain all of this to the Council of Elders. Then he looked at the tranquilized sleeping girl and decided that the council would just have to get used to it. He hoped the Miran lifecraft could cope with this load, or, if it couldn't, that they could ferry them to-and-fro.

Abret and Kretz were wrestling with the logistics too. "We'll have to do several trips, Kretz."

"We can hardly do anything else. We owe them. We are honor-bound to pay them back," said Kretz.

Abret nodded. It was such a psychologically soothing thing to be back with another Miran, a sane and pleasant one. "Yes. It's a concept they seem to understand too—and expect of us. It is strange how similar, in that aspect, the cultures are."

"Not really," said Kretz. "Thinking about it as an animal behavioralist, I suppose understanding an obligation is the cornerstone of any intelligent species' ability to act as a social unit. There isn't really any way out of it, if you want your social unit to function."

"There are always a few that try," said Abret, thinking of a few individuals.

"Inevitably," agreed Kretz. "I bet humans have them too, and like them just as little as we do."

# 35

"There are always a few who want to turn space into some kind of reserve. 'Preserved eternally unpolluted, pristine and unchanging. Like the rainforest ought to be.' Well, life is a pollutant. Twenty-five percent of particulate pollution alone is biological. Lichens eat rock. Plants spew chemicals. Animals respire, animals fart. And without that pollution, there is no rainforest. And the only eternal thing in the universe is change."

Transcript of the testimony of Dr. Michael Da Silva, Chair of Zoology, to Senate Select Committee on Space exploration, 1/4/2037.

"We're going have to do this in two trips," explained Kretz, when they arrived at the airlock. "Abret and I have decided that we'll take the people needing to go to

Icarus habitat first, then the uThani. It's a lot safer for both of us to pilot the lifecraft."

Howard knew that the time had come—and he was no nearer to a decision himself about where to go. All he was sure about was that he was going to stay with Lani. She was plainly thinking about the same thing. She squeezed his hand.

"Nama-ti needs to come with us for surgery and rehab first," said Zoë. "And we'd like Mister Ji and his daughter for a while for some psychological counseling."

Dandani grunted. He'd been very silent on the trip back. "Nama-ti go die," he said. "Even if no die, hand gone. He no pull a bow again. Better dead than no hunt."

"Believe me, we can fix, at least partly. One thing about a danger-sport culture, we're good at orthopedics and prosthetics."

Dandani looked incredulously at her. "Fix?"

Zoë nodded. "So that he at least has *some* use again." She turned to one of the other two fliers. "What do you think, Isaac?"

The flier nodded. "Forty percent use at least. He'll keep the index finger and thumb anyway."

Dandani was smiling again. "You fix, I bring pile of feathers, high as you." He looked at Lani and winked. "You know, healer woman even better wife than strong woman."

"He's back to normal," said Lani shaking her head. "Look, take them and move them out of here. We— Howard and I and the locals—will get into the airlock as soon as you've cycled it. We'll get everyone suited up and ready to go."

Howard nodded, and looked thoughtful. "That translator device you took off the other Miran body: would it work for English to Ji's language?"

Kretz looked at Abret. "It could be set to do that, yes," said Abret.

"Could you leave it with us? Then I can explain what they have to do."

So Howard was left with Derfel's Transcomp, and the Miran and fliers, and the uThani set out. Farewells were brief—time and danger pressed.

"Be happy together," said Howard, awkwardly, to Amber and Zoë. It was . . . unnatural, he still felt. Not as much as he had at first, though. You grew accustomed to it and realized that they were still the same likeable people. They weren't hurting anyone. If they were so plainly transparently joyful together, was it wrong? It was a bit too complex for Howard. God was better fitted to understand and judge than he was. He seemed to have blessed the relationship with a degree of bliss, and that was enough for Howard.

Dandani made things more complicated. "I speak for you with chief. Place in uThani for you. Brother." He winked at Lani. "Or you can leave him behind and come with me." He ducked and laughed.

And they went into the airlock, and closed the door.

With his fingers twined with Lani's, Howard watched until the red airlock light turned green. Then he cleared his throat and turned to the watching locals. "It is time for us to go. Don't worry. There is a better world out there. It is different, but you will be looked after."

The woman holding her children, with a small cloth bundle as their sole possessions, nodded. "Yes, he-who-brings-the-ancestor. We are ready."

They'd have to learn to call him something else. "Good. Let's go. Once we're in there and suited up, you're safe."

Inside the airlock he showed them where the suits were kept. He and Lani helped to fit the children and bemused adults into them.

When they were sorted it was their turn.

At the end of suiting up, Howard had done his thinking and reached his decisions. He turned to her. "Lani, New Eden would be your idea of hell. You might love me now, but you'd come to hate me, I think. You would be miserable."

She looked coolly at him. "Are you giving me the push, Howard? Are you telling me to go back to Diana and get out of your life?"

He shook his head and took her gauntleted hand. "No. I don't, at this stage, see any place except New Eden for these people. I can't send them back there alone. I want you now and always to be my wife. My partner. Call it what you like. I love you, and I want you beside me. I can't change that. So I am asking you to come back to New Eden with me, and help me change it."

"You already belong to me," she said gruffly. "And I'm a cop. If you go without me, I'll have to follow you, and keep you in safe custody." She put her arms around him. "Like this." She looked up at him. "It's not everyone who has someone offer to change the world for her. I don't think I could have refused that, even if you didn't already belong to me. Now kiss me, before I put this helmet on." Her eyes were very moist.

He did. For a long time. When he came up for air he touched her cheek and said, "With you beside me, I could change any number of worlds."

Abret looked at the lifecraft almost unbelievingly. Not long ago it had seemed improbable that he would ever see it again. Now . . . he would be heading toward the spacecraft. One more stepping stone towards that long journey home. To a place that smelled right to nest.

They got in through the airlocks, settled their passengers. Took their seats, and began the wonderful familiar mantra of pre-flight checks. Kretz clicked on the radio.

"This is the lifecraft to the spacecraft. Selna, are you receiving us?"

There was a silence.

And then Selna's voice. Cold. Angry. "Kretz. I've started the pre-lift sequences. I won't interrupt them for you."

"We're on our way, Selna," said Kretz, soothingly. "I have rescued Abret from the alien habitat."

It didn't have the desired effect. "I told you to come here. Not to risk yourself. Get here *now*. Once final sequence checks begin, I can't interrupt them."

"Stop them now, Selna. You must interrupt them. We're coming. We just can't get there yet. We have some . . . debts we have to pay."

"Debts?" she asked.

"Aliens that helped us survive and get free. They need to be returned to their habitats. We've got them on board."

She screamed. Loud enough to make Kretz and Abret tear the earpieces away from their ears. "Get the filth off the lifecraft! Get here now! I've *got* to get back. Get here before the launch sequence is done. Get here. Get here! Get here! Or stay with those filth forever. I've had your excuses. You lied about checks so you could rescue Abret. You have less than a third of a TU or you can stay there with him."

Abret looked at Kretz. Selna had been his lover, and those relationships often re-established after changeover.

Kretz looked back at him. Spoke into the radio unit again. "Please wait, Selna. It won't take us more than a TU. And we're not even in the optimum launch window yet."

"You have less than a third of a TU," she said again.

Abret took a deep breath. "I'll fly. You keep talking to her."

Kretz nodded. "We deliver these. Pick up Howard. And then we run straight for the spacecraft. We should do it easily. She'll stop when we get there. You can embark and I'll get Howard and the others back. That way . . ."

"It is my debt of honor too, friend. You could have left me there, when you got to the lifecraft. We need to get to her, hopefully get her sedated into trance-sleep."

"It may not work," said Kretz grimly. "There have been no trials on females. There are a lot of physiological changes."

"What else can we do?" said Abret. "First stop, next habitat?"

"Yes. And then the one beyond that."

"We have to rush," said Kretz to them, "Please disembark as quickly as possible." And then he turned to Dandani and spoke to him in his language.

The uThani's mouth fell open. And then he laughed.

Dandani turned to Amber. "He is good enough sneaky to make uThani too."

Amber wished she could speak Miran. Because she'd love to know what it was that made the sudden rush necessary. The best launch window for a return to their homeworld—not due for the last bead for nearly six months—was definitely some time off.

Still, she was willing enough to scramble off the ship and be helped toward the airlock. It was odd to think that they'd never see each other again. Sad. Kretz was alien . . . but very human too.

Howard greeted Kretz with a smile and a ready, roped-together group of space-suits in various sizes. "We must run," said Kretz. "Abret is ready for a hot lift."

Abret had managed to set down right next to the airlock, tricky though that must have been.

Dandani was still aboard. "Why?" asked Howard.

"He could not do the space-walk alone. And we did not have time."

Abret was already lifting, not even waiting for them to find seats.

Howard had spent too much time with Kretz not to read his expressions. "What's wrong," he asked calmly.

The tone seemed to help Kretz.

"Selna. The other Miran survivor. She is back on the spacecraft threatening to launch without us. We cannot get home if she does that. This craft is far too small and far too slow. It has no trance-equipment or drugs. And we have insufficient supplies."

"Surely she won't do that to you?"

"It . . . is possible, yes," said Kretz reluctantly. "She's changed sex. She *needs* her nesting territory. Miran always return to the area of their birth to breed, Howard. And, well, Amber was telling me you humans have something called PMS."

Howard had not the vaguest idea what Kretz was talking about. But Lani obviously did. She nodded. "Yeah. Um. You'll get used to it, Howard. Do you aliens have this problem?"

Kretz nodded. "Only at changeover. There are huge physiological and hormonal changes. On Miran . . . we stay a long way from someone during changeover. Once it is over—Miran females are territorial, never move out of their nesting territory again. But they are everything else we males are not. Sensible. Conservative. But Selna . . ."

"Is having a whole life-time's PMS. Can't get to her nesting territory," said Lani, pulling a face.

Kretz nodded. "So we are going to the last habitat first. Abret will alight, try and calm her and stop the launch sequence. Then we, or rather I, will fly you back to your habitats."

"Kretz!" yelled Abret. The rest of what he said was a gabble of alien, but Kretz left at a run, shouting: "Get them into seats and strapped in."

Howard set about doing so with Lani.

Then they strapped in.

He was glad of it.

# 36

Without hope, without dreams, we have no future.
                    —Abraham Lee. Colonist.

"The side-boosters are flaring," said Abret, as Kretz
dived into his seat. "Tell her we're nearly there! She's
got to stop the sequence. Abort! Abort! ABORT!"

And then as Abret flung the ship into a skidding landing on the end surface of the last habitat . . .

It was too late.

Their hopes of ever returning home were a shrinking speck.

Howard was the first to get out of his seat. The two
aliens were keening gently. He looked out of the forward

ndows. All he could see were some mounds of white stuff and a gaping opening where the airlock should be. Some of the metal walkways were also hanging—as if torn aside by some tremendous force. There was no sign of anything that could be an alien spaceship.

"What happened here?" said Lani coming up behind him.

"Their ship must have gone without them," he said quietly.

"And there?" Lani pointed at the ruined lock.

"It appears that the last habitat . . . is not a habitat any more."

"What do you think happened?" she asked.

"I don't know," Howard admitted. "Could anyone survive that?"

"I doubt it. They probably died fast, anyway. Well, Kretz doesn't need to worry about invasion any more."

Howard was silenced by it. How many humans, no matter how evil, had died there? "Do you think she did it on purpose?"

Lani shrugged. "I would have."

It was a horrific thought. Howard wondered what decision he would have made. His species against a single act of genocide?

Kretz stood up. "Go back to your seats, please," he said in a curiously flat voice. "We must take you back to your homes."

"But what are you going to do, Kretz?" asked Lani, taking his arm and ignoring the request to return to her seat.

Kretz shrugged. It was a very human gesture, and a very sad one.

"What can we do? Abret and I have not enough hormone supplements, food, or a ship that could reach our home. I suppose we will complete such research as can and see if we can launch the lifecraft toward Miran. He pointed at the distant double star. "I think then we will choose a quick death," he said.

Howard had come to stand between the two aliens. He put an arm around Kretz's shoulders, and a hand onto Abret.

"You will always have a place with us," he said quietly.

"We'll even cope with super-PMS," said Lani. "And at least there are two of you."

Kretz shook his head. "Brother Howard. I did not know what brother meant, in the deeper sense of the word, when I was in your habitat. I know now. But it cannot work. Miran must go home to breed. It was that, rather than anything else that drove Selna to this desperate, doomed, illogical step. I thank you—because we are brothers across the species line, across space, across evolution. But it cannot be."

Howard squeezed his shoulder. "Then we'll have to send you home. We don't abandon our brothers either."

Kretz smiled. It was a slight, tragic smile, as Howard judged these things. "I do not believe that even the people of Icarus could build us another ship."

Howard grinned at him. "There is another answer. I believe, from what Amber was telling me—that we have five months until the final habitat is launched, to rehabilitate it. We'll send you and Abret home in it."

The two Miran looked at him, uncomprehending.

"This is a spacecraft too." Howard pointed to the bulk of the habitat below them. "It's programmed to reach your system. When one door closes another opens. Knock and it shall be opened unto you."

Kretz looked at Abret. Abret looked back at Kretz. "I think he means we have to repair the airlock," said Abret,

vly. "One door closes there before another opens.
umans have odd ways of saying things, but you get
quite used to them."

Lani shook her head. "You and the uThani. Now, lets
get this tub moving. To Icarus, I think. I thought it was
all over but I think that now we need to consult Amber
and her girlfriend and the clever box of tricks."

# 37

"Like it or not, a part of the payload of each habitat must be habitat building equipment. To some of you this is a dumping exercise. To others it is a research experiment in sociodynamics. But to the vast majority of the electorate it will become our outreach. Their dream-by-proxy. The feedback will stop it being forgotten. Sabotage it and history will not be forgiving."

—Frank Darcy, Representative,
Irish subregion, in the Slowtrain Funding
Debate in the Lower House of SysGov.

"The first thing we need to establish is if we can synthesize enough male hormones to keep you guys from super-PMS," said Amber. "Holy Susan, that's a frightening

...ught. Food—well, at worst you can make do on the ...nthesized auto-cannibal's diet and some human sources of starches, fats and sugars. Although, I'd like to examine whatever rations there are in the lifecraft and see if we can manage synthesis."

Then she looked at the Icarus people. "Second, the question as to whether the final habitat can be made habitable, or not, needs to be investigated."

"It ought to be," said Zoë. "But whether we have the expendable resources or not is another question. Still, I can promise you that every flight cooperative will have engineers queuing to go and look. It's what we plan to be doing, when we get to Signy. This is a chance to practice. Might not do any harm to involve other habitats, if it is practical. Good training opportunity."

"We can take your engineers," said the bemused looking Abret.

"Do you have enough fuel for lots of these little hops?"

"Several thousand of them, I would estimate."

"Good," said Zoë. "Because I believe that we've got some protein-vat parts for Diana, that need delivering, as well as a blasted uThani with half our stock in spare iron, in the shape of arrow-heads and machetes. We need to get him out of here before we go broke."

"And I need to go back to New Eden. There are some things that need to be corrected," said Howard. "It is time that they came to terms with the Universe outside of New Eden. I need to arrange for settling space for Ji and his family."

"Well, give me a few minutes to make some calls," said Zoë. "It's actually a good thing this. The fault lines between the flight cooperatives had become pretty sharp. Now, suddenly, they're pulling together, when faced with real problems and challenges."

A few minutes later she returned, smiling from ⌐ to-ear. "You have caused more fun than the annual fligh. acrobatics competition. Can you transport five of the best in a few minutes? Ji and the uThani will just have to wait, apparently."

Amber sighed. "I'd better go too. If there is a computer net still working . . . If there is any air in there . . . well, the guys in that habitat sound like a bunch of murderers at best. It'd be wise to see if we can detect them rather than getting killed by them."

It was several hours before they returned. Beaming. Especially Amber.

"We can send them home. First . . . "

She looked at Howard. "I know you were upset about the idea that the Miran might have blown that airlock. It appears that the guilty party were the geniuses inside the habitat. I was able to hook up to the datanet and habitat brain and find out just what happened. They've apparently been making their own weaponry and ammunition and explosives for centuries. They packed the airlock—solid, just about—with high explosive. Set a timer and blew open what they thought was the route to the aliens. The habitat had explosive decompression of about sixty percent of the air pressure before an emergency shutter could be put in place by the surviving repair-'bots." She pulled a grim face. "There is pretty little left alive. No people at all According to the habitat brain they were down to about a thousand anyway, and had long gone to cannibalism. Real cannibalism. The environment was poisoned, damaged and dying. The macro-'bots were mostly destroyed in the fighting, that's why the repairs took so long.

Anyway . . . the other news is that the habitat brain
is reordered from its allocation in the tender. Atmosphere is being replenished. The 'bots have an inner door
to the airlock in place. We're hoping to place an outer
one, fabricated from colonist stock in the last bead. With
some work, Abret and Kretz will be going home."

Howard hugged her. That didn't seem very hard now.
The two aliens stood smiling, too.

"We have something to suggest," said Abret tentatively.

"It's a very large habitat," said Kretz.

"And very empty, for two of us," said Abret. "We
wondered . . . Miran do not occupy space well. We have
discovered humans—the right humans—are a species we
wish to be friends with. Our world . . . is our world. We
do not think humans would enjoy it much. Even the
cooler regions are warmer than you would find comfortable. But we would welcome you in our space. Well. We
would welcome some humans—such as our friends here.
If you wished for a place of your own: There is Miran's
sun's companion. It has a gaseous world you might be
able to use as a fliers' haven. There are some rocky
planetoids . . . "

He trailed off.

Kretz turned to Howard and Lani. "You once said you
dreamed of a world of your own, you two. Would you
come with us? We would leave you a world of your own?"

"The habitat belonged to your species. You have a
claim to it," said Abret.

Howard looked at Lani. She looked back at him.

"It's not genetically practicable," said Amber. "Not
two of you."

"Oh. I think we can recruit a few other sets of genes,"
said Lani cheerfully. "If that is okay with the Miran, that

is. I quite fancy the companion star. We wouldn't quite in each other's sandwiches. But we'd be clos enough."

"What are sandwiches . . . ?"

"Details. Along with the many other details, I will explain them to you. Howard will probably show you with pieces of dead parrot and bread."

Sister Thirsdaughter often found some reason to walk down to the airlock, through Howard Dansson's lands. In another month, the council might just accede to brother Galsson's pointed suggestions that the area be reallocated. It was a shame, really. Howard had been a nice boy, and a good husbandman. She was surprised at how many young men—and women—had troubled her for the story. They regarded the poor boy as something of a hero, it seemed.

She was too old for the shock of seeing him standing on the path looking at the wilderness that his tomatoes had become. He, and the young woman with him, had to catch her as she fell.

She sat there, looking at them holding hands. Howard certainly had found some courage out there, as well as a rather striking-looking girl. He, and she, shone with happiness and almost crackled with an energy of purpose. The Howard who had left here had not known what to do with his life. This Howard seemed to have found out.

"Well," she said. "Did you get Brother Kretz back to his people?"

"At least one of them," replied Howard. "I'm taking steps for him to go the rest of the way, soon."

"I'm glad to have you back, Howard," she said. "I always wondered if it was possible to go out into the outside world and return."

Howard smiled. "Yes. It is possible, and indeed, neces-sary. Every elder from New Eden must do it, and soon, if you are to survive. There is God's universe out there, and we're part of it. Now, I need to find as many of the local elders as I can. I've got a lot to do, and I need their help as much as they need mine. I've removed the bones from this airlock doorway, and it is ready for use. And I've found where the repair 'bots are in storage. This place needs some repair, before you get to the prom-ised land."

"But . . . " said Sister Thirsdaughter, feeling like a leaf in the recirc of this new Howard's purpose. "This *is* the promised land, Howard."

He shook his head, and the girl at his side said, "No. There has been some confusion over the years. This is just the ship, getting us there. It's such a big ship that people forgot they were onboard."

"New Eden was just the Ark," said Howard. "Mount Ararat is ahead and you need to get ready or you'll cap-size after four hundred and thirty years of safe journey."

He took Sister Thirsdaughter's arm, and the woman took her other one.

"I'm looking forward to taking Brother Galsson to look on the glory of the Almighty," he said cheerfully. "I don't think he's going to like discovering how great it is and how small he is."

"I hear that you were the midwife who delivered How-ard," said the young woman with him, as if this were the sort of conversation women had in front of men. "I'm expecting his baby."

The screen showed a long procession of people. Respectful people, come to pay their respects to the ancestor, and perhaps hear his words of encouragement and advice. It was strange advice at times, but it he led to a remarkable disappearance of the men in brown uniforms with red braid and gold buttons.

"We have nearly eighty years to bring them up to speed," said the Osprey technician. "Then they've got thirty years on their own before they'll drop into orbit around a new sun. Mr. Ji will be able to help us. There has been a big call for Mr. Ji to stay here. We're transmitting and receiving from the head . . . "

That gentleman shook his head. "No," he said. "I go with Brother Howard. Is atheist place this." He smiled wryly. "I sinned much. Now have found God. Need to be close to God. And my wife say Howard he is the hand of the ancestor. She will not stay here. We recruit fifty people for the new farms." He scowled. "Need them to counter those uThani. And the women who do no work."

Unity—the habitat once called "Aryan Freedom" —went into the final and most dangerous phase of a Slowtrain habitat's existence: deceleration. Cameras from the surface of New Eden recorded it. Unity's own human and Miran cargo were in gel cases, deep in the safety of the water at the far pole, in the combination cosmic ray storm/crash shelter. They traveled with genetic material—plant and animal tissue—from uThani and New Eden and even some rice seedlings from the Workers' Paradise.

The chemical severing of the cable midway between habitats happened so unspectacularly—as planned—as to be virtually unfelt by the occupants of New Eden. The equatorial spin ion jets had shifted slightly to separate the now decoupled Unity from merely fellow-traveling with rest of the Slowtrain because of their matching momentum. The jets now turned Unity so that it was no longer spinning on its axis, ninety degrees from the direction of travel. Instead it turned to spin in the direction of travel. The huge probe-cable that was the equatorial ridge began to uncoil.

To the cameras on New Eden's surface, sending images to the watchers in four habitats, Unity looked like a ball, with whirling, barely visible rings around the equator and at either pole. Close examination showed how the forward momentum of Unity was transferred at the crucial moments into the launch of a sequence of probes—which is what the whole equatorial ridge had been. Some went on to explore wider before using their momentum to head back to Earth. Others, containing a sea of sociological and psychological data about the behavior of isolated humans, were heading home directly.

By the time the last probe had been launched, the rotation of Unity was almost entirely damped. The cable, which had been undergoing its own chemical metamorphosis, began to fray out into a vast gossamer sheet—into two enormous lateen butterfly wings, several thousand times the size of Unity itself.

And then, in a blaze of terawatt laser, came the Slowtrain's fusion plant's parting blessing. The sudden flash on those braking wings that had alerted the Miranese astronomers. The Slowtrain proceeded onward at its steady pace, to drop the next seed of humanity—New Eden—at a star 7.7 light-years away.

Unity continued its braking infall on Miran's sun and her companion. It would take two years to get into a suitable orbit before the solar sails must be converted to solar harvesters, and a lifecraft set out on the final leg of the journey home for the two Mirans aboard.

# EPILOGUE

"Gentlemen, you miss the point of space engineering. The equipment needed to build a single habitat by melting an m-class asteroid, spinning it so that we centrifugally separate the metals, and then using the 'mosquito' to remove the fraction wanted for other purposes, and then injecting water to 'blow' it into a bubble is expensive, yes. But the process itself is simple and relatively cheap, even if getting there and setting up isn't. The point is—once we've got there and set up we're not just going to build one bubble. Even when humans get to other stars, the first thing they'll do is build more.

"We build. That's what we do. That's what we are."

Transcript of Dr. W. Andrea Asiago's address to the new-formed Interstellar Colonization and Exploration society, considered by many to be the ɔerminal point of the Slowtrain Project. From: *A Concise History of Human Space Colonization*. P233, Chipattari, H, and Shah, G.D. (Ed)

---

There was much work to be done, but Howard made time to come to the observation pod. It was accessible from within the habitat through an airlock, having been hidden under the equatorial ridge. Now, as Unity spun on her axis, he could look through the floor and see the Slowtrain—an ever-shrinking, racing string of beads lit by their future sun. Then, when the habitat turned, he could see Miran's suns.

And in between, the vast emptiness. The glory of stars and space.

Lani put her arm around him. It was good to have him to herself for a bit—and to get his nose out of a screen. He read too much. He wanted to read everything.

He smiled at her.

"A penny for your thoughts. As long as they involve me and supper," she said lightly.

"Actually, I was being philosophical."

"Oh, dear. Why did I ask?" She gave him a squeeze. "Tell me."

"Well . . . Earth sent out its misfits. I suspect it also, unwittingly, sent out many of its best. I don't know that they realized that the two were one and the same, a lot of the time, and that they needed us, not that we needed them. They sent us their danger-loving probes, their troublemakers, their fighters, their radicals and their arch-conservatives. From what I have now read they sent us the stock that have always founded colonies. I think humans are like plants. You can't plant the same crop on the same ground forever. The plants use up the soil, even if they die there and fertilize it. Our species is a colonist one. A frontier one. We need to move and mix and dream."

Looking at the double star they were heading for, and the endless panoply beyond, Lani squeezed his hand. This was the dream. This infinity was space enough— just—for the biggest dream. She looked away from it and back at Howard, also looking out at infinity, at the same dream. She touched his cheek and kissed him. "Do you realize that—populated or not—each of the habitats is a laser relay station? We can send messages back to Earth . . . at lightspeed."

"Then we should," he said.

She shrugged. Earth's solar system seemed very far away and very insignificant. "What would we say to them? That people are not sociological experiments?"

He was silent for a while. "Maybe. But I would tell them that mankind is a colonist species and belongs on far frontiers. I would thank them for their unintended generosity. And what I would tell them was this: It's from a poem I recently read by an Earth poet called Emma Lazarus:

*"Give me your tired, your poor*
*Your huddled masses yearning to breathe free,*
*The wretched refuse of your teeming shore."*